PEACE TALKS

JIM BUTCHER

THE DRESDEN FILES

PEACE TALKS

orbit

www.orbitbooks.net

First published in Great Britain in 2020 by Orbit

1 3 5 7 9 10 8 6 4 2

Copyright © 2020 by Jim Butcher

A CIP catalogue record for this book
is available from the British Library.

HB ISBN 978-0-356-50091-1
C format 978-0-356-51529-8

Printed and bound in Great Britain by Clays Ltd, Elcograf S.p.A.

Papers used by Orbit are from well-managed forests
and other responsible sources.

Orbit
An imprint of
Little, Brown Book Group
Carmelite House
50 Victoria Embankment
London EC4Y 0DZ

An Hachette UK Company
www.hachette.co.uk

www.orbitbooks.net

For Frostbite Doomreaver McBane Butcher.
I miss you, little buddy.

1

My brother ruined a perfectly good run by saying, "Justine is pregnant."

That kicked me completely out of my mental zone, and suddenly I became aware of the burning in my legs, my heavy breathing. I dropped out of gear and gradually slowed down until I was walking. In the blue light of July predawn, Montrose Beach was deserted. It wasn't hot yet. That's why I was up at oh-God-thirty.

Thomas slowed down, too, until we were walking side by side. His dark hair was pulled back into a ponytail. Like me, he wore an old T-shirt, sweatpants, and sneakers. He was one of those men who were so good-looking that it made people check around to see if they were being pranked.

He was also a vampire.

"Let me get this right. You pick me up this morning," I said. "We came all the way down here. We did six miles in the sand and neither of us said a word. The whole city is still and quiet. We've barely seen a moving car."

"Yeah?" Thomas asked.

I scowled. "So why'd you have to go and ruin it?"

His mouth twitched at the corner. "Sorry to spoil your man time, there, Hemingway."

"Nnngh," I said. We had reached the end of our last lap and were almost back to the cars anyway. I stopped and turned toward the lake and breathed. The weighted vest I was wearing pinched at something on my shoulder, restricting its movement, and I rolled it irritably.

Far out over the lake, the blue had begun to lighten. Sunrise would be soon.

"You sure?" I asked.

"Very," he said.

I glanced aside at him. The ideal symmetry of his face was stretched tight with tension. His eyes, which were sometimes blue, usually grey, were tinting toward reflective silver. I knew the look. He was Hungry.

"How did that happen?" I asked him.

He looked aside at me without turning his head and lifted his eyebrows. "Did no one ever have this talk with you?"

I scowled. "I mean, weren't you careful?"

"Yes," Thomas said. "And my kind are all but infertile to boot. Happened anyway."

"What happens now?"

"The usual, mostly. Except that the baby's Hunger will draw life energy from Justine. She's going to be fed upon continuously for the next seven and a half months."

I studied him. "Is that dangerous?"

He swallowed. "According to the family records, just over fifty percent either don't survive the delivery or die shortly after."

"Hell's bells," I said. I kept staring out at the water. Blue had given way to lighter blue and then to the first wash of gold. Chicago was starting to wake up around us. The burble of noise from the freeways had begun to escalate by slow degrees. Birds in the sanctuary at the end of the beach were beginning to sing.

"I don't know what to do," Thomas said. "If I lose her . . ."

He didn't continue. He didn't have to. There was a universe of pain residing in that ellipsis.

"You'll be fine," I said. "I'll help."

"You?" Thomas asked. A faint smile lightened his profile for a second.

"I'll have you know I've been a full-time dad for well over a month, and Maggie isn't dead yet. I clearly have mad parenting skills."

The smile faded. "Right. But . . . Harry . . ."

I put my hand on his shoulder. "Don't borrow trouble," I said. "There's plenty of that going around without looking for more of it. She needs taking care of. So whatever needs to happen, we'll do it."

He stared at me for a silent moment and nodded once.

"Meanwhile," I said, "you should probably focus on taking care of yourself so you can be there for her."

"I'm fine," he said, waving one hand.

"You don't look fine."

That made him jerk his head toward me and glare. The expression changed him. Suddenly he looked less like a human being and more like something carved from marble. Angry, angry marble. I felt my shoulders tense up in the presence of a creature I knew was genuinely dangerous.

He glared at me, but he had to look up to do it. My older brother is right around six feet tall, but I'm six nine. Usually, I have a commanding advantage when looking down at him. Today, I had less than usual, since I was standing in a depression in the sand.

His voice was cool. "Leave it, Harry."

"If I don't," I asked, "are you gonna punch me?"

He scowled at me.

"Because you know. I'm all Captain Winter now. It might not go the way you assume it would."

He sneered. "Please. I'd hog-tie you with your entrails."

I squinted at him. Then I spoke carefully and slowly. "If you don't take care of yourself and act like a sane person," I said, "maybe we'll find out."

He scowled and started to speak, his expression darkening.

"No," I said simply. "No, you don't get to do that. You don't get to go into an emo vampire angst spiral over this. Because that's selfish, and you can't afford to think that way. Not anymore."

He stared at me for a while, his expression furious, then thoughtful, then disturbed.

Waves rolled in on the beach.

"I have to think of them," he said.

"Good man would," I said.

His grey eyes stared out at the lake. "Everything is going to change," he said.

"Yeah."

"I'm scared," he said.

"Yeah."

Something in his body language relaxed, and suddenly he was just my brother again. "I'm sorry," he said. "That I got edgy. I . . . don't like to talk vampire stuff with you."

"You'd rather pretend we were just normal brothers, with normal problems," I said.

"Wouldn't you?" he asked.

I squinted down at my feet for a while. "Maybe. But you can't ignore things that are real just because they're uncomfortable. I'll sit on you and make you take care of yourself if I have to. But it's probably better for them if you do it."

He nodded. "Probably. I have a solution in mind," he said. "I'll work on it. Good enough?"

I raised both of my hands, palms out. "I'm not your dad," I said. Then it was my turn to frown. "Your dad's side of the family going to be an issue?"

"When aren't they an issue?"

"Heh," I said. Silence stretched. Over the lake, the sky began to swell with the first faint band of deep orange. It had already gotten to the sky-scrapers behind us. The light moved steadily down the buildings' sides.

"Sometimes," Thomas said, "I hate what I am. I hate being me."

"Maybe it's time to work on that," I said to him. "Isn't really the kind of thing you want to teach to a little kid."

He glowered at me. Then he said, "When the hell did you get deep?"

"Through experience, wisdom I have earned," I said in Yoda's voice. But it tickled my throat weirdly and made me start coughing. I dealt with that for longer than I should have needed to and was straightening up again when Thomas said, his tone suddenly tighter, "Harry."

I looked up to see a young man approaching us.

Carlos Ramirez was of average height, maybe of a little more than average muscle. He was filling out, getting that solid adult look to him, though for some reason I still expected to see a gangly kid in his early twenties whenever I saw him. He'd grown his dark hair out longer. His

skin was bronzed from inclination and the sun. He walked with difficulty, limping and leaning on a thick cane carved with symbols—his
wizard's staff. He wore jeans and a tank top and a light jacket. Ramirez
was solid, a proven fighter, a good man to have at your back, and was one
of a very few people on the White Council of Wizardry whom I considered a friend.

"Harry," he said. He nodded warily at Thomas. "Raith."

My brother nodded back. "Been a while."

"Since the Deeps," Ramirez agreed.

"Carlos," I said. "How's your back?"

"I know when it's going to rain now," he said, flashing me a quick
grin. "Won't be dancing much for a while. But I won't miss that damned
chair."

He held up a hand. I bumped fists with him. "What brings you out
from the coast?"

"Council business," he said.

Thomas nodded and said, "I'll go."

"No need," Ramirez said. "This is going public this morning. Mc-
Coy thought it would be good for someone you knew to tell you, Harry."

I grunted and unfastened the damned weighted vest. White Council
business, typically, gave me a headache. "What is it this time?"

"Peace talks," Ramirez said.

I arched an eyebrow. "What, seriously? With the Fomor?"

The supernatural world had been kind of topsy-turvy lately. Some
lunatic had managed to wipe out the Red Court of Vampires completely,
and the resulting vacuum had destabilized balances of power that were
centuries old. The biggest result of the chaos was that the Fomor, an
undersea power hardly anyone had spoken about during my lifetime,
had risen up with a vengeance, taking territory from various powers and
wreaking havoc on ordinary humans—mostly the poor, migrants, people without many champions to stand for them.

"A convocation of the Unseelie Accord signatories," Ramirez confirmed. "Every major power is coming to the meeting. Apparently, the
Fomor requested it. They want to resolve our differences. Everyone's
sending representatives."

I whistled. That would be something. A gathering of influential members of the greatest powers in the supernatural world, in a time where tensions were high and tempers hot. I pitied the poor town where that little dinner party was going to take place. In fact . . .

I felt my mouth open. "Wait. They're doing it here? *Here?* In Chicago?"

Ramirez shrugged. "Yeah, that's why McCoy sent me to tell you."

"Whose stupid idea was that?" I asked.

"That's the other reason McCoy sent me," Ramirez said, grinning. "The local baron offered his hospitality."

"*Marcone?*" I demanded. Gentleman Johnnie Marcone, former robber baron of Chicago's outfit, was now *Baron* Marcone, the only vanilla human being to sign the Unseelie Accords. He'd managed that a few years ago, and he'd been building his power base ever since.

"That stunt he pulled with Mab this spring," I said, scowling.

Ramirez shrugged and spread his hands. "Marcone maneuvered Nicodemus Archleone into a corner and took everything he had, without breaking a single one of the bylaws of the Accords. Say what you will about the man, but he's competent. It impressed a lot of people."

"Yeah," I said darkly. "That was all him. Tell me that the Council doesn't want me to be our emissary."

Ramirez blinked. "Wait, what? Oh . . . oh God, no, Harry. I mean . . . no. Just no."

My brother covered up his mouth with one hand and coughed. I chose to ignore the wrinkles at the corners of his eyes.

Ramirez cleared his throat before continuing. "But they will expect you to be the Council's liaison with Winter, if needed, and to provide security for the Senior Council members in attendance. Everyone will be conducting themselves under guest-right, but they'll all bring their own muscle, too."

"Trust but verify," I said. I took off the weighted vest with disgust and tossed it onto the beach. It made an extremely weighty *thump* when it hit.

Ramirez arched an eyebrow. "Christ, Harry. How much does that thing weigh?"

"Two-twenty," I replied.

He shook his head. His expression, for a moment, was probing and pensive. I'd learned to recognize the look—that "I wonder if Harry Dresden is still Harry Dresden or if the Queen of Air and Darkness has turned him into her personal monster" look.

I get that one a lot these days. Sometimes in the mirror.

I looked down at my feet again and studied the ground. I could see it better as the sun drew nearer the horizon.

"You sure the Senior Council wants me to be on the security team?" I asked.

Ramirez nodded firmly. "I'm heading it up. They told me I could pick my own team. I'm picking you. I want you there."

"Where you can more easily keep an eye on him," Thomas murmured.

Ramirez grinned and inclined his head. "Maybe. Or maybe I just want to see some more buildings burn down." He nodded to me and said, "Harry. I'll be in touch."

I nodded back. "Good to see you, 'Los."

"Raith," Ramirez said.

"Warden Ramirez," my brother answered.

Ramirez shambled off, leaning on his cane, moving without much grace but with considerable energy.

"Well," Thomas said. He watched Ramirez depart, and his eyes narrowed in thought. "It looks like I'd better get moving. Things are going to get complicated."

"You don't know that," I said. "Maybe it'll be a nice dinner, and everyone will sing 'Kumbaya' together."

He eyed me.

I looked down at my feet again and said, "Yeah. Maybe not."

He snorted, clapped my arm, and started walking back to the car without saying anything further. I knew he'd wait for me.

Once he was gone, I stepped out of the depression in the sand and picked up my weighted vest. Then I turned and studied it as the sun began to come up in earnest and I could finally see clearly.

I'd been standing in a humanoid footprint.

It was well over three feet long.

Once I looked, I saw that there was a line of them, with several yards stretching between each one and the next. The line led toward the water. The rising lakeshore breeze was already beginning to blur the footprints' outlines.

Maybe their appearance was a complete coincidence.

Yeah. Maybe not.

I slung the weighted vest over my shoulder and started trudging back to the car. I had that sinking feeling that things were about to get hectic again.

2

Thomas came with me back to my place for a post-exercise breakfast.

Well. Technically, it was Molly's place. But she wasn't around much, and I was living there.

The svartalf embassy in Chicago was a neat little building in the business district, with a lawn that was an absolute gaping expanse when you considered the cost of real estate in town. It looked like the kind of building that should be full of people in severely sober business attire, doing things with money and numbers that were too complicated, fussy, and god-awful boring to be widely understood.

As it happened, that was pretty close to the truth.

There was a little guardhouse on the drive in, a fairly recent feature, and a bland-looking man in a bland and expensive fitted suit and dark sunglasses looked up from his book. We stopped at the window and I said, "The purple mustang flies tonight."

The guard stared at me.

"Uh . . . hang on," I said, and racked my brain. "Sad Tuesdays present no problem to the local authorities?"

He kept staring at me. "State your names, please."

"Oh come *on*, Austri," I said. "Do we have to do this dance every single morning? You know who I am. Hell, we watched the kids play together for an hour last night."

"I wasn't on duty then," Austri said, his tone entirely neutral, his eyes flat. "State your names, please."

"Once," I said. "Just once, would it kill you to let security protocol slide?"

He gave me more of that blank stare, a slow blink, and said, "Potentially. Which is why we have security protocols."

I gave him my most wizardly glower, to no avail. Then I grumbled under my breath, making mostly Yosemite Sam noises, and started fumbling around in my gym bag. "My name is Harry Dresden, Winter Knight, vassal to Molly Carpenter, Lady Winter of the Sidhe Court, and under the protection of her guest-right. This is Thomas Raith, also her guest, friend to Lady Evanna."

"He is one of Evanna's lovers," Austri corrected me meticulously. He nodded at Thomas.

"'Sup, Austri," my brother said.

"Duty," Austri said seriously, and opened a folder, flipping through a number of profile pages with photographs in the top corner. He stopped on my page, carefully compared the image to me, and then another to Thomas, and nodded. "Passphrase, please."

"Yeah, one second." I finally found the folded-up piece of paper with the weekly passphrases on it in the depths of the gym bag. I unfolded it, shook sand off it, consulted it, and read, "'All of my base are belong to me.' What does that even mean?"

Austri stared at me in frustration for a moment and sighed. Then he looked at Thomas. "And yours?"

"'The itsy-bitsy spider went up the waterspout,'" Thomas said promptly, without referencing a cheat card. Because he has nothing better to do with his time than memorize random passphrases.

Austri nodded approvingly, flipped the folder closed, and put it away. "Please wait," he said. He hit a button and muttered a nearly silent word, which I knew would disarm about two thousand lethal magical wards between me and the front door. Then he nodded at me and said, "You may enter."

"Thank you," I said.

He leaned back in his chair a bit, relaxing, and the illusion of unremarkable humanity that covered the svartalf went liquid and translucent. Austri had grey skin with a gymnast's muscles beneath, a head a

little too big for the rest of him, and absolutely enormous black eyes, like
that alien in the autopsy video. Beneath the surface illusion, his expression was relaxed and pleasant. "My Ingri would like another playdate
with Maggie and Sir Mouse."

"Maggie would enjoy that as well. I'll contact Mrs. Austri?"

He nodded. "That is her designated area of responsibility. Cards
again tonight?"

"I'd like to, but I can't commit to it," I said.

He frowned slightly. "I prefer being able to plan my evening activities."

"Duty," I explained.

His frown vanished, and he picked up his book again. "That is different, of course. Please let me know when your duties permit you to
spare the time."

I gave him a nod and went forward.

Austri was the svartalves in a nutshell. Anal-retentive, a ferocious
stickler, inhumanly disciplined, inflexibly dedicated to his concepts of
honor and duty—but good people once you got to know him. It takes all
kinds, you know?

We passed through two more security checkpoints, one in the building's lobby and another at the elevator that led down to the embassy's
large subterranean complex. One of the other svartalves peered at my
driver's license, then at me, and insisted on measuring my height and
taking my fingerprints to further verify that it was actually me and not
an impostor wearing a Harry suit.

I guess I shouldn't have minded it so much. Adding more checks did
mean more security, even if it was occasionally applied somewhat mali-
ciously by guys like Gedwig here. Still, the svartalves' particular blend
of paranoia and punctiliousness meant that my daughter would be that
much safer under their roof. But some days it chafed, and this was one
of them.

We slipped into the apartment and found it still dim and dark and
cool. I stopped for a moment to marvel at the miracle of air-conditioning
in the summer. Magic and technology don't get along, and the aura of
energy around a wizard like me plays merry hell with pretty much any-

thing developed after the Second World War. I'd never lived in a place whose AC survived more than a few days, but the svartalves had constructed this apartment especially for Molly. It had lights that worked, and a radio that worked, and hot water that worked, and an AC that worked, and I had no idea how the clever folk had managed that. The svartalves were famous craftsmen. Word was, if you wanted something made, they could make it.

Maybe I should get Molly to ask for a TV. Or an Internet . . . thing. Device. One of those Internet thingies. I figure everyone is so insane about the Internet, there must be something cool there.

Anyway, when we finally came all the way into the living room, Mister, my big grey tomcat, appeared as he always did and flung himself at my shins in a welcome-home shoulder block. I leaned down to rub the base of his ears the way he liked, which he received with great magnanimity, before dismissing me to continue my day. He walked by Thomas, rubbing his cheek against my brother's leg once and once only to mark him as Mister's property; then he walked off in regal disinterest. Mister wasn't as young as he used to be, but he still knew who ruled the apartment.

My daughter was still sleeping on the couch, covered by a heavy blanket. Next to her lay a shaggy grey behemoth about the size of a Budweiser horse, my Temple dog, Mouse. He didn't even lift his head or open his eyes when we came in. He just yawned and wriggled into a slightly more comfortable position before huffing out a breath and going back to sleep. Maggie's breathing caught in a little hitch; then she put out her hand and sank it into the dog's fur. They both sighed in their sleep and went motionless again.

I stood there for a moment, just looking down at them.

Thomas usually busied himself with coffee in the kitchen at moments like this. But today, he stepped up beside me and stood there, looking at the girl and the dog.

"Damn," he said.

I nodded. "Big responsibility."

"Yeah."

"You can do it."

I turned to look at him. There was some expression I couldn't define on his face, some mix of longing and gentle, exquisite pain.

"I don't think so, Harry," he said.

"Don't be a dope," I said. "You love her. You'll love the kid. Of course you can."

A faint sad smile mixed in with the other expressions on his face.

We both turned back to the sleeping child.

There was a quality to the stillness that I had never experienced before I'd started taking care of Maggie. A sense of . . . intense satisfaction like nothing I'd ever known. There she was, sleeping, happy, healthy—safe.

I took a deep stabilizing breath. Weariness fled, not from my body, but from somewhere deeper and infinitely more important. My brother exhaled at the same time and thumped his fist on my shoulder. Then he turned for the kitchen and I headed for the shower.

I broiled myself for as long as seemed appropriate, and as I was getting dressed I heard voices from the kitchen.

"Milk doesn't have feelings," Maggie was saying.

"Why not?" piped a voice even younger.

"Because milk is inanimate," Maggie said cheerfully.

"Oh." There was a pause. "But it is moving."

"I moved it," Maggie said. "And then it sloshes around for a while."

"Why?"

"Because of gravity, I think," Maggie said. "Or maybe memontum."

"Do you mean momentum?" the littler voice asked.

"I might," Maggie said seriously.

"How do you know, then?"

"When you're ten, you'll know things, too," Maggie said.

"Why?"

I walked into the apartment's little kitchen to find Maggie, in her pajamas, making a mess with the attentive help of Mouse and a skull carved from wood. Little green dots of light glowed in the skull's eye sockets, like the embers of some bizarre fire. Half the contents of the apartment's little pantry were crowded onto the kitchen counter.

I eyed Thomas, who was sitting at the kitchen table with a mug of coffee. He'd already poured mine. I walked over to him and took my cup, murmuring, "You didn't think to step in here?"

"You got in the shower so long ago, I forget exactly what I was thinking back in those days," he shot back.

I lowered my voice a little. "How'd she do?" I asked him.

He spoke in kind. "Pretty good. We exchanged good-mornings, made eye contact, and she seemed happy to do it," he said. "She asked me if I wanted pancakes."

"And you said yes?"

"Harry," Thomas said, "be real. Everyone wants someone to make us pancakes; we're all just too grown-up to say it."

I sipped coffee, because it was impossible to argue with logic like that.

He sipped, too. "You going to stop her?"

I savored the perfection that is coffee and enjoyed that first swallow before responding. "Think I'd better scout it out."

I took my cup into the kitchen and heard Thomas get up to tag along. When I came into its line of sight, the little wooden skull's eyes swiveled to me, and her voice proclaimed proudly, "Pancakes are inanimate!"

"Correct," I said, speaking to the spirit inside the skull. Better inside that wooden one than mine, let me tell you. Ever since the new-formed spirit of intellect had coalesced inside my mind, it had grown until it was too big for the space, which admittedly had not taken her very long. We'd managed to successfully get her out of my head, and she'd taken up residence in the carved wooden skull prepared for her. Ever since, we'd been teaching her and answering a river of endless questions. "Good morning, Bonea."

"Morning is when the sun comes up!" the little skull said. "It ends at noon!"

Bonea was full of points of information that didn't connect to anything else. She could tell you the particulars of all sorts of secrets of the universe, but she'd have no idea what kind of an effect those secrets could have on the actual world. Which made her . . . someone to be carefully managed. "Correct again," I said. "Good morning, Maggie."

"Hi, Dad," Maggie said. "I am making us all pancakes for breakfast."

"Which is awesome," Thomas said, nudging me in the small of the back.

Maggie threw him a swift glance and a shy smile.

I didn't have to look to know he winked back at her.

I lifted my eyebrows. "Yeah. Pancakes. That's new."

"Molly says you have to be brave and try new things to grow," my daughter said seriously. "And Thomas says everyone likes pancakes."

"Everyone likes pancakes," Thomas said.

I gave him a narrow-eyed look over my shoulder to tell him to stop helping me. He returned it with a guileless smile.

"Well. They're not wrong," I said seriously. "Do you want any help?"

"I can do it by myself," she said. "I know how to work the stove and Bonnie knows the recipe."

"I know two hundred and twenty-seven individual pancake recipes!" Bonnie said. "Sixteen can be made with the current inventory of the kitchen!"

"We're using number seven," Maggie said seriously. "From scratch is best."

That sounded like the makings of a huge mess to me. Mouse gave me what I swear was a smug look and licked his chops. It would be extra work to clean up afterward—but it would probably be good for Maggie to try it. So I leaned down and kissed her on the head and said, "Be careful of the stove. And let me know if you need help with anything, punkin."

"See there, Miss Maggie?" Thomas said. "I told you so."

I stopped and eyed him. "Did you set all this up so you could get pancakes?"

Thomas put on a serious expression and widened his eyes a little at Maggie. "I'm not saying that I didn't."

I rolled my eyes at him.

My daughter giggled. "Mister Thomas is okay, Dad."

"You are very young. Tell you what. You let me deal with him," I said. "You keep your mind on what you're doing, okay? Be safe."

"'Kay," she said. She turned back to the task, and though her eyes were still puffy with sleep, she focused on the work with the instant morning energy that can be possessed only by someone who has not yet discovered the immutable necessity of coffee.

I settled down on the couch, nearby. The apartment was basically a single large room, sharing the kitchen, the dining room, and a living room with no walls between. There were two doors to the two bedrooms—Molly's and mine. Well, technically the room was Molly's. As far as I knew, she hadn't actually been in it since I'd moved in, except for a couple of times she'd breezed through, petted Mouse, tickled Maggie, shared some sunny chat with me, and departed again.

It had been a while since we'd really talked.

The apartment reminded me of my old place in the basement of Mrs. Spunkelcrief's boardinghouse. Only there was no musty, moldy smell of old basement. And it was bigger. And it was more brightly lit. And newer. And quite a bit cleaner. And it just didn't *feel* right.

As dumpy as it had been, that grotty little apartment had been my home. Damn the vampires, for burning it down. Damn Marcone, for buying the property and putting up his new headquarters on the ground where home used to be.

I missed it.

Ah, well. There was no sense in brooding over it. Life never stays the same. There's always some kind of curveball coming at you. Nothing to do but swing away.

Thomas picked a spot of wall to lean against where he could see the kitchen and sipped his coffee. His eyes were focused on Maggie with thoughtful intensity. "Living dangerously, eh?"

"Mouse will let me know if there's a problem," I said.

"Good dog, there," Thomas said.

"You want," I said, "I could write to Brother Wang. Tell him you want a puppy."

"You already stole that one from him." Thomas snorted.

"Accidentally," I said. "Plus I think the furball stowed away on purpose. Even if Brother Wang doesn't like it, I figure he won't gainsay the dog."

"Well," Thomas mused, "he is a pretty good dog."

"Damned right he is," I said.

"Let me think about it," Thomas said. "There's a lot going on."

He still hadn't taken his eyes off Maggie.

"Hey, man," I said. "You okay?"

He glanced aside at me and offered me a faint smile. "Just . . . thinking real hard about the future."

"Well," I said. "That's understandable." I closed my eyes and felt my limbs aching in dull, steady throbs that kept time with my heartbeat. Suddenly, I sneezed, hard.

"God bless you," Maggie said promptly from the kitchen.

"Nnngh," I called. "Thank you." The sneeze had sent a surge of aching sensation through my limbs that took several seconds to fade. I opened one eye. That wasn't right.

The mantle of power of the Winter Knight was what let me keep pace with my brother the vampire while running in sand and wearing two hundred pounds of extra weight. One of the things the mantle did was to dull pain, to the point where I experienced it only as a kind of tense, silvery sensation. Broken bones were sort of annoying. A bleeding wound was something of a distraction—but I didn't ever, ever just ache.

Except now I was.

Stupid Winter mantle. It kept up a constant assault of primal, feral emotions and desires that were like supercharged versions of my own instincts. I didn't go out for intense exercise every morning because I enjoyed it. I did it because discipline and routine helped me keep the more primal instincts in check. Daily intense exercise forced the mantle to expend energy in keeping my body going—on my schedule, at my will—and as a result reduced the amount of pressure it could apply to my conscious thoughts. And while it did make me able to ignore pain and to push my body well beyond the normal limits of human endurance, the mantle's influence was a steady nuisance that required constant effort to keep buttoned up.

"Whoa," Thomas said. "You okay there, nerd?"

"That was weird," I said.

Mister prowled up onto the couch and settled on my lap, thrusting his head beneath my hand. I petted him automatically, and his body rumbled with a purr that sounded like a pot of boiling water.

A second or two after that thought, I sneezed again, harder, and this time the aching surge sent a wave of exhaustion flooding through me, so hard that I nearly fell over onto my side.

Also, there was a clang and a splashing sound. Mister leapt out of my lap and bolted. It took me a couple of tries to get my eyes to focus, but when I did, I saw that a metal pot with a black plastic handle was lying on its side on the carpet in front of me. Little wisps of steam rose from the soaking carpet next to the pot.

I blinked up at Thomas and traded a look with him. His face told me that he had no idea what had just happened. We both looked back at the pot.

I frowned and leaned down to touch it. It wasn't quite hot enough to burn me, but it was close. I blinked at it and reached for the handle. I picked up the pot. The handle felt oddly squishy for a couple of seconds—and then suddenly, plastic and metal and water alike shuddered and melted into a clear gelatinous fluid that fell out of my fingers to splat on the carpet. Ectoplasm, the raw matter of the spirit world.

What the hell?

Ectoplasm was a strange substance. It could be shaped by magic and fed energy, and as long as the energy kept pouring in, it would hold its form. Spirits from the Nevernever could forge bodies to be used in the material world and run around in them like their own version of going on a spacewalk. But once the energy stopped pouring in, the construct body would revert to its original form—mucus-like ectoplasm, which would itself sublimate from the material world and back to the Nevernever within moments.

So where the hell had the pot come from?

The Guard? The little faeries who loitered about my home certainly had a mischievous streak a mile wide. Could one of them have played a prank on me?

Maybe. But if so, how had the prankster known what I was thinking about?

It was damned peculiar.

"Harry?" Thomas asked.

"Damned peculiar," I said, and swiped at my nose, which was suddenly all but overflowing. "Even for me."

"Dad?" Maggie called.

"Hmmm?"

"I'm not supposed to flip the pancake until it's golden brown, Bonnie says. But I can't *see* the cooked part. How do I know?"

I pushed myself up off the couch, grabbed a handful of tissues, and headed for the kitchen. "It's a little tricky," I said. "You can tell from what the batter on the uncooked side looks like. I'll show you."

"Okay."

I started instructing my daughter in the fine art of pancake flipping. We had just gotten the second one started when a tiny bell began to ring very rapidly from somewhere in one of the walls—the apartment's security alarm.

Mouse whipped his head around to the source of the sound and let out a low growl. Maggie blinked and then looked at me uncertainly.

Thomas came off the wall in a tense little bound of tightly leashed energy. He glanced at me and then went to the kitchen and took one of the big chef knives from the block.

"Someone's coming," I said. "Let's see what's happening first. Now, just like we practiced. Take Bonnie, go to my room, and put her in her box. Stay in there with her, stay low to the ground, and keep quiet. Okay?"

Maggie looked uncertain but she nodded. "Okay."

"Go on."

I shut the bedroom door behind her and picked up my wizard's staff from its spot near the fireplace. I suddenly wished that I'd found a way to spend more hours on my personal magical arsenal. I hadn't, because I'd been busy being a father, which took up way more time than I had believed possible. There'd been very little time to actively work on my gear—a very wizard-hours-intensive endeavor. All I had was the staff I'd carved out on the lost island of Demonreach in the middle of Lake Michigan, my blasting rod, and a slapdash version of my old shield bracelet—but they would have to do.

Whatever had set off the alarm, it seemed unlikely that it could march all the way through the svartalves' security—but if it hadn't done so, then why was my security alarm ringing?

"What do you think?" Thomas asked.

"I think anything that goes through svartalf security to get here has me a little edgy," I said.

"Oh, so it's not just me. That's nice."

A few seconds later, a heavy hand rapped hard on the door to the apartment.

I checked to make absolutely sure that the door to the room with my daughter inside was firmly shut. And then, gripping my staff much like a rifle, I paced silently forward to answer the door, my brother falling into step beside me.

3

I summoned my will and channeled power into my staff. The runes spiraling along its length smoldered with emerald fire, and tiny wisps of smoke rose from it. The clean, smoky scent of fresh-scorched wood laced the air. Runes and sigils of green light spangled the walls.

A wizard's staff is a versatile tool. I could use one to project any number of forces or effects as the need arose, and I made sure mine was ready to wreak havoc or reflect energy as needed. Thomas moved in utter silence to the wall beside the door, where he would be within arm's reach of anyone who came through it. He gripped the knife low along his leg and nodded to me when he was ready.

And I calmly opened the apartment's front door.

An old man stood there. He was a couple of inches shorter than average, and stout. Like me, he carried a staff, though his was a good deal shorter and, like him, stouter than my own. Some wisps of white and silver hair drifted around his otherwise shining head, though there seemed to be more liver spots on the skin than I remembered from the last time I'd seen him. His dark eyes were bright, though, behind his spectacles, and he wore a plain white cotton T-shirt with his blue overalls and steel-toed work boots. He was my mentor, Ebenezar McCoy, senior member of the White Council of Wizardry.

He was also my grandfather.

The old man eyed me, his brow furrowing in thought, studying me as I stood there, and then my green-glowing staff.

"New work," he noted. "Dense, though. Maybe a little rough."

"All I had was a pocketknife," I said. "No sandpaper. Had to use rocks."

"Ah," he said. "May I come in?"

I looked past Ebenezar to where Austri stood in the hall, one hand inside his suit, a couple of fingers pressed to one ear. His lips were moving, though I couldn't hear what he was saying. "Austri? What's with the alarm?"

Austri apparently listened to something coming into his ear that only he could hear and nodded. He didn't take his hand out of his coat when he answered me. "This person is known to the svartalves," he said. "He is an enforcer for the White Council of Wizardry and is known to be extremely dangerous. He did not follow security protocols."

"I don't have forty-eight hours to wait for DNA tests to come back, even if I'd give you any," Ebenezar growled. "I told you. Etri knows me. He'll vouch for me."

There was an odd, almost rippling sound, and suddenly a dozen more svartalves like Austri just slid up out of the floor as if it had been made of water. They were grasping a number of weapons, both modern and ancient—but they didn't move to attack. Impulsive responses were not a part of their nature. Their expressions were unreadable, but definitely not friendly.

Austri eyed Ebenezar and then looked to me. "Wizard Dresden? Is this person to be considered a guest of Miss Carpenter?"

"That would be simplest for all involved, I think," I said.

"Simple?" Austri asked. "It is irrelevant how simple or how complicated it may be. Is he Miss Carpenter's guest or not?"

"He is," I said. "Let him come in. I'll take responsibility for his conduct while he is here."

Austri frowned for a long moment, his expression taking on several nuanced shades of doubt. But he only lowered his hand from his jacket and nodded to me. At a gesture, he and the rest of the svartalf security team filed down the hallway and out of sight.

"Sticklers, aren't they?" I said.

"Goes a great deal deeper than that," Ebenezar said.

"You pushed their buttons on purpose," I said.

"Not at first. But one of them got snotty with me."

"So you just started walking over them?"

Something mischievous sparkled in the back of his eyes. "It's good for them, from time to time, for someone to remind them that they can't exercise control over everything, and that a member of the Senior Council can walk where he chooses to walk." His eyes crinkled at the corners. "That last guy really got to me."

"Gedwig," I said. "The grouchy. He's always extra paranoid." I let the power ease out of my staff, and the runes stopped glowing, the light dying away. I made a gesture toward Thomas with one hand, and my brother eased away from the door. Then I stood aside and opened the door wider for my grandfather. "Come in."

The old man didn't miss much. He came in with the calm, wary look of a man who isn't focused on one thing because he's taking in everything—and immediately spun his staff to point squarely at Thomas.

"What is that thing doing here?" Ebenezar demanded.

Thomas lifted his eyebrows. "Thing? Pretty bold assertion of righteousness from the White Council's hatchetman."

As far as I knew, my grandfather didn't know that Thomas and I shared a mother, his daughter. He didn't know he had another grandson. Ebenezar had . . . kind of a thing about White Court vampires.

(The Paranet called them "whampires," but I refused to cave in to such silliness, unless it became entirely convenient.)

"Vampire," my grandfather growled, "you've been a useful ally to young Dresden up until now. Don't go ruining things by getting my attention."

Thomas's eyes glittered a shade brighter, and he put on the smile he wore when he was exceptionally furious. "I'm hearing a lot of loud talk from a guy who let himself get this close to someone like me without having a shield already up."

"Why, you slick little punk," my grandfather began.

The stench of burning batter filled the air, and I stalked over to the stove, where I flipped the pancake, which had burned during the altercation. Then I slapped the spatula back down onto the counter with unnecessary force and said, words sizzling with vitriol, "Gentlemen, I should not need to remind either of you that you are *guests* in my *home*."

And that hit them both like a bucket of cold water.

In our world, maybe the closest thing to inviolable laws are the ancient traditions of guest-right and host-right. In them, guests are to be honored and treated as members of the host's own family. And they, in turn, are expected to *behave* as respectful members of the host's own family.

And in this case we all were actual family, only my grandfather didn't know it.

But Thomas backed off a bit more, his tense frame easing out of its predatory stance, and my grandfather lowered his staff and turned until he was partially facing away from Thomas.

"Sorry, Harry," Thomas said. "Won't happen again."

I nodded at him and glanced at the old man.

"I owe you an apology," my grandfather said to me, with heavy emphasis on the pronouns. "Shouldn't have behaved like that in your home. I'm sorry."

Well, clearly this morning wasn't going in anyone's photo album. But it wasn't going to result in a funeral, either. Take your wins where you can get them, I guess.

"Thank you," I said to them both. I held out my hand, and Thomas passed me the chef knife's handle.

I put the knife away and cleared my throat at my grandfather.

He eyed Thomas, the look a threat. Then he abruptly eased his stance and spoke in conversational tones. "Those pancakes I smell?" he asked, setting his staff in the corner by the door.

I put mine with his. "Yeah. Just making us some breakfast."

"Harry," Thomas said, "I'm going to go."

"You don't have to," I said.

He eyed Ebenezar, his lips compressed. "Yeah. I do."

"Thomas," I began.

My brother held up his hand to forestall me, his face a thundercloud, and stalked out.

My grandfather watched him go until the door closed behind him. Then he glanced up at me from behind the ridge of his shaggy eyebrows.

"Thanks for that," I said.

"You should thank me," he said without heat. "Telling you, you don't know them like you think you do."

"The White Court might be bad on average," I said. "But that one's okay."

"Which is exactly what everyone they've ever seduced will tell you about them," my grandfather said, scowling. But he held up a hand and his tone turned apologetic. "Look, Hoss. Your business is your own. I don't come riding in here all the time trying to run your life. And I shouldn't have thrown a wrench in whatever you had going with the vampire. But you're young, and I got experiences with them and perspective on them that you don't. I don't want you to figure it out the hard way, that's all."

I frowned at the old man.

If he was explaining his reasoning instead of leaving me to do it myself, he was worried.

"There he is!" Ebenezar said, smiling as Mouse came shambling over to greet him. He ruffled the dog's ears with brisk fondness. "I don't have much time, so I'll come right to it. You're in trouble."

"Uh-huh," I said. I went back into the kitchen and poured batter onto the griddle. "First time we've spoken face-to-face since Chichén Itzá. All business, huh, sir?"

He took that in for a moment, his eyes narrowing slightly. "We've all had our hands full since that night," he said. "People have been dying. You don't know what it's been like out there."

"I missed you, too," I said. "I'm likewise glad to see you alive and in one piece."

"There isn't time for this," he said.

"Pancakes?" I asked. "I'm always pretty hungry after my morning constitutional."

The old man's voice hardened. "I'm not kidding, grandson," he said. "There has been a motion raised before the general Council to strip you of your status as a member of the White Council entirely."

I arched an eyebrow sharply. "Huh. First the Council forces me to wear one of those damned grey cloaks whether I want one or not. Now they're talking about kicking me out? I'm going to get whiplash."

"You're going to get more than that if the motion passes," he said, heat in his tone. Then he visibly took a moment to forcibly calm himself. "Harry, I want to get caught up, too. I want to talk. Clear the air. And we will. But right now is no moment to let your emotions run your life."

I scowled down at the pancake. I'd had all kinds of practice in keeping my emotions in check lately. "All right," I said. "Truce. For now. What pretext is the Council basing this upon?"

"An aggregate of various factors," he replied. "Your nonstandard elevation to full wizard, for example. The number of times you've involved yourself in high-profile cases. Your insistence on operating openly as a wizard for over a decade. Not least of which, the conflict of interest they claim now lies upon you due to your service to Queen Mab. A service that has apparently also brought a proven warlock into Mab's influence beside you."

"It's all true," I said. "I haven't lied to anyone about any of it. It's all on the record. So what's the problem?"

"The problem is that trust is getting harder and harder to come by in the White Council," Ebenezar said. "Your choices have made you an outlier. Suspicion naturally falls upon someone in your position in times of strain."

I flipped the pancake. I'd timed it right. It was golden brown.

"If they boot me," I said, thinking through it aloud, "it means that I will no longer have the protection of the Council. I won't be an official wizard."

"You've made a great many enemies over the years," Ebenezar said. "So have I. If you were outcast from the Council, your enemies—and mine—would see you occupying a weakened position. They'll do something about it. How much protection can Mab provide you?"

"Mab," I said, "is not all that into safety. She mostly provides the opposite of that, actually. The way she figures it, the only way she could make me perfectly safe would be to cut my throat and entomb me in amber."

The quip did not draw a smile from the old man. He stared at me with craggy non-amusement.

I sighed. "It isn't Mab's job to protect her Knight. It's supposed to be the other way around. If something comes along and kills me, I clearly wasn't strong enough to be her Knight in the first place."

"You aren't taking this seriously," he said.

I flipped the pancake onto the pile and poured out batter for the next. "If it gets bad, I can always fall back to Demonreach."

"God, if they knew the whole truth about that place," Ebenezar muttered. "And then what? Stay trapped on your island for the rest of your life, afraid to step off it?"

"So don't let the motion go to a general vote," I said. "You're on the Senior Council. Pull rank. Assume control of it."

"I can't," Ebenezar said. "Without a quorum, it's got to be a general vote, and four of the Senior Council are going to be at the peace talks when the vote takes place."

My stomach twisted a little. "Which four?"

"Me, Cristos, Listens-to-Wind, and Martha Liberty."

"Oh," I said quietly. My grandfather was a cagey old fox, with a thick network of alliances throughout the White Council—and almost as many enemies. The Merlin himself couldn't stand Ebenezar, and of the three Senior Council members who would preside over the next Council meeting, only the Gatekeeper had ever shown me any kind of fondness. Even if the vote could go to the Senior Council, I'd lose two to one.

Of course, I wasn't sure about how I would fare among the general population of the White Council, either. Wizards live a long time, and they don't do it by taking unnecessary risks. If you look up *unnecessary risk* in the White Council's dictionary, my picture is there. And my address. And all my personal contact information. And my permanent record from middle school.

"You need to talk to some of them face-to-face," Ebenezar said. "Shake some hands. Make sure they know who you are. Reassure them. You only have a few days, but if you move fast, I think you can gather enough support to defeat the motion."

"No," I said. "I can't. Not without neglecting my duties as a Warden and the Winter Knight both."

"What?" he asked.

I told him about my meeting with Ramirez that morning. "I've been assigned to look out for you at the summit and to liaise with Winter."

The old man spat a curse.

"Yeah," I said.

Most of my support in the Senior Council was getting sent away at exactly the same time I was given a high-profile assignment providing security for the peace summit. Meanwhile, of the wizards who actually did know me, Ramirez and his bunch were the ones who would probably speak on my behalf—and they'd been sent to the summit, too.

"I'm being set up."

"Hngh," Ebenezar agreed.

"Was it the Merlin?" I asked. "Kind of feels like his style."

"Maybe," my grandfather said. "On the other hand, Cristos is throwing around a lot of orders these days, too. Hard to say where it comes from."

I flipped the pancake. If I hadn't spent years with the old man, I wouldn't have noticed anything in his tone, but there was a peculiar shade of emphasis to his phrasing that made me glance up at him. He'd said *Cristos*, but what he meant was . . .

"The Black Council," I said.

He grimaced at me and then at the walls.

The Black Council was secret stuff. Some unknown folks in the wizarding community had been causing a great deal of mischief in my life over the past decade and more. Their goals were no clearer than their identities, but it was obvious that they were damned dangerous. Wizard Cristos had ascended to the Senior Council under odd circumstances—circumstances that seemed to indicate that the Black Council was exercising power within the Council itself. A White Council that was bumbling and fussy and not interested in anything but its own politics was a fairly terrible but normal thing—but a White Council that was being directed by the kind of people I'd run into over the years was a nightmare that barely bore thinking upon.

A few of us had gotten together to see if we could stop it from happening. Because secret societies within the White Council were seen as evidence of plotting to overthrow it, we had to be really, really careful about our little cabal. Especially since we *were* kind of plotting against the White Council, even if we were doing it for its own good.

"I sweep it three times a day and have the Little Folk on the lookout for any possible eavesdropping," I said. "No one is listening in on us."

"Good," Ebenezar said. "Yes. Whether Cristos is an open servant of the Black Council or just their puppet, I think it's safe to say that they want you gone."

"So what else is new?" I asked.

"Don't be cute," Ebenezar said. "They've been running operations and sometimes you've interfered—but they've never come at you directly."

"Guess I was a headache one time too many."

"My point is," he said, "whatever's happening here . . . your removal has become a priority to them."

I flipped another pancake. I bobbled it. Some of the batter splattered and smeared. I wasn't scared, exactly . . . but the Black Council had done some scary stuff.

"What do you think?" I asked him.

"I think that these people aren't going to announce themselves," he said. "They aren't going to come at you directly, they aren't going to be obvious, and they aren't going to give up." He squinted at me and said, "This vote that's going—that's just the storm they're brewing up to distract you."

"So we ignore it?"

"Storm can still kill you, whether you pay attention to it or not," he said. "We still have to deal with it. That's what makes it an excellent distraction."

"Then what do we do?"

"Don't get too focused on the situation that's being set up. They want you locked in on that so that you never see the real problem coming."

I finished another pancake and brought the plate of them over to the table. I divided them out, and my grandfather and I ate in quiet.

"Good," he said.

"Thanks."

We wrapped up breakfast and my mentor shook his head. "I'll see what I can do about this vote. Meanwhile, you do whatever you need to."

"To do what?" I asked.

"To survive," he said. He squinted at nothing in particular and said, "You've had it easy so far, in some ways."

"Easy?" I asked.

"You've had troubles," he said. "But you've gotten to play Lancelot at all of them. You've ridden forth to do open battle and you've won the day."

"Not all of them."

"More than most would have," he said. "I was like that once. Like you, now."

Silence stretched and I didn't try to fill it.

"You're getting into deeper weeds now, boy. The stakes are getting higher."

"Meaning what?"

"The past few years have shown them that you aren't someone who is easily removed the direct way. They're going to start trying alternate methods."

"Like what?" I asked.

"The old way," he said, his voice weary. "The way it always happens. I think someone you don't expect is going to stab you in the back, Hoss."

4

There was a very soft sound from the back of the apartment and the old man came to his feet with the speed of an alley cat. Before he'd even gotten there, he'd hissed a word, and his staff flew across the room and into his hand.

"Whoa, whoa, whoa," I said, rising, my hands spread. "Would you relax, please?"

"Who is that?" he demanded. He shot me a hard look. "Who?"

"I just fed you pancakes," I muttered. How tense were things in the old man's world that he would react like that? "Stars and stones."

"Don't say that," he said, his tone slipping into a more familiar, grouchier cadence. "You don't even know what it means."

"The guy I learned it from wouldn't teach me," I said back. "Would you relax for five seconds, please? Please?"

He glowered at me. He lowered the staff only slightly. "Why should I?"

"Because I'd rather my *daughter* didn't have her *great-grandad* scare her to death on their first meeting," I said.

At that, the old man blinked. Twice. He lowered his staff abruptly. "What? She's *here*? She *was* here? This whole time?"

"She has trouble with new people," I said quietly. "It's hard on her." I looked down at Mouse and jerked my chin at the door to the bedroom. The big dog got up obediently and padded over to the door to be a reassuring presence for the girl.

"You let the *vampire* around her?" my grandfather whispered, his expression shocked.

"Maggie?" I called quietly. "Please come out. There's someone I guess you should meet."

The door opened only a little. I could see a sliver of her face and one brown eye peering out warily.

"I want you to come meet your great-grandfather," I said quietly. "I hadn't actually pictured it quite like this," I said, with a glance at the old man. "But I guess we've got what we've got. Come on, punkin."

The door opened a little more. She reached out and felt around with one hand until her fingers found Mouse's fur. She curled them into his mane and then, very slowly, opened the door. She faced Ebenezar without moving or speaking.

"Maggie," he said quietly. His voice sounded rough. "Hello, young lady."

She nodded at him a little.

Ebenezar nodded back. Then he turned to me, and an anger I had never seen before smoldered in his eyes. He opened his mouth to speak.

Before he could, I gave him a warning glance and said, "How about we go up to the garden, and Mouse can stretch his legs?"

"Okay," Maggie said.

The old man glared daggers at me. Then schooled his expression and turned back to my daughter with a gentle smile. "That sounds nice," he said.

I stood with Ebenezar and watched Maggie and Mouse play with svartalf children.

The garden was gorgeous, centered on a couple of trees that grew in the courtyard in the middle of the svartalf embassy. Grass and flowers had been planted in tasteful balance, leaving enough room for the children to run about and play hide-and-seek. Svartalf children are odd-looking little creatures, with their parents' grey skin and absolutely enormous eyes—adorable, really. There were half a dozen kids in residence at the embassy of an age to play with Maggie, and all of them loved

Mouse, who was engaging them all in a game of tag, lightly springing away from them and twisting and dodging despite all his mass of muscle.

Several svartalves were in the garden. They kept a polite physical and psychological distance from us, clearly savvy to the tension that currently existed between me and the old man.

"Are you insane?" Ebenezar asked me.

"I'm making a choice," I said.

"You might as well get her a shirt with a series of bull's-eyes on it," he said. He kept his voice pitched too low for the children to hear him. "You raise that child near you, and you're making her a target. My God, the vampires already know about her."

"She was in a safe house far away from me for a long time," I said. "It didn't work out so well."

"What was wrong with the Carpenters' house?" he said. "Short of headquarters in Edinburgh, you couldn't find a better-protected place. Why not leave her there?"

"Because her father doesn't live there," I said.

The old man looked up at the sky as though imploring the Almighty to give him patience. "You're a damned fool."

I ground my teeth. "You have a better idea?"

"She needs to be somewhere safe. Somewhere away from you. At least until such time as she shows potential talent of her own, so that she can learn to protect herself."

"Assuming she ever does."

"If she doesn't, our world will get her killed."

At that, I felt my own temper rising. "I guess you'd do it differently," I said.

"I *did* do it differently," he snapped. "I made sure your mother grew up far away from the dangers of my life."

"How'd that work out?" I asked him. "Let's ask Mom. Oh, wait. We can't. She's dead."

There was a sudden silence. I'm not sure if the sunlight literally dimmed for a few seconds or not. But the svartalves suddenly drifted even farther away from us.

The old man's voice was a quiet rumble.

"What did you say to me, boy?"

"She's dead," I said, enunciating. "Your daughter, who you stashed somewhere safe for her protection, is dead now. You have no stones to throw at me."

The old man looked like something carven from old ivory. He said nothing.

"The monsters already *did* try to kill Maggie. And I stopped them," I said. "And if they try again, I'll stop them again. She doesn't need somewhere *safe*. But she does need her *dad*."

"How dare you," the old man whispered.

"I might not be the best parent in the whole world," I said. "But I'm *here*. I'm in her life. And there's no substitute for that. None. There never was. There never will be."

"You idiot," Ebenezar said through clenched teeth. "Do you know what these hosts of yours are capable of?"

"Living up to their word," I spat.

"Boy," he said, "don't push me."

"Why? What are you going to do? Let me vanish into the foster care system? For my own good, of course."

The old man's head rocked back as if I'd slapped him.

"Mom died when I was born," I said in a monotone. "Dad when I was coming up on kindergarten. And you just let me be alone."

Ebenezar turned from me and hunched his shoulders.

"Maybe you thought you were protecting me," I continued, without inflection. "But you were also abandoning me. And it hurt. It left scars. I didn't even know you existed, and I was still angry with you." I watched the children pursue Mouse. He could run for hours without getting winded. They were all having a ball. "She's been through enough. I'm not putting her through that, too."

The back of his neck and his bald pate were both turning red. I heard his knuckles pop as his blunt, strong hands clenched into fists.

"Boy," he growled. "You aren't thinking straight. You aren't thinking this through."

"One of us isn't."

"Your mother is dead," Ebenezar said. "Your father is dead. The woman who bore your child is dead. And you are the common denominator. Can't you see that? Can't you see that it's necessary to set your own feelings aside?"

I felt a flash of rage and pain so intense that for a second I thought I was about to lose control—and it had nothing to do with the Winter mantle.

"What I see," I said, "is a little girl who needs her father to love her. I can't do that if I'm not there."

"You're wrong."

"Maybe," I said. "But she's my child. It's my call."

He shook his head.

"And since I've noticed that my life at times resembles a badly written Mexican soap opera," I continued, "I want you to know something."

"What?"

"I think that right now you're considering protecting her by grabbing her and stashing her somewhere safe. If you go through with it, I'm going to take her back. Over your dead body if necessary, sir."

The old man turned to stare at me, his face a thundercloud.

I stared back. I didn't blink.

"Lad," Ebenezar said. The faint burr of a Scots accent had entered his voice. "You're walking somewhere you don't want to go."

"Not the first time. Not the last."

The old man thrust out a pugnacious jaw and drew in a breath.

"Gentlemen," said a new voice, deep and rich. "Gentlemen, excuse me."

The old man and I both turned our glares on the intruder.

A svartalf stood before us, clad in a suit of dark blue silk. He was taller than Austri, and heavier with muscle. His expression was calm and absolutely resolute. "Gentlemen, you are guests in my home. This display of yours is unseemly at best."

I blinked and looked around slowly. The play in the garden had stopped. The svartalf children had withdrawn to hide behind their parents. Maggie stood halfway between the other children and her family, poised on one foot as if set to flee, both her hands clutching desperately at Mouse's mane. The big dog stood between the child and us, giving me a very disapproving look.

I guess we hadn't kept our voices as quiet as we thought we had.

"Etri," my grandfather said. He nodded his head once and said, "We're having a . . . personal discussion."

Etri, the head of the svartalf embassy, gave Ebenezar a look devoid of sympathy or understanding. "Have it elsewhere. You are frightening my people's children. While you are in my house, McCoy, you will conduct yourself with courtesy and decorum."

The statement was flat, uncompromising, and there was not even the subtle hint that it might entertain the possibility of some other outcome. I raised an eyebrow at the svartalf. I knew he was well respected in the supernatural community, which generally translated to considerable personal power, but only a fool squared off against Ebenezar McCoy.

(Yes. I'm aware of the implications of that statement; I'd been doing it for like ten minutes.)

The old man took a deliberate breath and then looked around. His eyes lingered on Maggie, and suddenly he seemed to deflate slightly. It was like watching him age a decade or two over the course of a few sentences.

And I suddenly really thought about the things I'd said in anger, and I felt ashamed.

"Of course," the old man said. "I formally apologize that the discussion got out of hand and that I disturbed your people's children. I offer no excuse and ask you to overlook my discourtesy."

"Yeah," I said. "Same here. Me, too."

Etri regarded Ebenezar for a moment and then glanced at me and rolled his eyes a little before nodding. "I believe this visit is over, Wizard McCoy. I will send your effects to the front gate."

"No, wait," I said. "Sir, I didn't mean—"

"Of course you are right, Etri," Ebenezar said, his voice brusque. He started to turn away.

"Sir," I said.

"Time to go," Ebenezar said, his voice weary. "Work to be done."

And he walked out.

I hadn't seen Austri enter the garden, but the security guard quietly stepped forward to tail the old man. I made a go-easy gesture at Austri.

The svartalf kept his expression stiff for a second, but then something like compassion softened it, and he nodded in reply to me.

Etri watched him go. Then he gave me an unreadable look, shook his head, and walked away. The other svartalves went with him.

Once everyone was gone, Maggie hurried over to me and threw her arms around my waist. I peeled her off and picked her up and held her.

"Was it my fault?" she asked me, her voice quavering. "I wanted . . . wanted to talk to Grandpa, but I couldn't make the words happen. I didn't mean to make him mad and go away."

My throat grew tight and I closed my eyes before any tears escaped. "Not your fault, punkin. That was so not your fault. You did fine."

She clung to my neck, hard enough to be uncomfortable. "But why was he mad?"

"Sometimes grown-ups disagree with each other," I said. "Sometimes they get angry and say things that hurt when they don't mean to. But it will pass. You'll see."

"Oh," she said.

Mouse came up to me and leaned against my legs in silent support.

"Will Grandpa come for Christmas?" she asked.

"Maybe he will."

"Okay," she said. "Are you mad at me?"

"No," I said, and kissed the side of her head. "You're my punkin."

"Good," she said. "I still want pancakes."

"Let's go make them," I said.

Mouse's tail thumped hopefully against my leg.

But first, we all stood there for a moment, the three of us, taking comfort in one another's proximity.

5

Of course it went badly," Karrin said. "It was a fight with someone in your family. Believe me, family fights are the worst."

"The family hasn't even been assembled yet and there's fights," I complained.

"Looks pretty assembled to me, from what I've seen," she said, her tone dry.

"Yeah, well. I've never had much opportunity to fight with family," I said.

"I have," she said. "Everyone cares about everyone else, so when you get mad and say something horrible, it hurts that much more. And too many things go unsaid. That's the worst, I think. Everyone thinks they know one another better than they probably do, so you fill in the silences with things the other person never actually said. Or thought. Or thought about saying."

I scowled and said, "Is that your professional opinion, Doctor Murphy?"

She snorted, fell silent, and squeezed my hand with hers. Her grip was small and strong and warm. We held hands a lot these days.

I'd come over to cook her some dinner. My cooking skills are modest but serviceable, and we'd both had our fill of oven-roasted chicken and potatoes and a fresh salad. Karrin was having a hard time moving around in the kitchen, between her knee, her shoulder, and all the braces she had to wear to keep them more or less immobilized. And she'd gotten sick of the available delivery food after only a few weeks of being laid up.

I came over a couple of nights a week and cooked for her, when the Carpenter kids were available to babysit Maggie.

"Speaking of doctors," I said, all smooth, "what did the doctor say today?"

"Round one of surgery went okay," she said. She exhaled and laid her head against my arm. We were sitting on the couch in her living room, with her injured leg propped up on an ottoman I'd gotten for her. She was a bitty thing, five and not much, if a very muscular five and not much. Blond hair, clean but bedraggled. Hard to keep it styled when you've got to do everything with one hand. No makeup.

And she looked tired. Karrin Murphy found the lack of work during her recovery exhausting.

She'd collected the injuries on my behalf. They weren't my fault, or that's what I kept telling myself, but at the end of the day she'd put herself in a place to get hurt because I'd asked her to be there. You could argue free will and causality and personal choice all you wanted, but the fact was that if I hadn't gotten her involved, she'd probably have been in one of her martial arts classes at this time of evening.

"Round two can start next week," she continued, speaking in her professional voice, the detached one that didn't have any emotion in it, used mostly when something really, really upset her. "Then it's just three more months of casts and stupid braces and then I can start six months of therapy while they wean me off the painkillers, and after all of that is done, if it goes very, very well, he thinks I might be able to walk without a cane. As long as I don't have to do it very fast."

I frowned. "What about your training?"

"There was damage," she said, her voice becoming not so much quiet as . . . dead. "In the knee, shoulder, elbow. They're hoping to get me back to fifty percent. Of basic function. Not athletic activity."

I remembered her scream when Nicodemus had kicked in her knee. The ugly, wet crunching sound when he'd calmly forced her arm out of its socket, tearing apart her rotator and hyperextending her elbow at the same time. He'd done it deliberately, inflicted as much damage, as much pain, as he could.

"I don't get to be me anymore," she whispered.

She'd been injured before, and she'd come back from it.

But everyone has limits. She was only human.

We sat in the silence while her old grandfather clock ticked steadily.

"Is there anything that . . ." she began.

I shook my head. "When it comes to healing, magic isn't much ahead of medicine at this point. Our people go to study from yours. Unless you want to get Faustian."

"No," she said firmly.

I nodded. There wasn't much else I could say. "I'm sorry," I said finally.

She gave her head a tiny shake. "Don't," she said. "I cried about it earlier. And I'll do it again later. But right now I don't want to think about it. Talk about something else."

I tried to think of something. I came up empty. So instead, I kissed her.

"You are the last of the red-hot raconteurs, Dresden," she murmured against my mouth. But then she closed her eyes and leaned into the kiss, and everything else started going away.

Kissing was something I had to be cautious about. After about twenty seconds of feeling her breath mingling with mine, the Winter mantle started going berserk with naked lust. The damned aura of power Mab had given me let me do some incredible things, but the constant drum-beat of sex and violence it kept playing at my thoughts and emotions never went away. So at twenty seconds, I started breathing faster, and at thirty my head was besieged by impulses of Things to Do with Karrin, and by the time a minute had gone by I was forcing myself to remember that I was stronger than I realized and to be careful not to clench my hands on her and haul her bodily against me.

Though, to be fair, she was reacting in almost exactly the same way and she didn't have an aura of wicked Faerie power to blame it on.

So maybe it wasn't the mantle at all. Maybe it was just me, which was scary.

Or maybe it was just . . . us.

Which was actually kind of an amazing thought.

Her fingers twined in my hair and gripped hard and she gasped, "Okay. You are a genius of conversation. This is exactly what I need."

"Are you su—" I began to ask.

"God, stop talking, Harry," she growled, and her hand got more intimate, sliding under my shirt. "I'm tired of waiting. You're tired of waiting. We're tired of waiting."

I made a vague sound of agreement that sort of turned into a growl. Then her mouth found mine again and muffled the sound and my heart rate accelerated to the level of frantic teenager. So did hers. Our breaths were coming out faster, synced, and then my hand slid over her hip and she let out a sound of need that robbed me of the ability to think about anything at all.

"Now," she gasped. Then she made a bunch of sounds that sort of had a consonant and a vowel as clothes got removed, or at least re-arranged. I helped her a little with mine, because after all, she only had one hand to work with. She kept urging me to hurry, though without words. And then I was kneeling on the floor and she was spread beneath me on the couch, our hips aligning, and I leaned down to find her mouth again and—

—and I felt her stiffen with sudden pain, felt the catch in her breath as it hit her. Her shoulder or her leg, I couldn't tell, but, dammit, she was supposed to be recovering, not . . . being athletic.

Her eyes opened all the way. She blinked at me a few times and asked, "What?"

"I . . ." I mumbled. "I don't know if . . ."

She seized my shirt in her good hand and dragged me toward her, eyes lambent. "I am not made of glass. Harry, I want this. For once in your life, would you please shut your mouth, stop thinking, and just do me."

I looked down and said, "Um."

Karrin looked down, and then up at me. She rolled her eyes to the ceiling for a second, and I swear to you, she must have had an even bet-ter sexual frustration face than I did. Then she sort of deflated, which made two of us, and let out her breath in a slow sigh.

"Dresden," she said, "this chivalrous self-identity thing you have go-ing is often endearing. But right now, I want to kick it in the nuts."

"I can't hurt you," I said. "I'm sorry."

She rolled her eyes again and pulled me down so that she could put an arm around my neck, while I carefully kept any weight off her. She kissed my temple and said, very gently, "I know. You dear idiot."

I put my arms around her carefully and hugged her back. And that was when someone knocked briskly at the front door.

I jumped up, *en déshabillé*, and tried to rearrange my clothes. Murphy sort of flopped about, trying to do the same with one hand and two largely immobile limbs. We both stopped to notice, and then to notice the other noticing, and then burst out into absurd laughter while we continued trying to dress.

"The door," Murphy tittered, dragging a quilted throw across her bare legs. I managed to stagger to it, glanced out the peephole and recognized the caller, and opened the door slightly while using it to hide the fact that my pants had fallen back to my knees.

The fuzz stood on the porch.

Two men were waiting there politely, with polite, neutral cop faces. I recognized one of them, though it had been a while since I'd seen him. He was on the tall side of medium height, good-looking, with a regulation high-and-tight for his dark hair, although he'd added a thick mustache to his look that, admittedly, set off his blue eyes very well. He wore a suit too expensive for his pay grade and had a thick manila envelope tucked under one arm.

"Detective Rudolph," I said as I finished pulling my pants on. In a tone of voice generally reserved for phrases like *Crucify him* or *I'm going to cut your throat*, I continued, "How nice to see you again."

"Dresden," Rudolph said, smirking for a moment. "Great. Two birds with one stone. Is Ms. Murphy home?"

He put a little emphasis on the title, just to remind everyone that she wasn't a cop anymore. I wanted to smack him. I restrained myself in a manly fashion and said, "It isn't a good time. She's still recuperating from her injuries."

"The ones from last winter," Rudolph noted.

I arched a brow. Murphy's injuries from our little outing with a pack of psychotic killers and sociopathic malcontents hadn't involved gunshot wounds, and they hadn't happened at a crime scene. The medical establishment hadn't needed to report them to the police—which meant that the cops had gone sniffing around to find out about them. That wasn't good.

Murphy had been helping me with a smash-and-grab operation. We'd robbed Hell. Or at least, *a* hell. The target hadn't been anything inside Chicago PD's jurisdiction, but we'd kind of had to get there through the basement of a bank, and it had gotten pretty thoroughly wrecked as a result. Plus there'd been the guards. And the police who had surrounded the bank. And the cops we'd gone through on the way out. We'd worked hard to make sure no one would be killed, but one of our associates had slaughtered a guard anyway.

That made us accomplices to murder at least, as far as the law was concerned. And they weren't wrong.

"Yeah, those injuries," I told him. "So buzz off."

"Or what?" Rudolph asked mildly.

"Or, unless you have a warrant to enter, or some kind of believable probable cause, I imagine Murph sues your department's ass to kingdom come."

"Maybe I'll insist," Rudolph said, smiling.

"I'd love to see that," I told him, and I meant it. The mantle was talking to me again, advising me that if I wasn't going to vent some of my built-up tension on a willing woman, then beating the arrogant stuffing out of Rudolph would be an appropriate substitute.

"Nah," the second cop said in a bored, distant voice. "You wouldn't, sir."

I eyed the other guy. He was about five feet, six inches—in all three dimensions. I seriously couldn't remember the last time I'd seen a guy built so solidly. He wore a tailored suit, because I doubted anything fit him off the rack, but it was made of neutral, plain materials, meant to blend into the background of the business world. His salt-and-pepper hair was buzzed short, and his face was rough with beard shadow that I suspected appeared about ten seconds after he was done shaving. Something about the way he held himself, the way his eyes were focused on nothing in particular, put me on notice that he knew what he was doing better than most.

I wasn't familiar with the cops in Internal Affairs the way I was with

Special Investigations, or the beat cops in the neighborhoods I knew. "They partnered you with Rudy, huh?" I said. "Harry Dresden."

"Detective Bradley," he said. "Sir, it would be in Ms. Murphy's best interests to speak to us now."

"Or we could do it downtown," Rudolph said. "I don't care which."

"Rudolph," I said in a pleasant voice, "do you know how long it takes to wash dried blood from a broken nose out of a mustache?"

"Harry," Karrin said from the couch, reproof in her voice. "Dial it down a notch?" She waved an apologetic hand at me, out of sight of the men at the door. "Let's just get it over with, huh?"

I glowered at the men and said, "I reserve the right to kick—"

"Harry," Murphy sighed.

"—ask you to leave if it looks like she's getting tired," I continued smoothly. I looked past Rudolph to the older man and said, "Okay?"

"Why, you—" Rudolph said.

Bradley the human tank put a hand on Rudolph's shoulder. His fingers squeezed slightly, and Rudolph shut his mouth and then shot him a quick, hard look.

"Sir," Bradley said, "it's in no one's interests to strain an injured woman unnecessarily. We'll be brief."

I growled and said, "Fine. Come in."

They did and asked to sit. Whatever. I didn't sit down. I went and stood behind Karrin, leaning against the wall with my arms folded.

"Murphy," Bradley said.

Karrin nodded at him warily. I knew her enough to recognize some respect in the gesture, if no affection. "Bradley. Out with it, Rudolph. What are you doing here?"

Rudolph opened the manila envelope and tugged out several pieces of paper with color prints of photos on them. He tossed them onto the coffee table. I picked them up and gave them to Karrin without taking my eyes off the cops.

She leafed through the pictures, and I felt her tension growing as she did. She passed me the pictures.

One of them was a still from a security take on a Chicago street. I didn't recognize the location exactly, but I did recognize the blurred shot of Murphy, in her little SUV, speeding down the street in heavy winter conditions.

The others were shots from outside the bank, and from security cameras inside. There'd been enough bad weather and enough magic in the air that the shots were all blurry and distorted, but one of them was of a couple of guys coming out the bank door. One of them was average height, and the second was very tall.

It was a shot of me and a mercenary named Grey during our egress of the heist, taken from a distance. The veil we'd been under must have flickered, or else the shot was from before it solidified and hid us from everyone. As it was, there wasn't much but outlines. Our faces couldn't really be made out in the distorted images. Still, there aren't a lot of NBA-sized guys robbing banks in Chicago. Or anywhere. All of the other images were just as vague, or worse, but had the recognizable silhouette of the same tall fellow, though none of them showed my face, except the last one. In that one, I was sprinting down a sidewalk, and anyone with eyes, which is to say most people who might wind up on a jury, could recognize the image as me.

"That shot of you," Rudolph said to Karrin, "came from the same day you wound up with your injuries. Hell of a coincidence."

"How?" she asked calmly. "Rudolph, everybody in Chicago gets on a security camera or three every day of their lives."

"They aren't all speeding in dangerous conditions," Rudolph said.

"Does Chicago have IA doing traffic stops?" Karrin asked. "Now that you've cleaned up all the corruption in town?"

"Speeding down main streets during an ice storm," Bradley said. "Near reports of gang violence at the same time."

"I was trying to make it home in time for my shows," she said, her tone dry.

"Car ended up wrecked, didn't it?"

"The follies of youthful impatience," Karrin said, and pointed at her casts. "Been pretty clear about that."

Bradley nodded. "Talked to your doctor. Says he hasn't ever seen injuries like yours from a wreck. Too precise. Says they're clearly directed violence."

"He's wrong," Karrin said. "And violating HIPAA."

"And your known associate," Bradley continued, as though she hadn't spoken. "We got images of him, too."

"Beautiful picture of you, Dresden," Rudolph said. "On the sidewalk outside a building where we found a body the next day." He consulted a little notebook in his pocket. "One Harvey Morrison, CPA."

Karrin gave him her cop face, and I made do with my wizard face, but it was tough. My stomach had just dropped out. Harvey Morrison had died badly, despite my efforts to save his life. Cops get a little funny about the corpses of murdered men and women, particularly when they're squares, unconnected to the world of crime.

Failing to save someone isn't quite the same thing as murdering them—but from the outside, the two can look almost identical.

Bradley continued. "Morrison was a frequent customer at Verity Trust Bank. Which was robbed the next day. His specific vault was opened during the robbery. During which a number of explosions and a great deal of gunfire occurred." He nodded at the pictures. "Those other images are of a suspect between six foot eight and six foot eleven, presumably one of the bank robbers." He looked up at me blandly. "Six . . . nine? Isn't it, Dresden?"

"I ate all of my Wheaties every morning at breakfast," I said.

"Wiseass," Rudolph hissed. "Keep on cracking wise. I've got your ass now."

"Cracking wise?" I asked him. I shook my head at Bradley and hooked a thumb at Rudolph. "Who talks like that?"

"He might be right," Bradley said quietly. He looked from me to Karrin. "We're digging. We're good at it."

"You are," Karrin acknowledged.

Bradley nodded. "Your family's done good work in this town, Murphy. Might be a good thing for you both if you talked to us before we dig up anything more."

Karrin didn't look at me, and I didn't look at her. We didn't need to check in on this particular subject. Like most of the rest of the world, the cops didn't have much time for the world of the supernatural. They would look at us blankly if we tried to tell them about a heist run by demon-possessed, two-thousand-year-old maniacs, and including our-selves, a shapeshifter, a Sasquatch, a one-man army, and a pyromancer. They'd figure we were going for an insanity plea and run us in.

The capacity of humanity to deny what is right in front of it is stag-gering. Hell, Rudolph had seen a loup-garou tear apart a Chicago police station with his own eyes, and he was still in denial.

"I don't know what to tell you," Karrin said. "In that picture, I'm just trying to get home out of the storm. I don't know anything about this accountant."

"And I barely know anything about anything," I said. "Except that there are maybe a thousand people in Chicagoland who are six foot eight or taller. These pictures could be of any of them. Hope you got a real big lineup room."

"And this picture? The one of you?" Bradley asked politely.

"I think I was running to catch a train," I said. I was trying for guileless.

Bradley clearly wasn't buying it. He eyed us both and then nodded and let out a breath. "Yeah. Okay."

Rudolph stood up briskly and said, "Well, we tried."

Bradley gave Rudolph a steady look. Then he stood and said, quietly, "I'll be right out. Wait for me."

"I am not your fucking junior partner," Rudolph snarled. "I am your superior officer."

"Yes, sir," Bradley said. "And I'll be right out."

Rudolph gave him a disgusted look. Then he eyed me, pointed at me with his index finger, and said, "I'm looking forward to seeing you locked up, Dresden."

"Yeah, keep looking," I told him.

Rudolph smirked at me. Then at Karrin.

She stared at him. She's got a good stare. Rudolph's smirk faded and he abruptly left without another word.

"Prick," Karrin breathed after the door closed behind him. She eyed Bradley and said, "Him? Really?"

Bradley shrugged, a tectonic shift of massive shoulders. "Job's gotta get done. Someone's gotta do it."

"Yeah," Karrin said quietly.

"Dogs are out," he said. "Matter of time before they get a scent. You and Dresden both cut it close for a long time. This time you went over the line."

"Don't know what you're talking about," Karrin said.

"Crap," Bradley replied. He rubbed a hand over his buzzed scalp. "Okay. That's how you want it, we play it all the way out."

"Do your job," Karrin said. "You always have."

"Yeah." Bradley shook his head. "Rudolph let it get personal. Unprofessional. Sorry about that."

"I don't expect any better from him," Karrin said. "Not your fault."

"Hey," I said. "Why does Internal Affairs have this one? Why not Homicide?"

He shrugged. "Murphy was one of ours, I guess. You were, too, sort of."

Karrin stared at him intently for a moment. Then she said, "Thanks for coming by, Bradley."

Bradley nodded politely. "Yeah. Thanks for your time. I hope you feel better soon, Ms. Murphy."

He left, too, shutting the door carefully behind him, as if he wanted to avoid cracking it in half by accident. Maybe it had been a problem for him before.

I let out a long breath after he left. Then I went to the door and watched them depart and nodded to Karrin once they were gone.

"What'd you get from him?" I asked. "I didn't catch it."

"Because I was one of theirs, *he guesses*," Murphy said. "Bradley doesn't guess about anything. He doesn't know why IA has the case."

I rubbed at the spot between my eyes and growled. "Someone is pulling strings behind the scenes. They got the case bumped over to one of their people. Rudolph."

"And Marcone owns Rudolph," Karrin said. She pursed her lips. "Or so we've assumed."

I grunted. "Who else could have him? Who else has so much influence in this town?"

She shook her head. "Asking the wrong person in this room."

"Hah," I said. "Something else to look into. What can we expect?"

"Bradley's like a starving dog with a bone," she said. "He gets on a trail, he doesn't get off it. He doesn't sweep things under the rug. Doesn't play the game."

"No wonder he's his age and still junior to Rudolph," I said. "Fortunately, we have a little thing called fact on our side: We didn't kill Harvey. Or the guy at the bank."

Karrin snorted. "We were there, and we're lying to the police about it. That would get us put away for a while all by itself. But our DNA was at the scene, and they might turn up eyewitnesses who saw us on the street or find more images from a camera somewhere. Or . . ."

"Or someone could make some more evidence happen," I said.

She nodded. "They could make a case out of it. This could . . . wind up badly."

"What do we do about it, then?"

She arched an eyebrow at me. "Do? What are we, the villains in Bradley's detective novel? Should we try to warn him off the case? Destroy some evidence? Set someone else up to take the fall?"

I grunted. "Still."

"Not much we can do," she said quietly. "Except find out more about what's going on. I've got a few channels left. I'll check them."

"I'll add looking into Rudolph's sponsor to my list," I said.

She nodded. "Think this will interfere with the weirdness convention?"

"Might be meant to," I said. I thought about it for a long moment and then said, "When I go, call Butters."

Karrin quirked an eyebrow at me.

"This shows every sign of becoming a sharknado," I said. "Have him get the word out. To everyone. I mean *everyone* on the Paranet."

"What word?"

"To keep their eyes open, sing out if they see anything, and to be ready," I said. "Someone's cooking something big. I can smell it."

Karrin nodded, and her gaze flicked to the grandfather clock against the wall. "You've still got a little time before you need to be back," she said.

"Yeah?"

She nodded. Her blue eyes were very direct. "Come here."

I arched an eyebrow. "Um. Things haven't really changed on that score. I'm not sure that—"

She let out a wicked little laugh. "Adapt and overcome, Harry. I'm intelligent. And you've at least got a decent imagination. Between the two of us, we'll come up with something." Her eyes narrowed. "Now. Come. Here."

It would have been incredibly impolite to refuse a lady.

So I went.

6

I might have been feeling pretty smug on my way back to the car.

But my babysitter had an early morning, so as pleasant as it sounded, there would be no staying around for more. I had to go do the responsible dad thing.

I was whistling as I got in the Munstermobile and got it to roar to life. The car was an old hearse from the forties, painted in shades of dark blue and purple, with flames on the hood and front fenders. It was not subtle. It was not anywhere close to subtle. But I figured that since I wasn't, either, that made it an entirely appropriate vehicle for me.

The car growled its way to life, and I turned and put one arm on the backrest of the front seat, to look behind me as I pulled out of Karrin's driveway, and nearly had a freaking heart attack.

Two monsters sat in the backseat.

My reflexes kicked in as I flinched, twisting at the waist to bring up my left hand, the one with my makeshift shield bracelet. I let out a garbled, incoherent cry as my will slammed through it and the copper band exploded with a small cloud of green-yellow sparks as the shield came up between me and the threat. My right hand locked into a rigid claw and a small sphere of the same color of green-yellow energy gathered within the cage of my fingers, spitting and hissing with vicious heat.

The wavering, unsteady light flickered and flashed with manic irregularity, and I got a chance to process the threat.

Neither of the monsters was moving, and both of them were beautiful.

The one on my left was a woman who looked like she had come to a glorious autumn of youthful beauty. Her hair was darker than an undertaker's grave, and her silver-grey eyes threw back the light of my readied magic in flashes of green and gold. Her teeth were white and perfect, and her smile looked sharp enough to cut a throat. She was wearing a white suit and sat with her legs crossed, gorgeously, and her hands folded in her lap.

"New colors," she said, her voice velvety smooth and calm. "The shield used to be blue. What changed?"

"He made an alliance with a powerful guardian entity," said the second monster, a woman seated beside the first. She was as lean as a rod of rebar, but colder and harder, and her opalescent green eyes were too big to be strictly human. Silver-white hair fell to her shoulders, today in a fine silken sheet. Her voice sounded calm and precise, and she wore a glacier blue dress that belonged on a runway. "It does not interfere with his duties."

I looked back and forth between the two women. My heart rate began to slow as my conscious mind started to catch on to the fact that I was not, apparently, under attack.

Which was not to say that I was not in danger.

I silently counted to five while I took a slow breath and decided to be calm and cautious—and polite. "Lara Raith," I said to the first monster, inclining my head slightly. Then I turned to the second and did the same, only a shade more deeply. "Queen Mab."

"So nice to see you again, Harry," Lara said, her sharp smile widening as she tucked a lock of dark hair behind her ear. "I love your hair. You look absolutely wolfish. How long has it been?"

"Since that mess on the island," I said. "How's the Vampire Queen business?"

There was something merry in her eyes as she widened them. "Booming. I sometimes think I might be about to explode at the prospect of all the marvelous opportunities that have been opening to me."

"As long as you don't do it in my car," I said. "Hi, Mab."

The second monster stared at me for a silent moment. Mab was the OG wicked faerie, the Queen of Air and Darkness, and her tolerance for my usual insouciance had limits. It had such limits that I still had a small lump on my skull that hadn't gone away, ever since she'd smashed my noggin against the inside of an elevator. She stared at me the way a cat stares at any creature of about the right size to be eaten, and said, "It is, in fact, my car."

"Ah," I said. "Right. Well. It's a company car."

Mab continued as if I hadn't spoken. "And Ms. Raith is welcome to explode within it or not, as she sees fit."

"Uh," I said, "I think she was employing a metapho—"

"Particularly during such a shocking display of bad grace as you are engaging in at the moment." She gave my hands a pointed look and then stared back at my eyes. "Do you mean to attack my person and my guest or not, my Knight?"

I twitched and remembered that my shield and the energy for an offensive strike were still glowing and pulsing between us. I relaxed my will and let the spells fade out, until there was nothing left but a drizzle of inefficiently transferred energies falling as campfire sparks from my bracelet. "Oh, right," I said. "Um. Excuse me."

"I regret my Knight's . . . excessive impulse-control issues," Mab said, turning to Lara. "I trust it has not cast a sour tone upon this meeting."

"On the contrary," Lara said. "I find it rather charming."

Mab's expression was entirely unreadable. "Your response does nothing to increase my good opinion of you, Ms. Raith. My Knight needs no encouragement."

"Hey!" I said.

Lara's eyes wrinkled at the corners. "Think of it as you would someone who had encountered a novel kind of food." She looked at me, and her eyes turned a few shades paler. "Something substantial and rarely obtained."

Mab considered that for a moment. Then she smiled. Her scary smile. I mean, most of what Mab does is sort of scary, but her smile is just unnerving. "Just so long as you understand that my Knight is a part of my house. Do not attempt to eat my porridge, Ms. Raith. You will find it neither hot nor cold nor just right, because, unlike Goldilocks, the bears will have eaten you. Am I understood?"

"Entirely," Lara said, inclining her head to Mab. Her eyes lingered on me for a moment. "Are you sure what I ask isn't too much trouble?"

"Such things are part and parcel of his duties," Mab said. "Assuming you find him acceptable."

"Oh my," Lara said, glancing at me again. "Oh yes."

I didn't much like the sound of where this conversation was going, so I cleared my throat and said, "Ladies. I'm sitting right here. I can hear you."

"Then you shall have no trouble understanding your orders," Mab said. "Ms. Raith is owed three favors by the Winter Court."

"Three?" I blurted. "I had to fight for my life through Arctis Tor and slug it out with an Elder Phobophage just to earn *one* favor!"

Mab's eyes swiveled to me. "And you were repaid appropriately for your deeds."

"I got a *doughnut!*"

"It is hardly my concern if you wasted your favor upon something so frivolous," Mab said.

I scowled. "What the hell did *she* do?"

"She used her mind," Mab said. "Unlike some."

"Hey!" I said.

"She has indicated that she wishes to collect upon these favors," Mab said. "I have already agreed to one. I place the responsibility for providing the substance of the remaining two in your hands."

I blinked and then narrowed my eyes. "You . . . what?"

Mab blinked her eyes and appeared to, just barely, avoid rolling them in exasperation. "Two favors. She may ask them of you during the approaching summit. You will provide whatever she asks, with as much energy and sincerity and forethought . . . as you are capable of employing. You will not fail me in this."

"Here's the thing," I said. "I'm already kind of busy. You know that. I'm guarding the Senior Council and liaisoning between the Council and Faerie already."

"My time and attention are infinitely more important than yours," Mab said. "You now have more work. Cease your whining, desist from your dalliances, and do your duty."

"Two favors," I said.

"No more, no less," Mab said.

"Just . . . anything she asks, you expect me to do."

"I expect her to show respect for my Court and my resources," Mab said. "I expect her to ask nothing of you that she would be unwilling to ask from me. Within those constraints—yes."

I sputtered and said, "Suppose she asks me to steal something?"

"I expect you to acquire it."

"Suppose she asks me to burn down a building?"

"I expect a mountain of fine ash."

"Suppose she asks me to kill someone?"

"I expect their corpse to be properly disposed of," Mab said. She leaned forward and narrowed her eyes slightly. "For you to do anything less would be for you to cast shame and dishonor upon my name, upon my throne, and upon all of Winter." Her voice dropped to a whisper. "I invite you to contemplate the consequences of that."

I didn't meet her eyes. I'd seen the kind of thing Mab would do to someone who merely displeased her, much less made her look bad. My predecessor begged me to kill him. He'd been a monster when he'd had my job—but Mab had crushed him into a broken, whimpering mass of cells before she'd allowed him to die.

And if I gave her reason, she would do the same to me.

No.

She'd do worse. A lot worse.

I glanced at Lara, who was watching me with a much less inhuman but no less unreadable version of Mab's feline expression. As the effective queen of the White Court, Lara was a card-carrying monster. She was intelligent, driven, and dangerous as hell. Rumor was that she owned politicians coast to coast in the United States now, and that her ambition was driving her to reach even further. Lara was perfectly capable of asking me to do something beyond the pale of any functioning conscience.

But Lara was damned smart, too. She had to know that I had limits—that my compact with Mab hadn't changed that. If she told me to do something unconscionable, I was going to tell her where she could shove it.

Which would get me killed. Overkilled. Überkilled.

I looked back at Mab. Her face was blank granite, immovable.

Lara was a ruling peer under the Unseelie Accords, the Geneva Conventions of the supernatural world. If I said no, if I defied Mab in front of her, I was pretty sure I would get the Prometheus treatment at the very least. But if I said yes, I could find myself in even more trouble. If I knew one thing about paying off favors that were part of a Faerie bargain, it was that they were never, ever simple.

I had nothing but lousy choices. So what else was new?

"Fine," I said. "Whatever."

"Excellent," Mab said. "Ms. Raith?"

Lara nodded, her large, luminous eyes never leaving my face. "Acceptable."

"Then our business is concluded, for now," Mab said.

There was a sudden surge of icy cold wind, so out of place in the summer evening that the windows of the car glazed over with misty condensation and I was forced to blink my eyes and shield them with one hand.

When I could see again, Mab and Lara were gone, and I was alone in the Munstermobile.

"Drama queen," I muttered, and started rolling down the windows. A few minutes later, the glass was clear and I was on the road, muttering imprecations about the ruthless nature of Faerie Queens as I drove back to the apartment.

I heard the sirens a couple of blocks out. I nudged the accelerator as I came down the street toward the svartalf embassy, suddenly anxious.

I became a lot more anxious when I saw the haze of smoke in the air—and when I saw the fire department's emergency vehicles deploying onto the grounds, anxiety blossomed into pure panic.

Flames leapt forty feet into the air above the compound as the building burned.

The embassy was on fire—and my daughter was inside.

7

I parked the Munstermobile a block away and ran in. I didn't really feel like being stopped by a well-meaning first responder, so I ran in under a veil. I also didn't feel like being away any longer than necessary, so I ran in at something like Olympic speed. It probably would have been more subtle if I hadn't vaulted the hood of the last police car in the way. The cop standing next to the driver's-side door goggled and fumbled his radio, which I guess is understandable when something resembling a low-budget Predator goes by.

There's no point in having a soul-threatening source of power to draw on if you aren't going to draw on it when your daughter is in danger.

That's exactly the reasoning that got you into this mess in the first place, Dresden, isn't it?

Shut up, me.

The svartalves must have disabled the wards all over the exterior grounds, or else CFD wouldn't have been able to get near the place. It must have pained Austri to no end to lower the defenses for a gang of humans. I went by the little security shack outside the place and saw no one in it.

The front door of the building was open, and smoke was billowing from it, hazing out everything more than thirty or forty feet away. Two teams of firefighters with hoses had already deployed up to the door and were flooding the place with water, evidently preparing to work their way inside. I didn't feel like getting hosed down or set on fire, so I skirted the front door, circling the building. There was an emergency exit on the side of the building, and a secondary entrance in the rear where deliveries came in.

The earth abruptly became liquid under my feet and forced me to slow my pace or pitch forward into it. The svartalves manipulated earth the way mortals do plastic, only with magic, obviously, and I dropped my veil at once, lifting my hands. "Whoa, whoa, it's me! Harry Dresden!"

A svartalf's head came up out of the ground without any kind of accompanying illusion, enormous dark eyes blinking twice and staring at me. "Ah," the svartalf said, rising higher out of the ground, and I recognized the voice. It was Etri's sister, Evanna, his second-in-command. Her hair was pale and so silken-fine that it hung rather lankly around her head. More of her rose out of the ground, clothed in a simple shift the same color as her hair. "Wizard, I was told to watch for you. I need you to come with me."

"My daughter," I said. "I have to get to her."

"Precisely," Evanna said, her voice crisp. She held out her hand to me.

I gritted my teeth and said, "We're going to earthwalk?"

"If you please," she said.

"I hate this," I said. "No offense." Then I took a deep breath and took her hand.

I can earthwalk. Technically. I mean, if I really, really, really wanted to, I could do it. Wizards can pull off almost anything other supernatural beings can do, if we want to work at it.

But why would I *want* to?

Evanna's hand pulled me down and I sank into the ground as if it had suddenly become thick Jell-O. Dirt-flavored Jell-O. We began moving, and the ground passed *through* us in the most unsettling way imaginable. I could feel the earth grinding at every inch of my skin, as if I was thrashing my way through fine sand, and my clothes didn't do a thing to stop the sensation. Worse, it gritted away at my eyelashes, forcing me to blink and hold my hand up over my eyes—which also did no good whatsoever.

Worst was the phantom sensation of earth in my mouth and my nose and tickling at my throat. Technically, I think she was using magic to slide our molecules around and through those of the ground around us. Practically, I was enjoying the experience of a slow and torturous sand-blasting, including getting punched in the taste buds with overwhelming mineral sensations.

Seriously. It's revolting.

We emerged from the earth into one of the residential corridors below the main building, which was presumably burning merrily somewhere above us. You couldn't have guessed it. There was no smoke in the air, no sound of any fire, no leak of water from above.

I fought against the urge to spit as Evanna let go of my hand—and looked up at my grimace with amusement. "Mortals find it unpleasant, I know. Do you need a cup of water?"

I lifted an eyebrow and looked down at her. Way, way, down. Evanna is six inches shorter than Karrin, though the two of them shared something in the way of the same solid, muscular frame. "Are you patronizing me?"

"Wizard. Would I do such a thing?" She started walking and I set out behind her.

"I'm not familiar with this level," I said.

"We're a level below our guest apartments and staff homes. These are the family quarters," Evanna replied. "Etri, myself, our mates and children, a few cousins from time to time," she said. Her feet made no sound on the stone floor.

"Uh. Shouldn't everyone be leaving? You know, the fire and all?"

Evanna cocked her head to look back and up at me. "We took precautions."

"Precautions?"

"With guests like yourself, it seemed wise," she said. Her delivery was stone-faced, completely dry. "We had heard rumors of other buildings burning down. The upper levels have been isolated from the quarters below. If the administrative offices burn to a pile of ash, it will not touch these levels."

I let out a breath in a sharp exhale, a sound of relief.

She inclined her head to me. "Your daughter is safe. We assume."

"What do you mean, you assume?" I asked.

"Once the fire began, security forces attempted to enter your quarters," she said. "The Guardian would not permit us to remove her."

I suddenly felt a little sick. "Mouse. You guys didn't . . ."

Evanna stared hard at me for a moment. Then her expression softened very slightly. "No, of course not. The character of the Temple Guardians is well-known. We would never desire to harm such a being unless at great need. And we do not harm children. That is why I was sent to watch for you."

I arched an eyebrow. "Wait. You're saying that you *couldn't* go get her."

Evanna shrugged a slender shoulder. "The Guardian seemed very determined."

I walked a few steps, thinking. She was right about Mouse. He was a good dog. Or maybe even a Good dog. But he had an unerring ability to determine when someone or something was hostile. He'd die before he let any harm come to Maggie.

Which meant that if Mouse was defending her from the svartalves . . .

I had to consider that they might be up to something he considered to be no good. They were a very insular people, and they weren't human. They might not necessarily think or feel about things the way I would expect them to. I'd lived among them for a time now, and while I was comfortable interacting with them, I wasn't fool enough to think that I knew them.

Evanna stared at up my face as I thought, and I suddenly realized that she was reading my expression. Her own face went completely blank, completely empty of any emotion, as she regarded me.

"What's going on here?" I asked her carefully.

"You tell me," she said.

I made an exasperated sound. "Hell's bells, Evanna, how should I know? I've been at my girlfriend's all evening. I just got here."

She turned abruptly, in front of me, confronting me exactly as if I wasn't two feet taller and two hundred pounds heavier than her. "Stop," she said firmly.

I did.

She narrowed her eyes and said, "Say that again."

"Why is everyone so shocked that I have a girlfriend?" I asked.

She closed her eyes for a moment, as if silently counting to three, and opened them again. "Not that part. Your explanation of events."

"Oh," I said. I began to speak but stopped myself at the last second and took a moment to think. I'd only met Evanna in passing, but she was looking remarkably intense by svartalf standards—which is to say, she was working as hard as she could to give away nothing by her expression or body language. I had to wonder what else she was concealing.

I looked around us. Then I focused and used my wizard senses, looking deeper. I could feel the energy moving around us, feel the disturbances in the stone beneath my feet, in several discrete locations.

Evanna wasn't alone. There were half a dozen of the embassy's security personnel shadowing us, earthwalking through the safety of the stone.

The svartalves were being polite about it and had sent a pretty and charming captor to round me up—but subtle or not, I suddenly realized that I was a prisoner being escorted. And that my next words were going to count for more than most.

In moments like this, I generally try to tell the truth, because I don't have the intellectual horsepower to keep track of very many lies. They add up.

"I've been at my girlfriend's all evening," I said. "I just got here. I don't know what's going on."

As I spoke, her eyes closed. She opened them again slowly after I finished speaking and said quietly, "You speak the truth."

"No kidding!" I blurted. "Evanna, I know that I'm a guest, but you are officially starting to freak me out. I want to see my daughter, please."

"You *are* under guest-right," she said quietly. Then she nodded once and said, "This way."

We went up the stairs, down a hall, and through a set of doors and were suddenly in territory I recognized—the hall outside of the apartment. There were a number of svartalf security staff gathered outside the door, and they were talking among themselves as Evanna and I approached.

". . . doesn't make any sense," one of them said. "The lock is disengaged. It should open."

"It must be a spell holding the lock closed," said another.

The first twisted the doorknob by way of demonstration. It turned freely the way unlocked doorknobs do. "Behold."

"A ram, then," said the second.

"You'd ruin the wood," I told them as we approached. "And you still wouldn't be able to get past."

The second svartalf rounded on me with a scowl. "You installed additional security precautions without notifying security?"

"Clearly."

"That is explicitly against our corporate policy!"

"Oh, get over it, Gedwig," I said. "For a guy who puts magical land mines all over his lawn, you're being awfully sensitive."

"You could have threatened the safety of everyone here."

I shook my head. "It's a completely passive plane of force. Extends across the walls on either side, too. Won't hurt anyone, and you'd need a tank to break it down." And it had cost me a very long weekend of work installing it.

Gedwig scowled. "This display of your distrust could be considered an insult to svartalf hospitality."

"*My* distrust!?" I blurted. "Are you freaking kidding m—" I cocked an eyebrow, turned to Evanna, and asked, "By any chance, does your people's tongue not have a word for *irony*?"

"Peace, Gedwig," Evanna said. "Mister Dresden, can you open the door?"

"It's easy if you have the key," I said. I produced the metal door key from my pocket and flipped it around so that she could see the pentacle inscribed on its base. "I think it would be best if I went in alone to talk to Mouse. All right?"

Evanna nodded once. "So be it."

"But, my lady," Gedwig began.

She flicked a hand up, palm toward him, and the guard shut his mouth instantly.

I nodded and touched the key to the doorknob. The energy bound in the key was conducted through the metal into the plane of force beyond it, disrupting its flow and shorting out its field. "Be right back," I said, and opened the door while watching the two security guys. Gedwig looked like he wanted to push in past me, but he held his position behind Evanna as I entered and shut the door behind me.

"Dad!" Maggie said. "You're home! What's happening?"

My daughter was sitting on the dinner table, as close to the middle of it as she could get, and her babysitter, Hope Carpenter, sat next to her with an arm protectively around her shoulders. Mouse was pacing steadily around the table, his head down, nose whuffling. He glanced up at me once and shook his ears a little by way of greeting before returning to his rounds.

"Harry," Hope said. She was a very serious young woman to whom adolescence had been uncommonly generous. Having become an expert father and all, over the past three or four months, I had new insights into how worried Michael would be about how his lovely dark blond daughter might be treated, especially given that . . .

Stars and stones, Maggie wasn't all that much younger than Hope, really. In a few more years, would *I* be the one writhing with protective paternal concern? I *would*. And that thought was fairly terrifying. Or maybe humiliating. Or both.

Augh. You already have trouble enough on your plate without borrowing more, Dresden.

"Heya, Hobbit," I told her, and gave them my most reassuring smile. "Uh. How come you guys are up on the table?"

"Because they keep trying to come through the floor and get us!" Maggie said, her voice wavery with fright.

Just then, Mouse whirled his entire body around, his grey mane flying. Maybe three feet to one side of the table, the stone floor suddenly rippled and a svartalf began earthwalking up out of the ground.

Mouse rushed over to the intruder, rose on his hind legs at the last second, and then plunged down onto his front paws, directly onto the inbound svartalf, letting out a dishes-rattling sound that could only technically have been described as a bark. It was more of an explosive roar, and flickering blue sparks leapt from his mane as he struck, even as a wave of supernatural energy washed through the room like a burst of spectral lightning. There was just enough time to see the svartalf flinch, and then suddenly the floor was the floor again, and Mouse had resumed his protective pacing around the table.

"Like *that*," Maggie said. "We didn't even break any rules at all. Get 'em, Mouse!"

"How long has this been going on?" I asked.

Hope shook her head and said, "T-twenty minutes? Half an hour? One minute we were on the couch and then there were these things trying to grab us. If it hadn't been for Mouse, they would have."

I felt my jaw clench so hard that my teeth squeaked in protest. Then I turned, picked up my staff, and said, "Stay right there. Good job, boy, keep it up. I'm going to try to sort this out."

Mouse whuffed an acknowledgment without ceasing his patrol around the girls.

I turned around and went back out to the hall. I might have looked a little angry, because Gedwig and his companion took one look at me, drew their weapons—a pistol in one hand and a slender wavy-bladed dagger in the other—and backed away from each other so that they were flanking me. They didn't point the guns directly at me or lunge at me with their knives, but everything about their body language suggested to me that they would shoot without hesitation if they had to.

Evanna stood her ground, her expression blandly neutral, and looked up at me expectantly.

I didn't raise my voice—but I didn't try to hide the anger in it, either. "Why are your people terrifying two children? What have they done to offend you?"

"Nothing," Evanna said. "We only sought to put them in protective custody and escort them out of the building through the escape tunnel."

"I thought you said there was no danger of fire."

"I did," Evanna said.

"I just saw one of your people try to grab them," I said. "Tell them to knock it off. Right now."

Evanna blinked at me once, then turned and snarled something to Gedwig. He clenched his jaw but nodded, holstered his weapon, and sank into the floor.

"Your anger is misplaced, wizard," Evanna said, her words clipped.

"You are not the one who has been wronged. Blood has been spilled, and those responsible will be made to repay the debt."

"What the *hell* does that have to do with me?" I demanded.

Evanna stared at me with her huge dark eyes and said, "I will show you, if you wish."

"I wish," I said.

She gestured for the other security guard to lower his weapon, then turned and started walking. She moved quickly for such a bitty thing, and I hurried to keep pace with her.

"An assassin entered the stronghold this evening," she said.

"What?" I asked. "How did that happen? Your security measures are insane."

"The way such things generally happen," she said. "Through treachery. The assassin reached my brother's business chambers. There were explosions, which started the fire. Several guards were wounded. One threw himself between Etri and harm and paid with his life for his loyalty."

I leaned my head back and felt the anger evaporating, rapidly transmuting to pure anxiety. Someone had tried to knock off what amounted to a head of state and had gotten close. Etri was no insignificant figure in the supernatural world—he was the heaviest hitter I knew of among his people, and they in turn were the most skilled and serious smiths and crafters and designers on the planet. Hell, I'd bought materials I had needed for magical components from them myself, on a regular basis. They were expensive and worth every penny, even back when I hadn't had an athletic sock filled with diamonds tucked under my mattress for a rainy day.

"I didn't know," I said in a much quieter voice. "Who did you lose?"

"Austri," Evanna said, "who has served our family faithfully for seven hundred years."

That hit me like a punch in the gut. Austri had been weird, but he'd been a decent guy, and a man who loved his children very much.

"Hell's bells," I said. "I . . . I'm sorry for your loss."

Evanna nodded at me once.

She led me down a hall I'd never been down, and into what could only have been a war room.

It was a huge chamber with twenty-foot ceilings broken into specific organized areas. In one corner was an armory that bristled with weapons— not only modern ones, not only archaic ones, but weapons that I could not so much as identify. Across from it was a medical triage, biologically isolated behind transparent plastic curtains. Svartalves in very normal-looking medical scrubs were moving about busily on the other side.

One gurney sat silently, ignored. There was a small figure on it, completely covered with a bloodstained sheet. Austri.

I turned my eyes past that to a small vehicle park, containing a number of cars, what looked like a chariot, a Viking longboat that appeared to be made out of some kind of glimmering silver, and a number of objects that, again, defied definition. At the far end of the room was what must have been a command-and-control area, with a number of tables in circled ranks around a central work area, glowing with the light of dozens of sheets of thin crystal that the svartalves were using like monitor screens.

While I was goggling, Etri approached, wearing the usual outfit for a male svartalf who wasn't pretending to be human—a brief loincloth. He looked awful. There was a swelling bruise on one of his cheekbones and what had to have been an incredibly painful burn on one bare shoulder. His huge dark eyes were not calm. There was an anger in them so deep that I could all but feel the earth trembling beneath his feet.

He held up his right hand. Evanna lifted her left, rested her hand against his for a moment, and said, "My lord brother."

"Sister," Etri replied. He looked at me. "What did you learn?"

"He seems ignorant of events," she said.

Etri actually scowled for a second. Then he said, "You are sure?"

"As sure as I may be," Evanna said.

"I *am* ignorant," I said. "For crying out loud, do you think I'd try to kill you, or help kill you while my own daughter was right here in your stronghold?"

Etri looked at me and made a growling sound. Then a svartalf called out in their native tongue, and Etri looked over his shoulder toward the command center. "I must go. Sister, please excuse me." He turned to walk away and said, over his shoulder, "Transparency is our policy with allies. Show him."

"Show me what?" I asked.

"This way," Evanna said, and walked deeper into the war room, to the last section—a series of cubes about five feet square, made of thick, heavy bars of some kind of dark metal I couldn't identify, walled off behind a couple of layers of similar bars—a detention area.

We had to pass through a couple of gates to get inside, and they locked behind us with heavy, very final-sounding thumps of metal on metal. Only one of the cells within was occupied, and it was surrounded by a number of very alert-looking, very heavily equipped svartalves, each carrying some kind of organic-looking, swirly implement made of something like silver and wearing body armor.

"The assassin," Evanna said without emotion. "A creature well-known to be your frequent ally."

My heart suddenly fell out of my chest.

The shirtless man curled on the floor of the cage had been beaten savagely. He was shuddering with pain, and maybe shock. There was hardly an inch of skin showing that wasn't covered in bruises and cuts and drying blood. One of his feet had been . . . I don't know what. It looked as if he'd gotten it caught in some kind of industrial machine. It was twisted at an impossible angle and seemed to be given shape only by the shoe containing it.

I recognized the shoe.

I'd seen it on the beach that morning.

The assassin lifted his head toward us. He was missing teeth from a mouth caked with blood. His face was grotesquely swollen, one eye completely shut.

It was my brother.

It was Thomas.

8

My brother stared back at me. His face twitched in the beginning of a sad, helpless little smile, but the gesture made him wince in pain even as he formed it. His head sank down again and he lay shuddering, too weak to look up.

I stood there staring in shock for a really long, silent moment. I could feel the pressure of Evanna's attention on me.

"I know he visited here sometimes," I said. My brother lived his life terrified that he was slowly killing Justine, feeding on her life force. So he would find other willing partners, sometimes. Which was, in his situation, maybe the most moral thing he could have done.

When you're an incubus, life is weird like that.

"He visited me, specifically," Evanna said, "as well as some of the other women of the Court, from time to time. My people have always been enamored of beauty, above all." She took a step closer to the cage and said, to Thomas, "And this wondrous creature did not make love so much as he made art. Blindingly beautiful, passionate art." Her voice turned harder. "Blinding, indeed. Such a waste."

I looked down, closed my eyes, and pictured the cells, then the war room, then the swiftest un-burnt route out of the svartalf embassy. I tried to add in everything I knew about where the security forces were, because depending on the answer to my next question, I might be about to take them all on.

That's the thing about living behind all that security: If it can keep threats out, it can just as easily keep you in.

"What will happen to him?" I asked.

"Justice," Evanna replied, a distinct note of contempt in the word. "He began his attack seven minutes after the official treaty period for the peace summit went into effect. By the law of the Accords, that makes his offense one that must be judged by the guidelines outlined within. A neutral emissary will be appointed to investigate and serve as arbiter of his fate."

I focused my eyes hard on my toes and relaxed a little. If this was a matter to be handled by the Accords, it meant that there was time. An emissary would have to be chosen, consented to by both the svartalves and the White Court, and the following inquiry would take time. Which meant I didn't have to go out in a blaze of glory, or at least gory, that very moment.

Evanna walked closer to the cage and lowered herself to sit on her ankles, facing Thomas. "Austri was a dear friend. Were it up to me alone, I would entomb you in stone with just enough air to give you time to feel yourself gasping to death, Thomas Raith. You will die for this. Or there will be a war such as this world has not seen in a millennium."

And then she spat on him.

My hands clenched hard on the solid oak of my staff, and I took half a step forward.

Instantly, the four guards trained their weapons on me. And considering I didn't even know what the hell they were or what they were supposed to do, it might have been just a little bit dicey to try to defend myself against them.

And besides. The Accords were in play. While they were, I was basically a one-man nation, with my actions reflecting upon the White Council as a whole—and upon the Winter Court, to boot. For Pete's sake. I was *two* one-man nations: not for purposes of power, only for potential disaster.

Hell's bells.

Evanna never looked away from Thomas and paid so little attention to me that I had to figure that she was confident her people could obliterate me before I could work any mischief. Given who the svartalves were—people even the Norse gods hadn't cared to make angry—I was inclined to take her seriously.

"Well, Raith?" she said in a quiet voice. "Have you anything to say?"

It looked like neither her anger, nor her contempt, nor her question had really registered with him. My brother stayed silent and still, except for involuntary spasms of muscles and shudders of pain.

"I thought better of you, Thomas," Evanna said. "If you had a problem with my people, you could have come to us as a friend." Then she rose and walked away, her back rigid. She didn't seem to care if I followed her or not, and I felt a little nervous that I might wind up locked inside the detention area if I didn't leave when I had the opportunity—so I followed her.

As we were leaving, a voice croaked, "Ha'ay."

The sound of it hurt. I steeled myself to look calm and confident, and turned back to face my brother.

A tear was cutting a slow pale scarlet trail across the dried blood on his cheek. "Junghg. S'Jnngh."

He couldn't say *Justine.*

"It's okay," I said gently. "I know. I'll look after her."

At my words, something in him broke. He started to contract with racking sobs. The sounds he made were those of an animal dying in a bewildering amount of pain.

I closed my eyes and breathed, willing away tears before they could fall. Then I turned my back on him and left him in the grip of the people who had hurt him so badly and who had every intention of taking his life.

What choice did I have?

My brother, my only brother, had just given the gathering of the oldest and most powerful supernatural beings on the planet a surpassingly excellent reason to kill him. In an hour, he had managed to put himself into a position where he was going to get more attention and more trouble from more excessively dangerous people than I'd ever managed to do in my life.

Trust me. I do it for my day job. I know what I'm talking about.

Stars and stones, Thomas, you idiot. What have you done?

9

What's wrong, Dad?" Maggie asked me.

We were back in the apartment, and when I asked her to, she had dutifully retrieved her bugout bag from the closet.

Yeah, I know, it sounds a little paranoid to teach a child to keep a bag full of spare clothes, snacks, basic medical and survival supplies, and water, just in case she needs to suddenly go on the run. But then, most kids didn't have to contend with the possibility of enemies coming up through the floor and grabbing them, either.

I'm raising my daughter to survive the kind of thing she might occasionally be adjacent to because of who her father is, and for the time being her best survival strategy was almost always to be ready to run away.

"I can't explain it right now," I said. I slid past her into her room and snagged the bowling bag that held Bonea's wooden skull, then secured the rest of my own limited gear, along with a bugout bag of my own. "We're going to drive Hobbit home, and you can stay with the Carpenters for a few days. How does that sound?"

Maggie looked at me with very serious young eyes for a moment. "Are you in trouble?"

"I don't get in trouble," I said, and winked at her. "I get bad guys in trouble."

"It'll be fine, munchkin," Hope said, and slid a sisterly arm around my daughter's shoulders. "I totally know this drill. You can sleep in my room. I've got a laptop. We can Netflix some fun stuff until as late as we want."

Maggie leaned against Hope a little, but her eyes never left me. "Dad, why are the svartalves mad at us?"

"They aren't mad, but something gave them a scare," I said. "They're going to be edgy for a while. Hope, could you get some tuna out of the fridge and put it at the back of Mister's carrier so he'll jump in? I don't want to leave him here alone."

"Sure, Harry," Hope said, and set about it.

"They're edgy? And that's why you're sending me back?" Maggie asked.

I'd been all ready to march out, efficiently and quickly, because I had a hundred things to do and sleep had just become a non-possibility for the foreseeable future—and while I'd prepared to do so, I'd forgotten that my daughter was still, in some ways, very small. So I paused. I put everything else out of my head, and I turned to drop to a knee in front of her and give her a hug. She hugged me back tightly, her thin little arms around my neck. Mouse ceased his pacing and came over to settle down at Maggie's back and lean a shoulder against her.

"Oh, punkin," I said. "I'm not sending you away. I just need someone to look out for you until I get back."

"Because there's monsters?"

"It's looking that way," I said.

"And you fight the monsters?" she asked.

"When they need fighting," I said. Though sometimes that was a much harder thing to determine than I had always assumed it would be.

Her hug grew a little tighter and more desperate. "What if you don't come back?"

This was the part where, in the movies, a quasi-hero dad is supposed to promise his little girl that he will be just fine and not to worry about him. In the movies, they have a lot to do, and they have to get the plot moving or the audience will get bored and start texting.

I hadn't been a dad very long. But Maggie deserved better than a quick sound bite and a four-second hug while I looked tormented for the camera.

So I leaned back from her and kept my hands on her shoulders. They felt very thin and fragile, though I objectively knew that she was as sturdy as any child. Her eyes were very big and very brown and her expression was very uncertain.

"First, you should know that your dad is one tough son of a bitch," I said quietly.

Her eyes widened. "Dad!"

"I have to tell the truth," I said. "And I will fight to come home to you safe and sound. Always. I'm strong, and I'm sort of smart, and I have a lot of tough, smart allies to help me. But second, you should know that I've made arrangements to take care of you. If something happens to me, Michael and Charity have already agreed that they will watch over you. We signed the official papers and everything. And you'll have Mouse with you, always. You will always be loved. Always."

"*Woof,*" said Mouse, quietly but firmly.

"And even if I die," I said gently, "there will be a part of me here. Even if you can't see me or hear me, I'll be near you. Death can't take you out of my sight, punkin. I'll just be watching over you from the next room."

I wasn't kidding. I'd collaborated with an ectomancer and everything. If someone managed to take me out, my daughter would still have one extremely ferocious shade watching over her sleep, protecting her from spiritual predation, and guarding her dreams—and a consulting archangel to monitor that shade's mental and emotional function.

Not only that, but she would have teachers waiting for her, should she ever develop talents that ran toward the weird side of the street. People I knew and trusted who were not psychotic Winter fae. I'd made my wishes known to Mab, who regarded devotion to her duties as a liege lord as a force considerably more constant than gravity. She had agreed to make the arrangements on my behalf, should I die as a loyal henchman—and on promises such as that, I trusted Mab more than almost anyone else I had ever met.

Every dad who loves his little girl would take out that kind of insurance policy if he could.

I can.

Maggie nodded to me several times and then said, very seriously, "You're a little scary sometimes. You should know that. Regular dads don't say things like this."

I tried to smile at her, but my eyes got all blurry.

She hugged me tight again and said, "I'd rather have you. Making me pancakes."

"Me, too," I said, and kissed her hair.

"Don't let them get you," she said. "Make things right and kick their . . . their butts."

"When you're eighteen," I said, "you can say *asses*."

She let out a titter and nodded against my neck.

"Make things right?" I asked. "Where did you learn that one?"

"From Mr. Carpenter," she said. "He says making things right is the first and last thing you should do every day. And that it's what you always try to do."

"Well," I said, "he's an expert on that stuff."

"He says you are," Maggie said. "That you're a good man. One of the best he knows."

I didn't say anything back. I couldn't. My throat was all tight. Mouse's tail whumped like a fluffy baseball bat against my ankle.

"Harry," Hope called out. "Mister's in his carrier."

I coughed and harrumphed and rose. "All right, guys," I said. "Get your stuff and stay close. We'll get you guys settled."

"Then what?" my daughter asked.

I took her hand and winked at her. "Then your dad goes to work."

10

I dropped the girls off at Michael and Charity's place. I'd spoken to Michael for less than three seconds before he volunteered to watch over Maggie until I was done. And, given that the retired Knight of the Cross's home was an impregnable fortress against supernatural forces, she would be safer there than anywhere else in town.

Michael's angelic security agency's only flaw was that it could do nothing to protect him and his family against mortals—which is why Molly had secretly purchased a house that had been for sale across the street, three doors down, and ordered a contingent of Winter Court fae into position. Any conventional forces attacking the Carpenter place would find themselves facing a war band of angry Sidhe with body armor, assault rifles, superhuman agility—and overwhelming backup already on the way.

Molly and I have similar attitudes about protecting family.

Speaking of which.

Carlos and the Council would be hearing what happened before very long, and I had no doubt that they would want to meet about the ramifications of an apparent assassination attempt by the White Court on Etri on the eve of a peace conference. Once that happened, I would doubtless be given chores—so the time to start looking out for my brother was now.

I went to see Justine.

I'd visited my brother at his home often enough that the doorman recognized me, and he buzzed me in with a nod. Thomas and Justine lived in one of the ritzier buildings in the Gold Coast, and it looked it.

I went up to Thomas's place and knocked, and Justine let me in with a warm smile and a hug. She smelled like strawberries. "Hi, Harry."

"Justine," I said. She was a woman of medium height and gorgeous on a level you rarely see off the cover of a magazine. Long hair that had gone silver-white about four decades early, huge dark eyes, pale skin, all arranged as prettily as you please. She was wearing thin cotton men's pajamas that hung about her comfortably and her hair was loosely braided, with strands escaping everywhere.

She wasn't showing as yet, except for . . . Well, they talk about a glow that pregnant women get. They don't literally glow, but the strength of a pregnant woman's aura often seems reinforced by the presence of the unborn child, burning more brightly and visibly to those who can see. I wasn't making any effort to perceive the energies in question, and I'm not a particularly sensitive sort, but even I could see the flickering, ghostly colors dancing elusively about her head and shoulders.

Justine had been abed when the doorman had called up to let her know I was coming, but even blurred and disoriented from sleep, it took her only seconds to realize something was wrong. She'd survived a long time in a world of monsters by being quite a bit brighter than she let on and by becoming very, very observant. She took one look at my face and stiffened. She didn't speak at once—instead, I could see her take a moment to actively compose herself, keeping her expression neutral, and when she did speak, it was in measured tones that would not reveal her emotions. "What's happened?"

Justine was a sweet and gentle person. I hated to say anything that I knew would hurt her. But there was no way this wasn't going to hurt.

So I told her. In short sentences.

She stared at me, stunned, her eyes huge. "I . . ." She swallowed. "Does Lara know?"

I arched a brow. That was a smart question, but not one I would have expected from Justine, first thing. When people learn about a loved one under threat, their reactions are rarely rational right out of the gate—there's an emotional response first, as fear has its say, and only after that immediate emotional response does logic start kicking in. Thomas was in trouble, and there were a couple of ways to get him out of it. The smartest way would be a political solution—and for that kind of fix, Lara was a much heavier hitter than I could ever be.

My brother was frequently on the outs with his big sister, something about having issues with authority figures, which I know nothing about. Lately, though, he'd been in better odor with the White Court and consequently with Lara. It was her job to protect her people against all comers on a political level, and it was a natural thought to seek out her protection from a political threat.

Lara was also a monster. A predator. She might have been a very attractive, very pleasant, polite, and urbane monster—but only a fool would forget what she was, even for a second. You don't show predators weakness. You don't ask them for help. And those factors alone should have put Lara at *least* second on a panicked girlfriend's list of people who might help.

But . . . Lara was probably the *smart* person to seek help from. I had just expected it to take a few minutes and an effort of dispassionate reasoning to get that through to Justine. My bad, maybe. Maybe I'd made the unthinking assumption that Justine was too pretty to be smart, and too enamored of my brother to be rational.

You have to be careful with assumptions. In my line of work, they can get you killed.

"If she doesn't, she will soon," I said. "I came straight to you."

She nodded jerkily. "How is he?"

"He'll live," I said. I'd seen him worse off. Once. But there was no point in torturing her with the details. "And the svartalves are sticklers for protocol. They won't just kill him. They'll abide by the Accords."

"You're sure?" Justine asked me.

"If you knew them," I said, "you wouldn't ask that. I'm sure."

Justine exhaled slowly. "I . . . Where are my manners? Come in, please. Sit."

"Thank you," I said, and did. Thomas's apartment had been done all in art deco and stainless steel. It had been aesthetically excellent, and I'd hated it. Justine's ongoing presence there had changed things. The furniture was softer and comfier than it had been in the past, and there was more pleasant clutter, including books and a number of different kinds of craft projects, plus a small sewing area added to a corner that had previously contained only a large and expensive vase.

I sat down in the corner of the couch closest to the love seat, where Thomas and Justine habitually resided, generally together.

Justine sat down on her side of the love seat, curling her legs up beneath her, and looked very small.

"This is bad," she said quietly. "Isn't it?"

"It's . . ." I blew out a breath, choosing my words carefully. "Sticky. This isn't a problem I can blow up or burn down."

"You think he'll get out of it?" she asked.

Hell's bells. If there was any getting out of this one, I didn't see how he was going to manage it. The svartalves had the vices of their virtues: Those who labor never to wrong another see scant value in forgiveness. Thomas had betrayed them. They weren't going to rest until the scales had been balanced to their satisfaction.

"I think," I said, "that it isn't over until it's over. It's possible that the emissary will find a way to resolve the situation without further loss of life."

Her dark eyes watched my face closely. "Do you think that's what will happen?"

"I don't know," I said. "We didn't get to talk much, but Thomas wanted me to come see you and make sure you know that he loves you."

She made an impatient sound and folded her arms. "If he *loved* me, then why . . ." She bit off the words and bowed her head, the composed veneer cracking. She shuddered in silence for a moment before her voice came out again, faded and cracked around the edges. "Why? Why, Harry? I don't understand why he would do that."

Hell. I didn't, either. Things had been moving so fast that there'd been no time to sit down and ask myself some pretty basic questions. Like, why the hell had my brother tried to kill the svartalf king? Was that what had happened at all? Or was it only what had happened from the svartalves' point of view?

What had my brother been doing? Why had he been doing it?

More questions that needed answers. At this rate, I was going to need a roll of newsprint to get them all written down.

Well then. Answer some questions. Starting with why my brother had gotten violent with the svartalves. And why was Etri still alive, if my brother had set out to kill him? Say what you will about Thomas, he's good in a fight. Really good. I'd seen him take up gun and blade more times than I could count.

And every time he'd done it, my brother had gone into a fight clear-headed and purposeful. Thomas could fight, but he didn't do it for fun. So that answered one question, right there.

"Whatever he did," I said, "he had a good reason."

"What reason?" she asked, her voice breaking.

"Hell if I know," I said.

"He told you," she said. "About me. Us." She put a hand on her stomach.

"Yeah," I said. "Um. Congratulations."

"But what if he . . . if he doesn't come home . . ."

I sat there, feeling helpless. "Hey . . . Justine, hey . . . He's still alive. And I'm going to make sure he stays that way."

She looked up at me, loose hairs stuck to the tear streaks on her face. "You are?"

Oh my.

As she looked at me, I realized some part of me had made decisions without checking in with my conscious brain. Again.

I was going to keep my brother alive or die in the effort. It didn't matter who was standing in the way. Not even if it was Etri and Mab and Lara and the whole White Council to boot.

Oh dear.

Cyclical winds rising. Unprecedented numbers of sharks schooling. Studio execs lurking with contracts for numbered sequels, ad infinitum.

"Yeah," I said quietly. "I am."

She leaned forward, her eyes beseeching. "Do you promise, Harry? You?"

"Yeah," I said. "Me. My word on it, Justine."

She cracked then, doubling over the hands she held cradling her still-flat tummy, and sobbed.

I couldn't sit down in the spot on the love seat where my brother should have been. But I knelt on the other side of her and put an arm around her shoulders. "Hey. Hey. I'm right here."

Justine went limp and wept.

11

I stood in the hall after Justine shut the door behind me and felt terrible.

My brother was going to die if I didn't do something.

Justine was falling to pieces. I hadn't been able to do much about that, other than just sit there like a giant wooden statue and put an arm around her and say, "There, there."

My apartment at the svartalves' place was clearly a thing of the past at this point. No matter how things played out with Thomas, I wasn't going to keep Maggie in the same building with people who had either killed my brother or else thirsted for vengeance against him. So even if I got through the next several days alive, I was going to be looking at a move on the other end, which is always awesome.

And then there was the little matter of the peace talks with the Fomor, and the political turmoil within the White Council, and the possibility that I might be cast out of it. Which, personally, I didn't much mind. The White Council had been mainly a pain in my neck my whole life, but . . . they also gave me the shelter of their community. I'd made a lot of enemies over the years. One of the reasons they didn't just openly come to kill me all the time was that the White Council was lurking in the background, the keepers of the secrets of the universe, the men and women who could reach out from anywhere in the world and lay the smack down on their enemies. The last time someone from an Accorded nation had openly set out to attack me directly, some rascal had pulled a satellite out of orbit and right down onto his head.

Granted, he'd had his own reasons for doing it—but as far as the world at large was concerned, the White Council had spoken in a simple and clear voice: Mess with one of us, and you mess with all of us.

If they voted me out, that aegis would be gone. No one would have my back, even theoretically.

No one but Mab.

Granted, I trusted Mab with my back, within certain circumstances, more than almost anyone alive. A monster she might be, but she kept her word and stood by her people. Even so, though, I had no illusions about the fact that she wanted me to be more malleable to her various needs. She wanted me meaner, colder, darker, more vicious, because it would make me better able to do the job of being the Winter Knight. Mab couldn't push me too hard in that direction, I knew, because it would anger certain people on the Council—and the united White Council was a force not even Mab could casually defy.

But if I was cast out of the Council's graces . . . Well. Without the threat of action up to and including all-out war to protect a wizard in good standing, Mab would be free to do a heck of a lot more than offer me fresh cookies when it came to pushing me toward the dark side.

I stood there for a moment, thinking. Thomas had gone gunning for Etri. Had it been personal? Unlikely. Thomas had been, ahem, in the good graces of the svartalves. Especially their females. I don't think he'd even spoken to Etri.

Had it had something to do with jealousy, then? Had Thomas been defending himself against, or maybe trying to make a point to, a jealous boyfriend? Or brother?

Again, unlikely. Svartalves didn't understand the concept of sexual monogamy. Their pairings were based upon shared assets, biological or otherwise, and beyond an ironclad code of honor when it came to taking care of one's progeny, they found the usual human approach to sexuality baffling. If I'd sat down to dinner with Etri and announced that I'd boinked his sister, Etri would have found the remark of casual interest and inquired as to whether or not I had enjoyed myself.

Okay, I'm going to say something a little mean, here: My brother is not exactly a complicated guy. He likes, in order, Justine, sex, exercise, food and drink, and occasionally fighting someone who needs fighting. That last would not seem to include Etri and his people, who as a group were about as threatening as the Amish on your average day. So there just weren't many reasons Thomas would have wanted to kill Etri.

So maybe he didn't want to. Assume I was your average world-conquering, troublemaking megalomaniac, and I wanted Thomas to whack someone for me. How would I get him to do it?

Obvious answer. She'd still been dabbing at the occasional tear when I left.

If someone had threatened Justine, then at the very least they'd have her under surveillance. But who would do that?

To answer that question, I supposed I had to find out who was watching her and ask them.

I cracked my knuckles and got to work.

I did a quick sweep of the hallway outside their apartment and found nothing, which I expected. Lara and her security teams already had the place covered, and my brother had inherited vestiges of Mom's power. He wasn't anything close to a wizard, but he had enough juice to be aware of magical patterns, and it would be a hell of a job to slip around this hallway laying down surveillance spells for an hour or two without being noticed.

I did a second, more careful sweep to be sure, and then went outside, slowly, senses open to perceive any magical forces that might be present. I even took a quick peek at the doorman with my Sight—the dangerous practice of opening one's mind to the raw input of the energy of the universe. Under the Sight, you see things for what they are, and you remember everything you see, and no enchantment can hide from it.

I got nothing. The doorman was clean, magically speaking, or at least unwounded by the kind of psychic attack it would take to coerce him. Someone could have bribed him just as easily, I supposed, though I felt confident that Lara's security people would have had that one covered fairly well. Hell, for that matter, I assumed that the doorman *was* one of Lara's people. It would be exactly her kind of move to do that.

So I took my search outside, as alert to any kind of magical mischief as I was to any purely vanilla suspicious activity. I circled the building carefully, all my senses open, and found . . . absolutely nothing.

Which made no damned sense, so I did it again, only slower and more thoroughly, not finishing until after midnight. Apparently, there was a whole lot of nothing going around. But at least it had taken me an hour and a half to determine as much.

I growled to myself, turned to go again, and readied my Sight to make absolutely sure I hadn't missed anything.

"When a hound goes too hard after a scent," said a man's voice behind me, "he ain't watching his own back trail. A wizard ought to do better."

I absolutely did not jump in surprise. Not even a little. I turned calmly and with immense dignity and regarded the speaker with stoic calm, and not one of you can prove otherwise.

I turned to find Ebenezar stepping forward out of a veil, stumpy staff in hand. He stared at me for a good long moment, his craggy face devoid of emotion.

"Little late to be your apprentice now, sir," I said.

"You'd be surprised," the old man replied. "Hoss—"

"Busy," I said brusquely. "I'm working. How'd you find me?"

The old man clenched his jaw and looked out at nothing for a minute. "Harry, word is out, about Thomas Raith. Once I knew who the svartalves were holding, I figured you'd be in one of a couple places. This was the first one."

"You want to be a detective, you could apprentice with me for a year," I said. "If my license is still current. Gotta be honest, I've been too busy to give the city of Chicago as much attention as it thinks it needs."

"Hoss, Thomas Raith is not your responsibility," Ebenezar said.

The hell he wasn't.

"The hell he isn't, sir," I said. "I owe him my life, several times."

"It ain't about that, boy," Ebenezar said, keeping his voice calm with an effort. "This one ain't about right and wrong. It's about authority and territory."

My feet hurt. And I wasn't a child to be lectured about the way of the goddamned world. "You know, it's funny how many times I hear something isn't about right and wrong from people who are about to do something awful," I said. "It's almost as if they know they're about to do something awful, and they just don't want to face any of the negative consequences associated with their choice."

The muscles at the base of the old man's jaws clenched until it looked like he was smuggling walnuts in his jowls. "Excuse me?"

"He's my ally," I said. "My friend. I recall you telling me about how one should respond to loyalty, once upon a time. That when you get it, you gotta give it back, or else a man starts looking at those people like they're things to be used."

"I said like coins to be spent," the old man snapped, heat everywhere in his tone. Which was an admission that I was right, as much as anything.

We traded a look, and his expression told me that he knew what I was thinking, and it made him angrier.

"You think you know the world," the old man said. "You're barely *in* it yet. You ain't seen what it gets like. How bad it can get. How cruel."

I thought of Susan's face. At the last. And the rage that went through me was incandescent, yet weirdly remote, like seeing fireworks from a passing jet. The scent of woodsmoke came to me, and the alley was suddenly filling with green-gold light from the runes of my staff.

"Maybe I've seen a thing or two," I said back, and my voice sounded perfectly calm.

The wrinkles on the old man's face were heavier and thicker in the harsh lighting as his expression darkened, even as his voice became gentler, pleading. "You've put your feet in the water and you think you know the ocean. My God, boy, I hope you never see the things I've seen. But if you keep going the way you're going, you'll get that and worse. I'm trying to protect you from the mistakes that damn near killed me. That *did* kill so many of the people I cared about."

I thought of Karrin. Of Nicodemus deliberately, efficiently breaking her body. For good. It had been one of those quiet, close winter nights. I had been near enough to hear the cartilage tearing.

The edges of the carved runes on my staff began to blacken, and my vision began to narrow.

In my head, Karrin's voice warned me quietly about how fights with family hurt so much more. But the voice of my anger was so much louder. By now, the Winter mantle was alert and interested in what was going on, sending jolts of adrenaline into my system, preparing me for a fight.

I poured as much of my anger into my voice as I could, my only outlet. "Susan tried your way. And if they'd been smart instead of obsessed with revenge, the Red Court could have killed Maggie that same day, along with her mother and you and me. So tell me again what a great plan it is to send her away."

"You never should have gotten mixed up in vampire business in the first place," Ebenezar snarled. "My God, boy. Don't you see what you've done?"

"I've done what is *right*," I spat.

"How righteous of you," the old man shot back. "I'm sure that is a great comfort to the families of those who have been killed so you could be right." He slammed the end of his staff on the ground in frustration, and cracks sprang out through the concrete around it. "*Dammit*, boy. The extended consequences of your actions have cost lives. They keep costing lives. And if you do this, if you defend that vampire, there's no chance at all you'll keep the protection of the White Council."

"If I do what is right, they'll throw me to the wolves, huh?"

"Look in the mirror," Ebenezar said harshly. "You *are* a wolf. That's the *point*."

That one hit me like a punch in the gut.

And everything went quiet.

There was just the sound of me breathing, harshly.

"When the Red Court took Susan," I said finally, "the White Council thought I should have done nothing."

I'm not sure what I sounded like. But the old man looked at me with an expression I had never seen on his face before. And then he slowly, slowly ground in his heels, planting his feet, his eyes focused on the middle of my chest.

"When they took Maggie," I said, and my throat felt strange, "the White Council would have had me do the same."

"This is different," Ebenezar said, his voice suddenly hard, a clear warning. "The vampire is no innocent. He has drawn first blood. The scales *will* be balanced. There is no escaping that."

I don't remember calling up my shield, but my copper-band shield bracelet was suddenly drizzling green-gold sparks and ready to go. "He was used."

The old man shifted his shoulders, lifting his left hand, fingers spread. He didn't bother to use the toys like I did, except for his staff. When the master brawler of the White Council wanted a shield, he willed it to be. No trinkets required. "This isn't a place we have authority," he pressed, as if trying to drill the words through my thick skull. "He's not one of ours."

"He's one of *mine*!" I shouted, slamming my own staff down, and fire sizzled out where it struck the ground, a flashing circle of flame that left a black ring scorched on the concrete.

The old man glowered at me and thrust out his jaw. "Boy, tell me you ain't dumb enough to try this."

The Winter mantle immediately bayed for blood, for defiance, for violence.

I started drawing in power.

The old man sensed it and did the same.

The universe yawed slightly in his direction as he did, a subtle bending of light, a minor wobble of gravity, a shudder in the very ground as Ebenezar drank power from the earth itself. That's how much more juice the old man was taking in than me.

In my head, all I could hear was Maggie screaming. She had a lot of nightmares, of when the Red Court had come for her foster family. And he wanted to put the interests of the Council ahead of that? Of *her*?

"Oh, I'm more than dumb enough," I said through clenched teeth.

And that was when every hair on my neck suddenly rose and stood on end, all the way down to my heels. Gooseflesh erupted over my entire body at once, and a primal, primeval wave of utter terror flickered through my lizard brain, utterly dislodging every rational thought in my head.

For a wizard, that's . . . less than ideal. Control of our own thoughts and emotions is vital. Otherwise, all kinds of horrible things can happen. The first lesson every practitioner learns is how to quiet and focus his or her mind. And in the face of that mindless fear, I ran to that first lesson, allowing emotions to slough away, seeking calm, patience, balance.

I didn't get any of those. But it was enough to let me shove the terror back and to start processing some degree of rational thought.

That hadn't been the result of some random eddy of energy. Terror that focused was nothing less than a psychic disruption, a mental attack, the psychic equivalent of an ear-piercing shriek, loud enough to burst eardrums—and whatever had done it wasn't even in sight yet.

In the sleeping city around me, hundreds or thousands of people had just been seized in the talons of nightmares of pursuit and mindless fear. Those who were awake and didn't know what they were dealing with would interpret it as a brief, frightening hallucination or a migraine or simply a dizzy spell.

The old man had recovered faster than me, and by the time I'd cleared my head, he was already staring out at the night, his jaw set.

"Is that what I think it is?" I asked him, my voice shaking.

"Outsiders," he confirmed grimly. "Someone just whistled them in."

"Super," I said. "Just once, I'd like to be wrong about these things."

The old man snorted. "Now, if you were an Outsider, what would you be doing in Chicago the night before a big peace conference?"

The question was almost meaningless. Outsiders were creatures from beyond the borders of reality, from outside of our universe. They weren't human. They weren't anything close to human. They were hideous, and they were dangerous, and they . . . were just too alien to be understood. There are Outsiders who want to eat your face off, and then there are the rest of them, who don't go in for that kind of namby-pamby cuddly stuff.

Demons they might be. But demons summoned by mortals, the only way for them to get into our reality. They always have a mortal purpose, if not always a rational one.

"Trying to interfere with it in some way," I suggested. "If a senior member of the Council was torn apart by monsters, it would tend to tilt blame toward the Fomor."

"Definitely a poor way to begin negotiations," Ebenezar agreed. "And I don't think that we—"

He suddenly froze and stared.

I followed his gaze.

In a corner of the alley, where one of the building's cornices formed a shadowy alcove, blue lines of light had appeared at the intersection of the ground and the two walls.

"Oh, Hell's bells," I breathed. "Is that what I think it is?"

"Belike," growled the old man, his eyes shifting around. "How well do you know this block?"

"It's Chicago," I said.

"Good. We need a place without people or much that can catch fire."

I eyed him and said, "It's *Chicago*."

The light in the corner shifted weirdly, warped, spun into curlicues and spirals that should have existed only in Escher drawings. The stone of the building twisted and stretched, and then rock rippled and bubbled like pancake batter, and something started hauling itself out of the surface of the stone at the intersection of the three lines of light. My chest suddenly vibrated as if I'd been standing in a pool in front of an outflow pipe, and a surge of nausea nearly knocked me down.

The thing that slithered into our world was the size of a horse, but lower, longer, and leaner. It was canine in shape, generally—a quadruped, the legs more or less right, and everything else subtly wrong. A row of short, powerful-looking tentacles ran along its flanks. A longer, thicker tentacle lashed like a whip where its tail should have been. The feet were spread out, wide, for grasping, kind of like an eagle's talons, and where its head should have been was nothing but a thick nest of more of the tendrils. It had something like scales made of mucus, rather than fur, and flesh squelched on flesh.

"Cornerhound," Ebenezar said, his voice purely disgusted. "Damned things."

The old man looked weary and obdurate, like a stone that had been resisting the sea since the last ice age. His expression was annoyed.

But then I noticed one of the more terrifying sights I'd seen in my life.

Ebenezar McCoy's hands were unsteady.

The end of his staff quivered as they trembled.

My mentor, my teacher, the most feared wizard on the planet, was frightened.

He stepped between the hound and me and lifted his left hand as the thing stood there for a second, dripping slime onto the ground beneath it and seething. Dozens of little mouths lined with serrated teeth opened along its flanks, gasping at the thick summer air as though it was something that the creature found only partially breathable.

Then the cornerhound crouched, its body turning toward us with serpentine fluidity. The cluster of tentacles around its head began to quiver and undulate in weird unison, the motion becoming more and more energetic, and a weird moaning sound erupted from the creature, descending swiftly down the scale of audible sound until the tentacles all undulated together in a single quivering movement, and suddenly flew forward at the same instant, with a sound so deep I could feel it more than hear it.

The old man lifted his hand with a single sharp word, and a wall of pure arcane power blazed into light between us, its surface covered in sigils and formulae and runes I had never seen before, a wall of such density and complexity that it made me feel young and clumsy for the first time in years.

Something hit the wall with a visible impact, sending out ripples of energetic transfer through its surface, making it suddenly opaque with spreading concentric circles of light, and the ground quivered so sharply that it buzzed and tickled at the soles of my feet clear through my shoes.

Ebenezar shouted, "Concentrated fire works best!"

And then there was a flash of light and a huge sound and an invisible tsunami grabbed me and threw me off my feet.

As I went down, I saw the old man's shield wall shatter, as a thousand pounds of Outsider came crashing through it. Broken shards of light streaked in every direction as the cornerhound's talons ripped the shield apart. The energies released were tremendous, and in their wake, rune-shaped patches of fire burned on the cornerhound's flesh—but the creature shook itself in a twisting shimmy as it landed, shedding the flame like water, and slashed an impossibly fast claw at the old man.

I lay there stunned, but Ebenezar had been to this dance a few times before. The old man didn't even try to pit his speed against the Outsider's. He was already on the way out of talon range by the time the thing decided to attack, and it missed him by inches. The nest of tentacles sprouting from the thing's neck snaked toward the old man, and the cornerhound's body followed.

The old man lifted his right hand overhead and brought it down with another ringing word, and unseen force came smashing down on the cornerhound from overhead like an invisible pile driver. But as the magical strike slammed home, the cornerhound's scales undulated in a nauseating wave, tentacles flickering. There was an enormous crushing, grinding sound, and in a circle around the terrible hound, the concrete was crushed to gravel, though the hound only staggered.

Before the Outsider could recover, the old man shoved the end of his staff to within six inches of its head, shouted a word, and unleashed a beam of fire no thicker than a thread and brighter than the noonday freaking sun.

The cornerhound rolled, and instead of cutting the creature in half, my grandfather's spell sliced off the little tentacles upon the creature's flank and two-thirds of its tail.

The Outsider's tentacle cluster swept toward Ebenezar, quivering wildly, and though I couldn't hear anything, the air shook like the speakers at a major concert, the air around them rippling with something that looked like summer heat waves on asphalt.

The edge of that cone of quivering air emanating from the Outsider's tentacle face brushed against my grandfather. The old man sucked in a short huff of surprised breath, staggered, and collapsed.

Sudden terror for my grandfather crashed over me, mingling with my frustration and rage from moments before, like gasoline being mixed with petroleum jelly.

And the Winter mantle gleefully threw a lit match.

I thrust the end of my staff at the creature and shouted, *"Forzare!"*

Once again, the cornerhound crouched defensively, tentacles quivering—but the old man's fire spell had seared half of them away, and on that side, my spell hammered into the hound like a runaway Volkswagen. There was a thump of impact, and the thousand-pound Outsider staggered several steps to one side, talons raking at the concrete in an effort to resist. The thing was incredibly powerful.

Right. See, the thing about supernatural strength is that to use it effectively, you've got to brace yourself against the ground or terrain or whatever—otherwise, all you do when you lob a supernaturally power-ful punch or toss a tractor truck is throw yourself a ways back. Get something super-strong off its balance or off the ground, and it isn't nearly as dangerous as it was a second before.

So while the cornerhound was still sliding across the concrete, I summoned my power, gathered it into a small point, focusing its pur-pose clearly in my mind, and shouted, *"Forzare!"* again, and flung the beastie straight up off of the ground. As it rocketed up, I gathered en-ergy frantically again, waiting to line my shot up with the side of the creature Ebenezar had wounded as it tumbled back toward the ground, and then I focused forward and shouted again, unleashing even more energy.

This time, the telekinetic blow struck the thing like some kind of enormous batter swinging for the fences, and it flew down the alley, across the nearest side street, and out of sight. A moment later, in the distance, I heard the sound of something smashing against what sounded like a mostly empty municipal trash bin.

I staggered, suddenly dizzy and weary from throwing the three energy-intensive spells back to back. I stumbled and had to lean on my staff to keep from falling, but I made it to Ebenezar's side and helped him sit up.

"What happened?" I asked him.

His voice came out rough. "Infrasonic attack. Like a tiger's roar. Super-low-pitched notes, below what humans can hear, capable of mak-ing your organs vibrate. Can have a bunch of effects . . ." He blinked his eyes several times, owlishly, and then said, "Hell of a thing to try to stop. Help me stand up."

I did, drunkenly. "How tough are these things?"

"Very," he said. He planted his staff and blinked several more times, then peered around and nodded. "Very damned hard to kill."

"Then we don't have very long," I said.

"Out of sight and clear of people," he said.

"Parking garage less than a block off," I said. "This w . . ."

My panting voice trailed off.

Because suddenly corners in buildings all around us had begun to glow with blue light.

"Stars and stones," breathed the old man. "They've sent the whole pack."

"We should get to my car," I said.

"Your car got any right-angle corners in it?" Ebenezar said. "Because if it does, we'll have those things coming at us out of the dashboard or through the backseat." He shook his head. "Our only chance is to bind and banish them. Move, boy, get us to that garage."

The buildings around us bulged and warped and deep bass-note sounds began to drop down below the range of human hearing all around us.

"Sooner'd be better than later," the old wizard said.

"Right," I said, and forced my weary body to start moving. "Come on."

12

We ran, and the cornerhounds followed us.

I wasn't sure how many of them had taken up our trail. It was more than half a dozen, but fewer than twenty. They made oddly light-sounding skittering noises and created small clouds of sparks when they moved on concrete, the result of those steel-hard claws striking the ground. They clung to the sides of buildings like giant spiders, those same talons biting into brick and concrete, easily supporting their weight.

I took us down the alley, in the direction opposite the one where I'd tossed the first cornerhound, across the street, a slight jog, and then down the alley beyond.

"They aren't following real close," I noted. All the cardio lately was standing me in good stead now. My heart was working and I was breathing hard and I barely noticed.

"They know we're dangerous," the old man panted. "They aren't used to dealing with our reality, or with beings that can actually hurt them. Makes them hesitate."

"Here," I said, and turned into the opening of a parking garage, weaving around the wooden arm that would swing up to allow cars in. I slowed down enough to let the old man catch up to me. He wasn't covering the ground as easy as I was.

Behind us, the cornerhounds . . . didn't lope so much as scuttle, as if they had to stop to consider each burst of motion before committing to it. They were deathly swift when they moved, absolutely oily with speed—and when they stopped, they were statue still, except for the quivering of the little tentacles running down their flanks. On any one of them, it might have looked a little silly. By the time you spread the sudden, darting motions out to a baker's dozen or so of them, it crossed the line to unnerving. There was something exceptionally primitive about the motion, something reptilian, even insectile about it. It would have been creepy if the hounds had been the size of beagles. When they were more the size of horses, it was downright terrifying.

"Fire's best," the old man continued, grimly keeping pace with me. "Anything magic they can shrug off to one degree or another. All-natural fire works just fine on 'em, though."

"What's the difference where the fire came from?" I asked.

"The difference is, anything we just make out of our will, they can slip most of the punch," he said. "I ain't got time to give you a graduate seminar on intention versus the natural operation of the universe until you've completed my 'why it's a damned stupid thing to trust vampires' course."

The parking garage was built under the apartment building above us, and the top level was mostly full. There wouldn't be room to do much fighting in there, which meant there was only one way to go: down. As a rule, when you're running from something, up or down tends to be a bad idea. The higher up or the farther down you go, the fewer and fewer ways there are out of the situation, and when something is chasing you, keeping your options open is another way of saying *staying alive*.

I gave the old man a worried glance as I headed down. He looked around and came to the same conclusion I had. "No help for it, Hoss. Head down."

"No need to drag the White Court into this," I said to him as I led the way. "They aren't involved yet."

"You're here in the first place because you think you're protecting the vampire's concubine," the old man groused. "And for all you know, they summoned these things and sent them after you."

I glanced back as the first couple or three cornerhounds slithered around the corner at the top of the ramp behind us and let out chest-shivering calls of discovery. Ahead of us, where walls and roof or floor formed a corner, sickly blue light began to glow.

"Not Lara's style," I panted, leading us down another level. "She does the cloak-and-dagger stuff for politics, but for her personal enemies, she's reliable. If she wanted me dead, she'd come at me with a knife. She's straightforward that way."

"Until the one time she isn't, and you're too dead to complain about how reliable vampires ain't," Ebenezar growled.

We spilled out onto the bottom level of the parking garage. It was mostly empty. We were near the limit of how low solid ground could go in this part of the city: The lowest depressions in the concrete were full of water that had the dank smell of long-standing sources of mold and mildew. We had to have been at the water level of the lake, or a little under.

"Place like this isn't going to react well to explosions and such," I noted, looking around.

"And it don't go quite low enough to get us enough water to get them immersed in it," he added. "All right, boy. Time to start teaching you this starborn business."

I blinked and almost tripped over my own feet. "Wait, what? You're going to start talking about it . . . *now*?!"

He cuffed me on the shoulder irritably. "We got maybe half a minute. Do you want to take a walk down memory lane?"

"Freaking wizards," I complained, rubbing at my shoulder. "Fine, tell me."

"Every couple or three wizard generations," Ebenezar said, "the stars line up just right, and what amounts to a spotlight plays over the earth for a few hours. Any child born within that light—"

"Is starborn. I get it," I said. "What does it *mean*?"

"Power against the Outsiders," the old man growled. "Among other things, that their minds can't be magically tainted by contact with anything from Outside. Which means . . ."

My eyes widened. "Hell's bells," I breathed.

See, when it comes to entities from way outside everyday reality, there are only a few options for dealing with them. In the first place, they aren't really here, in a strictly physical sense. They're coming in from outside of the mortal world, and that means constructing a body from ectoplasm and infusing it with enough energy and will to serve as a kind of avatar or drone for the supernatural being, still safely in its home reality. That's what the cornerhounds had done when they'd come to Chicago to mess with us.

Fighting something like that was often difficult. The bodies they inhabited tended to have no need for things like sensing pain, for example, and it took a considerable amount of extra energy to make a hit sink home. To fight them physically, you had to dismantle the machinery of the construct's body, breaking joints and bones until they just couldn't function anymore.

For any creature of the physical size and resilience of these cornerhounds, it was a far easier prospect to bind and banish them—to simply pit your will against their own and *force* them out of the bodies they inhabited when they came here. But that was sort of like rubbing your brain against a bus station toilet; you simply had no idea what you were going to pick up by doing it—and wizards who frequently tangled with Outsiders (or even the weirder entities from within our own reality) tended to go a little loopy due to the contamination of direct contact with alien, inhuman intelligences. That's why there was a whole Law of Magic about reaching beyond the Outer Gates.

But if I was insulated against such influences . . .

Was that why Nemesis, for example, had revealed itself to me but had never actually attacked me in an effort to take control of my thoughts and actions? Because it actually *couldn't*? It made sense, grouped with my previous experiences with Outsiders, where others had been disabled by their attacks while I had still been capable of taking action. It meant that not only could I resist their influences, but I could go up against these things, mind to mind, without fear of short-circuiting my brain along the way.

The old man meant for me to banish them, to trap them in a circle and will them straight out of reality.

"How are we going to get them into a circle?" I asked.

Ebenezar leaned his staff against his body, produced a pocketknife from his overalls, and said, "Bait."

He dug the knife into his arm and twisted, and a small rivulet of blood began to pour out of the wound and patter to the ground. The first of the cornerhounds appeared at the top of the ramp behind us and let out a pitch-dropping moan, its tentacles quivering in time with the sound of falling droplets. It moved several feet toward us in an oily blur, then went still again, like some kind of bizarre deep-sea predator.

"So, here's the exercise," Ebenezar said, and passed me the knife. If he was in pain, it didn't show up in his voice. "Defensive circle first. We go at the same time. The smell of the blood is going to drive them crazy, and they're going to try to get at me. While they do, you'll lay down a circle and activate it, then banish them." He eyed me. "And just so I'm certain you haven't missed the lesson, please also observe that every single point of the plan is vampire-free."

The corners of the lowest level of the parking garage began to glow with a sickly blue light.

"Sir," I growled, taking the knife. I bent over and walked around us in a quick circle, tip of the knife scoring the concrete as I went, until I had a closed shape that mostly looked like a circle. I stepped into it, touched the score mark, and made a minor effort of will, feeling the magical circle spring up around us like an invisible screen of energy. "There's a time and a place for everything. This is neither."

I offered him the knife back by the handle. The old man pumped his fist several times and made sure the blood kept dripping. Then he folded the pocketknife and put it away, taking up his staff and holding it upright and parallel to his spine with both hands, carefully keeping it inside the circle. Cornerhounds began to thrash and tear their way into our world. Half a dozen more joined the one coming down the ramp in erratic bursts of speed—then simply crouched and waited.

"You sure?" he asked. "How about we check with one of your stalwart vampire allies who are here in your hour of need?"

I glowered at him. "That's a cheap shot and you know it."

"Eleven, twelve," the old man counted, "thirteen, aye. The whole pack is here. Now they'll get serious."

"You think these things are smart?" I said.

"Damned smart," he said. "But so single-minded and alien you almost can't tell."

"They'll try to stop me from laying down a circle, then," I said. "We need a smoke screen—but they don't even have *eyes*. Do they? They don't have eyes at the backs of their throats or something, do they?"

"You don't want to know," said the old man.

Suddenly, three of the cornerhounds speed-slithered close to us, tentacles flailing. One of them struck against the boundary described by the circle. There was a flash of light, a cascade of angry fireplace sparks, and a shuddering bass note of pain, and then the three cornerhounds went still again. The one with a singed tentacle was no more than two feet away from me.

I swallowed and did a quick scan of the circle with my eyes. A magical circle was proof against beings summoned to the mortal world, Outsiders included, but if any solid object fell across the scratch in the concrete, the circle would lose integrity and collapse, and we'd be at the things' mercy.

"But they run on audio?" I asked him.

"Like bats."

The cornerhound near me rose onto its hind legs, tentacles probing, as if seeking a way around the curtain of force provided by the circle. There were sharp popping sounds as tentacle tips brushed against the circle and recoiled in little bursts of sparks and low rumbles of pain.

"No teeth," I noted, my throat dry. "Out of morbid curiosity, what happens to us if they, uh . . . get us?"

"They take us into one of those corners," Ebenezar said, "and drag us back to wherever they came from."

I swallowed. "Then what?"

The old man looked faintly disturbed and said something that, for wizards, is akin to dropping an F-bomb. "I don't know."

I blinked at him and felt my eyes widening. "Oh." I swallowed again and said, "These are major entities. Don't know if I can take them all on at once."

"There aren't multiple entities there," he said. "Just one, that happens to be running around in several different bodies. It's a package deal, Hoss. You can't banish one of them without banishing all of them."

I looked past Ebenezar to where an old pickup had been parked, the only car down on this lowest level.

"Then we have to turn up the pressure," I said, nodding at the old truck.

"Ring of fire?" he asked.

"Ring of fire," I said. "Damn. Sure wish I had a buck—"

The sneeze took me completely off guard. It came out of nowhere and was louder than it had any right to be, my voice cracking halfway through. There was a surge of tension and energy, a dizzying burst of involuntarily expended magical energy, and way too much ectoplasm coming out of my nose.

There was also a clatter, and a galvanized five-gallon steel bucket fell to the ground at my feet and started rolling. Ebenezar spat a curse and stabbed his staff at the bucket, pinning it to the ground an inch or two before it could break the circle and get us both killed.

"Bucket," I finished lamely, my nasal passages completely obstructed by ectoplasm. Ugh. "Sorry. It'll be gone in a second."

The old man blinked at the bucket. "Hell's bells, boy. Conjuritis? At your age?"

"Conjurwhatnow?" I asked.

The old man lifted his right hand and murmured a word, fingers curling into a complex little sequence, and there was a surge of will from the old man that enveloped the bucket—and instead of quivering and collapsing into ectoplasm, it held steady while the old man bent over and picked it up. "Conjuritis. I've told you about that."

"No, you haven't, sir," I said.

The old man scowled at me. "Are you sure? Maybe you just weren't listening. Like on vampire day."

"*Seriously? Really?*" I demanded of him and swiped an arm at the tentacular horrors closing in on us. "Right now?"

He thrust his jaw and the bucket at me. "Every time you get tangled up with them, you get burned," he said. "Boy, when are you gonna use your head?"

I seized the bucket from him.

Suddenly, without a sound, without any kind of signal, all of the hounds crouched in an identical stance, and their tentacles began to vibrate all together.

"Go!" Ebenezar thundered. "Fast!"

Right. Time to get my head in the game. Maybe the cornerhounds couldn't physically get to us, but if all thirteen of those things dropped the purely physical bass on us all at once, I was pretty sure we weren't walking out of this garage.

In a perfect world, I could have broken the circle, rendered myself undetectable to the enemy, and just slipped aside and let the old man keep their attention while I laid down the circle and came at them.

But I'd have to make do with a birthday prank I'd been getting ready for Butters, instead.

First, step out of the circle.

As I did, the cornerhounds tensed, muscles and tendrils quivering.

At the same time, Ebenezar began to backpedal to put his back to the nearest column supporting the garage, even as he brought up another bulwark of invisible force to take shelter behind. "Come on, ye great ugly beasties!"

The cornerhounds' tentacle heads flared out, tracking the old man, and rumbling, vibrating, subsonic thunderclaps filled the air and made me dizzy.

I rose, will gathered, and lifted my right hand, fingers spread to project energy, and snarled, *"Consulere rex!"*

The spell wasn't a terribly complicated one. It basically duplicated an air horn. Just . . . a little bigger. And it played a tune.

Okay, look. You're going to have to trust me on this one: Having a friggin' *Tyrannosaurus rex* roaring out the tune of "Happy Birthday to You" at full volume is an *entirely* appropriate birthday present for Waldo Butters.

The sound that filled the parking garage wasn't the volume of an air horn. Or a marching band. Or a train's horn. It did, in fact, check in at around a hundred and sixty decibels. It wasn't a hundred and sixty-five because when I'd tried that much, it broke all the glasses in the kitchen and set my hair on fire.

I'm not kidding.

For the record, that's about the same amount of sound a passenger jet makes at takeoff. Now imagine being in a relatively small, enclosed, acoustically reflective area with that much noise.

No, don't. If you haven't done it, you can't imagine.

The sound was less like noise than it was like being thrown into an enormous vat of petroleum jelly. Instantly, I felt like there was no way to get a good breath. There was pressure against all of my skin and pain in my ears, like when you dive to the bottom of a deep pool. I dropped my staff to the ground so that I could clap my hands over my ears, not that it did much good. This loud was a full-body, weapons-grade loud. It was a minor miracle I had the presence of mind to hang on to the bucket.

I had planned to run for the truck—but I hadn't really counted on how damned loud this spell was going to be. So I staggered that way instead, barely able to keep my feet and walk in a straight line.

The cornerhounds had it worse than I did. Under the assault of my "Dino Serenade," they crouched in pure agony, tendrils flailing, head tentacles flapping wildly, like some kind of flared-hood lizard receiving jolts of current. They weren't howling now, or if they were, it was kind of redundant.

Sometimes the best defense is a T. rex.

I drunkenly fell only twice on the way to the truck. Then came the hard part.

I had to take my hands off my ears, and the, uh, music felt like it was going to burst my eardrums. I put the bucket down, crouched beside the truck, and called upon Winter.

Being the Winter Knight isn't much fun. Having that mantle in my life on a daily basis meant that I had to fight and work, every day, to keep being more or less me. The damned thing made me think things I would rather not think, and want things I would rather not want. Being the Winter Knight doesn't help you be a good dad, or make better pancakes. It doesn't help you understand philosophy, create beauty, or garner knowledge.

What it *does* do is make you hell on wheels in a fight.

I seized the truck by its frame, used the hem of my spell-armored leather duster to protect my hands, tensed my back and my legs, and stood up.

It was hard. It hurt like hell as the edges of the frame and the mass behind them bit at my hands, even through the duster. My muscles screamed in protest—but the absolute cold of Winter ice filled my thoughts and my limbs, a counteragony that either dulled the physical pain or gave me so much additional pain that the mere physical torment seemed irrelevant by comparison.

The pickup truck quivered and creaked in my hands, and with a surge of my shoulders and legs I got my grip reversed and pushed the vehicle up onto its side.

Staggering under the assault of the ongoing "Dino Serenade," I clenched my right hand into a fist and peered at the truck until I found the plastic of the gas tank. Then I drove my fist into it and right through the tank's wall.

I ripped my fist out and brought the bucket up with the other hand at the same time. Gasoline flooded onto my shirt and then into the bucket. Five gallons fills up pretty damned quick from a fist-sized hole. Once it was sloshing over the brim, I turned and staggered back toward the circle.

And my "Dino Serenade" ended.

The silence hit me like a club. I staggered to a knee, barely able to hold on to the bucket, and gasped.

As I did, I became aware of the cornerhounds. Most of them were gathered around Ebenezar, who was protected by so many layers of energy that his actual bodily shape was distorted to my sight—but one of the hideous creatures wasn't three feet to my left.

Another was less than six inches to my right.

There was a stunned, frozen instant where none of us moved and the world was one big after-tone from a chime the size of a skyscraper. And then my own sadly unremarkable singing voice added, into the silence at the spell's finale, "And many moooooooooore!"

Tendrils flailed in excitement.

Tentacles flared in angry aggression.

I broke into a sprint, sloshing gasoline from my bucket.

"Sir!" I screamed.

A cornerhound leapt at me, a thousand pounds of tentacles and talons and muscle.

I ducked, reflexes as sharp and fast as the report of a gunshot on a clear winter evening.

Claws raked at my back.

My duster's protective spells held, and all the night's sweat and discomfort became worthwhile.

Ebenezer, meanwhile, had survived the blast of infrasound that the pack had begun to deliver just before my spell went off, and he hadn't wasted his time since. With a single word, he pointed at the concrete floor of the parking garage, and a cloud of fine chips of rubble flew upward in a perfect circle as the old man's will dug a trench two inches deep and four across in the obdurate flooring.

Three of the hounds hit him, one second motionless, the next moving like serpents guided by some singular, terrible will. The old man swatted one of them away with an upward blow of his staff and a detonation of kinetic energy that slammed the Outsider into the concrete ceiling and brought it back down in a shower of rubble from the impact. The second hit him square in the chest with outstretched talons, and there was a humming snap of expanding energy that sounded like a bug zapper the size of a Tesla coil. It recoiled from the old man, claws burned black. But the third cornerhound hit him in one leg, and while the old man's shield protected him from the impact, the natural consequences of Newton's First Law and having one leg slammed out abruptly from beneath him were harder on the old man. He went down with a gasp as another trio of cornerhounds blurred to within striking range at the base of the column.

The Outsiders closed on my grandfather, talons and tentacles tearing. Flashes of light, humming howls of electricity, the stench of charred flesh, and basso moans filled the air as the old man fought them, his body encased in armor of pure will that made my own defensive spells seem crude and primitive by comparison.

I sprinted to help him, and as I did, I felt the plummeting tone of a subsonic roar hit my back, a sensation weirdly like that of a low-pressure stream of water.

One second I was moving fine. The next I was staggering, the entire garage a sudden blur. My guts had turned to water, my knees to jelly. It was everything I could do to get a hand on the ground and shift to a modified three-point gait, in order to keep from simply falling over and spilling the bucket and its contents everywhere. As I moved forward, the ground kept rotating counterclockwise, no matter how much my rational brain insisted that couldn't be happening—my inner ears weren't having it.

Behind me, the hounds came forward in sudden streaks of oily speed.

I gollumed across the lower end of the circle the old man had cut in the floor around him, with the hounds in full pursuit—and two more flying toward me from the circle's upper end. They were already in midleap.

From the floor, from beneath a mound of foes, the old man shouted and a burst of wind suddenly swept up from the floor. It caught the two hounds with exactly enough force to lift them over my head and past me, sending them crashing into the pack pursuing me, briefly disrupting their advance.

And the old man did that from a under a pile of nine *more* of the things trying to seize him with their tentacles and tear him into quarters.

That is a wizard, people.

I covered the rest of the ground toward the uphill end of Ebenezar's circle. I couldn't have dropped the gas into the circle at its lower end. Gravity wouldn't have been our friend. But I got to the uphill side of the circle and poured out the gasoline as quickly as I could without sloshing it out of the little trench in the concrete.

One of the cornerhounds let out an ululating cry, the sound distressed, and half the creatures atop Ebenezar peeled off him and flung themselves at me.

The cornerhounds probably should have thought their way through taking pressure off a man of my grandfather's skills. A shouted word sent a burst of flame roaring out from the surface of his body in an expanding Ebenezar-shaped wave of blue-white fire, and the cornerhounds around him recoiled. The old man slammed his right palm on the earth, growling a low phrase, and gravity suddenly increased around the hounds coming toward me, dragging them to earth as they fought in vain against the weight of their own bodies.

The hounds on Ebenezar recovered from the blast of flame and threw themselves onto him again. Now he couldn't fight back—not and hold the hounds coming toward me, anyway.

The Outsiders went at him, and there was another light show as the old man's personal defenses resisted and spat sparks of defiance back at them. In that moment, only the power of my grandfather's mind and will stood between him and death.

Meanwhile, the four who'd originally been on me came darting spastically back into the fray, circling out around the field of increased gravity that held their companions.

I looked up to see cornerhounds blurring toward my face, which was exactly where I did not want them—but I flung my face into the circle, because that was where I absolutely *did* want them, spinning as I went so that I could look back and see the cornerhounds leaping toward me in a group so tight that each of the four hounds was touching the others, talons and tentacles outstretched, in one of those moments that, at the time, seemed to last forever.

And as I went, as their tails cleared the line of the circle, I focused my will on the trough in the floor, snapped my fingers, and shouted, *"Flickum bicus!"*

My will carried fire to the gasoline in the circle, a single small static spark of eye-searing brightness, and flame leapt up with a low sound like something huge taking a deep breath, the fire racing swiftly around the circle's exterior and burning with a clear, cold blue light.

Working magic inside of circles is intense. Doing it in a ring of fire, where the flames close the circle is . . . like being inside a room where the walls and floors and ceilings are all sheets of mirror, with infinities of reflection spinning in every direction. Anything you do with magic inside a ring of fire has a tendency to build power very, very rapidly, and to send fragments of energy rebounding around inside of it, recombining in potent and unpredictable ways—so potent and unpredictable, in fact, that while the technique was not black magic per se, it was nonetheless on the list of prescribed spells and actions that the Wardens used to assess the warlock potential of any given wizard. It was that dangerous.

Think of a ring of fire as, oh, an experimental fusion reactor. One way or another, something big is going to happen. If this banishing got out of hand, something closely resembling a small nuke could go off in the middle of the Gold Coast.

The good news was that this was the kind of magic I was good at—moving massive amounts of energy in a straight line. Even better, the fact that the Outsiders were *in* the circle with me meant that I didn't need any of their bits to create a channel for the spell.

Of course, it also meant they could rip my face off while I tried.

God, I love working under pressure.

I hit the ground and slid a ways as the first of the hounds closed on me. I kicked its squishy nest of tentacles as hard as I could with one booted heel along the way. That pushed me back a bit from the thing and seemed to disorient it long enough for me to shout, "Hounds of the corners, I banish thee!"

I infused my voice with my will, and the normally invisible screen of the circle suddenly came to green-gold life, myriad ribbons of tiny flame stretching up to the ceiling of the garage, but rather than remain a steady column, the ring of fire pulsed and swelled and subsided again. Flickers and sparks began to spit from the stone where Ebenezar's will held gravity against four of the hounds. More sparks began whirling off his defensive spells, larger and brighter, moving more like fireflies, with an eerie emulation of biological purpose.

When I added my voice to that, the flames brightened to an almost unbearable intensity—and a basso wail went up from thirteen throats at once, and every single hound turned to fling itself at me.

Once the old man was loose of them, he promptly raised his left hand and smacked his palm down on the concrete, and concrete groaned as gravity increased again, dragging at the hounds, who despite their resistance were crushed inexorably to the floor.

And the old man's face had gone purple with the effort of the spell, his expression twisted into an agonized rictus.

My God, he could be killing himself right in front of my eyes.

He couldn't keep up an effort like this for long.

"Cornerhounds, servants of the Outer Night, this world is not meant for you!" I shouted at them. "I banish thee!"

Again came a chorus of basso moans, but the helpless hounds couldn't break the grasp of Ebenezar McCoy's will.

Except for one—the one who happened to be nearest me.

The old man, while holding his defenses *and* an earth magic working that would take me at least a minute to even assemble, had done a *second* earth spell with such precision that he had excluded me from the excessive gravity while catching all the cornerhounds in his mind's net.

Well. Twelve out of thirteen. The last one began to drag itself out of the gravity well and toward me, pushing itself upright the moment its front talons cleared the increased gravity, its legs bunching for a leap that would end at my throat. It got clear and leapt.

The ring of fire began to make a howling sound, the light flickering and strobing through several spectrums of color that fire had no business emitting. The energy in the air became so thick that it made my eyes itch, and I hadn't even added my own gathered will to it yet. If I defended myself from the hound, abandoned the banishing, there would be no way to predict what would happen with all this gathered energy.

So I stood my ground as the hound tore free of the heavy gravity, and shouted, "Hounds of Tindalos, return to the Void that awaits thee! I banish thee!" I raised my staff in both hands and began to release my will.

And I *felt* them.

Inside my head.

Felt the Outside.

I'm not going to try to explain to you what it was like to experience that. If it hasn't happened to you, there's no common point of reference.

It hurt. That much I can tell you. The Winter mantle didn't do a damned thing against that kind of pain. Pain is as good a way to think of it as any. Touching their thoughts to yours is like licking frozen iron and giving yourself an ice-cream headache from it at the same time.

Their thoughts, or whatever madness it was that passed for them, began to devour mine. I felt like my mind was being chewed apart by a swarm of ants. And then for just an instant, the alien thought patterns made sense, and I saw an image from their point of view—a being made of coherent light, a column of glowing energy centers, and pure dread, standing like an obelisk before the cornerhounds, a bolt of terrible lightning gathered around its upraised fists, head, and shoulders, like a miniature storm front.

I saw what they saw when they looked at me.

And I felt their fear.

The Winter mantle howled with sudden hunger, Winter's power flooded into me, and frost gathered on every surface in the parking garage with a crackling like a swimming pool full of Pop Rocks. Certainty flooded over me, the sense of the fusion of purpose, will, desire, and belief—certainty that moments like this were precisely why I existed in the first place.

"BEGONE!" I roared, and slammed my staff down, unleashing my will as I did.

And within the ring of fire, reality became a storm of ghostly energy, of random light and sound, of darting bolts of light and color. I felt the cornerhounds raise their will against mine—and theirs crumbled like day-old corn bread. I tore them from their ectoplasmic bodies and sent their unseen, immaterial asses screaming back to the Void outside of all Creation.

The thirteenth hound's talons were maybe eight inches from the tip of my nose when energy howled and swirled in the circle as the banishing spell caught up the cornerhounds. There was a sudden indrawn-breath sound that moaned through the night all around us, a great shuddering in the air—and then they simply vanished.

So instead of being dismembered by a thousand-pound monster, a thousand pounds of gross, slimy ectoplasm smashed into my chest, promptly knocking me on my ass and sending me sliding fifteen feet across the floor.

Twelve more cornerhounds' worth of ectoplasm washed out over the now-extinguished ring of fire and began to ooze over the entire parking garage.

Ebenezar sagged down to lie on his side, then rolled onto his back, breathing as heavily as if he'd been running up stairs, while a sludgy flow of ectoplasm three or four inches deep went past him. It looked like the after-party on the set of *The Blob*.

I tried to flick goo from my fingers and had little luck. The stuff was like snot but stickier, and if not for the fact that it would sublimate and vanish within about a quarter of an hour, it would have put a real dent in my wardrobe over the years.

But for the moment, I was covered in clear, gelatinous snot.

We were both silent for a moment before Ebenezar croaked, "See? Not one vampire needed."

I eyed the old man, weary from the expenditure of so much energy. Then I asked, "Why do you hate them so much, sir?"

He glanced over at me and stared for a moment, pensive. Then he asked me, "Why did you hate those ghouls you killed at Camp Kaboom?"

I frowned and looked away. I wasn't proud of what I'd done that day. But I wasn't sure I'd do it any differently, either. The things those ghouls had done to a couple of kids I'd been helping to teach did not bear thinking upon.

Neither did the ghouls' endings.

I used ants.

The old man sighed. When I looked back at him, his eyes were closed. His cheeks seemed sunken. And there was a sense of desperate weariness to him that I had never seen before. When he spoke, he didn't open his eyes. "See? You know why. I hate them because I know them. Because they took someone from me."

"Mom?" I asked.

His jaw muscles tightened. "Her, too. What you did to the Reds was a hell of a thing, Hoss. But the part of me that knows them thinks it was only a good beginning. God help me, some days I'm not sure I don't agree."

"The Red Court got the way they were by killing a human being. Every one of them. The White Court is different. They're born that way. And they're not all the same," I said.

"Game they've played for a very long time, Hoss," he said. "You'll see it for yourself. If you live long enough."

He exhaled and sat up. Then he reclaimed his staff and shoved himself to his feet. His face didn't look right. It wasn't purple at least, but it was too pale, his lips maybe a little grey. His eyes belonged on a starving man.

"It's best if we get off the street and behind some wards," he said. "If they've got the gumption and resources, whoever sent those things might try it again."

"No," I said. "Not until I get something on this whole starborn thing."

His jaw flexed a couple of times. Then he said, "I told you. You were born at the right time and place. As a result, you . . ." He sighed as if struggling to find an explanation. "Your life force resonates at a frequency that is the mirror opposite and cancellation of the Outsiders. They can't take away your free will. They're vulnerable to your power. Hell, you can punch them and they'll actually feel pain from it."

Well. A kick to the sort-of face had made that cornerhound flinch for three-quarters of a second, anyway. "Let's call that one Plan B."

"Good idea," Ebenezar said.

I frowned. "This starborn thing. It happens all the time?"

The old man seemed to think about that one before he answered. "Once every six hundred and sixty-six years."

"Why?" I asked him. "What's it for? What's coming?"

The old man shook his head. "Lesson's over for tonight. I already said more'n I should've."

"Wait a minute," I said.

"Hoss," he said, his voice quiet and like granite, "there's nothing you can do for the vampire except go down with him. Drop it." He closed his eyes and spoke through clenched teeth. "Or I'll make you drop it."

I expected to feel fury at his words. I don't react well to authoritarian gestures.

But I didn't feel angry.

Just . . . hurt.

"You don't trust my judgment," I said quietly.

"Course I do," he said grumpily. "But I care about you even more— and you're ears-deep in alligators and you ain't thinking so straight right now." He pushed back a glob of ectoplasm that threatened to gloop down into his eyes. "You know me. I don't want to do this to you, Hoss. Don't make me."

I thought about what I was going to say for a moment.

I had always known Ebenezar McCoy as a gruff, abrasive, tough, fearless, and unfailingly kind human being, even before I knew he was my grandfather.

I wanted to tell him about his other grandson. But I understood the hate he felt. I understood it because I felt it myself. It was the kind of hate not many people in the first world are ever forced to feel—the hate that comes from blood and death, from having those near you hurt and killed. That was old-school hate. Weapons-grade. Primal.

If someone somehow revealed to me that a ghoul was actually my offspring, I wasn't sure how I'd react, beyond knowing that it wouldn't be reasonable and that fire was going to come into it somewhere.

I couldn't count on my grandfather. I might be all my brother had going for him.

"Sir," I said finally. "You know me. When someone I care about is in trouble, I'll go through whatever it takes to help them." My next words came out in a whisper, "Don't make me go through you, sir."

He narrowed his eyes for a long moment. "You figure you can, Hoss?"

"So far, so good."

"Said the man falling past the thirtieth floor."

We both stood there for a moment, dripping ectoplasm, neither one of us moving.

"Stars and stones," the old man sighed finally. "Go cool off. Think it over. Sleep on it." His voice hardened. "Maybe you'll change your mind."

"Maybe one of us will."

"One of *them*," he spat the last word as if it had been made of acid, "is not worth making an orphan of your daughter."

"It's not about who they are," I said quietly. "It's about who I am. And the example I'm setting."

The old man stared at me for a moment, his expression unreadable. Then he turned and stalked away, slowly, his shoulders slumped, his jaw clenched. As he went, he vanished behind a veil that was, like most of his magic, better than anything I could do. Then I was standing there alone in an empty parking garage.

I looked around at the wreckage and closed my eyes.

Family complicates everything.

Dammit.

13

Hounds of Tindalos are real, huh?" Butters asked. "Weird."

"Well. For some values of 'real,'" I said. "Lovecraft got kicked out of the Venatori Umbrorum for mucking about with Thule Society research. Don't know many of the details, but apparently it wasn't actually cancer that ate his guts out later. It was . . . something more literal."

I sat at the little table in Butters's apartment kitchen. I had my duster off and both arms resting on the table with my palms up. Butters sat across from me wearing loose exercise clothes. An EMT's toolbox sat on the table next to him, and he was currently peering at my hands through his thick glasses, which he now wore in the form of securely fastened athletic goggles.

Butters was a little guy in his early forties, even littler since he'd gotten in shape. Now he was all made of wire. Maybe five foot five, but if he weighed more than a hundred and forty pounds, I'd eat my duster without salt. His hair was a dark, curly, unkempt mess, but that might have been a factor of my showing up at his door after hours.

"God," Butters muttered, using a wipe to try to clean up the deep, gashing cuts on my hands. "You've got motor oil in the gashes."

"That a problem?"

He gave me a sleepy, unamused look. "Considering all the debris it collects, yes. Yes, it is." He sighed. "Gotta debride it. Sorry, man."

I nodded. "Just get it over with."

After that, it was about twenty minutes of water, Betadine solution, and a stiff-bristled brush being applied to the area around and inside the wound. Could have been worse. Butters could have used iodine. Could have been worse—but it wasn't exactly a picnic, either. Hands are sensitive.

Twenty minutes later, I was sweating and grumpy, and Butters was glowering at the injuries with dissatisfaction. "That's the best I can do here. I'll wrap them up, but you'll need to change the bandages every day and watch like hell for any sign of infection. But in the 'ounce of prevention' department, until you get invulnerable skin, buy some gloves to protect your hands, Hulk."

"Not a bad idea," I said. "How bad is the damage?"

I have this issue with feeling pain. It's part of the Winter Knight package. When something happens to me, I sort of notice it, but ongoing pain just fades into my background. So bad things can happen to me without my knowing it, if I don't use my head.

"I don't think there's damage to the actual working structure of your hands," Butters said. "But the human body isn't really made for flipping trucks, man. You're . . . developed to something like the maximum potential for your height and build, but your joints are still human joints. Your cartilage is still only cartilage, and even though your body will actually heal damage to it, it has a failure point. And your bones are still just made of bone." He shook his head. "Seriously. One of these days you're going to try to lift something too heavy, and even if your muscles can handle it, your bones and joints won't."

"What's that gonna look like?" I wondered aloud.

"An industrial accident," Butters said. He wiped down my hands one more time, thoroughly, and then began wrapping the injuries. "Okay. So the White Council wants to give you a hard time. So what else is new?"

Butters was not up on the concept of the Black Council, a covert group of wizards who were nebulous and impossible to identify with absolute certainty, working toward goals that seemed nefarious at best. That information was being held under wraps by the wizards dedicated to fighting them. Partly because we had little hard evidence about the Black Council, what they wanted, and who their members were, and partly because the bad guys would have more trouble taking action against us if they couldn't even be sure who was their enemy.

Butters was trustworthy, but the Black Council was a wizard problem.

"Yeah," I said. "Meet the new boss. Same as the old boss."

Butters gave me a look, because I'm not a very good spy, and lying to a friend doesn't come naturally to me. But he shrugged and let it pass. "Okay." He yawned. "When you called, you said something about health issues, plural. What else is bothering you?"

I told him about my sneezes and the conjuritis.

His eyes narrowed and he said, "This isn't some kind of prank you're playing on the new guy in the game, is it? Cause I've sort of been expecting that."

"What? No, that's crazy talk," I said, and tried hard not to think about my "Dino Serenade," due for his birthday. "This is a real problem, man."

"Sure," Butters said, snapping his rubber gloves off and beginning to clean up. "Whatever."

Augh, of all the crazy things to happen in my life, I wouldn't think that my randomly involuntarily conjuring objects out of nothing at the drop of a hat would really ping anyone's radar. All the things happening right now, and *this* is the point that Butters picks to decide to stonewall me on?

I sneezed again. Hard.

There was an enormous crash as a section of mortared stone wall, maybe four feet square, landed on Butters's kitchen floor so hard that the tables and chairs jumped off the floor. Butters yelped and fell over backwards out of his chair—into a backwards roll that brought him onto his feet right next to the steak-knife holder on the counter. He had his hand on a knife before I could get all the way to my feet.

Little guy. But fast. Knights of the Sword aren't ever to be underestimated.

"Dere," I said, swiping awkwardly at my nose with my forearms. "Dere, do yuh *see* dow?"

Butters just stared at the stone wall. Then he quivered when it shuddered, went transparent, and then collapsed into gallons and gallons of ectoplasm. The supernatural gelatin kind of spread out slowly over the floor, like a test shot for a remake of *The Blob*.

"Okay," Butters said. "So . . . that just happened." He regarded the ectoplasm and then me and shook his head. "Your life, Harry. What the hell?"

"Dod't asg be," I said. I sloshed across the kitchen floor, got a paper towel, and started trying to blow my nose clean. It was kind of a mess. It took several paper towels' worth of expelled ectoplasm to be able to breathe properly again. "Look, I can't be randomly making things appear out of nowhere."

"I'm a *medical examiner*," Butters wailed. "Christ, Harry! Some kind of virus that has an interaction with your nervous system, or your brain or your freaking subconscious? This is something to take to Mayo or Johns Hopkins. Or maybe Professor Xavier's school."

"None of those guys are weird enough. You do weird."

He put the knife back and threw up his hands. "Augh. Okay. Is there always a sneeze?"

"Yeah, so far," I said.

"Then go get whatever cold medicine you use when you have a cold. Maybe if you stop the sneezing, you'll stop the conjuring, too."

I eyed him blearily and then said, betrayed, "I could have worked that out for myself."

"Weird," he said, "it's almost as if you're a grown damned man who could make some commonsense health decisions for himself, if he chose to."

I flipped him a casual bird, idly noting the pain of my wounded hand as I did. "What about the nausea? I feel like I'm stuck on one of those rides where you go in circles."

"Infrasound is pretty wild and unexplored stuff," Butters said. "There's too many potential weapon and military communication applications for it, and it's hard to measure, so there hasn't been a ton of publicly available research. But, the Paranet being the Paranet, I found some Bigfoot researchers who say that the Bigfoot use it all the time to encourage people to leave the area. Tigers and other large predators use it, too, as part of the roar. You know when you hear stories about people freezing when a tiger roars? That's infrasound, having an effect on the parasympathetic nervous system."

"Thank you for confirming that infrasound is real and has real effects on people," I said, "but I sort of worked that one out for myself. How do we fix it?"

"According to the Bigfoot guys, mostly what it takes to recover is a solid sleep cycle. So if you're going to insist on treating me like your personal physician, here: Take two aspirin and call me in the morning."

I grimaced. "Yeah, sleep probably isn't an option, either."

"Course not." Butters sighed. He went to a cabinet, got a plastic bottle out, and tossed it to me.

"Allergy meds?" I asked skeptically.

"Are you a doctor now?" Butters went to the sink and filled a cup of water.

"Maybe I'm only a medical examiner."

Butters dipped a finger in the water and flicked it at me, then sloshed carefully through the slime and put the cup down on the table in front of me. "Diphenhydramine," he said. "Sneezing is usually a histamine reaction. This is an antihistamine. Should help. Take two."

I did as I was told without uttering any intelligible complaints, thus proving that I am not a contrary, obstreperous stiff neck who resents any authority figure telling him what to do. I mean, it's documented now. So that's settled.

I heard a soft sound and looked up at the doorway to the kitchen as a young woman appeared in it. Andi had long, wavy red hair and bombshell curves. She wore an emerald green terry-cloth robe, which she held closed with one hand, her eyes were sleepy, and she was possibly the most adorable werewolf I knew. "Waldo? What was that bang? What happened to the floor? Oh, Harry." She gathered the robe closed a little more closely and belted it. "I didn't realize you were here."

"Andi," I said. "Sorry. Didn't mean to wake you up."

She gave me a tired smile. "Word is that things are getting tense out there."

"Word's right," I said. "Be a good idea for you to get as much sleep as possible, in case you're needed."

"And yet," Butters protested, "here you are waking *me* up, I notice."

"For you, sleep time was yesterday," I said. "You're needed now."

There were soft footsteps and a second female voice said, "Is everything okay?"

Another young woman appeared, built slim but strong, legs like a long-distance runner's beneath an Avengers T-shirt big enough to serve her as a dress. She had very fine mousy brown hair to her shoulders, and she was squinting her large brown eyes against her lack of glasses, her narrow face disrupted by sleep marks on one cheek. "Oh," she said. "My goodness. Hello, Harry. I'm, um, sleeping over. After the LAN party. Oh, did you hurt your hands?"

"Marci," I said, to possibly the second-cutest werewolf I knew. "Um, hello. Yeah, just having ol' Doc Butters take a look and make sure I didn't void the warranty."

"Oh," Marci said. "Oh. I see."

There followed a long, awkward silence, in which Butters turned a sufficient shade of pink to advertise for breast cancer awareness and in which Marci looked at everything in the apartment except me.

"Oh for God's *sake*," Andi said. "He's an adult human being, guys. And I'm tired. Draw conclusions, Harry. You won't be far off. And I'm not cleaning this mess up." She turned, took Marci's hand, and walked firmly back toward the bedroom. Marci's cheeks flushed bright red, but she went with Andi.

I looked at Butters, whose earlobes could have been mistaken for tamales, and arched an eyebrow.

The little guy took a deep breath. Then he said, in a calm and sincere tone, "Harry, tease me about this or screw it up for me and I'll knock your teeth out."

And he said it right.

I mean, there's a way to convey your sincere willingness to commit violence. Most people seem to think it involves a lot of screaming and waving your arms. It doesn't. Really dangerous people don't feel a need to shout about it. Delivering that kind of warning, sincerely, takes mostly the sort of confidence that only comes from experience.

Butters had only had the Sword since the end of winter. He'd only been doing full-speed Knight work for about a month. But I'd seen him square off against maybe the scariest and most dangerous bad guy I personally knew—and Butters won.

And here he was, facing off with *me* like a grouchy badger. He told me to back off and made me want to do it.

Damn. Little guy had gotten all grown up on me.

I lifted my hands, palms out in a gesture of peace, and said, "Okay. But I reserve the right to talk to you about it later."

"Oh God, can we not?" Butters said. He went to rummage in the fridge, restless and uncomfortable as a schoolboy caught with adult magazines. "We're sort of keeping this low-key."

"Low-key, huh?"

"Look," he said plaintively, "I'm honestly not quite sure how this happened, and I am not going to let anyone screw it up."

"Butters," I said. I waited until he turned to look at me. Then I said, "You're not sitting in *my* kitchen asking for *my* help, man. I'm pretty sure you can make the choices for your own damned life. And there's too much glass in my house to throw stones at anyone."

His eyes searched my expression for a moment before some of the tension went out of him. "Yeah. Yeah, okay. Sorry, man."

"Nothing to be sorry for," I said. I glanced back toward where the women had disappeared to and opened my mouth. Then I ran my tongue thoughtfully over my teeth and closed it.

Honestly, it's really kind of startling how many problems that avoids. I should think about doing it more often.

"Well," Butters said, in the tone of a man getting back to business. "The Paranet has sent out advance warning. Everyone's been told to see something, say something. How about some details?"

I nodded and let him know what was up with the Accorded nations and their peace talks, and what had happened to Thomas.

He listened, his expression growing increasingly concerned. "That sounds, um, like it could get interesting."

Something in his tone made me look up at him. "Oh?"

"Sanya's in town," Butters explained. "Hotel by the airport. He was just transferring through O'Hare, but his flight got delayed. Seven times."

There were currently two Knights operating in the whole world. Two of them. And the Knights of the Sword (or Cross, depending on how you looked at their professional priorities) tended to wind up wherever they were needed most, always by pure coincidence. In fact, the coincidence was so freaking pure that it basically told me that it wasn't. I have a dubious relationship with God—but judging from the timing of the entrances of the Knights He sponsored, He would have made one hell of a travel agent.

"Ah," I said. "Um. Maybe Sanya could visit for a couple of days. You guys could swap some Knightly stories or something."

Butters gave me a tight smile. "Right. How do I help you?"

I shook my head. "I've learned by now that you guys are gonna show up exactly where the Almighty wants you, and I'm probably smart not to bump anybody's elbow. So it's up to you. How do you think you'll do the most good?"

He regarded me for a moment. Then he said quietly, "It's the Paranet crowd I'm worried about."

Magical talent is like the rest of it—not everybody gets the same amount. There are people like me who can sling around the forces of the universe as if they were their personal play toys. And then there are folks who, while gifted, just can't do that much. The have-nots of the magical world had an unenviable position in life—aware of the world of the paranormal, but without sufficient personal power to affect it.

Until the Paranet, anyway. Use of the Internet had done something for the have-nots that nothing else had before—it had united them. Meeting people, making friends, coordinating activities, had all become more possible to do in relative safety, and it had created something just as powerful as tremendous inborn magical talent: a community. Supernatural predators were having less and less luck against the have-nots these days, as they coordinated actions, communicated with one another about possible threats—and joined their individually unimpressive talents into coordinated efforts that made them, in some senses, damned near as strong as a wizard themselves.

But though they had gathered enough strength to keep the vermin at bay, they still couldn't stand against a storm like the one that was brewing.

"Agree," I said quietly. "And they know you. Trust you. Work with them. Get all the intelligence you can and coordinate it with Murphy."

"What about Thomas?" Butters didn't know Thomas was my brother, but he knew he was an ally we'd fought beside on too many occasions to consider leaving him behind.

"What I'm working on," I said. "Could be that a diplomatic solution is the best one."

Butters slipped on the slime and nearly fell on his ass. He caught the countertop and held himself up instead. Then he stared at me, fighting back a smile, and said, "Who are you, and what have you done with Harry Dresden?"

I glowered at him and rose, careful to keep my balance amid the ectoplasm on the floor. It was already sublimating. Maybe half of it was gone. I shrugged back into my duster. "I don't *prefer* to blow things up and burn things down. It just sort of works out that way."

Butters nodded. "What's your next move?"

"Diplomacy," I said, "with a Vampire Queen."

"You're not going out to the château alone, are you?"

Château Raith was White Court headquarters in these parts. "Yeah."

Butters sighed. "I'll get my bag."

"No need," I told him. "Mab and Lara have a deal going, and Mab's made it clear what Lara is and is not allowed to do. She'll play nice."

Butters frowned. "You sure?"

I nodded. "Rest up. Might need you for real in the next few days."

He looked from me toward the bedroom, his conscience at war with the rest of him.

"Okay," he said finally. "Good luck, Harry."

"I only have one kind of luck." I nodded my thanks to Butters, grabbed my staff, and set out to visit Lara Raith.

14

The Raith Estates are about an hour north of town, out in the country-side, where the nearest neighbor is too far away to hear you scream. The place is surrounded by a forest of old enormous trees, mostly oak, that look like they were transplanted from Sherwood Forest.

Hell, given how much money and power the White Court had, maybe they had been.

I pulled up to the gates of the estate in the Munstermobile to find them guarded by half a dozen men in full tactical gear and body armor. They weren't kidding around. As I stopped the car, five men pointed assault rifles at me, and one approached the car. His spine was rigid, his shoulders square, his manner relaxed. Lara recruited her personal security almost exclusively from former military, mostly Marines.

The man who approached my car had a solid blend of the lean ath-leticism of youth and the weather-beaten edges of experience. He wasn't even bothering with a friendly smile. I'd run into him before. His name was Riley.

"Can I help you, sir?"

"Those look like ARs," I said. I squinted at the guns pointing at me. "But with real big barrels. Beowulfs?"

Riley shrugged. "Can I help you?"

"I'm to see Ms. Raith," I said.

"The grounds are closed for the night."

I looked at him and rested my arm on the window, leaning back comfortably in my seat. Lara didn't hire chumps, so I was dealing with a professional. Most of the time, when something like this happened, I tended to react . . . adversely. But I was here to talk about a diplomatic solution. I was kind of new to this, but it seemed like me blowing things up and knocking Lara's people ass over teakettle probably wouldn't be an auspicious beginning.

And besides. I was willing to bet the other five or six guys I couldn't see right now would have a rocket launcher or something, and I didn't need to add getting blown up to my list of problems.

So I smiled at the guard and said, "Look. You and I crossed trails over the Luther case. Didn't turn out so good for your boss, but you kept it from being a real wreck—and we were both good to our word."

Riley eyed me and grunted acknowledgment.

"I'm here to help," I said. "Call the house. You won't regret it."

He stared down at me for a second. Then he walked to the guard-house and got on a phone while several extremely heavy-duty guns, known for their vehicle-stopping capability, pointed steadily at my noggin. His face turned a little paler than it had been, and he waved at the other guards, causing them to lower the weapons and get out of the way. He pointed at me and then at the gate, and the gate buzzed and began to swing open.

Before I could put the car in gear and pull in, a Humvee pulled out of the dark inside the fence. The military-style truck was painted all black and had an actual Ma Deuce machine gun on a pintle mount atop it. The Humvee preceded me, and as my car began to roll, a second truck, mounted with a second machine gun, pulled in behind me. Riley swung up onto the running board of the second vehicle, his rifle held up and ready with one hand as we began to move forward. I was, it seemed, to have an escort up to the house.

We all drove a couple of miles through Sherwood until we emerged from the trees onto the lawn of a grand estate I'd been to a few times before. As we drove, I could feel subtle webs of magic woven throughout the path along the road. We were moving too fast for me to get much out of what I could sense, but the implications were pretty clear—Lara had blanketed her grounds in magical protections of some kind.

Now, where had she gotten someone to do that for her?

Raith Manor was a brooding château, built in the rural French style from some point in the eighteenth century, only with more gargoyles and Gothic features that vaguely called Notre-Dame to mind. You know, before the fire. Our cars parked out front, and Riley came over to open my door for me.

"We'll secure your car while you're inside, sir," he said, and held out his hand for my keys.

Securing my car could mean a lot of things, among them tearing it apart to look for bugs and bombs. I eyed him. "After you've acknowledged my guest-right," I said.

"You are Ms. Raith's guest and are under her protection," he confirmed.

I grunted and handed him the keys. Then I walked up the steps for several seconds, Riley moving behind me. I opened the door and went inside like I owned the place.

The big old house was a dark and brooding structure, even on a sunny day. On a dark night, it looked like a set from a *Scooby-Doo* cartoon. There was little light inside, just a few subtle spots, here and there, on art that was scattered throughout the place. I started to turn to ask Riley where everyone was, but Riley had stopped at the door and shut it carefully, leaving me alone in the dimness.

I wasn't alone for long. There were the firm clicks of someone approaching in heels over hardwood floors. I didn't want to assume it was a woman. Raith Manor was that kind of place.

A tall figure in a close-fit black business suit approached me through one of the swaths of dim light. Dark red hair, cropped close to her head, intent sea green eyes—with scar tissue at their corners. She moved like an athlete and looked about thirty—but something about the way she regarded me as she came closer made me wary, and I took note of the fact that her knuckles were swollen with scars.

"Good evening, Mister Dresden," she said, smiling slightly. "If you will follow me, I'll take you to Ms. Raith."

"Yeah, okay," I said, and we started walking deeper into the manor.

The place looked like it had been furnished by the Louvre. I'd lived in apartments that cost less to build than a few square feet of the château.

It took me maybe twenty seconds to be pretty sure of my guess. "What, did Vadderung throw some kind of bargain-basement sale on renting out his Valkyries?"

"Monoc Securities provides consultants in many places, sir," the redhead said. She gave me a smile with maybe four teeth too many in it, and her voice turned into a purr. "Though I'd be interested to hear what you mean by *bargain-basement*."

Valkyries were superhumanly strong, swift, and tough and had the kind of experience that comes with agelessness. And they didn't just like fighting—they lusted for it. I'd seen a Valkyrie in action before. I didn't particularly want to take one on for funsies, and this Valkyrie walked with a kind of steady, inevitable confidence that said that walls would be well advised to stay out of her way.

"It wasn't an insult for you personally," I said. "I'm playing."

"Don't I look playful to you?" she asked.

"You look like you play rough," I said.

The woman let out a laugh that came up straight from her belly. "You've got eyes and you use them, *seidrmadr*." She regarded me speculatively. "Most men don't know to show some respect."

"You have much trouble correcting them?"

"No, I don't," she said calmly. "My sister says you're all right in a bad spot."

"Sister?" I asked. "Oh, Sigrun Gard?"

"Obviously," she said. She offered me her hand. "Freydis Gard."

"Harry." I took her hand. She had a grip like a pneumatic clamp, and my bandaged hands were sensitive. "Ouch, be gentle with me."

She laughed again. "I've heard some about you, but you must be something special. Lara doesn't let anyone interrupt this part of her day."

"It's probably easier than replacing the landscaping," I said.

"That must be it," Freydis said. She came to a door, stopped, and gave me an utterly incongruous Vanna White kind of gesture toward it. "And here we are."

So I opened the door and went through it, into the Raith Dojo.

I mean, when you've got five gazillion rooms in the house, one of them obviously needs to be a dojo. Sure.

The room was brightly lit, a stark contrast to the rest of the place. The walls were white and had a number of white silk banners hanging from them, marked with black kanji that had been painted on. I knew enough to recognize the lettering but not enough to read it. The practice floor was smooth wood with tatami matting over much of it.

A woman wearing a white kimono was in the middle of the practice floor, with one of the smooth round staves called a *bo* in her hands. She was flowing through a practice routine that had the weapon whirling in an arcing blur around her and before her. The sound of the weapon cutting the air, faster than a vanilla human could have moved it, was a steady hiss.

She turned and faced me, still striking, spinning, thrusting at the empty air. Lara Raith had cheekbones that could split atoms, bright grey-silver eyes capable of boring through plate steel, and a smile that could turn crueler than a hook-tipped knife. Her blue-black hair was long and would have fallen to the small of her back if it hadn't been bound up into a messy bun. She froze in the midst of her routine, body coming to an utter halt, transforming her from a dervish into a mannequin. The demonstration of perfect control was more than a little impressive. And interesting.

But that was Lara. I had never been in her presence without feeling an intense attraction for her, and I wasn't at all sure it was because she was a vampire of the White Court, and the closest thing to a succubus that you could find this side of Hell. It had more to do with *her*. Lara was as beautiful and dangerous as a hungry tigress, and very, very smart.

She met my eyes for a second and then gave me an edged smile. "You want to talk to me right now, Harry," she said, "take off your shoes and pick up a *bo*."

"Oh, come on," I said.

She arched an eyebrow. "I don't give anyone my practice time," she said. "This is my house. You came to me. Take my terms or leave them, Dresden."

I exhaled.

Doing what she asked was an acceptable way for her to get around the traditional protections of my guest-right. After all, if we were in the dojo, training, and something bad happened to me, it could be a regrettable accident. Combat training is dangerous in its own right, after all. Or, I supposed, she could claim I had attempted to assassinate her, just as Thomas had tried to take out Etri. In fact, I could see a sort of hare-brained logic in Lara attempting to muddy the waters around Thomas's situation by creating a similar one with me, and then casting blame at a wider conspiracy. Cockamamie nonsense, but someone desperate enough to help family might reason themselves into it.

I chewed on my lip. But not Lara Raith. Not her style at all.

Lara was the slipperiest and cagiest vampire in a basket of psychotic sociopaths. I didn't really see her as the same kind of hedonistic monster as many other White Court vamps I had met—she was something much more dangerous than that. She was disciplined, rigidly self-restrained, and she didn't give way to either the demonic parasite that made her a monster or anyone else who would try to force her into doing something she didn't want to do.

If Lara wanted me dead, it would have happened already. It would have been abrupt, swift, and well executed, and I probably wouldn't have had much of a chance to respond. I might never realize it had happened. I'd seen Lara fight—and she'd seen me do the same. Neither one of us would be interested in giving the other a chance to fight *back*.

But I was on the clock here. Wasting time wrangling with Lara over protocol wasn't going to help my brother. So I set my jaw and kicked off my sneakers.

Lara watched that and her smile turned a shade wicked. "Good boy."

"Now you're just being obvious," I said, and sat down to take off my socks. I rose, left my duster on, and picked up a *bo* of my own from a simple wooden rack of them to one side of the training floor. I flexed my injured hands and winced in discomfort. The pain was already growing more distant as the Winter mantle flooded distressed nerve endings with the distant sensation of nothing but cold.

I walked around Lara to stand in front of her and took up a ready position, gripping the staff loosely, with most of it extended out in front of me at waist level, like someone holding out a pitchfork of hay.

Lara turned to me and bowed at the waist, smiling. "European."

Murphy'd shown me plenty of Asian stuff, too, but I didn't want to let Lara know about that. "I learned in Hog Hollow, Missouri," I said. "But my first teacher was a Scot."

"I spent much of the eighteenth century in Japan." She took up a ready position of her own, staff held vertically with the lower end angled out toward me.

"I thought it was closed to all outsiders then."

She grinned and moved her hip in a little roll that made me want to stampede. "Have you looked at me?"

"Uh. Right," I said.

Her smile turned warmer. "What do you want, Harry?"

I snapped my staff at her in a simple thrust. She parried easily and countered with a hard beat that came so fast that it nearly took the weapon out of my hand. I recovered the weapon and my balance, retreating from a strike that hit the mat where my bare foot had been an instant earlier. The blow landed hard enough to send a crack like a home-run hit through the room.

"Hell's balls, Lara!" I said.

"Pain is the best teacher," she said. "I don't pull hits. You shouldn't, either."

She came at me in a hard, fast strike at the level of my ankles. I caught it on the end of my staff in the nick and flicked her weapon back. "You heard about Thomas."

"And your visit to him, and your visit to Justine later, yes," she said. "What did he tell you?"

I shook my head. "All he said was 'Justine.' And he barely said that. They'd busted up his mouth pretty good."

I launched another exchange from outside Lara's reach and drove her across the mat. She was tall for a woman, but I'm tall for anybody. I probably had most of a foot of advantage in reach on her, and I started using it. The staves cracked together over and over, and I barely avoided getting my knuckles shattered. She was faster than me, and more skilled in a purely technical sense. But that wasn't the only thing that decided real fights. This was bear versus mountain lion—if she got caught somewhere I could put my power and endurance to good use, she'd be the one in trouble. I kept pressing her toward the corners of the mat, and she kept slipping to one side without ever leaving it, one step ahead of me.

But there were other ways to slow people down.

"My people are covering Justine," Lara said. "She's as safe as I can make her without sequestering her here."

"She's pregnant," I said.

Lara missed a step, and I was ready. I thrust the tip of my *bo* at her knee. She avoided it, but only by taking the hit in the meat of her calf, through the kimono, and she hissed in pain. She countered with a strike to my head that I ducked, and then she came back up onto one leg, weapon ready to defend or attack, her eyes narrowed.

If this had been for real, the fight would be over in moments. Or at least, the foreplay would. We'd both be shifting toward using supernatural abilities, and God only knew how that kind of chaos would play out. I drew back, grounded the end of my *bo*, and bent at the waist in a slight bow.

Lara regarded me warily and then mirrored me as best she could on one leg, which was excellently. "You're sure?" Lara demanded a moment later, rolling the ankle on that leg several times.

"Thomas was," I said.

"And they didn't tell m . . ." Lara pressed her lips together. Then she shifted her grip to a more aggressive stance, something like mine, and I came onto guard to match her. We thrust and parried for a moment, circling. "Have you told his grandfather about him?" she asked.

I faltered at that, and Lara sent a thrust at me that hit me square in the belt buckle and shoved me off my feet and onto my ass.

I sat on the floor for a moment, eyeing Lara, who grounded her staff and bowed exactly as I had and regarded me calmly.

She knew about Thomas and me. I mean, I'd been aware of that, but she'd put together enough to work out who Ebenezar was, too. The White Court had a reputation for being insidious subversives. Connections to them, regardless of their source, were regarded with what most of the supernatural world considered healthy suspicion. If Ebenezar's connection (and mine) to the White Court became public knowledge, the ramifications for our current situation were . . . sticky.

And Ebenezar didn't just have issues with vampires: He had volumes and ongoing subscriptions. It had the potential for a real humdinger of a mess.

"I've known from the beginning," she said impatiently, as if she'd been reading my thoughts. "I was here when my father was so obsessed with your mother. He made me play nanny to Thomas. I often heard them talk, because apparently no one in my family understands what a deadly weapon the ability to listen can be, and she left Thomas in my care once when she visited McCoy. And after she died, I helped Father hang her portrait in his psychotic little egomaniac's gallery."

I nodded. "But you never brought it up. Never used it for leverage."

"No," she said. "Because I'm also the one who changed Thomas's diapers, after his mother escaped our father. Dressed him. Fed him his meals. Taught him to read." She shook her head, her eyes focused on one of the banners. "I'm more ruthless than most, Dresden. But even for me, there are limits. Most of those limits involve family."

"That's why you didn't use it against him," I said. "How come you didn't use it against me?"

"You never gave me a good reason to fight quite that dirty," she replied. "And I couldn't have used it against you without exposing my brother to trouble as well."

"Then you know why I want to help him," I said.

"We both do."

"Then get him out," I said. "You can do that, right? Work something out with Etri and his people?"

Her features shifted subtly, changed. Somehow they became paler, more like marble, less like something that belonged to a living human person. "Impossible."

"Nothing's impossible," I said.

She held up one slim white hand. "As the situation stands, yes, it is. I've been shown the preliminary evidence. Thomas entered their embassy under false pretenses, less than ten minutes after the beginning of the armistice for the peace talks, and attempted to murder their king. On *camera*. If I do anything but deny and disavow his actions, Etri will have little choice but to assume that I sent Thomas to kill him."

"Etri's people look all stuffy, but they have Viking sensibilities," I said quietly.

"Yes," Lara replied. "If they believe I've tried to harm Etri, they will begin a war I am not at all certain I care to fight." She let out a laugh that had something of a hysterical edge on it. "Thomas couldn't have screwed this up any harder if he'd had a year to plan it."

"There's got to be something you can do," I said. "What about a weregild?"

Lara grimaced. "The svartalf who died—"

"Austri," I said. "His name was Austri."

She regarded me for a moment, her expression troubled. "Austri, then. He died defending a head of state. This is an offense against the svartalves as a nation, not just an individual. Weregild is what leaders use when they both want to avoid conflict. Etri doesn't." She shook her head again. "Our brother is beyond my political reach."

I scowled. "Well, what have you got all these Marines for, then?"

Lara eyed me as if I'd been a child missing the slowest, easiest pitches she could throw at me. "If I tried to have him forcibly taken from svartalf territory, not only would it represent a major military effort to face the dragon in its den; it would mean violating their sovereign territory as defined in the Accords. Mab wouldn't remain neutral then—she'd be obligated to help them. She might even send her hatchetman after me." She shook her head. "I might be willing and able to go up against Etri and his people for my idiot brother, if there's no other way. But I cannot and will not lead my people into a mass suicide by svartalves *and* Mab *and* the rest of the Accorded nations." She looked away, at one of the banners and its kanji, and seemed, for a moment, ashamed. "Even within my own Court, my authority has limits. If I tried such an irrational thing, they'd depose me."

I exhaled slowly.

She said nothing for a moment.

"Why?" I asked her. "Why did he do it?"

She shook her head. "I had hoped that you would know something I didn't, wizard. It wasn't my doing, and he didn't give me the least indication that it was going to happen—presumably to provide me with enough deniability to avoid a war. Which I suppose indicates that somewhere within the idiocy, he meant well."

"Fighting is out," I said.

"Yes."

"And talking is out."

"So it would seem."

"But we've got to do something."

Lara's expression became entirely opaque. "Obviously. I am open to ideas."

"We have to create more options," I said.

She nodded, her expression pensive. "I'll be working the room at the fete tomorrow night. Perhaps some leverage might be obtainable there."

"Possible? Perhaps?" I shook my head as I rose. "Our brother is going to die if we don't do something. If you can't be bothered to—"

Lara came at me in a black-and-white-and-silver-eyed blur that covered twenty feet in less time than it took me to blink. She caught the front of my duster in her pale hands and whirled me into the mat with enough force to make me see stars. By the time I'd brushed a few of them out of my field of view, Lara was astride me, one hand twisted into my duster, one hand lifted knifelike and rigid, ready to sweep down at my throat.

"Do not," she hissed, leaning closer toward me, "presume to tell me what my family is worth to me. Or what I am willing to do for them."

I didn't have a whole lot to say to that. Both of us panted. I found myself staring at her mouth.

Lara's eyes brightened, glittered like mirrors. She stared at me for a second, breathing heavily herself with the exertion of moving so swiftly.

I was intensely aware of the sensation of her weight on me. So was my . . . body. But then my body is always overly enthusiastic.

More to the point, the Winter mantle was going berserk. The mantle didn't just come with access to nifty Fae power sources and greater physical speed and strength. Winter was the spiritual home of all things primal and primitive. They were hunters, raiders, takers. Don't search the Winter Court of the Sidhe for a hug. You won't find one anywhere that doesn't collapse your ribs into your spine—but if you want savage, animalistic sex, yeah. You've come to the right place. I mean, you might get torn to pieces in the process, but in Winter, them's the breaks.

The mantle thought that Lara was a fantastic idea. That she needed someone to tear those clothes off her and spend several hours with her in heavy physical exertion, and it thought that someone ought to be me. My body was backing up that concept. It backed it up so strongly that I felt the slow, sensual tension slide into my muscles, pressing my body against her a little more firmly wherever we were in contact.

"Oh," Lara breathed quietly. Her eyes shone like mirrors.

I looked down and away from them, lest things get even more complicated. It was little improvement. It meant I could see one of her legs, positioned out to one side, and it had come clear of the folds of the kimono. Her skin was flawless and pale over absolutely glorious musculature. Even her feet were pretty.

She leaned closer and inhaled through her nose. The proximity made me feel dizzy—among other things.

I focused through the . . . well, not pain, but the need was rapidly building in that direction. I pushed my body's stupid ideas away and spoke in a calm, level voice. "Lara," I said quietly.

"Yes?" she breathed.

"Is it involuntary," I asked her, "or are you using the come-hither on me on purpose?"

I tried for a calm, bright, conversational tone. It came out a hell of a lot lower and quieter and huskier than I meant. Because at the moment, the only thing I could really think very much about was how much I wanted to toss her onto a bed and start ripping off clothing. There wasn't any thought or emotion behind that drive—just the primal, physical need of a body screaming for satisfaction.

I wondered if she was feeling something similar.

Her pale eyes stared steadily at my face, and she looked like she was thinking about something else. It took her a moment to lick her lips and answer. "It's . . . some of both. I can use it whenever I wish to. But I can't always choose when *not* to use it."

I swallowed. "Then get off me." At least I'd gotten the words in the right order. "This is a business trip. I came here to try to find a way to help Thomas. Not to get frisky with an apex sexual predator."

Lara blinked at me, and her eyes darkened by several shades. Her mouth turned up into a slow, genuine smile. "What did you call me?" she asked.

"You heard me," I said.

Some of the tension eased out of her. A moment later, she flowed to her feet and withdrew a few steps from me. I had to force myself to leave my hands down, rather than grabbing at her clothes as she drew back. "Well," she said. "You aren't wrong."

I exhaled slowly and clubbed the Winter mantle and its stupid primal drives back into the backseat. I wasn't sure I was exactly relieved that Lara had withdrawn, but it was probably simpler that she had.

She turned away and said, "The more power one has, the less flexible it is, wizard." She shook her head. "The White Court is mine. But I cannot lead it to its destruction over actions this reckless. Not even for my idiot brother." She shook her head. "Unless things change, I will have no choice but to disavow him."

"Without your support," I said very quietly, "he has no chance at all."

She closed her eyes and exhaled. Then she turned to me, her gaze intense, her eyes now a grey so deep that they were nearly blue, and said, "No, Harry. He still has one."

I swallowed and said, "Oh."

Me.

15

The Munstermobile wasn't exactly designed for speed. It didn't have power steering or power brakes—just power—and it got about two gallons to the mile.

I settled in for the drive back. Riley and the Machinegun Hummer Revue escorted me back to the front gates. I turned out of the estate and onto an unlit country road that would take me back to the highway. We'd reached the witching hour, and the summer night was overcast, pregnant with heat and rain that hadn't fallen. The windows started steaming over as vampire Graceland receded behind me, and I cranked them down laboriously.

My brother was in trouble and Lara wasn't going to be any help.

I thought furiously about how to get him out. The White Council wasn't going to be of any use unless Lara went to them with a formal request—an action that would have to happen openly, and which Etri's people would be sure to regard as a tacit admission of guilt regarding Thomas. Mab wouldn't help Thomas. His only use to her was as a replacement Knight should anything happen to me, and she could have been deceiving me about that. She didn't do things for the sake of kindness. If I was unable to show her the profit to Winter in saving my brother, she would care no more about him than about the floor she walked on.

My only two sources of diplomatic muscle weren't going to be any help, and I was pretty sure that I couldn't get into a fully on-alert svartalf stronghold and drag him out all by myself. That would be a suicide mission, just as Thomas's had been. If I went in and took along friends for support, would it count as a murder-suicide?

God, I felt sick. And tired. Stupid cornerhounds. Stupid allergy meds. What was I going to do?

My stomach rumbled. I debated hitting an all-night hamburger franchise when I got to the highway. On the one hand, my body definitely needed the fuel. On the other hand, my stomach felt like it would probably object to adding much of anything to it. I was fumbling in my pockets for a coin to flip when grey shapes loomed up in the road in front of me. I stood on the brakes and left broad swaths of rubber on the road behind me as I fought the big old car to a halt.

I wound up with the nose of the car pointing into the weeds and the headlights casting a harsh cone of white light, partly over the road and partly over the thick trees that hemmed it in.

I killed the engine and stared out the driver's-side window at the four Wardens who barred my way.

Ramirez stood in the middle of the crew and slightly forward, leaning on his cane, his dark eyes steady. He'd have been the first one to meet bumper if I hadn't been able to stop the car. Gone were the casual civilian clothes—he was dressed in the White Council's version of tactical gear, complete with his grey Warden's cloak.

To his right stood "Wild Bill" Meyers. Wild Bill had filled out a lot as he got into his late twenties, adding on the muscle and solidity of a maturing body. He'd grown his beard out, and it wasn't all skinny and patchy like it used to be. He kind of reminded me of Grizzly Adams now. His cloak was shorter on him than it had been when we'd started the war with the Red Court—Wild Bill hadn't been done growing yet. Rather than one of the enchanted swords most of the established Wardens carried, Wild Bill had a bowie knife he'd been working on steadily for years. It rode his belt across from a .45-70 Big Frame Revolver that weighed as much as my leg.

In the shadows cast to the left side of the road by my headlights stood Yoshimo, who refused to let anyone call her by her first name. It had taken Ramirez a couple of years to find out that it was Yukie, and I'm pretty sure she hadn't forgiven him. She was a girl of Okinawan heritage, about five four, and she carried a katana on her hip and an assault rifle on a strap around one shoulder. She could use either of them like a Hong Kong action-movie star.

The fourth member of Ramirez's crew stood to his left, looking steadily into my headlights. He was a slim, very dapper young man dressed in a camel-colored bespoke suit and wearing a neatly complementary bowler hat. Chandler had indulged in experimental facial hair as well, and currently sported a thick, fierce Freddie Mercury mustache. It could have looked dopey with his outfit, but Chandler being Chandler, he carried it off with panache. Maybe the strictly ornamental walking cane helped. He was the only one of the four not geared up for a fight—but then Chandler had always made it a point to uphold the forms of civilization harder than were strictly necessary.

The five of us had been through more than a little together, though Chandler had been our handler and point of contact, not usually a field guy.

None of them were smiling.

I could recognize game faces when I saw them.

Harry, I thought to myself. *These kids might be here to hurt you.*

I sat in the car for a moment while the engine clicked. Then I said, "In the future, you guys should probably look for a crosswalk. Or maybe an adult to hold your hand."

"We need to talk, Harry," Ramirez said. "Got a minute?"

I eyed him and then mused, "How'd you pull off the tracking spell?"

"Right wrist," he said.

I eyed him, then held up my right hand and peered. I had to turn my thumb until it faced almost all the way away from me to spot the dot of black ink on the outside of my wrist.

Ramirez held up his right hand and wiggled his pinky finger, where an identically shaped ink spot marked his skin.

"Wow," I said in a level tone. "Mistrusting me right from the get-go, huh?"

He shrugged. "I was pretty clear about my intentions," he said. "If you don't want others to think you're shady, man, maybe you shouldn't be doing shady things at shady times with shady people." He nodded back the way I'd come, toward the Château. "Come on, Harry. It's us. Make this simple. Talk to me."

"Maybe you don't know about my life's relationship with simple," I said. I eyed Ramirez. Then the others. "Hey, guys. What's up?"

Yoshimo gave me her samurai face. Wild Bill lifted his chin, an almost unconscious gesture of acknowledgment. Chandler rolled his eyes at them and walked forward, extending his hand and speaking in a precise Oxford accent. "Harry, good to see you, man."

Ramirez and the others tensed as Chandler walked into their lines of fire—a term that among wizards could become especially literal. I took the opportunity to get out of the Munstermobile and regard his extended hand with a skeptically lifted eyebrow.

Chandler's cobalt blue eyes sparkled, and he held up his hand, showing me his fingers. I inspected them minutely, then traded grips with Chandler in a hearty handshake, eyeing Ramirez over the shorter man's head as I did.

"How's the PhD work coming?" I asked him.

"Viciously political," he said, smiling. "History is such a thorny thing on the Continent."

"Most people can't just go talk to folks who were alive for it, I imagine," I said.

"Precisely. Maddening," Chandler said. "I'm sorry we're doing this, Harry. But you've got to admit, old boy, you've had a damned peculiar day. Or so it would appear from the outside."

I responded with a genial frown and duplicated his accent badly. "Oh really? How so, if you do not mind me asking?"

Chandler's smile didn't falter. But it took on an aspect of granite, somehow. "No one's that disingenuous, Dresden. The Winter Lady gets you quarters inside the svartalf embassy. Not long after, a known personal agent of Lara Raith and a frequent ally of your own gets inside, somehow, and attempts to assassinate Etri. Hours later, you visit the assassin's significant other, then have a meeting with Ms. Raith."

"Um," I said. "Sure, I mean, when you put it like that, I see how that might look a little suspicious. . . ."

"We've a long tradition of twisty thinking in my homeland," Chandler said. "Perhaps it has made me cynical and uncharitable, but it occurs to me that there are a disturbing number of connections in these events. It makes one wonder if you've been entirely honest with us."

I held up my wrist so that the spot of black ink Ramirez had put there was showing. "You're going to lecture me about being open and honest? And, seriously, *ink*, after the last time around with an actual traitor in the Council? What were you thinking?"

Chandler arched an eyebrow. He glanced over his shoulder at Ramirez and said, "Fair points." He took a step closer and lowered his voice. "But all the same, Dresden. It's damned peculiar. Perhaps it's time you 'leveled' with us, I believe is the vernacular."

I studied Chandler's face for a moment and then looked at the other Wardens. "How'd you decide who would be the good cop?" I asked him quietly. "Rock, paper, scissors?"

"Don't be daft," Chandler replied, "As an academic, I find myself dealing with temperamental potential lunatics on a regular basis. I was the obvious choice. And we drew straws."

"Lunatic, eh?" I asked.

"There have been certain questions about how much of your will remains your own, yes," Chandler said frankly.

"I'm my own man, more or less," I told him.

"Yes, well, you would think that, wouldn't you?" Chandler said with a wry smile. "You see our predicament. Matters are unfolding here that we don't quite understand. We have an interest in learning as much as possible."

The way he said *we* was something new. He wasn't using the word as an inclusive one, like, *we are all friends*. He was using it as an exclusive term. *We, all of us, not you.*

He was referring to me as someone outside of the White Council. His bright blue eyes were direct, almost pleading as he said it, willing me to get the message. I saw recognition flicker in them as he saw me process what he was actually saying: *Be advised, Harry. The White Council now considers you a threat.*

Didn't bode too well for that vote.

"Got it," I said, looking away from his eyes hurriedly. I gave Chandler the faintest ghost of a nod of thanks, and he twitched his eyebrows in acknowledgment. "Look, you guys are worried about nothing. You told me you want me as a liaison with Winter. Fine. I'm liaising. Mab told me to keep an eye on Lara," I said, and was technically more or less not lying, "and I came out to talk to her."

Ramirez nodded. "What'd you find out?"

"She says she's got no idea why he did it," I said. "Right now it looks like she means to disavow him in front of the Accorded nations."

"And you believe her?" Ramirez asked.

"No reason not to," I said.

Yoshimo hissed, "Vampires are not to be trusted."

The intensity of the words was, uh, kind of threatening, really.

"I'm not trusting a vampire," I said to her. "I'm trusting my reason. Lara Raith has been all about supporting the Accords. These peace talks are going to be a major test of them. She wouldn't do anything to rock the boat this hard right before they're due to begin."

"Unless she has deeper plans, and this is only part of them," Ramirez said. He glanced at Yoshimo and nodded.

Yoshimo looked at me, frowned, and started to say something. Wild Bill put a hand on her shoulder. She glanced back and up at him, some strain visible briefly in her expression—then she smoothed it out into a mask again. Then she came toward me, hands empty, and stopped a couple feet in front of me. I found myself tensing.

When I did, up came Yoshimo's and Wild Bill's guns, not quite pointing at me, fingers not actually resting on triggers—but the barrels were only a twitch away from being locked on my chest, and at this range professionals wouldn't miss.

"Easy," Chandler said, his voice extremely calm and smooth. "Easy, everyone. Let's not make this into something it doesn't have to be."

"What the hell is going on here, people?" I asked.

"We're trying to help you, Harry," Ramirez said, his voice like stone. "But you sure as hell aren't making it easy."

"Putting a tracker on me?" I asked, much more mildly than I felt at

"Suddenly I remember why I have authority issues," I said. "Go fuck yourself, Ramirez. And tell whoever ordered you to do this to me to pound sand while you're at it."

"Captain Luccio ordered me to do this," Ramirez said quietly. "She's still your friend. She wants to help you, too."

"I don't need this kind of help," I said. "We're supposed to be on the same side."

"We *are*," Chandler said emphatically. Then his face fell. "Unless . . . we aren't, I suppose."

"Every word I've said to you is true," I snapped. Or at least not a lie. "I've had enough bullshit from the White Council for one night."

"Harry, let's sort this out with the captain," Chandler said. "Come back to Edinburgh with us. Let's talk this out, yes?"

It was a rational suggestion, and it was completely unacceptable—because Thomas did not have time for me to spend a full day in a hostile debriefing back in Edinburgh. Those things were thorough and exhausting. It was possible that I'd gone through them maybe once or twice.

That gave me little choice.

"I've *been* talking," I said. "You aren't *listening*. The problem is on your end." I glared at Ramirez. "I've got a lot of work to do. Get out of the road. Or arrest me." I grounded my staff and shook my shield bracelet clear of my sleeve. "If you can."

Things got real quiet. No one took their eyes off me, but everyone's attention was on Ramirez.

He exhaled slowly. Then he said, "My God, Harry, you don't make it easy, do you?"

"Of the two of us here," I said, "which of us has definitely wronged the other? You suspect that I *might* have done something wrong. You've *definitely* wronged me, trying to find out. And you did it *first*."

"We've both done things we'd rather not have, as Wardens," he answered. "That's the job." He shook his head and, leaning heavily on the cane, limped out of the road. "Six o'clock tomorrow, security meeting at the Four Seasons before the mixer. We're registered under McCoy."

I tilted my head and narrowed my eyes. "I'm still on the team, eh?"

"Keep your friends close," Ramirez said.

I huffed out a breath in a parody of a laugh and turned back toward the Munstermobile.

"Harry," Ramirez said.

I paused without looking back at him.

"I hope I'm wrong," he said. "I hope I need to apologize to you later. God, I would love to do that. Please believe that much is true."

For a second, I felt nothing but tired.

Secrets are heavy, heavy things. Carry around too many of them for too long and the weight will crush the life out of you.

I wanted to tell everyone to take a walk, talk to Ramirez alone, and tell him everything. Carlos was a good man. He'd do the right thing. But the professional paranoia of the White Council made that impossible. Hell, if they thought I'd been subverted, they would regard the fact that I wanted to talk to him alone as proof that I was, myself, trying to isolate Ramirez so that he could be subverted as well. The other Wardens might not even let me have the conversation. And even if I did, if Carlos really thought I'd been made into someone's sock puppet, he might talk with me and report everything I'd said back to the Council in an effort to discover what disinformation I'd been trying to give them. If he knew I meant to free Thomas, he'd have excellent reason to have me detained, to prevent an incident that could rapidly spiral out of control.

Fear is a prison. But when you combine it with secrets, it becomes especially toxic, vicious. It puts us all into solitary, unable to hear one another clearly.

"You are," I said tonelessly. "You do."

Then I got into my car and got moving again.

Alone.

16

I was tired and sick, which isn't the best frame of mind to be in when you're doing detail-oriented work, but I wasn't sure how else to proceed.

Screw it. If I had to do this alone, I would.

I started planning ahead.

So after eating some fast food, I stopped at the trucker station at the highway and bought a shower. I rinsed off meticulously and at length, until I was sure that Ramirez's tracking spell had lost its hold on me. I also scrubbed off the ink spot, along with a couple of layers of skin so that he wouldn't be able to get it to lock on again. Once that was done, I made some purchases and headed back out.

I needed some isolation, so I picked a random direction away from the crowds and started following my instincts, doing so until I was damned sure I wasn't being physically followed. I wound up at the Illinois Beach State Park as the sky in the east was just turning deep blue after several hours of black. It's about seven miles of the shoreline of Lake Michigan, mostly pebbles and dunes and marshes with low scrub brush and the occasional larger stand of trees. I found parking in a church lot not too far from the park, took my stuff, and headed in. The park wasn't due to open until well after sunrise, so I'd have to keep an eye out for rangers and other amateur meddlers. The professionals were at work here.

Which was just as well—when you summon a powerful extradimensional being, you're taking on a lot of responsibility.

First of all, you're bringing something powerful and dangerous into the world. It doesn't matter if you're trying to call down an angel or whistle up one of the Fallen; you've got to take that into account. Even benevolent beings, if they're big enough, can kill you without even realizing it's happening until it's too late. Malicious creatures are going to want to kill you as a matter of course. So location is pretty important, so you can maybe have a chance to run for it, first of all. If you can get a location that somehow parallels the nature of the creature you're summoning, it gives you an edge against them, costs less energy to bring them in.

Next, containment. In keeping with the theme of part one, you need some way to make sure that the thing you're calling can't just get out and do as it pleases. Most things will simply leave, rendering all that travel to the middle of nowhere a waste of time.

Finally, you need some motivation. Beings from beyond the mortal world don't generally work for free. After you talk them out of either leaving or murdering you outright, you'll need something to sweeten the pot.

I found the perfect spot after I'd hiked all the way in and reached the lakeshore, with the light changing, announcing the approach of dawn without actually getting any brighter. I wound up at the base of a spit of sandy, pebbly beach that met harshly with a stand of thick trees. At the base of the largest tree were the crumbled remains of a clearly illegal tree house someone had built a decade or two in the past. I could still find what was left of slats that had been nailed into the tree trunk to provide an improvised ladder up.

Perfect.

I set my bag of things down and began laying them out in a circle I drew in the sandy soil with my staff. At the top of the circle went a storm candle and a magazine featuring an image of the weirdest female pop singer operating at the time—she was wearing an outfit made mostly out of old tires and did not look any too warm. The next candle featured a can of cold Dr Pepper. I popped it open and listened to it hiss out the pressure, then crackle in the quiet of predawn, bubbles bubbling enthusiastically. Beside the next candle, I placed a watermelon Ring Pop in its plastic wrapper. I opened the wrapper, leaving the jewel-like candy atop it, and the smell of its sweetness and the tangy scent of artificial watermelon filled the air.

The next candle featured a sheet of coarse sandpaper, rough side up. I laid my hand on it and moved my palm slowly over the grit and adhesive, feeling it tear gently at my skin. And beside the fifth and last candle went a jar of Nutella.

I double-checked the positioning of the ingredients, made sure the circle was closed, and then leaned down and touched it with one finger and an effort of will. The energy whirled about the circle in the sand and sprang up at once in an invisible curtain, enclosing the ground within it, cutting off the circle's interior from the mortal world behind an insulative firewall.

Then I closed my eyes, cleared my head, and began whispering a Name.

"Margaret Katherine Amanda Carpenter," I chanted rhythmically, "I call you."

The candles flickered and danced, though there was no wind. Their colors began to shift and change, seemingly at random, through the spectrum.

"Margaret Katherine Amanda Carpenter," I whispered, "I need you."

Behind me, the trees exploded with movement, and I flinched and whirled. A flock of vultures, disturbed from their evening rest, burst into the air, wings flapping in miniature thunder. It took them several seconds to clear out, and then they were gone into the darkness of the air, leaving behind jitters and a few falling black feathers.

I took a deep breath and braced my will. "Margaret Katherine Amanda Carpenter," I said, louder and firmer. "We need to talk. Come on, Molls."

At the third Naming, energy rushed out of me and into the circle. The candles there burst into showers of sparks in a dozen colors, and I had to blink my eyes and look away.

When I looked back, the youngest Queen of Faerie stood in the circle of power.

Molly Carpenter was a tall young woman, and when I looked at her, I always thought of swords and knives, these days. She'd gone very lean, living on the streets and fighting the incursions of the Fomor, back when I'd been mostly dead, and though her situation had improved, apparently her diet hadn't. Her cheekbones looked like something the TSA would be nervous about letting onto a plane, and that leanness extended to her neck, creating shadows that were a little too deep and sharp. Her blue eyes had always been beautiful, but were they a hint more oblique than they had been, or was that just clever makeup?

The Winter Lady wore a grey business skirt suit with sensible heels and stood with one hip shot out to one side, her fist resting on it. Her silver-white hair was drawn back into a painstakingly neat braid that held it close to her head with no strands escaping. Her expression was nonplussed, and she held a smoldering cell phone in one hand.

She regarded the phone for a moment, sighed, and dropped the useless wreck onto the ground.

"Hey, Molls," I said.

"Harry," she said. "I *have* a phone for exactly this reason."

"This is a business call," I said in a quiet, low voice. "Knight to Lady."

Molly inhaled slowly. "I . . . oh. I see."

"Things are getting tense," I said. "The Wardens have decided I am a threat. I'm being monitored, and they're doing some kind of cheesy technical weirdness with cell phones now. Couldn't risk a call without Ramirez getting involved in the conversation."

Some ugly flicker went across Molly's face at the mention of the Wardens. She shook her head, put her hands on her stomach, and said, "Ugh. That's the strangest feeling, being summoned."

"That seems like it should be true," I said. "I apologize for the inconvenience."

The Winter Lady stared at me for an unnerving second before she said, in Molly's voice, "Apology accepted." She looked around the circle at the objects involved in the summoning and promptly pounced on the jar of Nutella. "Aha! Payment. Now we're square." She opened the jar, seized the Ring Pop, and put it on her left forefinger. Then she dipped the Ring Pop in, and closed her eyes as she licked the confection off it. "Oh God," she said. "I haven't had food in a day and a half."

"Hell's bells, Padawan," I said. "Nutella and corn syrup is probably not the place to start."

"Probably not," she agreed, and scooped out an even larger dollop. "You going to let me out of the circle or what?"

"Honestly," I said, "I'm a little curious to see if you can do it yourself. I mean, you're still human, too. That circle shouldn't be able to hold Molly."

She lifted her eyebrows. "Harry, you could put me through a wood chipper if you wanted. I'd get better. Immortal now, remember?" She lifted a hand and reached out to touch the plane of the circle. The tip of her finger flattened as if pressed against perfectly transparent glass. "I'm human. But this mantle isn't like yours. It's an order of magnitude more complex. It's not something you put on like a cloak. It's all through me now. Intermixed." She shook her head sadly. "I could leave this circle, I think—but not without leaving the largest part of me behind. Whatever was left wouldn't be . . . right. Find someone else to experiment with."

A cold feeling kind of spread through me, starting right behind my belt buckle.

Because that circle shouldn't have been able to hold Molly.

Which meant that the being talking to me . . . wasn't. Not the way I remembered. Molly had taken on the mantle of the Winter Lady and become something that wasn't quite human anymore. She was dealing with forces that I might literally be unable to comprehend. Those pressures might have changed the shape of her, made her into something else, something dangerous.

Which, I thought, *must be almost precisely what Ramirez is thinking about you.*

Molly had definitely become someone darker and more dangerous.

But she was still Molly. Still the girl I'd met years ago, still the young woman I'd trained, still the woman who'd fought by my side on too many occasions to easily count. My instincts told me that she was something to be feared. And my instincts were right.

But people are often more than one thing. Molly was a very pretty, very dangerous monster now. But she was also the Padawan. She was also my friend.

I leaned down and broke the circle with my hand, releasing its energy back into the universe with a subaudible popping sensation.

Molly exhaled and calmly stepped out of the circle. She regarded me for a long moment and said, "God, you look tired."

I tilted my head at her and suddenly smiled. "You mean 'old.'"

"Weathered," she countered. "Like Aragorn."

I laughed at that. As a wizard, I could expect three centuries and change. Maybe more. I still had a decade and change to go before my body started settling into what it would look like for most of my life. "Wanna know a secret?"

"Always."

"Only the young think being called old is an insult," I said, still smiling. "I am what I am, regardless of what anyone calls it. No one can change it, regardless of what anyone calls it. And it mostly means that nothing has managed to kill me yet."

Molly gave me a small, bitter smile. "One thing did."

"I asked for your help with that," I said sternly. "You had a hell of a tough choice to make, and you chose loyalty to your friend. I will never forget that, Molly."

"Neither will I," she said quietly.

I pursed my lips. There is no guilt like wizard guilt, because there is no arrogance like wizard arrogance. We get used to having so much power, so much ability to change things, that we also tend to assume that whatever happens is also our responsibility. Throw in a few shreds of human decency, where you actually worry about the results of your actions upon others, and you wind up with a lot of regrets.

Because it's hard, it's really, really *hard*, in fact damned near impossible, to exercise power without it having some unexpected consequences. Doesn't matter what kind of power it is—magic, muscle, political office, electricity, moral authority. Use any of it, and you're going to find out that as a result, things happen that you didn't expect.

When those consequences are a blown light bulb, no big deal.

But sometimes people get hurt. Sometimes they die. Sometimes innocents. Sometimes friends.

Molly probably wasn't going to forgive herself for assisting in what had amounted to a very complicated near suicide. There'd been a lot of fallout, on every conceivable scale. Very little of it had been Molly's fault, directly or otherwise, but she'd been a mover on that scene, and she probably felt at least as bad as I did about it, and I'd been way more in the middle of things.

And, being a wizard, I felt guilty as hell for walking her into that. I hadn't had much choice, if I wanted to save my daughter's life, but though the cost was worthy, it still had to be paid—and Molly had laid down cold, hard cash.

So cold and so hard that Mab had wound up choosing her to be the new Winter Lady, in fact.

Suddenly I wondered if maybe I hadn't been hard enough on myself. I mean, hell, at least when I'd become the Winter Knight, I'd made a choice. My back had been to a wall and my options had all sucked, but I'd at least sought out my bargain with Mab.

Molly hadn't been consulted, and Mab's policy on dissenting opinion was crystalline: *Deal with it or die.*

Of course, for inveterate dissenters like myself, it created a pretty simple counterpolicy for when I was tired of Mab's crap: *Deal with it or kill me.* Mab was a lot of things, but irrational wasn't one of them, and as long as it was easier to put up with me than replace me, we had attained a state of balance. I imagined that Molly had come to similar arrangements.

I put my hand on her shoulder, squeezed slightly, and gave her another smile. "Hey. It was hard, for everyone. But we came through it. And with all these scars, we have to have learned a lesson somewhere, right?"

"I'm not sure how well that logic holds up," she said, giving me a wry smile.

"I think of it as the idiot's version of optimism," I said. I eyed the lightening sky. "How up are you on current events?"

She glanced that way as well. "I've been working in eastern Russia for two weeks," she said. "I'm busy as hell."

"Okay," I said, and I caught her up on recent events. Everything. Except for Butters and Andi and Marci because Butters had asked me and because I wasn't quite sure what to think about that myself.

"Before we go any further and just to be clear," she asked, "did my apartment actually burn down?"

"No."

She nodded and exhaled. "So . . . let's see . . ." She closed her eyes and thought for a moment about what I had told her. "Oh God, you're going to go get Thomas, aren't you?"

"I'm exhausting all possibilities for a diplomatic solution first," I said. She gave me a wary look.

"I like the svartalves," I explained. "They're good people. And they've got kids. I'm not going to wade into them, guns blazing."

Her eyebrows went up. "And you think I can get something done?"

"The svartalves like you," I said. "As far as I can tell, you're an honorary svartalf. And every single one of them is a sucker for pretty girls, and that's you also."

A flicker of her hand acknowledged fact without preening. "I think you're overestimating my influence in the face of events like this," she said. "Etri and his people are old-school. Blood has been spilled. There's going to be an accounting, period, and they are not going to be interested in mercy."

"You underestimate how much faith I have in your creativity, intelligence, and resourcefulness, Molly."

She grimaced. "You understand that if it comes to that, I can't directly help you get him out. If a Faerie Queen violated the Accords so blatantly, they would collapse. It would mean worldwide havoc."

"I figured," I said.

Her expression turned into a lopsided smile. "You don't ask for much, do you?"

"This can't possibly be more difficult to handle than moving back into your parents' place after you got all the piercings and tattoos."

She bobbed her head to one side to acknowledge the point. "That seemed pretty impossible at the time, I suppose."

"Help me," I said. I helpfully bent down and picked up the can of Dr Pepper, offering it to her. "I got you Nutella and everything."

"All that did was give me an excuse not to bitch-slap you for daring to summon me," she said frankly. "Honestly, I do have a job, you know.

It's kind of important. I really can't afford to encourage people to interrupt me all the time."

She took the soda and sipped.

"It's Thomas," I said.

"It's Thomas," she agreed. She exhaled. "You understand that you've asked for my help. You know what that means, right?"

"Obligation," I said.

"Yes. You'll owe me. And those scales will have to be balanced. It's . . . like an itch I can't scratch until they are."

"You're still you, grasshopper."

She regarded me for a moment, her maybe-not-quite-as-human eyes huge, luminous, and unsettlingly, unnervingly beautiful in her gaunt face. Her voice came out in a whisper I had last heard in a greenly lit root-lined cavern on the island. "Not always."

I felt a little chill slide around inside me.

She shook her head and was abruptly the grasshopper again. "I'm willing to do whatever I can to help you. Are you willing to balance whatever I offer up?"

"He's my brother," I said. "Duh."

She nodded. "What is it you want?"

I told her.

She was quiet for a long time. Then she said, "Tricky. Difficult."

"If I could do it myself, I wouldn't be asking you, grasshopper. Can you do it?"

She sipped more of the drink, her eyes sparkling as they narrowed. "Are you questioning my phenomenal cosmic powers?"

"Well, you've been so busy globe-trotting doing Winter Lady stuff," I drawled. "Let's just say I'm curious if you've kept your wizard muscles in shape."

"Hah!" she said, grinning. Then her expression sobered. "I've done some work like it lately. The skills aren't the issue." She leaned toward me a little, her eyes intent. "Harry. I need you to be absolutely sure. Once a bargain is done, there's no going back. And I *will* hold you to it." Her expression flickered, for just a second suddenly looking much less sure. "I don't get a choice about that."

"He's my brother," I said. "I'm sure."

The Winter Lady nodded, her eyes suddenly luminous, suddenly something a man could drown in. Then she stepped over to me, stood on tiptoe, reached up, and drew my mouth down to hers. She gave me a soft kiss on the mouth that was about ninety-nine percent sisterly, and murmured, "Done."

There was a sensation of something setting firmly into place, somewhere inside me, as if I'd been made of Legos, one of them had come loose, and Molly had just pressed it solidly back into position. It sent a little frisson through me, and I shivered as the bargain was forged.

And, Hell's bells, did Molly have soft, lovely lips, which did not bear thinking on.

She stepped away from me much more slowly, her eyes down. She brushed her hand over her mouth and muttered, "Mab's going to be furious if I don't get the leshyie numbers up, but . . ." She nodded. "I'll build your toy for you."

"You're the best."

"I'm awesome," she agreed. "But this is a mess. I don't know how much direct help I'll be able to give."

"At this point," I said, "I'll take whatever I can get."

17

I drove Molly back to town and dropped her off at the svartalf embassy, where the security guard, a conspicuously unfamiliar face, welcomed her at once and with tremendous deference. I still wasn't clear on what the grasshopper had done for the svartalves to make them so gaga over her, but it was clear that whatever she'd done, she had impressed them with the fact that she was more than a pretty face.

I watched her go in and made sure she was safely in the building, as if I were a teenager dropping off his date five minutes early, and then started driving.

I felt awful.

I felt really, really awful.

And I wanted to go home.

Home, like *love*, *hate*, *war*, and *peace*, is one of those words that is so important that it doesn't need more than one syllable. Home is part of the fabric of who humans are. Doesn't matter if you're a vampire or a wizard or a secretary or a schoolteacher; you have to have a home, even if only in principle—there has to be a zero point from which you can make comparisons to everything else. Home tends to be it.

That can be a good thing, to help you stay oriented in a very confusing world. If you don't know where your feet are planted, you've got no way to know where you're heading when you start taking steps. It can be a bad thing, when you run into something so different from home that it scares you and makes you angry. That's also part of being human.

But there's a deeper meaning to home. Something simpler, more primal.

It's where you eat the best food because other predators can't take it from you very easily there.

It's where you and your mate are the most intimate.

It's where you raise your children, safe against a world that can do horrible things to them.

It's where you sleep, safe.

It's where you relax.

It's where you dream.

Home is where you embrace the present and plan the future.

It's where the *books* are.

And more than anything else, it's where you build that world that you want.

I drove through Chicago streets in the early morning and wished that I felt numb. My head hurt from lack of sleep and insufficient amounts of insufficiently nourishing food. My body ached, especially my hands and forearms. My head still spun with motion sickness, my guts sending up frequent complaints.

My brother was in trouble, and I didn't know if I could get him out.

I thought of Justine's misery and fear and the trust in her eyes when I'd promised to help Thomas, and suddenly felt very tired.

I very much wanted to go home.

And I didn't have one.

My comfy, dumpy old apartment was gone, flattened by Gentleman Johnnie Marcone to make way for his stupid little castle and the Bigger Better Brighter Future Society. I mean, that had only been after the Red Court of Vampires had burned my home down, but I guess I'd settled their hash not long after. I was willing to call that one even.

But I missed my couch and the comfy chairs in front of my fire. I missed reading for hours on end with Mouse snoozing comfortably beside me and Mister purring between my ankles. I missed my cluttered, thoroughly functional little magical laboratory in the subbasement, and

Bob on the shelf. I missed problems as simple as a rogue sorcerer trying to run his own drug cartel.

And I missed not being afraid for the people I loved.

I bowed my head at a light and wept. The guy behind me had to honk to get me to look up again. I considered blowing out his engine in a fit of pure pique and decided against it: I was the one who wasn't moving at a green light.

I didn't know what else to do.

I felt tired and lost and sick. Which left me only one place to go.

The sky had just begun to turn golden in the east when I pulled up to the Carpenters' house. As I got out of the car, a neighbor a few doors down, an elderly gentleman in a flannel shirt and a red ball cap, came out of the door and stumped down the driveway to get his morning paper. He gave me a gimlet glower as he did, as if I'd personally come and put all his newspaper pages out of order, then carefully folded it up again and walked stiffly back into his house.

Man. I wished I was old enough to be irrationally grumpy at some random guy on the street. I could have blown out his engine.

I didn't knock on the door. I went around to the backyard. There I found the Carpenter treehouse, which looked like something out of a Disney movie, in a massive old oak tree in the backyard. A bit behind it was the workshop, the rolling door of which was currently wide open. An old radio played classic rock in the background, and one of the better human beings I knew was on a weight bench, working out.

Michael Carpenter was in his fifties from the neck up, with silvering hair, grey eyes, and a well-kept salt-and-pepper beard. From the neck down, he could have been twenty or thirty years younger. He was performing basic bench presses with around two hundred and fifty pounds on the bar. Michael was doing slow reps with it.

I hadn't seen the start of his set, but I counted fourteen repetitions of the movement before he carefully set the bar back onto the rack, so he was probably doing twenties. The struts of the bench creaked a bit as the weight settled onto them.

Michael glanced up at me and smiled. He sat up, breathing heavily but in a controlled manner, and said, "Harry! Up early or late?"

"Late," I said, and bumped fists with him. "Going light this morning?"

He grinned a bit wider. "Most mornings. It's my shoulders. They just can't take the heavy stuff anymore."

I eyed the weights and said, "Yeah, you wimp."

He laughed. "Want a turn?"

I felt awful. And angry about it. The Winter mantle didn't care if I'd missed sleep and felt terrible. It wanted me to kill or have sex with something. Feeding it exercise was as close as I could get. Dammit. "Sure."

He got up amiably, using an aluminum cane lying beside the bench to stand. Michael had taken multiple hits from an AK-style assault rifle out on the island a few years back. He shouldn't have survived it. Instead, he'd come out of it with a bad hip, a bum leg, a bad eye, a severe limp, and the only non-posthumous retirement I'd ever heard about for a Knight of the Cross.

He limped gamely over to the head of the bench to spot me. I took off my duster, lay down, and started working.

"You look"—Michael paused, considering his words—"distracted."

He was my friend. I told him what was up. He listened gravely.

"Harry, you idiot," he said gently. "Go get some sleep."

I glared at him and kept working.

He was one of a relatively few people in my life upon whom my glare had no effect. "You aren't going to muscle your way through this one, and you aren't going to be able to think your way through it in your current condition. Help your brother. Get some sleep."

I thought about that one until the frozen chill of Winter had seeped into my arms and chest and I was breathing like a steam engine. Then I put the weight down.

"How many was that?" I asked.

"I stopped counting at forty." Michael put a hand on my shoulder and said, "Enough, Harry. Get some rest."

"I can't," I said, my voice suddenly harsh. I sat up, hard. "Somebody pushed my brother into this. Somehow. I have to stop them. I have to fight them."

"Yes," Michael said, his tone patient. "But you need to fight them smarter, not harder."

I scowled and glanced back over my shoulder at him.

"You're no kid anymore, Harry. But take it from someone who did this kind of thing for a very long time: Take your sleep wherever you can get it. You never know when you'll have no other choice."

I shook my head. "What if something happens while I'm sleeping? What if those lost hours are the difference between saving him and . . ."

"What if a meteor hits the planet tomorrow?" Michael replied. "Harry, there is very little in this world that we can control. You have to realize when you've reached the limits of what you can choose to do to change the situation."

"When you reach the limits," I said quietly, "maybe it's time to change your limits."

Those words fell on a very long silence.

When Michael spoke, his voice was frank. "How well did that work out for you, the last time?"

I tilted my head a little, in acceptance of the hit.

"Harry," he said, "over the years, I've talked to you many times about coming to church."

"Endlessly," I said.

He nodded cheerfully. "And the invitation is a standing one. But all I've ever wanted for you was to help you develop in your faith."

"I'm not sure how much Catholicism I've got to develop," I said.

Michael waved a hand. "Not religion, Harry. Faith. Faith isn't all about God, or a god, you know."

I peered at him.

"Mine is," he said. "This path is, to me, a very good path. It's brought me a very wonderful life. But maybe it isn't the only path. Many children learn things very differently, after all. It seems to me that God should be an excellent teacher enough to take that into account." He shook his head. "But faith is about more than that. Like Waldo, for example."

"How do you mean?" I asked.

"He's not particularly religious," Michael said. "But I've never, ever met an individual more dedicated to the idea that tomorrow can be better than today. That people, all of us, have the ability to take action to make things better—and that friends always help. Despite all the ugliness he's seen, in his job and in his other, ah, interests. He holds on to that."

"Polka in the morgue," I said.

Michael smiled. "Yes. Yes, exactly. But I think you miss my point."

I tilted my head at him.

"He has faith in *you*, Harry Dresden," Michael said. "In the path you've walked, and in which he now emulates you."

I felt my eyebrows slowly climb in horror. "He . . . what now?"

Michael nodded, amused. "You're an example. To Waldo." His voice softened. "To Molly."

I sighed. "Yeah."

"You might think about them, when you consider your next steps. And you might try to have a little faith, yourself."

"In what?"

"In you, man," he said, almost laughing. "Harry, do you really think you've found yourself where you have, time and time again, at the random whims of the universe? Have you noticed how often you've managed to emerge more or less triumphant?"

"Yeah," I said. "Sort of."

"Then perhaps you are the right person, in the right place, at the right time," Michael said. "Again. Have faith in that. And get some sleep."

I glared at him for a minute. "Seems an awfully egotistical way to look at the universe," I said darkly.

"How can it be egotistical when I'm the one who had to point it out to you?" Michael countered.

Michael was just better at this kind of talk than me. I glowered at him and then sneered in concession. "I'll try to sleep. No promises."

"Good," he said. He limped over to a small refrigerator and got out a couple of bottles of water. He brought one to me and I accepted it. We drank them together in silence. Then Michael said, "Harry?"

"Yeah?"

"Have you seen much of Molly lately?"

"A little," I said.

He hesitated for a long moment before saying slowly, "You might . . . ask her to check in with us?"

I lifted my eyebrows. "Hasn't she?"

"Not face-to-face," he said. "Not in some time."

"She's been very busy in her new job, I know, a lot of travel . . ." I began.

Michael gave me a very direct look. "Harry. Please don't assume that I do not realize secrets are being kept from me. Tolerance is not the same as ignorance. But I trust you. I trust Molly."

I keyed into what was going on. "Ah. But Charity doesn't."

Michael hedged. "She . . . is worried that her daughter is a very young person moving in a world that rewards inexperience with pain. She very much wants to be sure her daughter is all right. And I am not sure that is an unreasonable position."

It had begun to dawn on me, through all the awful, that Molly *still* hadn't told her mom and dad about her new gig as the Winter Lady. And it had been . . . how long now?

Hell's bells. My stomach sank a little. I wasn't at all sure how well Charity and Michael would react to the news that their daughter had gotten herself knit to the wicked Winter Fae. That was a far, far cry from merely hanging out with the wrong crowd. If she'd come directly to them, at the beginning, it might have been talked through immediately. But after a year and more of doubt and silence and avoidance and worry . . . Wow.

Family complicates things.

And, after all, they were both absolutely right to be worried about their daughter.

Hell. I was.

"Maybe it isn't," I allowed.

"Thank you," he said. "I know she's a grown woman now, but . . . she's also still our little girl."

"I'm sure she'd roll her eyes to hear it," I said.

"Likely," Michael said, his smile a little sad. "But perhaps she'll humor us."

"I'll talk to Molly," I promised.

And yawned.

Yeah. That's what I would do. Be sane. Be smart. *Get some rest and come at them fresh, Harry.*

Assuming you figure out who they are.

18

The Carpenters had a number of empty bedrooms these days, and I crashed in Daniel's old room. After recovering from his injuries, and avoiding what could have been a serious scrape with the law, Daniel had re-upped with the military. He was on a base in the Southwest somewhere, married, with the family's first grandchild on the way.

There was a very lonely quality to his old room—posters on the wall advertised bands that few people cared about anymore. The clothes hanging in the closet were years out of style, waiting faithfully for someone who might not even fit into them anymore. The bed seemed too small for the man I knew, who I'd seen fighting some genuine darkness, and paying the price for his courage, and it was certainly too small for the husband and father he'd become.

But I bet it would make a great room for grandkids to stay in when they visited fussy old Grandma and Grandpa Carpenter, the boring squares who never did anything interesting.

Hah.

And meanwhile, it would do quite well for a worried, world-weary wizard.

I slept, not long enough but very hard, and woke to a small face about two inches from mine and late-afternoon sunlight coming through the window.

"Hi," Maggie said when I managed to get an eye to creak open.

"Hmph," I said, in as gentle a tone as I could manage.

"Are you awake now?" she asked.

I blinked. It took about five minutes to accomplish that much. "Apparently."

"Okay," she said seriously. "I'm not supposed to bother you until you're awake." She pushed back from the bed and ran out of the room.

I took that under advisement for a sober moment and then heard her feet pounding back up the stairs. She was carrying a large box, wrapped in white paper and tied with a length of silver cord. She grunted and hefted it onto the general vicinity of my hips, with the inherent accuracy that small children and most animals seemed to possess.

I flinched and caught the box, preventing any real damage, and sat blearily up. "What is this?"

"It was on the porch this morning," Maggie said. "Mouse doesn't think there's a bomb or poison or anything."

I eyed the box. There was a paper tag on it. I caught it and squinted until I could make out Molly's handwriting:

I KNOW YOU MEANT TO GET ONE EVENTUALLY. M.

"Hmmm," I said, and opened the box with Maggie looking on in eager interest.

"Awww," she said in disappointment a moment later, as I drew a new suit out of the box. "It's just clothes."

"Nothing wrong with clothes," I said.

"Yeah, but it could have been a knife or a gun or a magic sword or something." She sighed. "You know. Cool wizard stuff to help you fight monsters." She picked up the silver-grey rough silk of the suit's coat. "And this is weird fabric."

I ran my hand over the cloth, musing. "Weird how?"

"It just . . . feels weird and looks weird. I mean, look at it. Does that look like something you'd see on TV?"

"It's spider silk," I mused. "I think it's a spider-silk suit."

"Ewg," Maggie said, jerking her hand back. Then she put it on again, more firmly. "That's so gross."

"And it's enchanted," I mused. I could feel the subtle currents of energy moving through the cloth, beneath my palms. I closed my eyes for a moment and felt the familiar shapes of my own defensive wardings, the same ones I worked into my leather coat. I'd taught the grasshopper the basics of enchanting gear by using my own most familiar formulae. She was probably the only person alive who could have duplicated my own work so closely. "Yeah, see? Once I'm wearing this, it's going to store the energy of my body heat, of my movements, and use it to help redirect incoming forces."

Maggie looked skeptical. "Well. Enchanted armored bug suit is better than just a suit, I guess."

"Yes, it is," I said. I checked the box. It included all the extras, including buttons and cuff links and a pinky crest ring in the glittering deep blue opals favored by the Winter Court.

The ring pulsed with stored power, with densely packed magical energy. I could feel it against my skin like the light of a tiny sun. I carefully pocketed it, then changed my mind and put it on. If I needed the thing, I was going to *really* need it, *tout de suite*. "It's also the same material the Warden capes are made of." I set the suit down and frowned for a moment. "So Molly wants to make a statement with my outfit."

"That you aren't afraid of spiders?" Maggie asked. "I mean, what else would that say?"

I pursed my lips. "You know . . . I'm not really sure."

So some other crosscurrents were swirling, only no one was saying anything about it. Par for the course when dealing with Mab, but I was used to more open communication with Molly. Only . . . taking on the mantle of the Winter Lady had given my former Padawan a lot of power, and whether you're talking about the supernatural world or any other one, more power meant more obligations, more responsibilities. Molly might not *have* entirely free will, as the concept was generally understood, anymore.

And Mab loved her some secrets. If she wanted them kept, I'm not sure Molly would be *able* to tell me.

Or maybe I was just being paranoid.

Well. I'd done pretty well, in the survival department, by assuming that my paranoia was justified. Maybe taking out an insurance policy wouldn't be a bad idea.

"Dad?" Maggie asked me. "What is it? You've been staring into space for like three minutes."

I blinked. "Could you please run and tell Michael that I need to borrow his office for a private phone call?" I asked her.

"Okay," she said, and hopped up with the energy of children on a sunny afternoon, running out. Mouse lumbered to his feet, nuzzled my face fondly with his big, slobbery mouth, and padded out after her.

I looked around helpless for a second, wiped off my face on the comforter, got out my wallet, found it empty, and started rummaging in my pockets for whatever change I could find there.

I got dressed and made a call in Michael's spartan, organized office. Once I shut the heavy wooden door, the sounds of the television out in the family room and the rap of wood on wood coming from the backyard were muted to nothing.

"It's Dresden," I said when he answered.

"Oh boy."

"I need your help," I said.

"With what?"

"Good cause."

He sounded skeptical. "Oh. Those."

"There's a cute girl."

"I like that."

"You can't have her," I said.

"I like that less."

"In or out?"

"Usual fee," he said.

"I only stole so many rocks."

He snorted. "So, get someone else."

"You're killing me, man."

"Only if it's for a good cause. Tell me about this girl."

I told him where to find Justine and what she looked like.

"You get that she's obviously a femme fatale, right?"

I arched an eyebrow. "She's . . . kind of not."

"Uh-huh," he said.

"She isn't."

"Customer's always right. What result do you want?"

I shuddered a bit. It wouldn't matter to him, personally, whether or not I asked him to save her or kill her. But the more experience I had in the world, the more I had come to think that monstrousness or a lack of it was a little less important than whether or not the monster would keep his word.

This one would.

"Covert surveillance. Make sure nothing bad happens to her."

"Am I a spy or a bodyguard?"

"Yes."

"Oh. You're floundering."

I was definitely not floundering. "I am definitely not floundering," I told him in a tone of perfect confidence. "I . . . just need more information before I can act appropriately."

"Uh-huh," he said. Only more annoyingly. "Opposition?"

"Unknown," I said.

He was quiet for a moment.

"To you," he said.

"Yeah."

"Now."

"Yeah."

"Here."

"Yeah."

"Oh," he said. "Super."

"If I get an easy job, I can call a temp agency."

"I don't do politics," he said. "The good causes mostly aren't."

"I'll handle that part," I said. "Your concern is solely the girl—and the baby. She's pregnant. Keep them safe from harm."

"Ah," he said, as though I had just simplified his life. "Rules of engagement?"

"Well, I think you should—"

"Trick question," he said, and hung up on me.

I eyed the phone.

Then I got into my pocket, got out the dollar bill that had been stuck in a pocket on a ride through the laundromat and was now a wadded block of solid pseudo-wood. I put it in an envelope, sealed it, and wrote **GREY** on it in pink highlighter. I stowed that in a pocket. *That'll put marzipan in your pie plate, bingo.*

Then I got up and headed outside.

Butters was a squirrely little guy—quick, bouncy, and bright-eyed.

The man pursuing him around the Carpenters' backyard was more of a bear—huge, powerful, and too fast for his size. He'd shaved his head entirely, and his scalp was the color of dark chocolate, covered with beads of sweat, and the blazing afternoon sun shone gratuitously upon all the muscle. Sanya was the size and build of an NFL linebacker, and his teeth showed in a broad smile the entire time he fought.

Even as I watched, the two men squared off, facing each other, each holding a length of wood carved to vaguely resemble a samurai sword. Butters held his in a two-handed grip, high over his head. The little guy was wearing his sports goggles, a tank top, and close-fit exercise pants. He looked like the protagonists in the old Hong Kong Theater movies—blade thin, flexible, and wiry with lean muscle that was all about speed and reflexes.

Sanya, dressed in battered blue jeans and biker boots, whirled his practice sword in one hand through a couple of flourishes and settled into a fencing stance in front of Butters and just out of his own reach, his off hand held out behind him.

"You have gotten much smoother," said Sanya, his voice a deep rumble inflected with a thick Russian accent on the vowels.

"Still not any faster," Butters said. And then his practice sword blurred as it swept down toward Sanya. Santa intercepted with a deflection parry, though he had enough muscle and mass on Butters that he probably didn't need to. His return thrust slithered down the haft of Butters's practice sword so fast that I heard it hit Waldo's thumb. He yelped and leapt back, shaking that hand for a moment—but he didn't lose his practice weapon.

"Smooth almost always better than fast," Sanya said, stepping back and lifting up a hand to signal a pause in the practice. "Smooth is technique. Grace. Smooth lets you think while you fight."

"And that's a big deal?" Butters asked.

"Is *everything*," Sanya said. "Fighting is least civilized thing one can do. Intellect is not made for fighting. You have been there, *da*?"

"Yeah. It's terrifying."

"*Da*," Sanya replied. "Hard to take test while some stinking thing shoving your face into stinking armpit." He set the practice sword carefully against the wall of the Carpenters' little workshop and then picked up an old, worn-looking cavalry saber with a wire-wrapped hilt in a battered leather scabbard. "Hard to get much thinking done in fight," Sanya said. He jabbed a thumb at one of his own biceps. "Muscle can be useful tool—or deadweight," Sanya said. He jabbed his thumb at his own forehead. "But this is most dangerous weapon."

Butters eyed the much, much larger man for a moment. "Yeah, everyone has one of those."

"Exactly true," Sanya said. "Dangerous place, planet Earth. Dangerous animals, humans." His grin became more wolfish. "Be more human than next guy. And pick up Sword."

Butters arched an eyebrow. "Um. Are you sure you want to play with these? I mean, there's like zero margin for error with that thing."

"Always zero margin for error," Sanya said calmly. He drew the old saber. Worn though the weapon might be, its blade shone nicked and bright and true in the sunlight. *Esperacchius*, the Sword of Hope, sang a bright, quiet song of power that I could feel against my face and chest like sunlight.

"Dude," Butters said. He stepped to one side and reached into an old messenger bag lying on the ground nearby. "I'm not sure what this thing will do to *Esperacchius*."

Sanya let out a rolling laugh. "Me, either. But have faith."

Butters frowned. "But what if it . . . ?"

The Russian shook his head. "If there is a sword that mine cannot stand against, I must know."

"What happened to having faith?" Butters asked.

Sanya gave Butters a nonplussed look before the smile resurged. "I suppose I have no objection to faith, in absence of knowledge," he said. "But knowledge good, too, *da*?"

"*Da*," I said, firmly.

Both men looked up at me, unsurprised at my presence. They'd just been busy. Butters bounced the hilt of *Fidelacchius* in his hand a couple of times, frowning. "You sure?"

"Worth knowing, isn't it?" I asked. "There's plenty of enchanted swords running around out there. They were the number one piece of military hardware for a very long time. The way I heard it, figuring out how to lay Power into that general mass of steel had been pretty much optimized. If what happened to the Sword of Faith represents a major escalation, a game-changer, that would be a good thing to know."

"Well, I don't want God yelling at me if I break His stuff." Butters sighed.

"Assuming there is one," Sanya said.

Butters gave Sanya a blank look and then said, "You are a very weird man."

"*Da*," Sanya agreed cheerfully. Then he lifted the Sword, all business again, and said, "*En garde.*"

Butters grimaced. But his feet settled into a fighting stance and he lifted *Fidelacchius*. He glanced around carefully at the neighboring houses to make sure no one was just out in their yard goggling and said, "But not for long. Okay?"

"*Da, da*," Sanya said.

Butters nodded once, grimly, and there was a hum of power and a flicker of extra sunlight as the Sword of Faith's shining blade sprang from its shattered hilt. The soft, wavering chord of ghostly choral music followed each motion of the blade as Butters raised it to an overhead guard position again.

"Always with the high guard," Sanya commented.

"Everyone's taller than me," Butters pointed out.

Then he swept the Sword of Faith at Sanya's arm.

Sanya moved smoothly, in a direct parry, pitting the strength of his Sword's steel and his arm directly against that of his opponent.

There was a flash of light, like when the mirror of a passing car briefly shows you the image of the sun, and the ghostly choral music swelled in volume and intensified for a moment. Sparks flew up from the contact of the weapons, and at the point where they met there was a light so white and so pure that I felt as if perhaps its like had not been seen for several billion years, at least. Maybe not since Someone said, "Let there be light."

Then the two men disengaged. Sanya held his blade out to one side and studied it, but its steel was shining, bright, and unchanged.

Butters frowned. Then he turned to an old stump in the yard that bore the remains of an old anvil fastened to it. About half of the anvil was gone, as if sliced away at an angle. Butters peered at the anvil for a second, took half a breath, and then swept the Sword of Faith at it. There was a howl from the sword, a cascade of sparks, and then a slice of the anvil about the thickness of a dinner plate fell away from it and onto the yard, where the sizzling-hot metal promptly started a small fire in the drying summer grass.

Butters yelped, seized a nearby water bottle, and put the fire out with a great deal of hissing, some stomping, and a small cloud of steam.

Sanya's expression, meanwhile, lit up into an even brighter version of his usual smile, and when he turned his eyes back to Butters, they shone brightly.

Butters regarded the other man's expression warily and then slowly smiled. "Yeah," he said. "Okay."

And without a word, the two Knights charged each other, Swords held high.

Once again, the swords clashed, only things were different now. Instead of Sanya dominating the fight, Butters had the edge. *Esperacchius* darted and whirled, liquid smooth, but as fast as Sanya was with his blade, the steel sword wasn't *weightless*.

Fidelacchius, the Sword of Faith, was.

Butters pressed the attack with absolute ruthlessness, never giving the Russian a break once he had the big man back on his heels. Sanya began retreating in earnest, parrying and returning attacks wherever he could—which was seldom, in the face of Butters's onslaught.

The big Russian tripped on a five-gallon bucket set neatly near an outdoor water spigot, fell back into a roll, and came back to his feet barely in time to catch the Sword of Faith on *Esperacchius*'s blade. He burst out into laughter as Butters drove him back relentlessly, and his flickering saber shifted to almost total defense. "Is not even fair! This is wonderful!"

Butters gasped out an answering laugh, and when he did, Sanya cheated. The taller Knight kicked some of Michael's lawn up at Butters's face, and the smaller man flinched back. Sanya took a risk and bulled in, and his timing was good. He got in close, his blade holding Butters's back, and swiped at Butters's head with his off hand.

He'd underestimated the little guy's reaction speed. Butters moved on pure instinct, shining blade of his sword sweeping to the side.

And directly through Sanya's wrist.

The big man screamed and fell to his knees, doubled up around his wrist.

"Sanya!" Butters cried. He stared at the shining sword for a moment, his eyes terrified—and then he dropped it. The blade flickered out and vanished as the hilt bounced off the lawn. Then he ran to the big man's side.

I turned to the house and bellowed, "Medic!" Then I joined Butters beside Sanya.

The big man rocked back and forth, shaking hard, the muscles on his back and shoulders standing out sharply.

"Oh, wow, we were warned and we did not listen," I muttered. "How many hands did we see go flying off?"

"I *know*," Butters said, his voice horrified. "Sanya, come on, man. Let me see it."

"Is all right," Sanya said through clenched teeth. "Only need one hand for saber. Can still be Knight."

"God, I am such an *idiot*," Butters said. "I shouldn't ever take that thing out unless evil's, like, right here. Let me see, man."

"Do not blame self, Waldo," Sanya said gravely. "Cannot see myself as Christian, but they have good ideas about forgiveness. I will forgive you, brother."

I stood up abruptly and folded my arms, arching an eyebrow.

"God, Sanya," Butters said. "It was an accident. I am *so* sorry. I . . ." He suddenly frowned. "Hey."

Sanya's deep voice rolled out in a bubbling laugh that came up from somewhere around his toes and rolled up through his belly and chest before finally spilling out his mouth. He held up the fingers of his "maimed" hand and wiggled them, still laughing.

"Oh," Butters stammered. "Oh, oh, oh. You *jerk*."

Sanya rose, still laughing, and swiped a hand over his shaven head. He went over to the discarded scabbard. He took a cloth from a small case on the scabbard's belt, wiped down the saber, and slid it neatly away. "Did not think so."

"Think what?" I asked.

He shrugged. "Was instinct. Did not feel like I was in danger from that sword."

"Instinct?" Butters demanded. He raked a hand back through his haystack of a hairdo. "For God's sake, man. If you'd been wrong . . ."

"Wasn't," Sanya pointed out with a smile.

Butters made an exasperated sound and snatched up *Fidelacchius*'s hilt, but his expression was puzzled. "What just happened?"

"Obviously, it failed to cut him," I said. "Question is why." I looked around the backyard. Honestly, there was very little danger of anyone seeing much of what was going on. Between the rosebushes planted along the fences, a few shrubs, an enormous tree, and some actual privacy fencing along the back of the yard, there weren't many places to see in. Michael had planned ahead.

As if the thought had summoned him, he came out the back door of the house, hurrying along in a heavy limp with his cane, the strap of a large medical kit slung over one shoulder. He slowed as he took in everyone's body language and gave me a questioning glance.

"Sanya was playing with us," I said.

"Cannot help it." Sanya chortled. "You are such simple provincial folk."

I knuckled him in the arm at the same time Butters kicked his shins. It only made him laugh again.

"What happened?" Michael asked calmly.

Butters told him.

"Huh," Michael said, lifting his eyebrows. "Have you ever touched the blade of the sword?"

"God no," Butters said. "I mean . . . come on, no. Just no."

"But it's cut people before," I said. "Right?"

"Yeah," Butters began. Then his voice trailed off. "No. It hasn't cut people. It's cut monsters."

The four of us considered that for a moment.

"Well," I said. "Light it up. Let's try it."

"I guess we have to." Butters sighed. He lifted the sword, simply holding it blade up, and it sprang to life with a choral hum.

Without hesitating an instant, Sanya held out his hand and put it squarely into the blade.

Absolutely nothing happened. It just passed into his flesh and then continued on the other side as if there'd been no interruption at all.

"Weird," Butters breathed. He reached up and tested it with a pinky finger—then put his whole hand into the beam as well. "Huh," he said. "It just feels a little warm."

Michael took his turn next, calmly passing his whole right hand into it on the first try. "Interesting."

"My turn," I said, and poked the burn-scarred forefinger of my left hand at the blade. There was heat there, uncomfortably warm but bearable, like washing dishes with the hot water turned up. I was sensing the raw energy of the sword, which absolutely seethed with stored potential, as if the power of a star could be bound into a physical form.

"But it still cuts things," I said. I gestured back toward the sliced anvil. "He did that not five minutes ago."

Michael pursed his lips for a moment. Then he looked at me and said, "Conservation of energy."

I frowned and then got what he was saying. "Oh. Yeah, I bet you're right. That makes sense."

Butters shook his head. "What makes sense?"

"Laws of the universe," I said. "Matter and energy cannot be created or destroyed. All you can do is change them around."

"Sure," Butters said. "What's that got to do with the Sword?"

I frowned, trying to figure out how to explain. "All the Swords have . . . a kind of supernatural mass, eh? Representative of their power in the world and their role in it. Okay?"

"Sure," Butters said slowly.

"When the Sword was vulnerable and Nicodemus broke *Fidelacchius*, he didn't destroy it," I said. "Maybe he couldn't destroy it. Maybe all he could do was change it. Now, ideally, for him, he'd have changed it to something nonfunctional. But the Swords are some of the most powerful artifacts I've ever seen. Things with that kind of power tend to resist being changed around, just like things with a lot of mass are hard to move."

"You're saying the Sword fought back," Butters said.

"He's saying," Michael said firmly, "that the operative word in *Sword of Faith* has never been *Sword*."

I gave Michael a reproving look. "I'm saying that even broken, the supernatural power of the Sword of Faith still had the same purpose—to support faith and defend the helpless against evil. While it was . . . in a state of flux, vulnerable to being damaged, it was still trying to find a way to fulfill its purpose. I think that when you touched it, Butters, it looked into your nerdy, nerdy heart and saw a way it could continue to do that."

"What?" Butters said in a tone of awe, looking at the shining blade.

"Sword looked at you," Sanya mused, "and saw Jedi. Saw way to keep fighting. So it became lightsaber."

"More powerful than a simple steel sword," Michael said. "But also less."

I nodded. "Because the scales have to stay balanced. It couldn't be more powerful than it was. But it also couldn't be less."

"It's further into the spiritual world than it was before it was broken," Michael said. "It's going to have less effect on the physical world."

I shook my head. "Not the physical world. The *mortal* world. It chops steel just fine. It's *people* it doesn't interact with anymore."

"How does it know the difference between people and monsters?" Butters asked.

"It could be something like a resonance with certain kinds of energy. Evil beings tend to put off negative energy—black magic. It's possible that the sword reacts to that. I mean, I can't think of any way to make that work, but someone smarter and better than me might not have that problem." I leaned back, thinking. Then I said slowly, "Or Occam's razor. Maybe because it *knows* the difference."

Michael frowned at me. "Harry?"

"The Knights of the Blackened Denarius each bear one of Judas's silver coins with a fallen angel trapped inside," I said. "You guys are their . . . their opposites. You each bear a sword worked with a nail from the Crucifixion . . ." I rolled one hand encouragingly.

"With an angel inside," breathed Butters.

There was a stunned silence around the little circle.

"Balance," I said. "I think it knows because it knows, Butters."

"Oh God," Butters breathed in a whisper. "I accidentally ran it through the laundry once."

Sanya let out a belly laugh.

Michael touched the blade of *Fidelacchius* again, more reverently. "Angels aren't allowed to interfere with mortals or their free will," he said. "If you're right, Harry . . . this blade of light is a direct expression of the will of an angel. It can't impinge upon the free will of a mortal. It can only fight evil beings who attempt the same."

"People can be evil," Butters said. "Would it have chopped up Chuck Manson?"

"People can be evil," Michael said. "They can be good. They can choose. That's . . . part of what makes us people." He shook his head. "I came to recognize the presence of evil over the years. True darkness is very different than mere rage or terror or greed, or desire for vengeance. I've met only a handful of mortals who were truly evil. Nicodemus and his like."

I nodded. "Angels are creatures of absolutes. You'd have to be pretty darned absolute to qualify as evil—or good—by their standards. It's why they like Michael so much."

Michael shrugged and nodded.

"So . . ." Butters said. "What's the takeaway here?"

"Your Sword isn't going to be of any use against mortals," I said quietly. "It's better than ever at handling monsters, but if one of them hires a bruiser from the outfit, that guy is going to bounce you off the ceiling."

Sanya clapped Butters on the shoulder, knocking him six inches, and suggested, "Time to get Kalashnikov."

"Fantastic," Butters muttered. He put the sword away and sighed. "Should we . . . like, talk to it or something? I feel like I've been super rude this whole time."

"Never hurts to be polite," I said.

"Did you read that in book somewhere, wizard?" Sanya asked innocently. "Perhaps a very long time ago?"

"If there are angels in the blades, they've been doing this for a while now," Michael said reassuringly to Butters. "I'm sure they understand our limits."

"But they would have told us, right?" Butters asked. "I mean, if that was true, it seems kind of important. They would have told us. Right?"

Michael shrugged. "Uriel is not generally free with information. He's fighting a war. The War. That means operational security."

"But why?" Sanya asked. "What difference if we knew?"

I shrugged. "Hey, I'm just trying to figure out why Butters has a safety sword."

Butters brightened. "I kind of do, don't I?"

"I will stick with steel," Sanya said. "And lead, of course."

I glanced up at the sun. "Hell's bells. I need to get moving. Little party tonight to get the peace talks started."

"What do you want us to do, Harry?" Butters asked.

I thought about it for a second and then put a hand on Butters's shoulder. "I'm still working in the dark. But you're the Knights of the Cross. If I work it out, I'll call you with details. But until then, do what you do, and we'll hope it comes out right in the wash."

Butters looked at me uncertainly.

"*Da*, is good plan," Sanya said. He clapped me on the shoulder hard enough to make me consider a chiropractor. "Dresden has been along on more Knight work than you so far. Is good plan. Wizard knows what he is talking about."

"No, I really don't," I said. "That's the problem."

"But you know that you do not know," Michael said. "Which is wise."

I snorted. "If knowing how clueless I am is the measure of wisdom, I am freaking Solomon, Walter Cronkite, and Judge Judy all rolled into one."

Sanya held up his hands with his fingers in a square, framing my face like a photographer. "Always thought you look more like a Judy."

I traded a round of goodbyes with the Knights, current and former, patted Mouse, hugged Maggie and told her I loved her and to be good, and headed out.

It was time to party.

19

We had a boring all-business meeting at six, the fete began at precisely seven thirty, no one showed up until at least eight, and the poor svartalf delegation must have spent half an hour wondering if they had come to the wrong address.

I hadn't needed directions. The fete was being hosted at the Brighter Future Society's headquarters, a small but genuine freaking castle that Gentleman Johnnie Marcone had flown over from somewhere in Scotland, stone by stone, and rebuilt on the lot of a burned-down boardinghouse.

My old house.

Gone now.

In fire.

I wanted to go home.

I pulled through all the familiar streets that led to my old home and my chest hurt as I did. Then I saw the castle and had it pointed out to my stupid heart, again, that home wasn't there anymore.

It wasn't a castle like you see at Disney World or anything. This one had been built for business, a no-nonsense block of stone that featured narrow, barred windows starting only on the second floor. It squatted on the lot like a fat frog taking up all of the lily pad, its walls starting not six inches from the sidewalk, and consequently managed to loom menacingly over pedestrians, despite being only three stories tall.

It stood out a little from my old neighborhood's aesthetic like a luchador at a Victorian tea party.

Tonight, the place's floodlights were on, glowing and golden, playing up over stone walls as dusk came on. When it got fully dark, Marcone's castle would look like it was holding a flashlight under its chin. A number of staff in red jackets were running a valet service. I parked on the street instead. Better to know where my car was and how to get back to it.

I sat behind the wheel, watching cars come and go, and waited until a pair of white, gold-chased stretch limos pulled up a few minutes later. The vehicles stopped in front of the castle and the staff leapt into action, opening doors and offering hands.

I exited my car at almost exactly the same time my grandfather got out of his. He was wearing his full formal attire, flowing dark wizard's robes with a purple stole hanging from his shoulders. Given his stocky frame and the width of the old man's still-muscular shoulders, the outfit made him look like a Weeble—those toys that wobble but won't fall down. He had shaved his usual fringe of wispy silver hair, and he looked younger for it, and he carried his staff in his right hand.

Ebenezar peered at the castle with narrowed eyes, then glanced sharply around and nodded when he saw me approaching.

"Hoss," he said.

"Sir."

Ebenezar turned to help the next person out, and I glanced back at the second limo to see Ramirez and his team pile out in rapid order, moving calmly and quickly into defensive positions around the lead limo. Carlos gave me a courteous, neutral nod as he went by.

I turned back to see a tall, sturdy woman with dark skin and thick silver hair wave off Ebenezar's offered hand. And when that didn't work, she took up a crutch from the vehicle's interior and poked my grandfather in the stomach. "I am not some wilting violet, Ebenezar McCoy. Move aside."

My grandfather shrugged and took a calm step back as Martha Liberty laboriously removed herself from the limo. She, too, was dressed in black robes and a purple stole, but in addition she sported an old-style white plaster cast around her right leg, evidently immobilizing the knee. I didn't know the woman well, but she always struck me as tough-minded, judgmental, and more or less fair. She swung her leg out, positioned her crutches, and lurched to her foot, holding the injured one slightly off the ground.

She glanced at me and gave me a short nod. "Warden Dresden."

"Senior Councilwoman," I replied politely, returning the nod.

"Excuse me, please," came a man's voice from the limo. "I should like to smooth things over with Etri before he has time to build up a head of steam."

Martha Liberty stepped aside so that Cristos, in the same robe and stole as the others, could emerge from the limo. The newly minted Senior Councilman had a thick mane of salt-and-pepper hair brushed straight back and falling to his collar. He wore an expensive suit beneath his formal robes, was a little taller than average, a little more muscular than average, and a little more possibly a member of the Black Council than average. He traded a neutral glance with Ebenezar, gave me a stiff nod, and strode quickly up to the castle's entrance.

"Always in a hurry, that one," came a voice from the limo. "Hey, Hoss Dresden. Give an old man your hand."

I grinned and stepped over to the car to clasp hands with Listens-to-Wind. He was one of the oldest members of the White Council and one of the most universally liked. A Native American shaman, he had seen the end of his people's world and the rise of a new one and had carried on unbowed. His skin was the color of smoke-smudged copper and covered in a map of leathery wrinkles. His silver braids were still thick, and if he stood with a slight stoop as he rose to his feet from the car, his dark eyes glittered very brightly within his seamed face. He wore the same outfit as the others, although he'd refused to trade in his sandals for formal shoes.

"Good to see you," I said, and meant it.

Listens-to-Wind squeezed my hand and gave me a brief, tired smile. "And you. You look better than the last time I saw you. More easy."

"Some, maybe," I said.

"We got a mutual friend here tonight," he said. "Crowds aren't really his thing, though. Maybe you can help me run interference for him at some point."

"Sure," I said. "Uh, who is it?"

"Heh," he said. "Mattie, shall we?"

Martha Liberty smiled, and the two of them started moving deliberately toward the castle, side by side.

Ebenezar came to stand at my side and look after them. "Good old Listens-to-Wind," the old man said. "The man loves his pranks." Then he cleared his throat and said, "Wardens, to me, please."

Ramirez walked over to us, giving the rally sign, and the rest of the Wardens came over, too.

"All right, people," Ebenezar said. "Remember that this is an Accorded event. The laws of hospitality are in full force, and I expect you to observe them rigorously. Understood?"

A murmur of assent went up.

"That said, do not assume others will be as courteous as we will. Eyes open, all night."

Wild Bill piped up. "What if we see something suspicious?"

"Use your best judgment," my grandfather replied, "while remembering that Mab, who is quite capable of enforcing the articles of the Unseelie Accords, will be in the room."

I snorted supportively. "She takes infractions kinda personal."

The younger Wardens exchanged uneasy looks.

"The wisest course is to observe the Accords and the laws of hospitality rigidly," Ebenezar said, his tone certain. "If you are not the first to break the laws, an argument can be made for reasonable self-defense."

"If we wait for an enemy to break the laws first, it might be too late to *enact* self-defense," Ramirez noted.

"Nobody ever said the job would be easy," I said. "Only that it would make us all rich."

At that a startled huff of laughter went up; Wardens were paid mainly in acrimony.

"Relax, guys," I said. "Believe me when I say that everyone else is just as afraid to piss off Mab as we are. Stay sharp, be polite, and we're home by ten."

"Warden Ramirez," Ebenezar said.

"You heard the man, folks." Ramirez sighed. "Let's mingle."

Technically, this wasn't my first visit to Marcone's little fortress, but it was the first time I'd done so physically. I'd been dead during the last visit, or mostly dead, or comatose and projecting my spirit there, or something.

I try not to get bogged down in details like that.

But as I approached the front door, I was struck by two things: First, a modest, plain bronze plaque fixed to the wall that spelled out the words BETTER FUTURE SOCIETY in letters an inch high. Second, that my magical senses were all but assaulted by the humming power of the defensive enchantments that had apparently been built into each individual stone of the castle. I had to pause for a moment and put up a mild mental defense against the hum of unfamiliar power, and I had the impression that the other wizards with me had to do the same.

Whoever had constructed this place, they'd warded it at least as heavily as the defenses of the White Council's own headquarters under Edinburgh. I could have hurled Power at this place all the ding-dong day, and it would have about as much effect as tossing handfuls of sand at sheet metal. It was similarly fortified against spiritual intrusion, with the only possible access points being the heavily armored entryways— and even those had been improved upon since I'd slipped my immaterial self through an open door.

Nothing was getting in now. The castle would make one hell of a defensive position.

Or, some nasty, suspicious part of me said, *nothing was getting out, making it one hell of a trap.*

"Huh," Ebenezar said, squinting at the castle. "That's old work. Real old."

"Our people, you think?" I asked him.

"Nnngh," he said, which meant that he didn't think so. "Maybe Tylwyth Teg. Maybe even Tuatha."

"Tuatha?"

The old man's mouth curled up at one corner, and his eyes were thoughtful and approving. "The ancient enemy of the Fomor," he said.

"Ah," I said. "Statements are being made."

"Better Future Society?" Ramirez asked, peering at the plaque.

"M— *Baron* Marcone, the White Court, and the Paranetters have formed an alliance against the Fomor here in Chicago the past few years," I said. "Too many kids had gone missing."

Wild Bill scowled darkly. "They turned to criminals and the White Court for help, did they?"

I straightened and turned slowly to Wild Bill, looking directly at him. "Their kids were being taken. And it wasn't like we were helping them."

Wild Bill quickly averted his gaze from mine. There was an uncomfortable silence.

"The reason for these talks is to try to undo a lot of bad calls," Ebenezar said wearily. "Come on, children. Let's get to work."

I walked in beside the old man. Inside the doorway was an antechamber where we were politely greeted by a handsome young man of heritage so mixed it was impossible to localize to so much as a given continent but might be generally covered by "Mediterranean." His hair was bleached white blond, and the man had truly unsettling eyes, somehow blending the colors of metallic gold with old-growth ivy. He wore a grey silk suit that didn't show the lines of any concealed weapons he might be carrying. I'd observed him once, while I was busy being dead. He was one of Marcone's troubleshooters, and his name was Childs.

A German shepherd dog stood calmly beside him, wearing a simple black nylon harness with one of those carrying handles on it.

"Hey there, Childs," I said. "How's tricks?" I extended my hand to the German shepherd, who gave it a polite sniff and then regarded me with considerably more calmness and professionalism than I was feeling.

"Good evening, ladies, gentlemen," he said politely. "Have we met, sir?"

"I met you, Childs," I said. "What's with the dog?"

The man looked decidedly uncomfortable. "My employer's main concern tonight is that no one brings any explosive compounds inside," he said calmly.

"Yeah. That would suck, if everything blew up and the place burned down," I said. "I speak from experience." I might have given him a toothy smile as I said it.

"Hoss," Ebenezar chided me gently.

Childs swallowed, probably exactly as hard as was warranted by the situation, but gave us a polite smile. "Please enjoy your evening, ladies and gentlemen."

"Hngh," Ebenezar said, and stumped inside. I let the younger Wardens follow the old man in and brought up the rear.

"Good work," I said to the dog as I went by. I hooked a thumb at Childs. "Make sure he gets a cookie later. Him such a gentleman."

The dog tilted his head, as dogs do, and his tail thumped once against Childs's leg. The troubleshooter gave me a somewhat sour smile and turned his attention deliberately back to the front door.

We proceeded into the main interior hallway. The castle was as I had remembered it: walls of grim stone, uncovered by plaster or paint, all rough-hewn blocks the size of a big man's torso. Candles burned in sconces every few steps, lighting the way, making the air smell of beeswax and something faintly floral. There was nothing like decoration on the walls, and the defensive power of the enchantments around the place was so strong that I could feel it through the soles of my shoes.

Ramirez glanced over his shoulder at me and said, "No guards."

"Don't count on it," I said. "Marcone keeps a platoon of Einherjaren on standby. Remember?"

"Yeah," Ramirez said grimly. "Those guys."

"What guys?" Wild Bill asked.

"Viking revenants with centuries of experience in every kind of warfare known to man," I clarified. "The guys doing the fighting and feasting in Valhalla. They don't mind dying. They've had practice."

"Consider them to be the most dangerous mortal warriors on the planet," Ebenezar growled from the front. "They are. Don't interact any more than you must. Many are berserkers, and safest left alone."

Ramirez lifted an eyebrow, nodded, and fell silent again. And as he did, we turned a corner and music came drifting down the hall from wide-open double doors ahead of us, along with a swelling of brighter lights.

Ebenezar glanced up at me, and his grizzled brows furrowed. "Hoss. You all right?"

I checked myself, trying to get my poker face back on. "Last time I went to one of these," I said, "things went kind of sideways."

"Heh," the old man said. "Me, too. Just you remember what I taught you."

"Never start the fight. Always finish it."

"Not that."

"Make your bed and do your chores?"

"Not *that*."

"Something, something, never let them see you sweat."

A grin flashed over the old man's seamed face, there and gone. "Close enough."

Then he gripped his stumpy staff and strode forward into the gathering.

I took a deep breath.

Then I followed him.

20

Marcone's little castle had a large central hall that took up what had to be a goodly portion of its ground floor.

The room was lit by chunks of glowing crystal mounted in sconces. Brownie work, unless I missed my guess, by the faint tinge of spring green and yellow coloring various pieces of white quartz—itself a potent charm against dark magic when properly attuned. That got my attention, right away. Summer Court work was unmistakable.

And apparently, Baron Marcone had convinced them to help him.

Music played from somewhere nearby, from live musicians, perhaps in an alcove behind some light curtains. I didn't recognize the composer of the little chamber orchestral piece, but that mostly meant that it wasn't Vivaldi. One of the Germans was as close as I could get. Whoever was playing, they weren't human. It held too much exactitude, too much unity in the tones, as if one mind had been playing all the instruments, and the shivering notes of perfect harmony it cast brought forth the ancient enchantment of music that had nothing to do with magic. That was Sidhe work, or I'd eat my tie, and from the sheer murderous precision of it, members of the Unseelie Court were responsible.

And they were playing for Marcone's party. Something that crowd did not do just for kicks—if they were doing this for a mortal, it was because they were paying off a favor.

I thought about the vaults we'd partially wrecked in the basement of Marcone's bank, where he'd been entrusted with protecting assets from a dozen different supernatural nations at least. Just how many markers had Marcone given out? How many truly scary beings were in the man's debt?

I frowned. The robber baron of Chicago was becoming a real concern.

And the hell of it was, I wasn't sure the residents of my town weren't at least partly better off for it. For all the harm he dealt out to the world, Marcone's people had taken the fight to the Fomor when they'd been hitting the town.

The swirl of attendees was a little dazzling, and I took a moment to just take it in.

Broad sheets of silk in a variety of colors decorated the roof and walls, streaming down from overhead to vaguely imitate the interior of an enormous tent, where negotiations would doubtless take place in the field between ancient armies. It took me a moment, but I recognized the various colors and patterns representing many of the nations of the Unseelie Accords, arranged subtly enough to be noticed only subliminally if one didn't go looking. But of course, here, *everyone* was looking. I regarded the various colors and patterns on the silk and realized the intention.

Our host had drawn up something of a seating arrangement.

Or, perhaps . . .

Battle lines.

A swirl of silver and onyx fabric patterned in strict geometric lines spilled down to backdrop a little area set with masterfully crafted furniture carved of . . . what looked like naturally ebony hardwood of some kind, chased with silver. Seated in a high-backed chair was King Etri of the Svartalves, appearing in his diminutive natural form, his grey skin and huge dark eyes striking against the backdrop. He was dressed in an impeccable suit of silver silk with black pinstripes and carried a cane of shining silver in his right hand.

Etri looked resolved—and exhausted. His broad forehead was wrinkled into a frown as he apparently listened to Senior Councilman Cristos, seated in the chair next to him. The wizard was in a conciliatory posture, bent forward slightly, his hands open, speaking quietly to the svartalf leader.

Etri's sister Evanna sat next to him, elegant in her own black suit, her fine silver-white hair spilling down over her shoulders like liquid metal. Her forehead was crossed by a band of some kind of metal that seemed to reflect colors that were not actually present in the room. Her dark eyes flicked toward mine and narrowed in immediate suspicion upon seeing me.

Five of Etri's warriors were spread out silently behind the pair, and every one of them turned their dark eyes toward me a beat after Evanna did. Their suspicion was a palpable force.

"What're they looking at?" muttered Wild Bill from next to me.

Yoshimo rested her hand calmly on his forearm. "Easy. They've done nothing."

"Pip-squeaks," Bill muttered.

"We're surrounded by stone right now," Ramirez said. "Not the best place to pick a fight with that crew. Especially since Mab would side with them if you did."

Wild Bill glowered at Ramirez but subsided. "I don't like side-eye is all."

"Oh, it's straight-eye," I noted. I nodded to Evanna, deeply enough to make it a small bow. Her expression became more neutral and she returned my nod precisely. But her eyes didn't change, even when she directed them elsewhere. "Maybe we should be covering the old folks, kids."

"Yeah," Ramirez said in his take-charge voice. "Yoshimo, stay with Senior Councilman Cristos. Bill, you've got McCoy's back. Chandler and I'll take Liberty and Listens-to-Wind."

Ah.

"Where do you want me?"

"Liaise," Ramirez said. "Head off trouble before it starts. And get me a scout of the room. You've met some of these people before."

I pursed my lips for a second and then said, "Who are you protecting here, Carlos?"

He clapped a hand lightly against my arm. "Hopefully everyone. Eyes open. Let's go, people."

The young Wardens moved out purposefully. I grimaced, snagged a champagne flute off a passing server's tray, and touched the rim of the glass to my lips for politeness's sake before continuing my slow perusal of the room.

Opposite the svartalves' colors was a streaming silken banner of pure white, intricately embroidered with sinuous shapes in silver thread, cascading down to a number of similarly upholstered sofas, where Lara Raith and her entourage had set up shop. Lara wore a simple white sheath dress cut to show a considerable length of leg and had her blue-black hair pinned up in elegant curls. Scarlet gems at her ears and wrist flickered with bloody red fire in the faerie lights. She sat in the center of one of the sofas as if it were a throne.

Freydis, dressed in a formfitting white bodysuit and a man's suit jacket, sat on the floor at Lara's feet like some kind of exotic pet, her green eyes bright in contrast to her close-cropped red hair. The Valkyrie looked distracted and sleepy and wasn't either one of those things. Behind Lara stood Riley and four of Lara's bodyguards, all of them looking lean and mean in matching buzz cuts and suits that didn't show the weapons they were undoubtedly carrying.

Lara looked up, met my eyes for a second, and gave me a serious nod. She moved her right hand in a tiny gesture, palm up, hand tilted toward the sofa beside her. I nodded and made my way over to her.

"Harry," she said, her tone light and delighted. "What a pleasure to see you. Won't you sit for a moment?"

"Very kind," I said, and settled next to her on the edge of the couch, where I could get up again quickly. I didn't touch her. "So, what's a nice girl like you doing in a dump like this?"

Lara threw back her head and laughed girlishly. It was patently false and impossible not to find appealing. "You're so funny. You're always so funny, Harry."

I blinked. Lara wasn't exactly a ditzy party girl, but she was doing a damned good impression.

She recognized when I got that something was up. Her eyes tracked over to one side and followed Ramirez as he limped slowly along behind Listens-to-Wind and Martha Liberty, leaning on his cane. Their color shifted from medium grey to a more sparkling color with flecks of metallic silver. "Oh, that poor boy. So pretty and wounded and so many hang-ups. Are you quite sure he isn't meant as a present?"

I heard a faint, sharp cracking sound, as if someone had snapped a couple of toothpicks. There was a whisper of power released into the air that I could barely detect, and a second later Freydis tucked a small, broken wooden plaque into her suit coat's pocket and said, firmly, "Clear."

Lara's giggling ceased and her smile vanished. "We've got about a minute before the happytalk illusion fades. What have you got?"

I pushed out my senses enough to feel the neat little combination privacy spell and external illusion now veiling us. "Little. I put a man I trust on Justine."

"My people are there."

"Can't be too safe," I said.

Lara grimaced. "Cristos is over there assuring Etri that the White Council will fully support him in this matter. Probably offering to dig my brother's grave for him."

"Etri isn't the sort to subcontract his work," I said. "And he's furious."

Lara narrowed her eyes at the svartalf king across the large room. "There must be a way he can be reasoned with."

"As a rule, yes," I said. "But he's got good reason to be angry right now."

"He's got my *brother*," Lara snarled.

"Etri and his people look like a batch of little geeks," I said. "You of all people shouldn't make the mistake of falling for appearances. If they were weak, someone would have offed them by now."

Lara clenched her jaw. "If I don't create some options, I'm going to have to leave Thomas to rot." She inhaled. "Or change my posture."

Which was a polite way to say *Start Killing People*.

I regarded Lara obliquely for a moment. Maybe she wasn't running on the kind of cold political calculation she'd led me to believe she had embraced. Maybe things weren't quite as clear where her baby brother was concerned as she had led me to believe.

I was pretty sure I hadn't been doing the peace process any favors lately, so I pondered as hard as I could. "When you have a problem, you have a problem," I said thoughtfully. I nodded at Cristos. "When you have *two* problems, sometimes one of them is a solution in disguise."

Lara eyed me and narrowed her eyes.

"Cristos thinks he's a statesman, brokering peace and justice, that kind of thing," I said. I took a deep breath. "Ask him for his help."

"Why would he do that?"

"Makes him look good if he can get both parties to concede something," I said. "He's out to gain face and reputation. Etri wants justice and he's upset enough not to be thinking clearly. If you can't negotiate something out of that, you aren't the person I think you are."

Lara gave me a direct, intense, silent look for a long moment. I could feel the soulgaze forming and averted my eyes before things got any more intimate.

"I want you to introduce me," she said.

"I'm happy to advise you," I said. "I'm not sure that it would be helpful to you for me t—"

Her voice hardened. "I am owed favors. You are obliged to repay them."

And, deep down inside of me, something *twisted* with acute discomfort, as if Lara's words had just reached into my guts and started kicking them, then waterboarded my conscience for good measure. Welling up from the Winter mantle was the sure and certain knowledge that Lara *was* owed, and that it was an injustice too deep to tolerate that she should not be repaid. No matter how inconvenient or personally humiliating it might be.

Wow.

So that's what it felt like from the faerie side of things.

No wonder so many of them didn't like me much.

"Fine," I growled. My voice came out tense, under pressure. I rose and offered her my arm, invisibly shattering the little illusion spell around us. "Come on."

"Everyone else stay here," Lara said firmly. She held up a finger to forestall both Freydis's and Riley's sudden words of protest. "No. I'm going alone." She rose and laid her hand lightly on my forearm and nodded to me. I started leading her across the room.

"I regret doing that to you," she said quietly after a few steps. "He's family."

"I didn't much like it, either," I said. I still felt faintly queasy, though the discomfort had rapidly begun fading the moment I'd acquiesced. "I get it. Don't make a habit of it."

She gave my arm a gentle squeeze of her fingers through the spider-silk suit and glanced up at me with a rather sad smile that showed no regret whatsoever. Her pale grey eyes were resolved. "Only if I must."

We went across the room to Etri's seating area, and I walked directly up to the svartalf king.

Cristos, who had been in the middle of saying something very sincerely, looked up at me and frowned. "Warden Dresden."

"Sorry to interrupt," I said, even more sincerely, "but I saw an opportunity for us to help out our neighbors."

Cristos arched an eyebrow and began to speak, but Etri held up a hand and the man fell silent. Yoshimo, standing six feet back and to one side of Cristos, gave me an inquiring glance.

"Etri," I said. "Please allow me to introduce Lara Raith, daughter of Lord Raith and his chancellor in the White Court."

"I know who she is," Etri said, his gaze level and not quite hostile. He nodded to Lara, who returned the gesture precisely. "I fear we have little to say to one another, Lady Lara."

"That depends on what is said, sir," Lara replied. "And when two potential foes meet, the presence of a trusted mutual ally can do much to allay suspicion and fear." She turned to bow her head to Cristos. "Sir, your reputation for skill in such matters is well-known. I am certain you are aware of the tensions between our realms at this delicate time. Perhaps the wider reconciliation we are all hoping for can begin here, between King Etri's people and my father's Court."

"Ridiculous," Evanna said, her voice brittle.

Etri gave his sister a weary look and held up his hand again. "Lady Lara, I see little hope for resolution of any kind in this matter but what is prescribed in the Accords."

Cristos's eyebrows beetled, and he folded his hands thoughtfully. "And yet, if you see little hope, then a little must be there. Perhaps a little hope is a good place to begin. Surely, Etri, there is no harm in speaking while we are all under the protection of guest-right."

The svartalf rubbed a few fingers wearily at his forehead, clearly ir-ritated, and glanced up at me. "Harry Dresden," he said. "You have been a guest and friend to my people. You were friends with Austri. Can this person be trusted?"

I eyed Lara and then turned back to Etri. "If she gives you her word, she'll keep it."

Which . . . wasn't exactly a lie. Lara was good to her word. So was Mab. So was Etri. And I didn't particularly trust any of them, beyond that.

But then, when you get right down to it, what else is there? And what more can you really ask for?

Etri studied me for a moment and then nodded, and I got the im-pression that he had intuited my exact meaning. His mouth set in a line that said he clearly didn't enjoy the prospect, but that he was also clearly resolved to treating his peers with courtesy. "Very well. Lady Lara, if you would please join us. May I send for a drink?"

Lara smiled warmly at me and settled down in a chair one of Etri's people carried over for her, to leave her, Etri, and Cristos seated at the points of a triangle. "Thank you, Warden Dresden, for the introduction."

"Sure," I said.

"Please," Cristos said, his voice mellow, his gaze annoyed, "do not let us keep you from your duties any longer, Warden."

"Yep," I said to Cristos, in a voice that was louder and more nasal than it had to be. "Okay. Bye-bye."

I shot Yoshimo with my forefinger and strode away. There was a buffet over in one corner of the hall. My nose caught a whiff of some-thing delicious and reported to my stomach, which instantly started growling. I realized I had been too distracted to have a meal today, which really seemed like something I should grow out of at some point.

Well. There was no sense in going hungry if I didn't have to, and I suspected that the more time I spent with my mouth full of food, the less time I would have to screw up at this stupid party. I went for the food.

The room was getting even fuller. Under a sickly green banner of cloth sat the LaChaise clan's representatives, centered on a ruddy-faced, burly man with big old muttonchops who looked like he enjoyed a lot of meat and potatoes. Carter LaChaise, leader of a large family of ghouls who ran a lot of supernatural business in Cajun country. They'd been seated at a table and were dining ravenously on steak tartare, I hoped, and looked weirdly like the painting of the Last Supper.

I considered setting them all on fire for a while, until I started getting looks from the table. It was only then that I noticed how widely I was smiling and moved along.

A black banner with black gemstones draped down into a semi-alcove shape, surrounding a single enormous chair in shadow. A very tall, very large man, apparently in his fifties, sat lazily in the chair, silently regarding the gathering. He held a pipe negligently in one hand, apparently unlit, but smoke trailed sinuously down from his nostrils with each breath, and his eyes reflected the light of the room like a cat's. Ferrovax, the dragon, disguised in human form. The last time we'd met had been at an event like this, and he'd tossed me around like a chew toy. I avoided his eyes, and his lips curled into a smirk as he tracked me going by. Some of my antics a few months back had disturbed some of his treasures, held in Marcone's vault. I had a feeling he was the type to take that personally.

I shivered at that. There was plenty of fallout from that job that was still due to come raining down, I was pretty sure.

There was a dizzying array of other delegations. The Summer Court of the Fae held the far corners of the room, in the complementary cardinal direction from the svartalves and the White Court, opposite the Winter Court on the other side. Both were centered around a single thronelike chair, but no principals were seated yet—only five of the Sidhe, in armor respective of their queens' colors, deep blues and greens and purples for winter, with more springlike greens and golds for summer.

Other beings were all over the place. I recognized a naga from a mess I'd gotten into on a rough weekend a few years back, at the moment disguised as a woman with smoky skin in a lovely white evening gown, chatting with Ivy the Archive, who was startlingly older than the last time I'd seen her, and dressed to match in a black evening gown without jewelry or other accoutrements.

Should Ivy even have hips yet? I did some math, making an effort not to count on my fingers, and realized that, yes, it really had been that long since I'd seen her. Now she looked like a girl going to prom, only way more self-assured—and she was evidently there alone, absent the bodyguard I'd come to associate with her as surely as I did coffee with doughnuts. Where was Kincaid? I tried to make eye contact with Ivy as I went by, but either she was too involved in the conversation to notice or she ignored me.

I felt awkward. I was never much good at parties.

I went by a sky blue banner swirling with cloudy whites and flashing lines of gold, opposite Ferrovax's cozy alcove, and exchanged a nod with Vadderung, CEO of Monoc Securities, seated in a comfortable stuffed chair that looked like it would be good for reading. Vadderung looked like a tall, muscular man in his early sixties who could probably bench-press a motorcycle. He wore a charcoal suit, his long wolf-grey hair and trimmed beard made rakish by a black eye patch on a leather thong. Like Ferrovax, he sat alone, without guards, with a rather large glass of wine in one hand and a smoldering pipe in the other.

I traded a nod with him as I passed, and he mouthed the word "Later" at me as I did.

I made it to the buffet without causing any major diplomatic incidents, which for me is remarkable. I picked up a plate and started with the platter of tiny tenderloin steaks. I mean, sure, they were *meant* to be little nothings, appetizers, but if you stacked a dozen of them together you had something that resembled a real steak.

I was moving on to look for something delicious to go with them when a hairy hand the size of a cafeteria tray, lumpy with scars and muscle, clamped down on my right shoulder.

I nearly flew out of my shoes as panic flashed through me, and my brain took me back to a few months before, when the owner of a hand like that had been stalking me through the burning ruins of one of the weapons vaults kept by the King of the Underworld, Hades himself. The Genoskwa had occupied more than the usual space in my nightmares since, and the sudden surge of adrenaline caused the Winter mantle to go berserk, readying my body for combat in an instant.

Only it was already too late. The fingers, thick as summer sausages, had already tightened down. It had me.

"Dresden," growled an enormous, rumbling voice. "Good. Finally, I can pay you back properly."

21

When someone has ahold of you, there's a basic rule of thumb to follow, which Murphy had taught me a while back. I called it the Rule of Thumb. The idea is to twist whatever part they've got hold of toward their thumb in a circling motion. The basic principle is that it's easier to overcome the power of one thumb than it is four fingers supported by the thumb. The Genoskwa's grip was incredibly strong—but the Winter mantle gave me enough physical capability, at moments like this, that I wasn't exactly a ninety-pound weakling, either.

His right hand was on my right shoulder. So I dipped suddenly, spinning clockwise and pulling sharply back and down, pitting the weight and power of my entire body against the monster's single thumb.

I did it just right—and even so, only barely managed to break the grip and pull away. I also managed to jostle the buffet table, setting the serving trays to clanking, and nearly knocked the thing over with my ass as I crouched, dropping my plate to lift my arms in what would probably be a useless gesture of self-defense.

Only it wasn't the Genoskwa.

Standing in front of me was a goddamned Sasquatch, a hairy humanoid figure a solid nine feet and change in height, layered with dark brown hair and muscle. He was wearing—I'm not even kidding—what looked like a Victorian-era tuxedo, tailored to his enormous size. He had spectacles across his broad, flat nose, their lenses the size of tea saucers, and they still looked a little small on him. His hair, all of it that was visible, had been shampooed and conditioned, and for a second I thought I was looking at a Wookie.

"Hah," rumbled the Sasquatch. His face spread into an uneasy smile that showed me broad teeth that looked like they could crunch through a fence post like it was a stalk of celery. "I heard you met my cousin."

I blinked several times and then realized that everyone in the room nearby was staring at us. I'd dropped both my staff and my snack plate, and the servers behind the buffet table looked like they wanted to quietly vanish. I huffed out a breath, pushed away the Winter mantle's scream to engage in bloody combat, and said, "Wow. River Shoulders? Is that you?"

"Ungh," River Shoulders grunted in the affirmative. He gestured down at the tuxedo awkwardly. "Had to put on this monkey suit. Didn't mean it to be a disguise."

Strength of a River in His Shoulders was a shaman of the Forest People who had apparently been living right under everyone's nose for hundreds of years. He'd hired me for some jobs in the past, and he was a decent guy. He also happened to be very large and very scary.

"What are you doing here?" I asked him.

He shrugged. His shoulders were a good five and a half feet across, so it was a fairly impressive motion. "After that mess in Oklahoma, I thought a lot about what you had to say, about my child. And you were right." He pursed his lips briefly. "Out of line, arrogant, but right."

I felt myself flash him a grin. "Seems about correct for a wizard."

"Eh, for a human," he agreed. "Called a council of my people. Told them to leave my son alone or I'd start breaking skulls. And then we decided to join the Accords."

I tilted my head. "After lying low for so long?" I asked. "Why?"

River Shoulders glanced around the room, maybe a little nervously. "So I could get the chance to pay you back. What you did for me, for my family, was more than just work for hire. You cared. You chanced making me mad to show me I was being foolish when no one else would. Even when I got mad. Pretty good friend stuff, there. And you gave me my son."

I cleared my throat and looked away. "Yeah, well. Okay."

"I heard you went up against one of the Forest People and beat him."

"Killed him," I said.

River Shoulders eyed me and repeated, "Beat him."

A little cold feeling went through me. "What?"

He nodded. "Big part of why I'm here. Wanted to warn you."

"How?" I demanded. "There was nothing left but ketchup."

River Shoulders shrugged again. "I don't know how. But I saw him not a moon ago. Blood on His Soul won't forget. Keep your eyes open, huh?" Once again, his eyes tracked nervously around the room. "Hey, does it feel hot in here to you?"

And suddenly I remembered Listens-to-Wind's cryptic words. River Shoulders wasn't a coward or anything, but it had to be tough to shift from a long lifetime of avoiding notice to showing up at a gathering of the most dangerous supernatural beings on the planet. "Oh, right," I said. I turned to one of the staff behind the buffet and said, "Is there somewhere a little quieter we can go?"

The staffer was mostly staring up at River Shoulders, but he said, "Uh. Yeah. Sure." He started to turn away.

River Shoulders put out a hand, rested fingertips lightly on the man's shoulders, and said, "Hey, Einherjar."

The man froze and turned to stare at River Shoulders, and then his hand, with hard eyes.

River nodded and withdrew his hand carefully. "Listen up. Grendel was a bad egg. Spawned mostly bad eggs. Most of my people thought he was a lunatic. So right now, the only quarrel you and me got is what you're bringing with you."

The man peered at River Shoulders and then at his tuxedo and spectacles. He gave a slow nod and said, "Yeah. Sir. Come up to the gym."

I took a look around the room and noted how many red jackets were casually blending in among the crowd. Yeah. Marcone had plenty of people here.

We followed the Einherjar back through a set of doors to a short hall, up a flight of stairs, and into the gym I'd visited before, in spirit. It wasn't big, but it had everything you needed, including a small boxing ring. There were a couple of lights on, but otherwise the place was dark and quiet. Our guide gave River Shoulders another thoughtful look and departed in silence.

River Shoulders let out a sigh and sank down to the stone floor, resting his back against a wall. He took the spectacles off and tucked them into a pocket.

"Why the glasses?" I asked.

"Make me look less threatening. Like that gorilla in the video game."

I arched an eyebrow. "You play video games?"

"I study human cultures," River Shoulders said. "How you guys think about us, and creatures you think are like us. Video-game gorilla thought of better than King Kong, you know?" He shook his head. "Humans are scared of just about everything. Problem is, their first reaction to being scared—"

"Is to kill it," I said, nodding. I considered my super-nice suit and decided that I didn't much like suits anyway. I sat down on the ground next to River. "I'm familiar with the problem."

"Hah," the big guy said. He shook his head. "Thank you, getting me out of there." He grimaced. "There's just too much tension there. Too much hatred. Lust. Greed. Fear."

I looked up at River for a moment and realized that he'd been frightened to be there. Exposed, in the midst of more noise and movement than he could adapt to readily. I knew River could wield Power in his own way, and if the poor guy was an empath, too, that room must have been torture. "Yeah, these parties are a hoot," I said.

He grunted, took a deep breath, and exhaled. He sounded like a racehorse. "Einherjaren here, too. That's always trouble."

"How come?" I asked.

He scrunched up his nose, enormous brows beetling. "My people follow three paths," he said. He gestured at himself. "Sky path, like me. We learn. We remember. Watch the stars. Read. Talk to you people, mostly on the rez. Think about things." He sighed. "There's not too many of us."

I frowned and said, "You're like wizards are to humans."

He shrugged. "Not entirely the wrong way to see it. Why you and me get on pretty good, probably."

"I'll buy that. Okay."

"Second path is the forest path. That's most of us, maybe nine in ten. Forest path thinks that humans are good example of what not to do. That we should stay close to nature. Avoid contact. Fire. Tools. All that. Stay quiet and unseen mostly and live in harmony with the natural world."

"And humans see them once in a while," I said.

River nodded. "Though me and the guys on the rez watch those shows about you looking for them. Pretty darned funny. Little bit sad."

I tilted my head and made a guess. "The Genoskwa. He's on the third path."

"War path," River agreed. "He thinks our people are the first people. Thinks we should kill most of you. Make the rest into cattle and slaves." He mused for a moment. "They're assholes," he said frankly. "Kind of stupid. But there's not too many of them, either, so they can't get what they want. Settle for hanging around national parks, making people disappear once in a while, when the sky path don't stop them."

"And the first Grendel was on the war path?"

River nodded. "Taught his tribe. They had numbers enough to make a go of it, back then. The other paths left them to their madness, walked over the ice, joined our people here. Grendel's people drove the humans from some places. Humans were tied to their lands, their crops. Not much they could do about it."

"What happened?"

"They picked a fight with the wrong humans," River Shoulders said. "Vikings. Vikings had a champion. A teacher."

"Beowulf?" I asked.

"Beowulf. Vadderung. He got a lot of names and faces." River Shoulders nodded. "Lived and fought like a mortal. Showed them how to have courage. Helped build a warrior culture. Fight the giants. Some of his people even came across the sea, found us, and didn't waste any time on talk. But there were too many of us here, and they left."

"So what was with confronting that guy before he brought us up here?"

River Shoulders shook his head. "Lot of the Einherjaren got to Valhalla fighting my people on the war path. They remember."

"So, the Genoskwa . . ."

"Our word for the war path," River Shoulders said. "Blood on His Soul is more arrogant than most. More dangerous, too. Thinks he is the ultimate genoskwa. A paragon." He pursed his lips and mused. "Maybe he is."

"He's a lot bigger than you," I noted.

"Yeah," River said amiably. He yawned. It was innocent and terrifying. A volleyball could fit in his mouth with room to spare. "I'm kind of a pip-squeak."

"Well, I know that was my first thought when I first saw you."

He grinned. That also was terrifying. But I was starting to get accustomed to it. "You not real used to talking to people taller than you, are you?"

"Probably some truth to that," I said. "How you feeling?"

"Better," he said. "Listens-to-Wind is a good kid, was helping shield me from all that"—he lifted a hand and flicked it around the side of his head, as if having difficulty putting a concept into words—"noise. But he's got duties of his own tonight."

A good kid?

"How old are you, exactly?" I asked.

River Shoulders put on a serious expression, exaggerated his northern, Native American accent, and said, "Many moons." He shrugged, returning to his usual tone. "Tough to keep track sometimes. Was born on the walk across the ice. Not much food at first. Probably why I grew up puny. Figure I'm about middle age."

Which, presumably, made him approximately the same age as the tale of Beowulf. That made him better than a thousand years old. Minimum.

No wonder he could do things with magic I'd never seen before.

"You know what, Hoss Dresden?"

"What?"

"You always treated me pretty good. Even when you were scared. Takes courage to do that to someone so different from you."

"Not so hard to be polite to someone who can punch me to the moon."

"Your personal history says otherwise," River Shoulders said, his tone gently teasing. "You pretty good about defying folk who need defying. And you're getting better about figuring out who those folk are. Listens-to-Wind says you had a tough childhood."

"Lot of people do," I said. "I was lucky to get a good teacher. Don't know about how much courage I have."

"Seem to have a bit," he replied. "Now, courage ain't everything. But you build everything else on it." He eyed me, and his features were both troubled and resolved, the expression of someone who had made a hard decision. "Sometime, you want to learn more, come find me."

"Should I blast calls and pound my staff on trees?" I asked lightly.

His eyes sparkled far back under his brows. "Maybe give my woman a call," he said. "Be quicker. And a little less silly-looking."

I frowned and said, "You're serious."

"Listens-to-Wind says you're a good investment. Just got some rough edges and need to learn more. Especially with that thing Mab hung on your shoulders."

I frowned. "Listens-to-Wind made an offer like that, too."

"Sure," River said. "But I taught him. And he's just about gotten to the end of his path." He looked uncomfortable. "Lot of the wizards who matter are near the end. Hanging on hard."

I tilted my head at him. "Why?"

"Not the right person, time, or place to tell you, starborn."

I pursed my lips. "Six hundred and sixty-six years," I said experimentally.

River's craggy brows rose, itself a feat of superhuman strength. "Huh," he said. "You learned some things."

"I learned that," I said.

"We pretty close to that time," he said. "Kinda promised not to tell you anything. Sucks. Necessary. But if I was you, I'd think hard about taking my offer." River's eyes flickered toward the door, and he started putting his spectacles carefully back on. "Someone coming."

It was a good ten seconds before I heard the whisper of light steps on stone, and then Molly swept into the room. The Winter Lady wore an opalescent formfitting gown that very heavily emphasized that she was my best friend's daughter and that I ought not to notice that about her, dammit.

"Harry," she said, and then paused, eyeing River Shoulders. "Uh, that is, Harry Dresden."

River Shoulders went from sitting down to standing in a light, liquid motion. "You want to insult me, you going to have to try something worse than calling me hairy, Miss Lady Winter," he said politely, and bowed a little at the waist. "If you will excuse me. Miss. Hoss."

"Good talk," I said. "Next time, a fire and steaks."

River Shoulders nodded and moved out of the room in long, silent, relaxed strides that carried him at about the same pace as me when I went jogging.

Molly waited until he had left and said, "What the hell, Harry? What are you doing up here?"

"Liaising," I said. "Listens-to-Wind asked me to keep an eye out for him."

"Well, I need you to do it some more," she said. "The fiddler decided he liked the look of Warden Yoshimo and tried to lay a whammy on her."

I stood up. "Hell's bells. Did it work?"

"Not for long. But it should be dealt with openly, in front of everyone, by you."

Right. As Mab's nominal enforcer, I was the guy she would send to, well, enforce the Accords, unless the infraction had been committed by someone out of my league.

"Okay," I said. "Show me."

She looked pointedly at my arm. I offered it to her, and we started back down to the main hall. "Molls, I talked to your dad today."

"Oh?" she asked, her tone utterly neutral.

"He says you haven't been home to visit in a while."

She glanced surreptitiously at me. "I've been busy. There's been no time."

I stopped and perforce she stopped with me. I frowned at her and said, "Kid. Make time."

Her voice turned sharper. "You aren't my father, Harry. You aren't my mentor anymore, either."

"No," I said agreeably. "But I am your friend."

"We can talk about this later," she said, tugging my arm.

I didn't budge. "Now seems to be a good time. Your family misses you. And you owe them better than this, Molls."

"Harry . . ."

"Just tell me you'll visit. The word of the Winter Lady is good."

"Harry, I *can't*," she said.

"Why not?"

She fretted her lower lip. "It's complicated."

"Going to Sunday dinner isn't complicated." I turned to her and put a hand on her shoulder. "You've got something precious. You've got a family. And they love you. And you're probably going to live for a very long time without them. It's idiotic to miss the chance to be with them while you can."

She looked away from me, and tears made her eyes glisten.

"Come on," I said, gently. "Don't get all famous and forget the people you started with, faerie princess. They've got to be proud to have a celebrity in the family."

Molly closed her eyes entirely as the tears fell.

Then she said, in a tiny voice, "They don't know."

I blinked exaggeratedly. "What?"

"I . . . I haven't told them. About being the Winter Lady."

"Yeah," I sighed. "I know. Stars and stones, Molls, what were you thinking?"

She shook her head. "It's . . . They're going to see it as a bargain made with dark powers. If they found out . . ."

"Not if," I said. "When. You can't keep things like this hidden forever."

She shook her head wordlessly.

"It needs to be done," I said. "You owe them the truth, at least."

"I *can't*," she hissed. She opened her eyes and met mine. "It's Papa. I've wanted to tell him, so many times. But he wouldn't understand. I just . . . just imagine the look on his face when he knows . . . and it *hurts*, Harry." She closed her eyes and shook her head again. "I can't face that. I can't."

She broke off, and her tears fell in silence.

It hurt to see her suffering.

So I gave her a hug.

She clung to me, hard.

"This is hurting you. And it's hurting them, too, even if they don't know it yet."

"I know," she said.

I said gently, firmly, "It has to be done."

"I can't."

"You can," I said. "I'll be there with you."

She shuddered and clung to me. "I can't ask you to do that."

"You didn't."

The shudders eased after a few moments. "You will?"

"What are friends for?"

Her weight leaned harder against me for a moment, in gratitude. "Thank you."

"Anytime."

We went back down to the main hall, where I immediately walked across the room to the musicians' alcove, reached up, and ripped down the swath of cloth covering it with an enormous rasp of tearing silk.

The music stopped instantly, and the entire gathering paused to stare at me with lifted eyebrows. I noted that Yoshimo, surrounded by her fellow Wardens and the Senior Council members, looked up with pained, furious eyes.

Behind the curtain, half a dozen Sidhe sat with musical instruments now silent in their hands and stared at me with their large jewel-like eyes. The ruling class of Faerie, the Sidhe were slim, beautiful, ancient, and deadly. The tallest among them was a male prettier than nine out of ten women on magazine covers, and he had silver-white hair and amber eyes. He carried a violin in one hand.

Without a word, I called upon Winter for strength and kicked him in the chest before he could rise fully to his feet.

The Sidhe crashed backward through the rest of the chamber orchestra, knocking over chairs and smashing instruments, and hit the stone wall with a crunch of broken bones. He staggered off the wall and fell to the ground, trying to scream in pain and unable to find enough breath to get it done.

I turned to Molly, hooked a thumb over my shoulder, and said, "That guy? He seemed the most douche-like."

Molly blinked once and nodded.

I nodded back and turned toward the fallen Sidhe. "These people are guests, under guest-right," I said in a voice meant to carry through the room.

"No harm was done," spat one of the other Sidhe, a female holding a cello. "It was but a game."

"Game over," I said. I raised my right hand, called upon Winter again, and thundered, *"Infriga!"*

In an instant, the air screamed in protest as near-absolute-zero cold rushed out of my hand and enveloped the fallen fiddler in a block of glacier blue ice. Even the other Winter Sidhe recoiled from the savage bite of the cold and wound up with their hair, ears, and fingertips coated in ice. All of them stared at me, frozen, ba-dump-bump, ching.

None of them moved.

Except the fiddler. His eyes moved, desperate and agonized.

I turned to find Molly approaching in full Winter Lady mode, her steps decisive, her posture regal. I inclined my head to her and said, "My lady, what is your will?"

"This sort of behavior cannot be tolerated," she said, her voice carrying to the entire room. "Though he is not one of mine, I offer my most sincere regrets to the White Council and to Warden Yoshimo for this incident." She looked around the room and said, "Baron Marcone has given his permission, as host, for me to deal with this matter. Place this lawbreaker on the buffet table. An ice sculpture is appropriate. Should he survive to thaw, he is banished from Winter lands and holdings upon pain of death."

She walked up to the block of ice and crouched down to face the fiddler's wide eyes. She simply stared for a moment, cold and icy, and then said, in a very calm, very hard tone, "It's not nice to do that to girls at parties."

She rose and made an imperious gesture with one hand. Evidently, she knew how to convey that she meant business. Half a dozen Einherjaren in their red caterers' coats immediately moved in, picked up the block of ice, and started carrying it toward the buffet table.

"Excellent," Molly said. She turned to the room and said, "Please excuse this disruption, honored ladies and gentlemen. I regret its necessity." She regarded the rest of the musicians, smiled, and said, with a very slight emphasis on the last word, "Please resume your duties."

And the music, altered considerably, started up again *tout de suite*.

The Sidhe are predators. One does not show predators weakness or hesitation. It's the easiest way to communicate with them. Molly had learned all about how to get her message across.

Within a minute, Lara swept up to us and gave Molly a polite bow of her head. Molly returned it.

"Lady Winter," Lara said, "I need a breath of air outside. I wonder if you would loan me your Knight as an escort for a few minutes. I shall return him directly."

Molly just stared at Lara, without expression. Then she moved her chin in the barest nod.

"Lovely," Lara said. She gave me a radiant smile and said, "Shall we?"

I offered her my arm, and the two of us left as the chatter of conversation resumed. Though I was ostensibly escorting her, Lara directed me with firm pressure on my arm, until we were outside the castle and walking down the sidewalk toward the other houses in the neighborhood.

I glanced at her and saw her jaw set with determination, and sharp excitement in her eyes. When we were several hundred feet from the castle, she said, "I did it."

"Did what?" I asked.

"I created options," she said. "It was always possible that Etri was holding Thomas because he wanted a ransom, but that apparently is not the case. He wants blood. I wasn't able to convince Etri to drop the charges against Thomas. But between Cristos and me, we convinced him that holding him prisoner in his own demesne made it appear as though vengeance was more important to him than justice."

I lifted my eyebrows. "How does that change anything?"

"Baron Marcone, as host of this gathering, offered to hold my brother prisoner until the matter had been settled through an Accorded emissary." Her eyes flashed. "My brother is being transferred to the castle."

"Still don't see how that changes anything," I said.

"Negotiations begin in earnest tomorrow night," she said. "Here. *Not* in svartalf territory."

I took a slow breath. "Oh no. Tell me you're not thinking what I think you're thinking."

"My brother will be here, in a building I know, and everyone will be preoccupied," she said. "And I won't be violating svartalf borders. I can work something out with Marcone after. He's reasonable about business."

She stopped and turned to face me, slate grey eyes as hard as stone.

"I tried to be reasonable. Etri declined to meet me halfway. It's time to create a better position. So, tomorrow night, while everyone is distracted, I'm taking my brother back. I'm going through anyone who gets in the way."

Oh, Hell's bells. I knew what came next.

So much for the diplomatic solution.

Her teeth showed very white as she saw my dawning comprehension. "And I'm calling in my second favor. You, Sir Knight, are going to help me."

22

Is she insane?" Karrin demanded.

I threw up my hands halfheartedly.

Her blue eyes stared hard at me for a moment before she said, in a calm, practical voice, "Oh God. You want to do it."

"I don't *want* to do it," I said. "But he's my *brother.*"

She lifted her good hand and pressed her fist against her nose. "God, Harry, there are times when I could just choke you."

"Yeah," I said tiredly. "Me, too."

Her grandmother's clock ticked steadily on the mantel over the little steel-lined gas fireplace, which must have been one of the fanciest things in the neighborhood when the house was first built. Karrin had been cleaning that day, which was a bad sign. It was one of her go-to reactions for stress. If she started cleaning the guns, I would know it was really bad.

"Things are already tense enough," she said. "If this disrupts the peace talks, there are going to be consequences."

"I know."

"My read is that this whole conference is Marcone's baby."

I grunted agreement. "He's actually *doing* what Cristos only *thinks* he is," I said. "Building alliances."

"And if you screw up Marcone's plan?" Karrin asked bluntly.

"His reputation takes a hit," I said.

"And he will respond to that."

"Marcone is acutely aware of the concept of payback," I agreed.

Karrin glowered. "I don't know all of the beings you deal with very well, Harry. But I know Marcone. And he scares me."

I stared at her for a moment.

I'm pretty sure there wasn't anyone else on the planet Karrin would say those words to.

She returned my gaze for a moment, and I had to look away. She knew what she'd just shown me. She'd decided to do it.

"Hey," I said, and went over to sit next to her on the couch. I put an arm around her. She fit very neatly into the space against my side. She pressed her cheek against my chest for a moment.

"What happens if you tell Lara no?" she asked.

"It . . . hurts," I said.

"You've done pain before," she said. "What will they do to you?"

"Mab is also all about payback," I said. "She'd act." I frowned and said, "Hell. If I get *caught* helping Lara disrupt the Accords, as her own damned enforcer, she'll have to act, too. Quickly. And publicly."

"Couldn't the White Council tell her to back off?"

I thought about that for a second and then said, "Maybe they could. Question is if they would. Pretty sure the answer is no."

"Useless," she muttered.

"I'm not exactly their poster child," I said. "It's likely they'd wrap me up in a bow for Mab to keep from crossing her."

"Can't your grandfather put a stop to that?"

I shook my head. "I don't think so. Last time, he had Martha Liberty's support. I don't know if he would, this time around. If that's the case, the Senior Council vote would definitely go against me. So he'd have to leave it to an open vote of the whole Council and . . . well . . ."

"Useless," Murphy repeated, more firmly. She pushed away from me, hauled herself to her feet, and hobbled out of the room stiffly on her cane.

When she came back in, she was carrying a blue plastic pistol case. She set it down on the table and sat down. Then she clicked open the case decisively.

Only instead of removing a pistol, she pulled out a handheld oscillating multitool and tossed me the end of its power cord. "Plug that in."

I clambered around until I found the power strip between the couch and the end table, and did. Then I withdrew a bit. Wizards and technology don't get along so well, but I'd been hitting new highs of self-restraint over the past few months. If I didn't get close to something as simple as an electric motor, I probably wouldn't screw it up, as long as I stayed calm. Probably. "What are you doing?" I asked.

Instead of answering, she snapped a saw blade onto the tool, flicked a switch that set it to buzzing, and immediately took the blade to the cast on her shoulder.

"Karrin," I blurted, rising.

"Back off before you short it out," she snapped. "Go stand over there in the kitchen. Go."

"What the hell do you think you're doing?" I asked.

She gave me a brief annoyed glare. "You're obviously doing this, no matter how stupid it is. I can't help you get away with it if I'm too busy being a starfish."

I clenched my fist against my nose and said, "There are times when I could choke you, too."

"Try it and I'll break your wrist," she said grimly.

I took a step toward her.

"No, don't come help me, you lummox. I can do it myself."

"*Karrin*," I said.

I might have sounded a little terrified.

She hesitated.

"Karrin," I said, more gently. "Murph. You can't keep doing this to yourself. You're hurt. You need time to heal. Please."

She looked away from me, into the middle distance, her lips tight. "This is probably as healed as I'm going to get, for all practical purposes," she said. Her voice was very thin.

"I can still use your help," I said. "Just coordinating communications with our friends—"

She shook her head several times. "No. No, Harry. I'm not changing how I live my life. This is my choice. And you've got no stones to throw when it comes to stupid plans. So either back me up or get out of the way."

Frustration flashed through me. Karrin might have been damned near superhuman, but she wasn't supernatural. She'd fought. She'd been beaten. She'd been hurt. She was in no condition to get involved in another one of my problems, and there was a very real chance that it could get her killed. She didn't have the protection of her badge anymore, and she no longer had the full use of a body that had spent a lifetime dealing with predators of one kind or another.

But she did have the enemies to show for it.

Granted, what made Karrin Murphy dangerous had never been her arms and legs. It had been the mind that directed them. But even there, I had doubts. She'd always had a lot to prove, to herself and to other people—and she had never been okay with showing weakness. Was that affecting her judgment now?

Or maybe it was something simpler than that.

Maybe she was just afraid for the man she loved.

I swallowed.

For a second, I debated killing the little saw. A simple hex would render it useless. And then I realized the manifest idiocy of *that* idea. Karrin would not readily forgive me that—and she'd just find another way to get the damned cast off when I wasn't looking anyhow. She probably had a second saw waiting in a box in the garage marked REPLACEMENTS FOR THINGS HARRY SCREWED UP. She believed in being prepared.

I couldn't stop her. It would be the same as telling her that she was weak and needed to stay home. That she wasn't strong enough to help me. It would break her.

And besides.

You can't go around making people's choices for them. Not if you love them.

So I stepped back over the line between the hardwood floor of the living room and the tiles of the kitchen.

"Thank you," Karrin said calmly.

"Murph," I said.

She paused with the saw resting against her cast and looked at me.

"What's happening now . . . you've got no standing at all in it. No protection from the Accords. No badge."

She watched my face, her expression serious.

"This is the jungle," I said. "And none of the players in this are going to have a problem burying inconveniences if it means holding the Accords together."

"You mean me," she said.

"I mean you," I said.

"You could have hexed the saw already," she said.

"No," I said. "I couldn't have."

"Well. You're not all dumb," she said, smiling faintly.

"Remains to be seen," I said. "I know you well enough to know there's no point trying to stop you. But I . . . I gotta know that you're walking into this with your eyes open, Murph."

She looked down for a long moment. Then she looked back up at me and said, "I *have* to do this."

I stared at her bandaged, broken body for a long moment.

Then I clenched my jaw and nodded once.

"Okay," I said. "I'll help."

Murphy's eyes softened for a moment.

Then she took the oscillating saw to the cast and started slicing away at it.

It didn't take her long to get the cuts made, though she hissed in discomfort a couple of times as she went.

"Don't cut yourself," I said. "If you bleed out it will take a week to clean up."

"They're burns," she said, annoyed. "The saw won't cut flesh, but it heats up the cast. I'm just too impatient."

"No kidding," I said lightly.

"Okay," she said. "Come help me pull it off."

I did.

Look, when you've been in as much cast as Karrin had for as long as she had, the results are kind of gross. There was a buildup of dead skin, flakes of it white and hard like scales where her skin had been. There's no dressing that up.

"Engh," Karrin said, wrinkling her nose as her arm came free. "It's the smell that bugs me."

"Junior high gym lockers were that bad," I said.

"Ew, boys," she said. She lifted her wounded arm a little, moving it slowly, wincing.

"Leg next," I said.

That one was worse. She hissed as the cast came free, and put a hand against her back. "Oh my God," she muttered. "My hips forgot how to be at this angle." She looked up at me, her face still pained. "I've got braces. We should put them o—"

She broke off when I simply picked her up, as carefully as I could. She got her good arm around my neck and helped as much as she was able.

"What do you think you're doing?" she asked.

"Taking you to a hot bath," I said. "Don't try to move. Just . . . let me do it. Okay?"

Her blue eyes went very soft for a moment, and she looked down.

"For a minute," she said.

I took her to the bathroom, moved aside the assistance equipment that was there, and set her down gently on the commode. It took me only a moment to get the bath going and then to help her out of her clothes and lower her carefully into the water.

We didn't speak. I moved slowly, sluicing warm water over dried-out skin where necessary, and let her soak in the warm water for a while. There was some gentle soap on hand, and after a time, I used that, with just my hands, being as careful as I could to get the area clean without stripping up layers of skin down to the raw new stuff at the bottom in the process.

Karrin watched me at first. After a while, she closed her eyes and just sort of sank back into the tub, her limbs loose. Her hair spread out a little in the water. She looked drawn, gaunt, in the face and neck—and peaceful.

"I love you," I said.

She opened her eyes and blinked a couple of times. Then she lifted one ear out of the water and said, "What did you say?"

I smiled at her. Then I went back to running my hands gently down her arm, encouraging some of the dead stuff to come off. It would take a few days for her to get back to normal.

"Oh," she said, studying my face.

Then she sat up in the water, twisted a little toward me, and slid both of her arms around my neck. She pulled my mouth down to hers with a strength that no longer surprised me.

But the sudden, sweet, almost desperate softness of the kiss that followed nearly knocked me into the tub.

And in the middle of it, she breathed, "I love you, too."

23

We were about halfway to Château Raith when Murphy asked, "You seeing this?"

"The Crown Vic behind us?" I asked. "Yeah."

"Yeah, them," Murphy said impatiently. "And also the other two cars."

I frowned. I was driving the Munstermobile, which Murphy hated riding in because the custom-sized seat wasn't adjustable, and her feet couldn't reach my pedals. By almost a foot. The old car wasn't exactly built with the driver's lines of sight in mind, but I scanned the early-morning traffic, frowning.

It took me a good minute of looking to spot what Murphy had already alerted me to—a dark blue Crown Vic was following about three cars back. Probably Rudolph and Bradley, in one of Internal Affairs' vehicles. Behind them, maybe three more cars back, was a battered old Jeep that looked like it would have been happier and more comfortable in the Rocky Mountains somewhere. And then there was a third car, a silver minivan, following along a ways behind the Jeep.

"You're a little popular," Murphy said.

"Hell's bells," I muttered. "Is it a whole surveillance team?"

"They'd be the worst one in the world," Murphy said. "If they had three of them working together, there's no reason for all of them to keep us in sight the entire time."

"Huh," I said, and watched the cars for a few minutes more. "They aren't working together. Three different parties tailing us?"

"Rudolph and Bradley are here for me," Murphy said. "Who are the other two?"

I chewed on the inside of my cheek for a second, thinking. "Um. Well, I suppose I could start driving like a lunatic and find out."

"In this old death trap?" she asked, and shuddered. "No, thank you. Should we let them follow us?"

"Tough to know that if we don't know who is back there," I said. "Rudolph I don't much care about, but I'd rather not have Bradley stick his head into a noose. He's just trying to do his job right."

"Well, you aren't going to lose a Crown Vic in this boat."

"True," I said. "So maybe we do this the other way."

"Magic?" she asked. "I don't really feel like walking the rest of the way, either."

I shook my head. "This old death trap was manufactured damned near a century ago," I said. "The whole point of driving it is because it can endure exposure to active magical forces and keep going vroom-vroom." I squinted at the road. "You know. For a while."

Murphy sighed. "What's your plan, Harry?"

"We're going to get out of sight for a second, and then I'm dropping a veil over us," I said. I thought about it for a second. "We'll have to stay on the highway. If we pull off to the side, there's no way I can veil the dust and debris we'd kick up driving on the shoulder."

"But other cars won't be able to see us," Murphy said.

"And we won't be able to see them very well, either," I said. "Be like driving in heavy rain."

She grimaced, clearly unhappy at the entire situation. "And we're riding in a brick with no handling."

"A brick that's heavier than a lot of the trucks on this highway right now," I said, "and made from all steel. Might not handle or accelerate like a modern car, but it's not made of drywall and cardboard, either."

Murphy gave me an impatient look. "Harry, do you even understand that modern engineering means that the lighter cars are actually considerably safer than cars like this one?"

"Not when they *hit* cars like this one," I noted.

"Yes, they're not meant to take dinosaurs into consideration," she growled.

"Exit coming up," I said. "Here we go."

I cut into the right-hand lane and accelerated smoothly and without noticeable effort from the old car. Between my old mechanic Mike and the tinker elves Mab had on call for maintenance and repairs, the Munstermobile purred like a three-thousand-pound kitten.

I went up the ramp with the accelerator mashed flat to the floor, and the cars following me had little choice but to emulate me. I'd timed my exit well, though. I gathered my will as I watched a couple of legitimate vehicles get in the way of my pursuers, and I reached the top of the ramp just in time for the green light. I went right through the intersection, back onto the entry ramp, and back down toward the highway, and as I went, I waved my hand in a gesture reminiscent of drawing a hood up over one's head, and murmured, *"Obscurata."*

There was an odd sensation, like a fine cold mist drifting down over me, and the interior of the car dimmed, as though heavy clouds had suddenly obscured the light, to the point where you'd have trouble telling what time it was by looking at the position of the sun.

Visibility dropped suddenly and dramatically. Magic is awesome, but you don't get anything for free—mess around with how much light is going to bounce off your body, and you're also futzing about with how much light makes it to your eyeballs, and for that matter how much light is available to do things like keep you warm. Going unseen isn't a super-complicated operation—doing it without blinding and freezing yourself is the hard part. I had settled on developing a veiling spell that would split the difference between visibility and comfort—by choice, obviously, and not because it was totally not my area of natural talent—and as a result, looking out of my veil was only a little easier than seeing *into* it. The world went dim, and just as it did, Murphy sat up straight, her eyes bright.

"Hey," she said. "Does this spell stop radar?"

"Uh," I said. I was already holding on to a veil and driving faster than was strictly safe, and my attention can only split so many ways. "Not mine. Molly's will stop almost everything, but I only bother with visible light becau—"

Murphy reached over while I was still talking and pushed down on my right knee, hard, pressing the accelerator flat again. "Faster."

I gave her an annoyed look and then did it. The old engine gave a game growl and we gathered speed going down the on-ramp, rapidly reaching speeds that would preclude any chance of getting off with a warning.

I checked the rearview mirror in time to see our entourage come barreling onto the entry ramp behind us—

—just as my more-or-less-invisible car passed a pair of highway patrol vehicles poised on the side of the ramp, watching for speeders to come sailing under the bridge.

I had a chance to see both highway patrol officers come to attention behind the wheel, their eyes on their radar-gun readouts, then switching to the apparently empty road—and both men locked eyes on our pursuers, the only apparent visible source of the readings on their instruments.

I flashed by them and just had time to see their bubs coming on before they vanished into the obscurement generated by my veil.

"Oh," I said to Murphy in admiration. "That's just mean."

"Right?" she asked me, smiling. She patted my leg and said, "Good job following directions."

Which was another way to say, *Thank you for trusting me.*

I chewed on my lip. If I drove in the right lane, I'd have to go slow to avoid problems, and I'd have to dodge anyone trying to make it over for the exits. If I drove in the far left, I'd run the risk of idiots just slamming into me from behind. I liked my chances better in a lower-speed accident, so I got behind a truck in the right-hand lane, crept up close enough that he couldn't have seen me in his mirrors, and stayed there.

"Aren't you worried about people flipping out when you appear all of a sudden?" she asked.

"Ah," I said. "Not so much. People work really hard not to notice unusual things, generally speaking. You know the drill by now." I shrugged. "Most people have encountered something that looks damned peculiar, that just doesn't fit. And mostly they explain it away, no matter how thin the explanation sounds, or they just don't think about it. Everyone says they want magic, but no one *really* wants to feel confused and frightened, or stay awake at night worried about dark forces they can do nothing about."

"And magic is that," she said.

"That's some of what magic is," I said. "It's also a lot of good stuff. Like all power. It depends on what you do with it."

"And yet, like all power," Murphy said, "it tends to corrupt."

Well.

Tough to argue with that.

The number of people capable of wielding Power, or power, responsibly was never exactly going to threaten the world food supply.

Out of the mist of my veil's obscurement, the Jeep that had been following us appeared. It pulled up directly behind me and then flashed its headlights in three quick signals.

"I handled the other two," Murphy said. "This one is yours."

"Yeah," I said, peering at the rearview mirror. Then I dropped the veil abruptly, hit my right blinker, and took the next exit ramp. Murphy arched an eyebrow but looked at me. I pulled off to the side of the road, and the Jeep pulled up behind me.

"Is that who I think it is?" Murphy asked.

"Uh-huh," I said. "Contracted him to help out."

Murphy eyed me and said, "Huh. Maybe you do learn. Eventually."

"Amazing, right?" I leaned back and way over and unlocked the rear passenger-side door.

Goodman Grey got into the backseat and slouched down wearily. He was perhaps one of the most forgettable people I'd ever seen. He was unremarkable in every way, a man of medium height and build, blandly not-bad-looking, and if you looked real close you could see Native American background in him somewhere. He was also one of the most dangerous shapeshifters in the world, he worked for one dollar per case, and he had saved me from meeting a truly ugly end in Tartarus.

"What the hell, man?" I asked as he settled in. "You're supposed to be watching Justine."

"Me and everyone else," he complained. "You should have asked me about my group rates. Hey, Ms. Murphy."

"Goodman," Murphy replied. "Still working for these unsavory characters, I see."

"Risk of the trade, ma'am," Grey replied.

"Hold on, now," I said. "Who else is watching Justine?"

"Who *isn't?*" Grey asked. "White Court, cops, Feds, some wackadoo who is either a perv or a nutcase, doing it all by hacking into surveillance cameras online—"

"That sounds like it's probably Paranoid Gary," I said. "He . . . has issues."

Murphy frowned and said, "Wait. How in the world did you find out all of this?"

Grey shrugged.

Murphy arched an eyebrow at him. "How sure are you about your information?"

"Ms. Murphy, please." Grey brushed imaginary lint off his shoulder and sniffed. "Like Dresden here, I do some of the work myself, and for some of it I have people."

"Feds, though?" she asked. "I mean, locals I could understand. But what are the Feds doing involved?"

"We tipped off Agent Tilly, remember?" I asked.

Grey nodded. "Isn't Tilly, but it's some of his guys from the local field office."

I grunted. "Everyone know about everyone else?" I asked.

"They know in part and they understand in part," Grey said, somewhat smugly. "I know about all of them."

"Unless you don't," Murphy pointed out.

"Unless I don't," Grey allowed, unperturbed. "But anyone who makes a move on the girl is going to set off about three different groups of dangerous people, and I figured you needed to know what was up."

"Yeah," I muttered. "Maybe I do." I closed my eyes for a second, thinking.

"Don't hurt yourself," Grey said.

I opened an eye and gave him an annoyed look that was, by necessity, at only half strength. It didn't seem to damage him. Then I closed my eye again and kept thinking.

"One of the people surveilling Justine is the person who threatened her," Murphy said. "And they must have given Thomas an ultimatum. And because he's an idiot like you, Harry, he didn't tell her about it."

"Yeah, feels like that's the right ballpark," I said.

"Oh crap," Grey sighed. "This is about the assassination attempt?"

"Yeah," I said. "I think someone leveraged him into it by threatening the girl."

"Huh," Grey said, sitting back. "Well, he's a dead man now. Svart-alves don't kid around."

I opened my eyes and looked at Grey in the mirror.

The shapeshifter shrugged and returned my gaze with a blank expression that showed neither hostility nor fear. "Oh. It's personal. You and him, huh?"

"He stood beside me when it was bad," I said.

"Ah," Grey said, as if enlightened. "Okay."

I nodded, and so did Murphy.

"So what do you want I should do?" Grey asked.

"Nothing's changed," I said. "Protect Justine."

"Yeah," he said, drawing the word out. "But there's a lot of players here. Sometimes the best defense is a good offense, right?"

I scowled. "Hey, who is putting up the money around here?"

Grey shrugged and said to Murphy, "Do you want to explain it to him?"

"He's one person, Harry, as remarkable as his abilities might be," Murphy said thoughtfully. "Given that there are multiple threats, if he isn't standing in arm's reach of her, there's not much he can do if someone decides to shoot her through the window."

My chest panged a bit. It did that sometimes, when I imagined someone I knew getting shot. It did that every time when I imagined it being me.

"Let me get closer and find out more," Grey said. "More information might help a lot. And if I can't get anything useful, or turn up the actual threat, I can vanish the girl, get her to a safe house."

"You have one of those?" Murphy asked.

Grey winked at her. "Let's just say I can borrow one."

I nodded, frowning. "Can you do email?"

"Who doesn't do email . . ." Grey began, but then he looked at me. "Oh. Yes."

"Murph, can you give him Paranoid Gary's email?" I asked.

"My last fresh one was before I got hurt," she said. "He may have moved on by now." She took a notepad out of her jacket pocket and flipped through pages. She found the one she wanted, turned to a fresh page, and started writing. Murphy hadn't been on the force for a while, but her habits had not changed much. She tore off the page and gave it to Grey. The email address was a string of gibberish letters and numbers. "Here. Make sure you tell him who gave you the address or he'll assume you're one of Them."

He accepted the note, glanced at it once, and handed it back to her. "And why are you trusting this guy again?"

"It's possible that Lara is playing games with me," I said. "So her people might be behind it. The local cops are probably in Marcone's pocket, and I don't trust him any further than I can kick him. I don't know why the Feds are involved or who is pushing them, but even though I like Tilly, he's a square and this seems like a damned odd play for him. And I've never really been comfortable dealing with government agents."

"Ah," Grey said. "And the Internet guy is safe?"

"Paranoid Gary is a creep and a weirdo, but he's our creepy weirdo," I said. "If he's the one doing the hacking thing, he can probably assist you. If it isn't him doing it, he can probably find out who it is."

"If he will," Murphy said.

"Sure," Grey said, almost jovially. "Because paranoid." He shook his head. "Well. You don't ever bore me, Dresden."

"I'm good like that," I said.

"At least you pay well," he said, and nodded to Murphy. "Ma'am."

"You're going to need someone to relieve you eventually," Murphy said.

"Only if we do this for a couple of weeks," he said. He nodded to her; then he got out of the Munstermobile and walked back to his old Jeep.

"Useful guy," she noted as Grey cranked up the vehicle and left, turning back toward Chicago.

"Very."

"You trust him?"

"Well. I hired him. I trust him to live up to that."

"So did Nicodemus," Murphy noted. "But someone else had hired him first. So what if someone else hired him first, again?"

I grimaced. "Thanks for bringing that up."

"You're a good person, Harry. You trust people too easily." She shifted in her seat, wincing.

"The leg?" I asked.

"Hip," she said shortly. "Don't forget your cold medicine."

Murphy had given me something that promised to remove mucus and sneezing and coughing and aching for eight hours at a time, about seven hours ago. I opened the little bottle and took more of it.

"Are we getting old?" I asked her. "Is this what that's like?"

She smiled slightly and shook her head. "It is what it is." She eyed me. "Do you think Lara is behind this?"

"My instinct says no. But she's tricky enough to try it, and it's called treachery because you don't see it coming," I said. "Wow, though. She's standing really close to Mab's toes on this one, no matter how you look at it."

"How she reacts to the proposal is going to tell us a lot," Murphy said.

"You ever get involved in one of my cases and find yourself drowning in an overabundance of information?" I asked.

She snorted. "Point."

"It might tell us something," I said. "Best we can hope for."

"We're moving ahead blind," she noted.

"Maybe." I pulled the car back onto the road and toward the highway. "But there's no use in wasting time."

24

Freydis met us at the door of Château Raith and said, "Seriously? You just drive here and walk up to the front door? Obvious much?"

"Aw," I said. "It's so cute when you guys try to employ the vernacular. It's just never quite on point. You know?"

The ginger Valkyrie gave me a narrow-eyed look and said, "Don't make me stop this car."

"Somehow worse and better at the same time," I said approvingly.

Freydis snorted. "Who is the mortal?"

"Please," Murphy said. "You know who I am, and you know what I do."

Freydis showed her teeth. "The Einherjaren like you, Ms. Murphy. But that doesn't give you a pass. This is an internal matter. You aren't coming into it."

"I already have," Murphy said. "Years ago. Unless Ms. Raith would prefer me to make a non-secret of her open secret about her father."

"Are you threatening my employer?" Freydis asked in a very level tone.

"I *am* a threat to your employer," Murphy replied calmly. "But there's no reason we can't be civilized about it."

"I could kill you right now," Freydis noted.

"You could try," Murphy answered. "But however that turned out, your boss would be working without Dresden's help."

Freydis narrowed her eyes and then looked at me. "What do you say, Dresden?"

"Good morning," I said. "Nothing further to add."

"The woman speaks for you?"

"For herself. But I don't see the point in repeating her."

"Her injuries . . ." Freydis began.

Murphy didn't seem to move quickly, but everything happened with smooth precision as she stepped forward and to one side. She drove the elbow of her injured arm at Freydis's midsection. It didn't hit hard, but it forced the Valkyrie's balance off, and Murphy followed up with a step into her as her cane clattered to the porch. She stepped into the Valkyrie, pinning her against the side of the doorway—and Murphy's gun came out and nestled up under Freydis's chin.

"I am getting tired," Murphy said, in a faintly annoyed tone, "of people using that phrase as if I was not standing right here."

Freydis stared down at Murphy for a long moment. If she was bothered by the gun under her chin, it didn't show on her face. She nodded and turned her palms up. "Enter, warrior."

Murphy met her eyes and nodded. She withdrew carefully, keeping the gun on Freydis until the last possible second, then took a limping step back. I picked up her cane and held it for her while she put the gun away, her eyes still on the Valkyrie. She accepted the cane with a nod.

I gestured toward the house and said, "Lead on, then?"

Freydis lifted a hand and rubbed briefly at the spot on her chin where the gun's muzzle had left a mild indentation. Then she said, to Murphy, "Are you seeing anyone?"

Murphy blinked.

"Mortals make the best lovers by far," Freydis explained. "And this job means I'm basically sexually frustrated around the clock. But it's hard to find mortals I respect."

Murphy's cheeks turned bright pink. "Um."

Freydis frowned slightly and glanced from Murphy to me and back. "I don't mind sharing."

"I'm . . . I'm Catholic," Murphy said.

Freydis's eyes shone with a wicked sparkle. "I don't mind conflicted, either."

Murphy gave me a somewhat desperate glance.

Huh. I'd officially seen everything now. Murphy asking for a rescue. From monsters and madmen, she'd never cried uncle.

It had taken a redhead.

"Business first, maybe?" I suggested.

"We could all die tonight," Freydis said. "But as you wish."

Freydis led us to the rear of the château and outside, to gardens I had never seen before. There was even a hedge maze, or maybe *an* hedge maze, depending on who you asked, a good ten feet high, and Freydis led us right into it.

"I apologize for the walk, Ms. Murphy," Freydis said.

Murphy limped along grimly, leaning on her cane. "I'm fine."

Freydis nodded but glanced my way, and it was possible that her steps gradually, imperceptibly slowed a bit over the next couple of minutes, until we reached the center of the maze.

We stepped into a grassy bower where apple trees had been planted beside a beautifully laid-out . . . not pond; it was definitely a water feature, complete with an abstract statue of a pair of faceless lovers intertwined in its center, with water rippling down over them. A party had taken place the night before, apparently. There were bottles and plates scattered with the remnants of food lying about on the grass, along with articles of clothing. Many of them ripped.

The center of the bower was . . . Well, I'm sure it had some kind of official garden title, but it amounted to a giant canopy bed, big enough for at least half a dozen people, and probably more if you squeezed, gauzy white curtains all around it. The morning light made them misty-translucent, and the breeze, enough to keep away the promise of another hot day, for the moment, stirred them in rippling waves.

Sitting cross-legged at the head of the bed, sipping a tiny cup of espresso, was Lara Raith. She was wearing an oversized blue T-shirt and old cutoff sweatpants with paint stains on them. Her hair was rumpled, and she wasn't wearing any makeup at all. As we entered, she looked up, and her eyes were absolutely sapphire blue, almost gemlike. She stretched, as anyone might in the morning, though not many of us would have made it look that good in those clothes, and smiled at us. "Harry. Ms. Murphy. Good morning."

I looked around. "Late night?"

"Your people and the svartalves aren't the only ones I'm practicing diplomacy with," she replied. "And it's always a good idea to eat a large meal before one expects difficulty."

Murphy leaned on her cane. "You prepare for trouble by having sex?"

"I'm a vampire, Ms. Murphy," Lara said calmly. "I have certain physiological needs. So yes. It is also often necessary for celebrating a victory. Or recovering from a defeat."

"I'm sensing a pattern," Murphy said in a very dry voice.

Lara laughed. It was just a laugh, with none of the supernatural come-hither in her voice I'd heard before. "Our information suggested you'd be in the casts for another week."

"Four days," Murphy corrected her. "And I got bored. But this isn't really a social call."

"Oh, how unprofessional of me," Lara said.

I peered around and said, "Someone bugged your office, didn't they?"

Lara lifted her little cup to me in a salute. "And they say you're a mindless thug."

"Who?" I asked.

"Even if I felt like sharing my"—she fluttered her lashes—"intimate details with you, Harry, what makes you think it would be wise to do so?"

"Just asking," I said. "One professional to another."

"I know you meant that to be flattery," Lara said, her tone wry. "So I'm going to take your intention into consideration." She visibly considered it for a moment before saying, "I'm not sure. But too many leaks have happened in the past few weeks. I'm secure against strictly technical means of doing it. And I've never had issues with my people betraying me."

"Not even in the Raith Deeps?" I asked.

She waved a dismissive hand. "Oh, that was just everyday treachery. That's different."

"How?"

"It was kept mostly in-house," she said. "It benefits all of the White

Court to have the strongest and most capable leadership possible. Challenging that leadership for control of our people's aims is good for everyone."

I sputtered. "I almost died. So did you."

"Don't be a whiner, Harry," Lara said. "Neither of us did. When my people turn on me, we keep it mainly between us. This information has been falling into outside hands. I work with consultants in such matters, of course, but they haven't been able to find any magical surveillance, either. My working theory is that it would take one of your people to manage a spell they couldn't detect."

I frowned. The White Council tended to wage information-based warfare whenever it could, right up until it was time to start ripping satellites out of orbit and triggering volcanic eruptions, on the theory that with enough knowledge, leverage would be far more effective, obviating the necessity for open war. It was an obnoxious, arrogant stance to take on such matters—and it worked.

Mostly.

That didn't mean being the target of a full-court press on surveillance was fun. I hadn't much liked it when they'd been monitoring me more closely, earlier in my career.

Wizards could be really annoying sometimes.

"Would either of you care for coffee?" she asked.

We did. Freydis set us up, her eyes always looking at nothing specific, as if she was trying to take in everything around us at once.

"So," Lara said. "Why are you here?"

"It's about tonight," I said.

She gave me a sharp look and then glanced at Murphy.

"You demanded my help," I said. "You're getting it. My way."

Something that very nearly resembled anger changed the shape of her face, made it look remote and cold. It was gone again after a breath. "I see." Her eyes went to Murphy. "I apologize that you were dragged into the matter."

"Then why'd you do it?" Murphy asked.

I shifted my weight a little so that my hip pressed against Murphy's. Well. It pressed against her upper arm.

Lara took that in for a moment and nodded slowly. "I see. I trust that you can keep this matter a professional one?"

"Try to stab us in the back or feed on either one of us, and I'll make holes in your skull," Murphy said. "Play it straight with us and we'll all be fine. I like your brother."

"Did you just threaten me in my own garden?" Lara asked.

"I just explained our stance to you," Murphy said.

Lara glanced at me.

I shrugged. "Better to have it out in the open than under the table."

She smiled and shook her head. "I suppose we are all here for Thomas, are we not?"

"Which is why we've come," I said. "This can't be a smash-and-grab run."

Lara frowned. "Given the security around him, I don't see any option."

"Do you *want* a war with Svartalfheim? What happened to avoiding open conflict?"

She gave me a pained glower and looked abruptly away. "The equation changed when they moved my brother. I'll be facing considerable in-house trouble if my own sibling is put to death. My enemies within the Court will use it as a justification to rally against me. If I can't protect my own family, how can I protect them, et cetera." She shook her head. "Allies outside the Court will also be watching. A quick conflict and a brokered peace could make my position stronger than it currently is."

"So this is all about power," Murphy noted.

"It is *also* about power," Lara corrected her. "For people in positions like mine, power concerns are a constant. But Thomas is my only brother. He's frequently vexing, but . . ." She shrugged. "I like him. Family isn't something one discards lightly."

I thought of the old man. "No, it isn't," I said quietly. "So what if I told you I thought we could get Thomas out clean, no bloodshed."

"To what advantage?" she asked. "Etri's people would track him and kill him. The Accorded nations will, theoretically, be honor bound to help."

"I think I can keep him hidden," I said. "From all of them."

"Even your own people?"

"Especially those assholes," I said.

Lara's eyebrows climbed.

"If we do it smoothly enough," Murphy said, "we can do this without violence and it will be a fait accompli. He'll be out of their hands and unreachable. You'll have time to talk things down. And since you'll have done it without shedding more blood, there will be pressure from the Accorded nations for Etri to restore peace and resolve the matter via weregild."

"A very steep weregild," Lara noted.

"Still cheaper than slugging it out with the svartalves," I said, "or slapping down another rebellion among your own people."

Lara frowned, narrowing her eyes in thought for a full minute. Her chin bobbed up and down very slightly. "I take it Mab is fine with this?"

"Mab can be very creative about what she notices or doesn't," I said. "Particularly if the forms are observed correctly. The lack of bloodshed at what amounts to her party will go a long way toward pacifying her."

"But she doesn't know," Lara pressed.

"She loaned me to you so that she wouldn't *have* to know."

Lara finished the last of her espresso. "Meaning . . . that there might well be consequences for you in the aftermath."

"Especially if we screw it up," I said.

"If we attempt and fail," Lara noted, "my position is even worse than if I do nothing."

"He's family."

Her sapphire eyes met mine for a dangerous second and then turned to Murphy. "I take it this is your plan?"

"I don't get weepy about who gets credit," Murphy said. "As long as the plan gets results."

Lara took a deep breath.

Then she said, "All right. Walk me through it."

25

It's not complicated," Murphy said.

Lara tilted her head and said, "Please don't assume I'm too thick to see the obvious options."

"You've been in the building for meetings of the Brighter Future Society," Murphy said. "I trained there on a daily basis for more than a year. With the guards."

Lara arched an eyebrow. "I assumed you were watchdogging the imperiled families who were staying there."

"I was," Murphy said. "I was also learning everything I could about the place." She snorted. "Marcone owns it. Keep your friends close."

Lara's smile was somehow both appreciative and predatory. "So you have information I didn't when I was making plans."

"The strong rooms are in the basement," Murphy said.

"Only one way in and out," Lara noted.

"That's not the first problem to plan for," Murphy said.

I nodded. "Before we go in, we need to set up a way out."

I arrived at the reception on time, wearing my silver suit and my Warden's cloak. It wasn't the original, which I preferred, sort of. It was a dress cloak, made of shimmery grey silk of some kind, and it didn't have any tears or burns or patches on it. Once again, I walked in with the Wardens and the members of the Senior Council, though this time Ramirez, dressed as I was, lagged a bit behind, leaning more heavily on his cane than the day before.

Predators would note that he was an easy target, isolated and falling behind like that, and this summit could be fairly described as a convocation of some of the deadliest predators around. I slowed my pace to walk next to him. That way he wouldn't be alone.

It was a muggy night, with light, sullen rainfall that made the warm air smell like hot asphalt and motor oil and cut grass. The rain was something to be expected when powerful delegates of both Summer and Winter were in proximity for any length of time.

"Hey, man," I said quietly. "You okay?"

Ramirez set his jaw, glanced at me for a second, and then said, "I will be. Right now it's inconvenient. At least I'm not stuck in a wheelchair anymore."

"What happened?" I asked.

The muscles in his jaw flexed before he spoke. "Tangled with the wrong monster."

"Line of duty?"

He shrugged a shoulder. "As it turned out."

I frowned. There were enormous anger and pain in the spaces between his words. I'd seen Carlos get hurt, during the war with the Red Court. It hadn't ever stopped his smile for very long.

This had.

"I'm sorry," I said.

His lips pressed into a line. "Yeah." He gave his head a little shake, as if dislodging an insect. "I heard about the vote in the Council, man. It's bullshit. However inconvenient you might be for them, whether any of them like it or not, you're a wizard, Harry."

"Yer a wizard, Harry," I growled.

He didn't smile, but an amused glint came to his eyes. "Point is, I've already cast my vote on your behalf. So have most of the other Wardens."

I was quiet for a second, with my throat a little tight. "Oh. Thanks."

"Yeah, well. We're just the guys who have to do the fighting and the dirty work," he said bitterly. "All the wizards who sit on their fat asses all day, who knows? To them, you're scary."

"You didn't used to curse so much," I noted. And he'd never sounded so bitter doing it, either. Man.

Something had done a number on Ramirez.

I made a mental note to grab a bottle of something very flammable and have a long talk with Carlos before long.

"How's Karrin doing?" he asked.

"Like always, but slower and grouchier."

"I heard what she did. Went hand to hand with Nicodemus Archleone and survived."

"You got that backwards, but yeah," I said. "Difference is, she can still live in her house."

"Hah," he said, with a flash of teeth. "Yeah. You wouldn't believe how many people have come to the Council asking us to help them find him."

"Are we?"

"Hell, yes," Ramirez said. "Guy's a goddamned monster. But he's slippery as hell."

"Sounds about right."

"Someone's going to get him, sooner or later."

"Can't be soon enough for me," I said. "So what's the deal with another reception? I thought that was last night. Is one party not enough?"

"Oh, God no," Ramirez said. "That was just an icebreaker. Tonight is opening ceremonies."

"Which is another party."

"Obviously. The Accords provide space for a lot of business at a summit meeting. New applicants, addressal of grievances, public announcements, explicitly stating the purpose of the summit, that kind of thing. That's what opening ceremonies are for, before the actual haggling starts."

I grunted. "Whee."

"Don't you like parties, Harry?" Ramirez asked. A ghost of his old humor came into his voice and face.

"Well," I said. "I heard that at least there will be cute girls."

Wham. It was nearly audible, how fast his expression became a closed door.

"'Los?" I asked.

He shook his head once and said, "Just hurting. I'll get some pain-killers after the reception."

I nodded. Like fire, pain was something that seemed to have its own extra-heavy existential mass. Magic could dull or erase pain, but not without side effects that were nearly as serious as those of medicinal palliatives. It took someone with centuries of experience in that kind of magic to do it safely, and that was neither one of us. I had eight years on Carlos, but by wizard standards, both of us were entry-level noobs in a lot of ways. It made sense that he wouldn't want to have his senses dulled on a night like this one.

Which made what I was about to do difficult, as well as painful.

And necessary.

I put a hand on his shoulder and said, "Hang in there, man. Once we get through this, maybe we should get Wild Bill and Yoshimo and go camping again or something."

"Sure," he said in a neutral voice. "That might be good."

He didn't notice the little ampule in my hand, or how it broke and spread the liquid inside onto his cloak and my skin. No one would notice one extra splash of liquid on his clothes. I lowered my hand, palming the broken ampule, and Ramirez didn't notice a thing.

Why would he?

He was a friend. He trusted me.

I felt sick.

"Are you sure you can pull that off on another wizard, Dresden?" Lara asked, her voice intent.

"No reason it shouldn't work," I said. "And if I do it to anyone *but* another wizard, I'm definitely crossing the line, just like that stupid bastard with the violin."

"If you're caught—"

"If any of us are caught, we're all screwed," I said. "No risk, no reward."

"Point," Lara said. "What next?"

"Next is plausibly getting you both out of the reception," Murphy said.

"What do we use to do that?" Lara asked.

Murphy smiled grimly. "Expectations."

We passed by Childs and his security dog again, to reenter the great hall. Once more, the room had been arranged by camps, borders subtly marked by style of furniture and swaths of overhead silk, giving the whole place a bit of a circus atmosphere, with a single difference—in the exact center of the room, at the focus of all the camps, a small circular speaking stage had been erected.

Music was playing, violins again. Evidently Marcone had managed to replace the offending Sidhe fiddler from the night before. Or maybe the guy lived. I had the same emotions either way.

Speaking of which, the man himself was present tonight, sitting and speaking with Etri on a deep green and dark carved-redwood old-world leather sofa, stuffed thick with cushioning, with gold studs as upholstery pins. Baron Marcone was a handsome man of middle years dressed in an immaculate grey business suit. Perhaps slightly taller than average, he had barely changed in all the years I'd known him. The few marks of age that had come upon him only made him look more reserved, severe, and dangerous.

He was flanked by Sigrun Gard and Hendricks, like always. Gard was a woman who was tall enough to play basketball and built like a powerlifter, visibly girded with muscle. She wore a suit that was every bit as nice as Marcone's, and her golden blond hair was held back in a tight, complicated, neat braid that left nothing much to grab onto. The lines of the suit were marred by the axe she wore strapped to her back, but it didn't look like the fashion police were going to have the courage to give her a hard time about it.

Hendricks, who stood at the other end of the couch, was a ginger Mack truck wearing a suit. He had a heavy brow ridge and had grown out a short beard that had come out several shades darker than his hair, and he had hands like shovels. His suit had been custom-made, but not to fit him—it was spending all its time trying not to show off the weapons he was doubtless carrying underneath it.

Marcone glanced up as the White Council's delegation entered together, and he looked at me for a moment, his expression neutral. The last time I'd taken a big case, I'd done considerable damage to his vault's exterior, if not much to the contents inside, and one of his people had been killed by the lunatics I'd been working with. I'd paid the weregild for the man's death—but appeasing someone and being at peace with them were two very different things.

I returned the look with as much of a poker face as I could, and we both looked elsewhere at the same moment, as if we'd planned it. I clenched my jaw. Jerk. I couldn't think of a time when I hadn't wanted to punch the guy right in his strong-jawed mouth.

I briefly toyed with the image of Marcone, with several missing teeth, reclining in a dentist's chair for repair work while Gard and Hendricks menaced the poor DDS with their glowers, and it made me smile. There. Who says I can't put on a proper party face? I knew the outfit had doctors. Did they also have dentists?

If any underworld boss in the world had a dental plan for his employees, it would be Marcone.

Which reminded me, I should probably be looking into a checkup for Maggie before she went to her new school in the fall, and— No, wait. Focus, Dresden. Survive the evening now; plan Maggie's dental appointments later.

So I plunged into the party. I exchanged brief words with River Shoulders as he spoke to Evanna. Across from Winter's blue and purple silks were Summer's golden and green colors, and I stepped up to the edge of their camp to trade nods with the Summer Lady, Sarissa, and a firm handshake with Fix, the Summer Knight, my opposite number on that side of things and a decent guy, all while being eyed by the Summer Sidhe security detachment they had with them.

I walked past the LaChaise clan and received several dark glares, which I returned with interest. I'm not particularly tolerant on the subject of ghouls, due to the fact that I'd seen them eat some kids I'd been teaching during the war with the now-deceased Red Court. Their particular clan hadn't been all that easy on people living in the Mississippi delta region, either, and I'd butted heads with them on side cases in the past. Some of LaChaise's people looked like they wanted to start a fight, but a few glances toward Mab's still-empty black chair in Winter's camp seemed to make them think better of it.

I'd be fine with fighting them, if they wanted to start things. I'm not saying that the only good ghoul was a dead ghoul, but I'd never met one that made me think otherwise, and I'd seen too many corpses they'd made to let it bother me. But as long as they respected the truce, they were guests and under the protection of their host. Maybe I could hope for some kind of misunderstanding later on, when the talks were done and everyone was heading home.

There were actually a few folks dancing in the center of the floor, in the open space around the speaker's podium. Evanna and River Shoulders made a particularly odd couple, with River holding the svartalf lady completely off the ground, with one hand, while walking through the steps of a cautious, stately waltz.

Freydis absolutely slinked up to me, looking fabulous in her white and silver dress. Granted, most ladies wouldn't have had quite so many fine old scars to show off as she did, but they only lent her a dangerously sexy aura. The red-haired Valkyrie gave me a dazzling smile, ran her hand over my arm, and said, "Hey there, *seidrmadr*. Who's a girl gotta stab to get a dance around here?"

I smiled and said, very quietly, "Mab's not even here yet."

Freydis ignored my concern and sidled close to me, sliding her left hand up to my shoulder and taking my left hand with her right. "Oh no. You have to dance with a stunning woman for a few extra moments. Whatever will you do, poor bastard?"

Well. She had a point there. So I lifted my arm, put a hand on her waist, and stepped into a simple waltz.

Freydis hadn't waltzed before, but she picked it up fast and within a minute was flowing gracefully through the steps with me. She squeezed my left hand and asked, "The scars. Burns?"

"Black Court vampire had an office building in a psychic armlock," I said. "One of her Renfields had a makeshift flamethrower."

"Just the hand? Or does it go all the way up?"

"To the wrist, on the front," I said. "Less on the back. I was holding up a shield with that hand."

"You killed them, I take it?"

"Why would you say that?"

"In my experience, burns make mortals rather vengeful."

"It's . . . a long story," I said. "Vamp got away. Mavra."

"Ah, that one," Freydis said. "She's earned a bit of a reputation over the years."

"Oh?"

"I probably shouldn't tell you this for free, but I adore dancing, I rarely get the chance, and my boss likes you," Freydis said.

I stopped to glance over at Vadderung in his chair. Once more he was seated across from Ferrovax- and the two were regarding each other steadily.

"He seems like the kind of guy who would tell you to say something like that when he asked you to pass on some information to me," I said.

Her green eyes flashed with appreciation. "Oh. You just went from a three to a six, *seidermadr*. I like men who look past the surface of things. And you can dance."

"Lucky me," I said. "So?"

"So if you get me drunk enough, and no one else more interesting turns up, I could show you all kinds of interesting scars. Bring your woman and we can skip some of the drinking."

That made my cheeks feel warm. "Um. I meant Mavra," I said.

"Just that we last spotted her movements about a year ago," Freydis said, unperturbed at the change of subject. "If you were counting on her never coming back, you might need to go over your numbers again."

"Reunion week around here," I complained.

"Oh, poor boy," Freydis said, thrusting out her lower lip mockingly. "Live as long as I have and you'll realize that none of us ever really escapes the past. It just keeps coming back to haunt you."

"I haven't seen much to suggest otherwise," I admitted. The piece ended and we segued from a waltz into a fox-trot, which again she picked up almost immediately, and during one of the turns I saw movement out of the corner of my eye and the temperature of the room seemed to drop about three degrees. "There. Is that her?"

"Cold, pretty, and scary?" Freydis asked. "Yes, that's her. Should we do it now?"

"Wait for her to get settled," I said.

Her green eyes tracked past my shoulder, watching intently. "She's talking to the big grendelkin."

"He's not a grendelkin," I muttered.

She arched a brow at me.

"You'll have to trust me. The Forest People are different than the grendelkin."

"Big, hairy, strong, stinky . . . If it walks like a Grendel and talks like a—"

"You and I," I said, meeting the Valkyrie's eyes, "are about to have a serious argument."

Freydis's eyes flared with defiance—but she looked away first.

"That's River Shoulders. He's okay. Tell your boss I said that."

"Why don't you do it yourself?"

"Because as long as he's using a messenger, I will, too," I said. "Not sure why he's keeping his distance, but I'll respect it. Could be he doesn't want to look too chummy with me here. Point is, tell him that River Shoulders isn't a grendelkin."

"He's chatty enough to be one," Freydis growled. The next turn let me see River Shoulders speaking earnestly—how else?—to Mab. Mab was listening to him with intense focus. How else? I saw her nod, speak a short phrase, and turn to continue toward her chair in her appointed camp. Molly was walking a step behind her and to her right. She paused to put a hand on River's massive arm and say something that made him let out a rumbling chuckle. She beamed up at him, patted his arm again, and kept pace with Mab.

"There," Freydis said a moment later as the turn took Mab out of my sight. "She's sitting."

I leaned down close to Freydis's ear and said, "Well. I guess we should do it, then."

"Nothing personal, tiger," she murmured back into mine.

Then Freydis drew back, her face drawn up in an expression of outrage, and smacked me.

Okay.

Maybe that was understating it.

The Valkyrie, who could potentially have lifted an entire automobile and chucked it a short distance, dealt me an open-hand blow to the cheekbone with the full power of her body. It was like taking a right cross from a professional slugger. If I hadn't rolled with it, she'd have knocked my startled ass completely unconscious.

The script called for me to grope her a bit as she pulled away from me, exactly the kind of behavior everyone expected from the Winter Knight, but my brains were so scrambled I could barely manage to make it look like a socially awkward hug she was avoiding. She stalked over to the White Court's camp, straight up to Lara. The redhead looked fantastic and drew the attention of the room as she did it. She reported to Lara in low tones, thrusting a fingertip at me along the way, her expression going from outrage to strain to visible distress.

Lara glared daggers at me from across the floor, sliding a supportive arm around Freydis's shoulders. She guided the other woman across the room, pausing at the same doorway where I'd gotten some quiet space last night. She spoke to one of the caterers and then stepped through with Freydis.

The room had gone quiet except for the musicians, and everyone was looking at me.

"Sir Knight," came Mab's voice, very clearly and very calmly.

That got everyone's attention, though they mostly tried not to be obvious about it. Even Vadderung and Ferrovax broke their casual staring contest to regard what else was happening in the room.

I could have sworn Mab's gown was deep purple when she entered the hall a moment ago, but when I looked back up at her seat, the cloth had turned as dark as midnight, and streaks of black were flowing through her silver-white hair.

We were about ten seconds into this heist and Mab was already halfway into her full form as judge, jury, and executioner of Winter. Perfect.

I looked aside and found myself facing my grandfather. Ebenezar gave me a look that was as panicked as I'd ever seen him give. I wanted to reassure him, somehow, to throw a wink at him. But I didn't want anyone to see that gesture, not with what was coming up. So instead, I gave him a small shrug, turned back to Mab, and bowed my head. Then I hurried over to her.

"Sir Knight," Mab said, her voice lowered to an intimate volume. "You have annoyed a valuable ally. Explain yourself."

"You don't want me to," I replied in a similar tone. "Look, I need to ask you for something I never really expected to want from you."

Mab arched a brow. "And that is?"

"Your trust," I said. "That I'm acting on your behalf."

Mab's eyes widened slightly.

"I need your assistance," I said. "Look at the door Lara just left through, and then at me like you want to murder me."

"For that, I shall hardly need to invoke a dramatic muse," Mab murmured. But she thrust her chin toward the door Lara had just departed through and then turned her wide dark eyes back to mine. "This is a public pantomime. You play for high stakes." Her eyes narrowed dangerously. "Do not bring me embarrassment with your failure."

"No, my queen," I said, loud enough for the room to hear. I stepped back from her and bowed deeply at the waist, before putting on an expression that I assumed looked angry and chagrined, and hurrying after Lara.

"What good is it going to do us to get into the gym?" Lara asked. "I've seen it. There's no way down to the holding cell from there."

Murphy smirked. "Like I said. You visited the place a few times. I lived there. Especially in the gym."

One of Marcone's people in the red jackets looked like he might disagree with me going up the stairs to the gym, but I pacified him with upraised hands and said, "I need to sort this out or my boss is gonna kill me. Just give me a minute."

It was one of the same guys from the night before. The guard looked from me over toward Marcone's camp. Marcone didn't look up from his conversation, but Hendricks, at his right hand, gave the guard a nod.

The guard stepped back with a grimace and said, "Watch that Freydis, man. She'll gut you as soon as look at you."

"Spoken like a three," I said. He looked confused. I kept moving.

I came up the stairs to the soft sounds of Freydis's sobs. Lara was standing by the nearest corner of the boxing ring with her arms around the Valkyrie's shoulders. I checked the stairs behind me to be sure that they were empty, closed the door, and said, "Clear."

"Od's blood, I should have been an actress," Freydis said in a pleased voice, standing clear of Lara.

"Well. The Einherjaren weren't buying it," I said. "Everyone knows you're up to something."

Lara smirked at me. Vampiric allure completely aside, the woman had a smirk that was to die for, and her little black dress was stylish and stunning. She flexed her hands like claws and said, "Getting my hooks into Mab's Knight, of course."

"Obviously," I said. I started for the back of the room, where the towels were stacked on a shelf, ready to be used. I shrugged out of my suit coat and vest as I went, and then out of the shoes, pants, and shirt, until I was left in just boxer briefs, an undershirt, and socks. It was necessary.

"I still believe this is a serious breach of security planning," Lara complained as she lifted her dress over her head and tossed it on a bench. She added her shoes, more carefully, and was wearing nothing else. Excellently. I averted my eyes.

"You don't know Einherjaren," Freydis insisted in a firm tone. "Once they get it in their heads that something needs to be one way, that's it. That's how it needs to be."

Lara sounded as if she was speaking with her nose wrinkled up. "Still. An old privy shaft?"

"Once they realized they could use it to drop their towels right next to the laundry room in the basement, instead of carrying them down in hampers, there was no stopping it," Freydis said. "They just knocked holes in the wall with the dumbbells and started dropping towels down the shaft. Marcone had to give in with grace and installed dumbwaiter doors."

I went to said door, flipped a latch, and opened it. It rolled up smoothly to reveal a shaft that began overhead and led straight down into the darkness. It was not excessively large.

There was an incredibly wonderful smell, flowers and cinnamon and something darker and sweeter, and then Lara was standing next to me, her bare shoulder against my elbow. My elbow approved, ecstatically— but Lara jumped and let out a little truncated sound of discomfort.

She glanced down at her shoulder, where a patch the shape, I guess, of the end of my elbow was turning red, as though she'd brushed it against a hot pan.

Vampires of the White Court had a severe allergy to sincere love, the way the Black Court doesn't like sunbathing. Skin-to-skin contact with people who love and who are loved in return is hardest of all on the White Court.

Which meant that . . .

Oh.

Well. I hadn't been thinking about having that aura of protection around me when Karrin and I got busy, but it was nice to have it.

And it was nice to know it was real. Very nice.

"Ouch," Lara said, her tone annoyed. Then she glanced up at me and her expression became suddenly pleased. "Oh. You and the police-woman? Congratulations, wizard."

"My relationships are none of your beeswax," I responded in a grumpy tone.

Lara nodded at the old privy shaft. "We're both about to crawl down that together, so I'd say I have a minor need to know if I'm going to receive second- and third-degree burns for bumping into you." She regarded the space gravely. "Small. Are you going to fit?"

"Stop setting me up for dirty jokes," I complained. "I'll manage. Are you sure you can handle the guard?"

Lara turned her head slightly toward me, her eyes down, and caught her lip between her teeth, before slowly looking up at me. Suddenly the light fled from the room, except where it touched the pale perfection of her skin.

I just about started howling and pounding my chest, I suddenly wanted her so badly. It took me a good long breath to get control of myself and force myself to avert my eyes.

"I'll manage," Lara murmured, and the painful pressure of my desire was abruptly mitigated.

I gritted my teeth and said, through them, "I meant the details. Are you sure he isn't going to see or hear anything else?"

"Give me sixty seconds," Lara said. "Once I get close enough, he's not going to notice anything else, even if you walked by him playing a trumpet and pounding drums. And even if he noticed, he'd not remember it."

"Sixty seconds," Freydis sighed. She was knotting towels together with mechanical precision. "Men."

Lara turned her eyes to Freydis, who suddenly caught her breath, her cheeks flushing with color.

"Darling, this isn't the same thing at all," Lara purred. "It's a pity your contract was so specific, or I'd demonstrate for you sometime."

Freydis let out a deep sigh and then went back to knotting towels without looking up.

Lara gave me an impish smile, held out her hands, and said, "Help me up, Harry."

"You don't need any help from me," I said, a little thickly. Even when she wasn't shining the come-hither flashlight right in my face, Lara Raith still left me feeling a little bit dazzled.

The de facto monarch of the White Court responded with an amused laugh and entered the shaft like a diver, silently vanishing down into the darkness.

"Sixty seconds," I muttered. "Going to take me twice that just to climb down."

"Going to lose my mind on this damned job," Freydis noted. "I'll have the rope ready in five."

"Cover," I said.

"Oh, right." She shook her head, dipped a hand into her dress, and took out a little wooden plaque. "If my head wasn't attached. I've never worked for a client this distracting."

She picked up my suit coat and Lara's dress and dropped them into the boxing ring. Then she touched the plaque to them, muttered something, and snapped the wood in her fingers. There was an eye-searing flash of light that left a Norse rune shaped like a lightning bolt burned on my retina in purple, and suddenly there I was, on top of Lara in the boxing ring, making out furiously.

As illusions went, it was excellent. Just really . . . detailed. Maybe too much so. I turned away, a little embarrassed.

"She likes you, you know," Freydis said, watching the illusion with amusement.

"From what I can tell, Lara mostly likes Lara," I said.

"Maybe. But she treats you differently than she does others."

I grunted and said, "Wonderful. Just the attention I need in my life."

And then I shoved my shoulders and head into a narrow, lightless, handleless stone shaft and started wriggling down it in my underwear.

26

Going headfirst down a three-story shaft in complete darkness isn't ever going to do well as a recreational business. I was completely reliant on keeping pressure against the walls to prevent me from falling. In that, the limited space was actually useful—it meant more of my body's surface area could be pressed against the walls, and less strain being placed on any one spot.

Unless the hand-cut stone shaft narrowed along the line and I got stuck, in which case I was just screwed. Or if it got a lot wider, in which case, also screwed. I might be kind of tough, but a three-story fall onto my head wasn't going to end well.

I started shimmying down. It was tough work, but I'd been doing a lot of cardio.

Lara had evidently left the dumbwaiter door open behind her, because there was dim light coming through, showing me a lumpy mass of white towels at the bottom of the shaft, as well as the shape of the walls. Once I had an idea of distance, it was possible to move more quickly—I could just relax a little and half slide down.

I paid with a little skin, but it wasn't as bad as it could have been. The stones of the castle were ancient. Time (and I didn't want to think too closely about what else) had worn off many of the rough edges. As long as I didn't start bleeding and making the walls slippery, I should be fine.

Fine. I felt like a wad of paper trying not to be blown through a straw, but other than that, everything was super.

I went down carefully, moving only one limb at a time, like the friendly neighborhood Spider-Man. Except that I couldn't actually stick to walls. And if I slipped, I didn't have any webbing to save myself with, and I'd fall and break my neck.

"'Friendly neighborhood Spider-Man,'" I sang under my breath, and inched lower.

My shoulders stuck.

My heart started beating a lot faster.

Not because I was scared or anything. This was just cardio.

It's not like I was experiencing claustrophobia. I was a wizard of the White Council. We don't let our emotions control us.

I forced myself to breathe slowly, to stop moving, to think. I was stuck because my muscles were contracted, holding me against the walls of the shaft. I had to relax. But if I relaxed, I would fall and die and that would be counterproductive, too. So the trick was going to be to relax *part* of me while keeping the rest of me tense.

I stretched out an arm, trying to get my shoulders unsquared to the walls, but it didn't work. I felt myself wedge in further, and my breathing increased. I strained harder and felt the pressure on my joints increase.

"'Can he swing, from a thread?'" I gasped.

Wait.

Stop, Harry. Think. Use your brain.

"'Take a look overhead,'" my brain kept on muttering.

Right. Overhead.

This was a Chinese finger-trap problem. The harder I tried to work directly against it, the more impossible it would be to escape it.

So I tensed and pushed myself back, upward. It was difficult, but I'd been working out a lot of late. Fighting the Winter mantle's pull had reaped me some physical benefits. I was able to back up several inches, readjust my shoulders, and slither past the close spot.

"'Hey there!'" I breathed, "'There goes the Spider-Man.'"

I kept going down, trying not to think of how hard it was to get my breath, or how I was trapped with my hands up over my head, and how if one of those giant spiders (they have those; I've seen them) started coming down the shaft after me, there wouldn't be a damned thing I could do about it.

Thanks, imagination. I didn't have enough problems, so I really appreciate you making up another one just to keep me on my toes.

I tried to keep my puffing as quiet as I could as I reached the bottom of the shaft and found a pile of sweaty towels and enough dim light to see them.

Well. There wasn't going to be a way to get out of this gracefully. I stuck my arms out through the door and started wiggling out after them, bending my neck to take my weight on my shoulders as I came out.

I finally shimmied my head out of the bottom of the shaft and into a wall of absolute lust.

Seriously. It was like suddenly being fifteen again, with my hormones exploding and me having no idea at all of how to deal with them. My skin turned hypersensitive, and I was suddenly, acutely aware of the sensation of stone against my back and legs, and that I'd gotten covered in dirt and dust on the way down. The pains of my body came rushing back onto me: soreness of muscle that should have been severely limiting my mobility, old injuries pounding with a steady ache, and the more recent damage to my hands throbbing insistently, all of which were normally muted by the Winter mantle.

Evidently, when a powerful vampire of the White Court wants you to pay attention to how your body feels, you do it. Period.

I turned my head and found my muscles responding only slowly, sluggishly.

The shaft had come out into a dim hallway, with the only lighting coming from a lamp on a desk, placed across one side of the hallway next to a heavy plastic frame that looked like some kind of metal detector.

One of the Einherjaren was standing in front of the desk. The man was at least as tall as me, only built with seventy or eighty more pounds of muscle, with a short buzz of black hair and a bristling black beard. He was standing in front of the desk, holding a heavy rifle, one of those ARs modified for anti-matériel rounds, at his shoulder, aiming down the barrel.

But he didn't matter.

The only thing that mattered was Lara Raith.

She stood maybe three feet from the Einherjar, balanced on her toes as one lovely leg slowly, slowly shifted, sliding forward. The motion made muscles stretch and bunch, and shadows rippled over her body in ways that should not have been *possible*, much less maddeningly arousing.

I forgot what I was doing on the floor of the castle.

That didn't matter.

Lara mattered.

I found myself just staring at her, at the most vibrant, dangerous, glorious woman I'd ever seen, only a few feet away, naked and pulsing with erotic energy. I didn't care about the smudges of dirt on that pale, perfect skin. I didn't care that my own body was smudged with filth. I didn't care about the mission, or the nightmare spider shaft I'd just slithered down, or the now-unfamiliar aches and pains, just so long as I didn't have to stop looking at the most incredible sight any man could ever s—

I sneezed, out of nowhere, hard, five or six times.

Magic surged out of me, energy pouring out with each involuntary contraction.

Lara's head whipped around toward me, her silver-blue eyes wide like a cat's.

Black widow spiders with bodies the size of basketballs came boiling out of the shaft behind me—five or six of them.

The Einherjar's glazed stare abruptly snapped into focus, and his cold grey eyes snapped from Lara to me to the spiders. His finger moved from ready position along the receiver to the trigger of the rifle.

Lara blurred.

She was inside the Einherjar's guard before I had fully realized she had begun to move, dipping down and coming up inside the circle of his arms, between the man and the rifle, her back to his chest. Before he'd begun to do much more than twitch in reaction, she had ahold of the weapon and had knocked his hand away from the trigger. The two struggled over the rifle. The Einherjar gave up trying to recover the rifle and clamped his huge right hand down on Lara's throat. Muscle and tendon in his forearms stood out like cord as he began to crush her neck.

Meanwhile, the spiders chittered and hissed and leapt toward the nearest target, which happened to be me.

"Glah!" I shouted. In a very manly fashion.

Look, big bugs are like a thing. I mean, imagine you looked down the length of your underwear-only-clad body and saw giant Alaskan crabs charging up it, pincers waving. You'd have shouted in a manly fashion as well, to prepare yourself for battle.

There wasn't much light, and even less time. I kicked frantically at one enormous spider and knocked it aside like a flabby kickball full of peanut butter. I shoved a second creature out of the air as it came at my face and then felt horrible puncture wounds happening as the other four bit into me. When teeth pierce your flesh, you don't feel much for a second or two—until whatever bit you starts worrying you, thrashing back and forth while tearing. Then it's like electricity flowing into you, lightning bolts of sharp silver sensation that surge up and down whatever limb is being bitten. Fangs pierced. Venom seared. My heart rate skyrocketed.

The other two widows rebounded from where I'd knocked them away and joined in.

And then, frantic breaths later, the forms of the spiders just wobbled and suddenly collapsed into translucent goo. One second, dozens of hard, tiny spider feet were poking into me everywhere while spider fangs sent pain scorching through me. The next, I was covered in ectoplasm and small wounds, having thoroughly slimed myself.

Goddamned conjuritis.

I would just have to hope that there weren't any negative interactions with ectoplasm being injected into my bloodstream—because whatever the venom had been, it was definitely reduced to ectoplasm now.

I flopped like a landed fish, ectogoo making the floor more slippery than your average waterslide, eventually thrashing until I could see Lara again.

She still stood with her back to the Einherjar. They'd dropped the gun in the struggle, and the man had both hands on her throat now. Her face was bright pink, her lips an ugly greyish color. I couldn't understand why she wasn't fighting back until I saw her hands, behind her, at the small of her back.

She wasn't trying to fight off his hold on her. She was going for the kill.

Lara arched, twisting and struggling, and the poor bastard hung on to her neck. He thought he was winning the fight.

Then his fatigue pants came loose. Lara's lips twisted into a triumphant snarl. There was a surge of bodies, and then the Einherjar let out a startled huffing sound. His eyes went wide and unfocused.

The struggle stopped. A slow smile spread over Lara's half-strangled face. She slid her hands up the Einherjar's arms and tugged gently at his fingers. His hands came away at once, sliding down her shoulders to her breasts. She coughed once, then let out a low purring sound, and her hips began to move in slow rhythm.

The Einherjar staggered. He sank back against his desk, balance wavering. Lara stayed with him, and though the motion should have been awkward, Lara moved smoothly and nimbly to match him, somewhere between a dance partner, a lover, and a hungry spider wrapping up its prey for the feast.

She looked back at her victim, teeth showing, and then looked at me. Her eyes were liquid silver, like mirrors. Deep pink finger marks on her neck promised bruises to come, but even as I stared at her, they were fading—as the Einherjar's breathing became heavier and more desperate.

"What the hell was that?" she demanded. Her voice was quiet and rough, as if she'd somehow spent ten years drinking whiskey. "Giant spiders? Dammit, Dresden."

I found myself just staring for a second. She wasn't putting out the same kind of aura she had before, but she was still one of the most erotic, terrifying sights I had looked upon. Her allure drew me, calling to my purely human hormones—and, needless to say, the Winter mantle was going absolutely insane with lust for her. It wanted nothing so much as to challenge the Einherjar, beat him to death, and then claim Lara as a prize of conquest.

But that wasn't me. Not the real me. That was just the mantle and the meat, wanting what they wanted. I pushed back against them both with my mind, with my will, until I remembered my purpose.

Thomas.

Save my brother.

I came to my sock feet, soaked with ectoplasm though they might be, and padded forward squishily.

"Don't kill him," I hissed intently, trying not to look at her. "All of this trouble is for nothing if you kill him."

"Don't be long," she countered, her voice throaty, sensual, a hint of a moan in every word. Her eyes had become almost completely white at this point, pupils like beads of black in their centers. Her eyes looked utterly inhuman—and exactly like those of the demon Hunger I'd observed with my wizard senses in my brother, years ago. "He's stronger than he looks. Hurt me badly. I'm still healing."

The Einherjar just remained locked where he was, his eyes blank, his expression one of a man in torment, moving only as needed to match Lara's motion. She was a tiny thing compared to his sheer muscular mass—and he clearly didn't have a chance in the world against her at this point. A man dedicated for centuries to his profession, and it meant nothing in the face of her power. There was no dignity to it.

Do we all look that goofy and clumsy during the act?

Yeah. Probably. Even when there wasn't a succubus involved.

I pushed past the vampire and her victim and tried to figure out exactly when I'd started taking the field *beside* the things that go bump in the night instead of *against* them.

And then I pushed those thoughts away, grabbed an armload of towels, and went looking for my brother.

27

At the end of the hallway, I found a heavy trapdoor set in the floor.

I froze.

My heart started beating faster.

The door didn't match the castle's décor. It wasn't lined up exactly right with the stones. It was old and made of heavy wood.

And there were scorch marks on it.

Because it was my door.

My door, *mine*, from my old apartment; the door to my subbasement lab. It still had the ring in it that I used to pull it up. And it had an additional bar on it that hadn't been there before.

I shook myself out of the freeze and stretched out a shaking hand to slide back the bar and open the door. It came up easily; it even squeaked at the right spot and felt, dammit, exactly like it always had. My chest suddenly hurt and my eyes burned.

Hell's bells, I wanted to feel like I was home again.

And instead, I was standing in Marcone's house.

Something stirred in me, down deep. It wasn't rage. It wasn't anything as ephemeral and temporary as rage. It wasn't predicated on my emotional pain. It felt older than that. Primordial. What was mine had been taken away.

It wasn't right. And no one was going to do anything about it.

Unless it was me.

Something went *click* somewhere inside.

Ever since the Red Court had taken my daughter, I'd been reeling from one disaster to the next, surviving. This entire situation was just one more entropy barrage hitting my life, forcing me to scramble once again, maybe getting me killed. (Again. Technically.)

Things were different now. I was a part of Maggie's life. And she might need me to walk her down an aisle one day.

Maybe it was time I started getting ahead of this stuff.

Maybe it was time to get serious.

My brother was lying curled up in a fetal position, naked and shockingly thin, as if he'd lost forty pounds of muscle in the past day. He looked better and worse—the bruises were gone, as was the blood. His hands still looked knotted and horrible, but his face was recognizable again. Being a vampire has its privileges, even if his skin looked like it needed to be a couple of sizes larger, drawn tight against what remained of his formerly muscular frame.

It was his expression that sickened me. He looked up with mercury-colored eyes, dull and glazed with simple animal pain.

"Thomas," I hissed. "It's Harry."

He blinked up at the light without speaking.

"Can you hear me, man?"

He stared and made a small choking sound.

"Hell's bells," I said. There was no ladder waiting for me below. So I grimaced, swung my legs over the opening, and then dropped down into it as quietly as I could.

It was a bit of a drop, but I managed not to land on Thomas or fall on my ass.

"Come on," I said. "We have to go."

For a long beat, nothing happened. Then he moved, and I felt myself let out a breath I hadn't realized I'd been holding. My brother was alive.

But there wasn't much left of him.

Stars and stones, the svartalves had worked him over badly. They hadn't put him in irons. They'd just beaten him until there was no possibility of him effecting his own escape. I wanted to be enraged about it, but among the supernatural nations, their actions would be considered effective, not sadistic. Hell, it would have been a simple matter for them to simply kill him out of hand and then announce that an assassin had made an attempt on Etri and been killed before he could do the job. But instead they were holding to the Accords.

He was alive. But his Hunger had evidently cannibalized his own body to keep him that way.

"Thomas, we haven't got much time," I said. "Get your lazy ass up. We have to go."

He looked at me, and his brow furrowed. I wasn't at all confident that he understood me.

"Of course," I said. "I have to do all the work myself."

I lifted my amulet and looked around the room, and my heart hurt. It was my old lab. I'd spent countless hours there, working, studying, brewing, casting, summoning, setting my hair on fire—you know, wizard stuff. So had Molly. There were smoke stains on the floor, and I could see the squares and rectangles where my old furniture had been, the feet of tables, the bases of bookshelves, the holes in the wall where I had screwed in the wire-frame storage shelving. My old copper summoning circle had survived, somehow, at the far end of the room. Maybe the floor of my old living room had collapsed over it, shielding it from the worst of the flames.

But it offered me no help.

I wouldn't have any trouble reaching up and grabbing the lip of the opening, then hauling myself out. But climbing out while carrying my brother would be a hell of a trick. Damn, I wished I had spent more of my time on earth magic. Altering gravity for a few seconds would make this really simple—but doing it at my current level of skill would take time that we did not have.

I'd have to go with the alternative and hope I didn't kill us both. Go, me.

I stooped down, wrapped exposed skin in towels as best as I could, and got hold of Thomas's arms. He hissed out a breath, but he didn't move, his body putting up all the resistance of boiled pasta. He was shockingly light, but even light, limp people are a pain and a half to move around. It took me a minute to get him up and over one shoulder in a fireman's carry. After that, I positioned myself under the exit, turning my body to, hopefully, make sure I didn't take any of Thomas's skin off on the way out.

"I should make a cloak of levitation," I muttered. "Doctor Strange would never have this problem."

I felt a flash of guilt at wasting time with smartassery and shoved it down. Time for that when my brother was safe.

And then I crouched, made the best guess I could, gathered my will, and thrust my right hand down at the floor while snarling, *"Forzare!"*

Raw kinetic force lashed down at the floor below me, and because of Sir Isaac Newton, it also propelled me up. I flew through the air, but I'd misjudged the amount of force needed. Magic is more art than science, and it was considerably harder to work with precision without a few tools to help me. So instead of gracefully sailing up to the level of the hallway's floor, I sort of lurched up to the level of my belt and then started to fall back down.

I grabbed at the floor of the hallway and desperately levered a knee up into the opening to give me a couple of points of tension—but it was hardly a solid position. I pushed as hard as I could with my right arm, but it was out straight, and there was only so much power in my shoulder and upper back. I strained to lift my brother onto the floor, but I had no leverage, and my position was too precarious to apply much of my strength. My muscles burned and then began, slowly, to falter. I ground my teeth, reaching deep, and strained to gain a few fractions of an inch that began to fade almost at once.

I started preparing to drop in a controlled fall that would, hopefully, protect my brother—but then his weight suddenly vanished from my shoulder.

Lara dragged him to one side with quick efficiency, blue eyes bright, cheeks still flushed, and then seized the guard's heavy leather jacket and tossed me one sleeve. I took it.

"You're taking forever," she said, and hauled me out of the hole.

"And yet you're the one literally fucking around on the job," I countered.

"That?" she asked, bobbing her head back toward the guard station and flashing me a wise, wicked smile. "No. That was just feeding. The other thing takes much, much longer. And preferably candles and champagne."

I pulled my legs out of the way, barely, before she shut the trapdoor—my trapdoor—and threw the bolt.

"How is he?" she asked.

I held up my amulet so that she could see her brother better.

"Empty night," she cursed. She crouched over him, peeling back one of his eyelids, and then his lips. His gums were swollen and blotchy with dark stains.

"What's happening?" I asked her.

"He's sustained too much trauma without feeding," she said. "His Hunger needs life energy. It's taking his. It's turned on him. It's killing him."

White Court vampires led a bizarre symbiotic existence: They were born bound to a demon that existed in immaterial tandem with them, called a Hunger. It was the demon who gave them their strength, their speed, their long lives, their capacity to recover from injury. In exchange they had to feed on the life force of others, to sustain the Hunger. My brother was, I knew, a rather potent example of the breed. That meant that his Hunger was strong, too.

And now he was paying for it.

"What can we do?"

She shook her head, her face hard. "This is how White Court vampires die. How my father will die, sooner or later."

"Justine," I said.

That word got through. Thomas lifted his head, mirrored eyes on me. He reached out a weak hand toward me in a gesture that died of exhaustion halfway.

"No," Lara said, her eyes intent on his face. "By the time a Hunger turns on one of us, it's mad, uncontrollable, insatiable. Even if we could redirect the Hunger, it would kill her and the child, and he'd die anyway." The muscles in her jaw tensed. "There's still part of him in there. I might be able to reach him if we get him out of here—if we *hurry*."

"Right," I said, and slung my brother back up onto my shoulder.

Lara gave me a nod of approval and rose with me, and we both padded as quietly as we could back toward the dumbwaiter shaft. We passed the enormous guard, who was sprawled on his desk, pants back on but unfastened. He reeked of bourbon. I hesitated beside the guard long enough to be sure I saw his chest rise and fall.

"He'll have a hell of a hangover," Lara noted.

"You were also *drinking*?" I asked. "When did you have *time*? Do you have vampire party superpowers I don't know about?"

"I found a bottle in his desk after he was finished and poured it on him," Lara said primly, as if she'd been wearing a Victorian schoolmarm's outfit instead of a whole lot of very well-tailored nothing. She strode to the dumbwaiter door and opened it. "Simple explanation for when he wakes up with a headache and a scrambled memory." She tilted her head. "What was with those spiders? Why did you conjure them?"

I made a frustrated sound. "It just . . . happened."

She frowned for a half second and then began fighting a smile from the corners of her mouth. "Oh, Empty Night. You've got conjuritis? I've heard about how awkward it can be when wizard kids get the disease. Aren't you a few . . . decades old for that?"

"It's not like I made an appointment."

"It would have been nice if you'd told me," Lara said. "That's all I'm saying."

"I took cold medicine," I said defensively.

Lara arched an eyebrow. "Seriously?"

"Does everybody know about this disease but me?" I complained. And I swiped at my nose with my forearm, fighting back another itch.

There was a soft thump, and a bundle of towels unrolled from the bottom of the shaft, their ends neatly knotted together.

"Hurry up," Freydis's voice hissed from the shaft above. "I only made the illusion a quickie."

"Help me," I said to Lara, and together we got the makeshift rope around Thomas.

*   *   *

Getting my brother back up that narrow shaft wasn't simple, even with Freydis's arms pulling him as steadily as any heavy-duty winch. He was too weak to even hold his head up steadily, and he collected some scrapes and bangs on the way up—but we got him there.

After that, we moved quick. Freydis pulled out some cleaning wipes and swept them over Lara's arms and legs, while Lara got her dress back on and stepped into her shoes. I was wearing the suit and had less exposed skin to clean. I used a wipe to swipe off my face, neck, and hands and flicked a comb through my hair, then dressed at my best speed.

The whole time I got dressed, I did my best to ignore the image in the boxing ring, of Lara and me sort of drowsily kissing and moving together in immediate postcoital languor. My image was breathing hard and gurgling out a self-satisfied chuckle against her throat. Her image's hair was a mess, and her face and throat were the palest shade of pink imaginable, and it was entirely too damned easy to consider what that must feel like against my image's lips.

"That's very sweet, really," Lara noted. "The personal bits in the afterglow. Perhaps not terribly believable, but a pretty fiction."

"I should get drunk and write fucking romance," Freydis agreed. She gave me a narrow-eyed glance. "I give the male leads too much credit. But this one seems less useless than some."

While smoothing her dress Lara gave me a glance that made me want to swing from the various equipment around the gym while pounding my chest, and I looked away, feeling my face heat up. The problem with high-pressure situations was that they forced a lot of basic, primal things out that you could normally keep buttoned down.

"Can we focus, please?" I said, my voice only a little rough.

There was a sudden snap in the air, like an enormous discharge of static electricity, and the image in the ring burst into a spectrum of color and faded, leaving behind only a blackened, smoking wooden plaque about the size of a small domino.

"A Freydis production," the Valkyrie noted. "Oh, one of the servers looked in and caught the show. He bought it and left discreetly, so as far as everyone at the peace talks is concerned, you guys are totally a thing as of, oh, an hour after tonight's business."

I blinked. "Um, what?"

"Potion," Lara said, producing a test tube from her tiny handbag. She shook it up, uncorked it, and wrinkled her nose at the muddled, messy liquid inside. Then she closed her eyes, downed a quick swallow, and passed the tube to Freydis.

The Valkyrie looked at it askance. "I don't normally accept drinks from guys like you, *seidrmadr*. What if this potion of yours makes me forget I'm protecting Lara?"

"Everyone who drinks it will be on the inside of the . . . the grey field," I said. "We'll be clear to each other. But to everyone else, we'll seem like bland, unobtrusive background, already identified and not worthy of noticing."

Freydis looked even more skeptical. "And this stuff actually works?"

"Too well, is the problem," I said darkly. "Drink."

She glowered but did. I took the tube and went to Thomas, dripping some into his mouth. He choked and twitched but he swallowed it down. Then it was my turn.

The details of all the contents aren't terribly important, but magical potions rarely taste like anything you'd feed to an actual human. This one tasted like, and had the texture of, stale and mushy cardboard that might have had a little mold growing on it. I sort of fought it down, wishing the *Mission: Impossible* plan had included bringing enough water to get the taste out of my mouth afterward.

It took a couple of heartbeats and then the world sort of shifted, changing by subtle degrees, like when clouds gradually cover the sun. Color began to bleed out of the room, until the world was left in all subtle shades of grey—except for the others. I could clearly see my brother, Lara, and Freydis in full color against the monochromatic background. The air turned a little chillier, a little clammier, or maybe we just thought it did. The psychic resonance that the potion set up had some weird blowback effects on the drinker, and I'd experienced them once before, a long time ago.

"Okay," I said. I hunched down and got one of Thomas's arms over my shoulder. Lara got his other arm and we hauled him to his feet. "Move smoothly and calmly. If we start running around, we'll wrinkle the seams at the edges of the glamour and make people take a second look. Once they do that, we're screwed. So stay cool and we'll be just fine."

Freydis traded a look with Lara, smirking, and said, "Kids."

"I think he's being very sweet," Lara said.

Right. Of the three of us in the conversation, I was the youngest by centuries at least. They had both probably faced enough dangerous situations to regard the entirety of my career as a promising rookie year. I felt like a bit of a jackass. When that happens, it's an excellent idea to shut your mouth.

So I just started walking, leaving Lara to keep up, which she did, without effort, her blue eyes bright. We had to support maybe ninety percent of Thomas's weight, and we stayed as close together as we could. Freydis paced along behind us, also keeping very near. Even in the realm of the supernatural, there are laws and limitations. Only so much power could go into the potion's glamour. The less physical space the glamour would have to cover, the denser and more effective it would be. Spread it out too much, and we'd be better off shouting for the world to pay no attention to that man behind the curtain.

It was an incredibly subtle working of magic—one that would have been far beyond my skill without the skull's tutelage, back in the day. It had hidden me so effectively that even screaming at people in an attempt to warn them they were about to die had gone unnoticed.

But those people hadn't been the most skillful, potent masters of the supernatural world and its various Arts. This would be a much, much tougher room. And I was about to pit the wiliness of Bob the Skull against the wariness and suspicion of some of the most powerful beings of the supernatural world—with utter disaster looming, should anything go amiss. We reached the doors back to the great hall, and I paused there, taking a breath and fighting down a slow shudder that tried to run up my spine.

"You're sure," Lara said, very quietly, "that the people here won't see through this . . . disguise?"

"It's the best I've got," I said.

"That wasn't exactly an answer."

"Yeah," I said, and put my hand on the door to open it. "But it's the best I've got."

28

My father, Malcolm, died when I was young. I don't have very many memories of him, even though I realized, maybe around the age of ten, that I would lose even those if I didn't keep them. So when I was young, I would lie awake quietly at night, thinking of him—of his face, his voice, the things he had said, and the things he had done.

Once, on the way to one of his gigs, we picked up two hitchhiking couples and drove them three hundred miles. Dad bought them a meal and replaced two of their pairs of shoes, even though we barely had enough to get by. He once found a sick and puny kitten in an alley outside a club he'd been playing, somewhere in Ohio, and spent the next three weeks carrying the little creature around with us so that he could nurse it back to health and find it a stable home. And he never passed a used bookstore. He loved books.

He took me to see Star Wars movies.

Him and me.

But it was always him and me. Until he was gone.

The brightest and best memories I had of him were getting lessons from him on magic. Not the Art—Dad was a performing illusionist.

"Everyone who comes to the show knows I'm going to try to trick them," my father said one night. We were sitting in an all-night diner when he said it, getting dinner on the way to a show he was playing in Colorado. He was a lean, dark-haired man, with serious eyes and a quick smile. He wore a denim jacket and a Cubs baseball cap. "I know that they know. And that's how you play the game."

"What game?" I asked him.

He picked up a coin and held it in his palm where I could see it.

"When someone is suspicious, they're looking for things to notice," he said. "Sometimes the best way to trick them is to *give* them something to notice. Once they're focused on that, you know where they're looking."

There was a loud crash and I jumped. The chair next to Dad had fallen backwards onto the floor.

When I looked back, his hand was still there, but the coin was gone.

"This example is pretty crude, but it works well enough. Once you know where they're looking, you also know where they *aren't* looking. That's when you have room to make the illusion happen. It's called misdirection. If I do it right, it looks like magic, and everyone is happy."

"What if you do it wrong?"

He smiled and reached for my ear. I caught his wrist. I might have been little, but I knew some of his moves by then. He had the quarter tucked into the fold of skin on the back of his hand, between his thumb and forefinger.

I grinned at him, took the coin, and pocketed it. That was the deal. If I ever was smart enough to catch him in the act, the coin was my reward, and I could put them in any video game I wanted.

"If I do it wrong, then it looks to the audience like I'm incompetent, like I'm stupid, and like I think they're stupid to be fooled by such a simple trick." He gave me a wry grin. "People don't react well to that."

Tough room, I thought to myself. *Not sure you ever played to a crowd that could react with as much . . . manifest* enthusiasm *as this one, Dad.*

I needed to stop talking to ghosts.

Showtime.

I pushed open the door behind the buffet table and surveyed the room. It seemed simple enough. Cristos was on the little speaking stage now, and all the illustrious bigwigs were watching him.

". . . and I'm very pleased to announce that we have been contacted by King Corb of the Fomor, who will be arriving shortly. Matters of state required his immediate attention, but they have been resolved, and His Majesty will arrive within moments."

There was a round of polite applause, which Cristos acknowledged with a beaming smile. "Recent events among the supernatural nations may have caused a great deal of confusion and turmoil—but they could also be an opportunity to forge even stronger bonds between the various nations. It is my hope that, should we reach a successful treaty, our neighbors the Fomor will work hand in hand with the rest of the Accorded nations. . . ."

It got dull after that, even for a black-and-white feature, despite Cristos's excellent speaking presence, and if all the supernatural grown-ups found him as cloying as I did, they hid it a hell of a lot better than I would have. Granted, the misdirection hadn't been specifically timed to interrupt Cristos and his speech.

That was merely a happy accident.

I took a second ampule, identical to the one I'd crushed on Ramirez, out of my suit's inner pocket and crushed it in the same hand I had the first. I'd been careful not to clean that spot on my palm, and the potion in the fresh ampule mixed with the residue from the one I'd slapped on Ramirez.

My hand quivered, clenched spasmodically once, and suddenly felt heavy, as if a large, slightly damp beach towel had been draped across it.

"On me," I whispered. "Here we go."

And then I spread my fingers out as if guiding a marionette, started wiggling them, and Lara and I started hauling Thomas out, Freydis close behind us.

The potion I'd slipped onto Ramirez's cloak had been half of the brew. The stuff currently on my hand was the other half. The two were magically linked by a drop of my blood, the most powerful agent for magical bindings known to reality. With that bond formed, it was a simple enough trick to send a pulse of energy from my hand over to poor Carlos's cloak.

The grey cloth abruptly flared, whipped wildly around as if in a hurricane wind, and promptly dragged the young Warden off his feet and across the floor—toward the back of the hall, in the opposite direction of the front door.

People and not-people let out noises of distress. Several dozen security teams bolted for their primaries. A lot of folks got tackled to the floor by their own retainers. I caught a glimpse of Molly being surrounded by a group of Sidhe and hustled to one side of the room—and I recognized one of them, the goddamned Redcap. The murderous Sidhe assassin had traded in his baseball cap for a scarlet headband of a leather whose origins I shuddered to consider.

We moved through the chaos as Carlos struggled with his cloak. He managed to unfasten it, and the damned thing promptly began flapping around like an enormous bat.

And it worked. The room stayed black-and-white. Everyone's paranoia was so focused on the potential threat that they didn't have enough cognitive cycles left to be paranoid about us.

The potion hadn't been a very potent one—I'd spent most of my effort on the actual blending potion to keep us concealed—and it wouldn't last long. The cloak's batteries already looked like they were getting weaker, its movements less frantic. We might not have time enough to make it to the door, in fact. I hurried my pace a little, as much as I dared.

And, halfway to the door, two figures abruptly flared into full color and looked right at us.

I froze as the dragon Ferrovax, still sitting in his chair, smoke dribbling from his nostrils, stared right at me—and gave me a slow, toothy smile.

Oh, Hell's bells.

If he raised the alarm, we were done.

Ferrovax inhaled in preparation to call out.

And, over the sounds of the room, I heard three sharp, quick raps of wood on stone.

I whipped my head in the other direction to see Vadderung, also in full color, still seated, still faced off against Ferrovax. His black eye patch lent him a particularly sinister aspect. He held a stylish cane of silvery hardwood in his right hand. Some trick of the light cast a shadow three times the length of the cane on the wall behind him. Vadderung stared at Ferrovax without blinking. A tiny smile touched the corner of his mouth.

Holy crap. The last time a dragon had been slain out here in the tangible, mortal world, it had been in a region called Tunguska. If Ferrovax decided to throw down in the middle of a city as large and as crowded as Chicago, the death toll could be the most catastrophic, concentrated loss of human life in *history*.

And it would kind of be my fault.

My heart began to pound. I looked back at the disguised dragon with wide eyes.

Ferrovax didn't look at me. I probably wasn't worth noticing, by his standards. My only noticeable feature, as far as he was concerned, was my ability to set myself on full smartass before conversing with dragons. He regarded Vadderung for a moment with hooded eyes. Then his partly open mouth twitched into a smirk and closed. He exhaled the breath he'd been going to use to call me out through his nose, along with two heavy plumes of acrid-smelling smoke.

I looked back at Vadderung. He didn't take his gaze from the dragon. He just twitched one of his knees toward the exit.

I gave him a tight nod and a wolfish grin, and we pressed on.

We made it out of the great hall and into the passage beyond just as the energy animating Ramirez's cape began to run out. From the entry antechamber, Childs appeared with his dog, and they both hurried toward us, and they both remained monochromatic as they passed us.

I picked up the pace even more. We hurried out the front, and I hoped to God that Murphy had remembered to drink her portion of the blending potion as well.

She had. She'd rented a car for the occasion, and Lara's people had provided false plates. The lights of the luxury sedan came up and she pulled smoothly into the street, coming to a halt nearby.

We hurried to the car. Murphy leaned out the window, and something in her eyes became easier when she saw me. "How'd it go?"

I winked at her. "I think we'll get away with it if we run fast enough," I said.

Lara got into the backseat first, and I pushed Thomas after her. Between the two of us, we got him wrestled in. Freydis followed him, and I circled toward the passenger-side door.

I had just opened it when a large truck rushed up toward us from the other direction, engine roaring, and I had a horrible flash of realization—the blending potion's real problem was that it was just too damned strong. It was entirely possible that the driver of the vehicle hadn't really noticed us *or* our car. The potion's magic might have influenced their subconscious to tell them that we were a large cardboard box or something, just aching to be run over.

But the truck swerved at the last minute, coming up onto the sidewalk with a couple of wheels, and screeched to a halt outside the Brighter Future Society.

The external valets and staff stood around confused by this turn of events, except for one security guard who was fumbling for both his weapon and his radio, shouting into it in a high-pitched, terrified voice.

He got a couple of words out before the doors to the truck rolled up and something that sounded like a broken piece of pneumatic machinery tore his torso to ribbons and sent a scarlet fan of blood onto the wall behind him. What hit the ground wasn't a person for much longer.

A dozen men in black tactical uniforms came pouring out of the back of the truck, holding suppressed semiautomatic carbines. They opened fire, the sound mostly a fuzzy cloud of clacks, hisses, and whumps.

It was over in maybe three seconds. None of the valets or staff survived. The ones still moving after they fell got bullets to the head.

"Holy shit," Murphy breathed. Her gun had appeared in her hand.

"Don't move," I warned. "Don't fire. Lara?"

The vampire's voice was tense. "They aren't mine."

"Clear!" snapped one of the soldiers, and I recognized him with a surge of rage. His name was Listen. He was medium-sized, of innocuous build, his head was as smooth as a cue ball, and he had led the tactical aspect of the Fomor's efforts here in Chicago—which was the polite way to say that he and his turtlenecks had spent years kidnapping minor magical talents and dragging them off to God knew what fate for his masters. He'd also killed or escaped from everyone who had tried to interfere with his mission.

I hate when the bad guys have good help.

Listen walked briskly back to the truck, bowed his head, and said, "Majesty, your will is done."

"Excellent," rasped a heavy, burbling voice. There was the sound of footsteps and a being descended from the truck. It stood nearly eight feet in height and reminded me of nothing so much as an enormous toad with an excellent tailor. He wore silk robes that were somehow reminiscent of Edo-style kimonos, but with the smooth lines subtly twisted. Between the design and the bizarre, disturbing imagery of the embroidery upon the sea-colored fabrics of each layer of robes, I was feeling a little queasy.

The guy wearing the robes was no looker, either. His face was too large and lumpy to be human. His mouth was so wide he could have eaten a banana sideways, and his lips were like rubbery, black, rotten fruits of the same variety. His skin was pocked and warty and a sickly blue-green where it wasn't ghostly pale, and his eyes were huge, watery, protruding, and disturbing. He had hair like withered black seaweed, draping over his head and shoulders in uneven clumps. He moved with a kind of frantic, jerky energy, and my instincts sized him up as someone dangerous and not particularly sane.

King Corb of the Fomor, I presumed.

The Fomor monarch leered down at the corpses for a moment before raising his gaze to Listen again. "Bring us within, Captain."

Listen snapped to attention and began barking orders to his "men." The turtlenecks were human, technically, but the Fomor had messed with them, sculpting flesh to their liking. The members of this crew would be quicker, tougher, and stronger than any normal bunch of mortals, and they could be damnably tough to kill, like ghouls. They responded at once, lining up on either side of the doorway.

Corb descended from the truck, spun on his heel, and, with a surprising amount of poise and grace, fell to one knee at the foot of the ramp, his head bowed.

I felt my eyebrows go up.

Footsteps sounded on the ramp once more, heavier this time. A generally humanoid, generally feminine figure in a heavy, hooded cloak of some oddly metallic fabric descended the ramp a deliberate step at a time.

Whoever she was, she was taller than Corb and had to unfold herself carefully from the truck. Her bare feet were visible, their proportions perfect, simply huge. They looked like she'd had them bronzed a long time ago, and the bronze had been covered with verdigris and then polished irregularly. It formed lumps and nodes over her skin like molten wax, but flexed and moved as if alive. Flickers of metallic and colored crystals were embedded in that bronze exoflesh.

She reached out a hand to touch Corb on the shoulder as she glided past him, showing more of the same metallic flesh. She was graceful despite her stature, her strides long and purposeful. Corb fell in at her side, a pace behind her. Without looking at him, she extended a hand. Corb reached into his robes and withdrew a length of chain maybe ten feet long from them. One end was attached to a steel band around the base of his throat, mostly concealed by his robes. He handed the other end to the Titanic woman.

She took it without breaking stride and strode into the castle, the soldiers falling in behind their leaders as they went in, weapons up.

"Stars and stones," I breathed.

A hit was going down.

Wars had begun that way.

I was arrested by a hideous, nauseating apprehension that went deep enough for my toes to have a bad feeling about this.

"Harry," Murphy hissed. "Get in."

"I can't," I decided. "I've got to see what's happening here." I leaned down to look at Murphy. "Get them to the island."

"Why?" Murphy demanded. "There's no point to it if you aren't there, too."

"I'll be along," I said. "Cross my heart."

Murphy's eyes widened. "You're scared."

"I need you to trust me on this," I said. "There's no time."

Murph looked like she wanted to argue, but instead she grimaced and put her gun away. "Goddammit."

"Dresden, this is not the plan," Lara said in a warning tone.

"No," I said. "It isn't. Get going and I'll meet you once I know what's happening."

"If you're caught—"

"I've still got the potion," I said. "In and out, Miss Law. Like the wind."

Lara looked from me to her brother, torn. The moment of indecision cost her. Murphy put the car in gear and accelerated smoothly eastbound, away from the castle.

I was left alone in the immediate vicinity of a number of ridiculously powerful supernatural beings and a small mound of bodies that seemed to promise that the night was young.

This showed every sign of working out very, very badly.

I swallowed and then set out to follow the murderous King of the Fomor and what was apparently the Power Behind the Throne into the peace talks.

29

King Corb and company strode into the great hall like they owned the place.

They entered amid the chaos in the wake of my previous departure. Voices were raised in tension, a chatter of sound in the crowded hall, as each nation, seemingly by reflex, withdrew to its originally assigned area.

I checked the hall and made my way toward where Ramirez and the Wardens were standing in front of the Senior Council members. That also put me within a few long steps of the high seat at the rear of the hall, where Mab currently stood with Molly, the Redcap, and four other Sidhe.

Corb and his retinue seemed to enjoy giving everyone time to settle into an uncomfortable silence. Then he strode forward, his chain clanking, and pitched something into the air with a casual underhand toss.

There was a heavy *clump* as the thing, about the size of my fist, bounced and then rolled.

It came to a halt at the foot of the dais where the high seat stood.

It was a very small severed head. It had been a while since the head had been taken, the skin shrunken tight, patches here and there beginning to fall to decay.

I recognized the features.

It was Gwynn ap Nudd, King of the Tylwyth Teg, one of the larger subnations of Faerie. I'd done business against him once in the past, and he still sent me season tickets to Cubs games once in a while. He'd been responsible for the famous Billy Goat Curse—and he'd been a signatory of the Unseelie Accords.

A gasp went through the room.

Mab stared down at the severed head for a solid three seconds. Silence stretched out into an endless crystalline moment.

The Queen of Air and Darkness lifted black, black eyes to King Corb. The temperature in the room plummeted. A film of frost crystals began to form over every metallic surface, and swirls of darkness appeared, spreading through Mab's silver-white hair and continuing through into her gown.

She spoke in a whisper that was heard by every ear in the hall. "Explain yourself."

The Fomor swaggered forward a step. "A peace gift," he said. His tone was velvety, completely sincere—and it was readily offset by the smile on his froggy face. His bugging eyes were coldly mocking, his sneer absolutely malevolent. "For an old woman past her time."

Corb flicked his hand and his men moved. A dozen suppressed weapons coughed and clacked, and every caterer and server in the hall dropped.

Marcone came out of his seat. Hendricks slammed a hand down onto his boss's shoulder, and Miss Gard stepped in front of him, her back to Marcone, her hand on her axe. A muffled cry of shock and horror went up from the guests.

Because they were *guests*.

Mab rose slowly, and by the time she stood, her hair and eyes and raven-claw nails were all black as pitch, her skin whiter than Death's horse. "You dare. *YOU DARE! YOU ARE A GUEST IN THIS HOUSE!*"

"Read your own laws, woman," Corb spat. "These hirelings were no members of a house, not vassals or lackeys. They're chattel at best." Corb turned to Marcone and with a contemptuous flick sent a velvet bag sailing through the air. It landed in front of Gard with an unmistakable metallic tinkle. "Your weregild, little man."

The room grew colder yet. Anxious, quickened breaths began to plume in front of tension-tightened faces.

"Old woman," Corb taunted. "I remember you as a bawling brat. I

remember your pimply face when you rode with the Conqueror. I remember how you wept when Merlin cast you out."

Mab's face . . .

. . . twisted into naked, ugly, absolute *rage*. Her body became so
rigid, so immobile, that it could not possibly have belonged to a living
thing.

"Tell me," Corb purred. "If he was yet among the living, do you think
he would still love you? Would he be so proud of what you've become?"

Mab did not descend from her high seat so much as reality itself
seemed to take a polite step to one side. One moment she was there; the
next there was a trail of falling snow and frost-blanketed floor in a laser-
straight line, and Mab stood within arm's length of Corb. "Your maggot
lips aren't worthy to speak his name," she hissed.

"*There* you are," Corb said, his tone approving. "I knew you had to
be inside all of that ice somewhere. Gather all the power you wish, old
woman. You know who you are, and so do I. You are no one."

Mab's face twisted in very human-looking fury, and that scared
me more than anything I'd seen in a good long while. Her lips lifted into
a snarl and she began to speak—before her black eyes widened. Her
focus shifted, her gaze swiftly tracking up the chain to the bronze-and-
crystalline fist of the woman who held it.

Corb let his head fall back and let out a delighted, crowing cackle.

The cloaked figure moved every bit as quickly as Mab had. One moment she was ten feet behind Corb. The next, there was a sound like
thunder.

There was no way to track what happened clearly. I think the cloaked
figure lashed out with a kick. I had the sense that there were defensive
energies beyond anything I could have managed around Mab, and that
the kick went through them as if they had not existed. The thunder was
followed almost instantly by a second sound, a roar of shattering stone.

I turned my head, feeling as if I had been encased in gelatin, and saw
the pieces of the high seat flying out in a cloud. There was a ragged hole
in the stone wall behind the seat about half the size of a coffin.

And the Queen of Air and Darkness was nowhere to be seen.

A stunned silence settled over the room.

The cloaked figure raised her hands in a very slow, deliberately dramatic gesture and slowly peeled back her hood.

The woman beneath the hood was made of bronze and crystal, and she was beautiful beyond mortal reckoning. Her hair, long and slick and close, as if she'd just emerged from water, looked like silk spun from silver.

It was her eyes that bothered me. Or rather, her eye. One of her eyes was a crystalline emerald green.

The other . . .

On that perfect bronze face, the mutilation of her eye stood out like a gallows in a public park. The orbital ridges around the socket were covered in white, granite-like scars, as if the biggest, ugliest cat you'd ever seen had scratched it out. It wasn't sunken, though the lid was closed. That mangled eye bulged ever so slightly, as if it had been meant for a being considerably larger than she was.

There was, around her, a humming throb of energy unlike anything I had ever sensed before, a power so ancient and terrible that the world had forgotten its like. That power demanded my respect, my obedience, my adoration, my abject terror, and suddenly I knew what was happening.

I was standing in the presence of a goddess.

I could barely breathe.

I couldn't have moved if I'd wanted to.

A moan went through the room, and I realized with a bit of alarm that one of the voices moaning was mine.

Some part of me noted that Vadderung and Ferrovax had both come to their feet, fists clenched—and they were not looking at each other any longer. Both stared hard at the woman.

The goddess swept her single-eyed gaze around the room, tracking from face to face. She gave the Winter Lady a look of pure contempt and delivered exactly the same expression to the rest of the gathered Accorded nations.

Her voice . . .

Oh God.

Her voice was sex and chocolate and hot soup and a bath on a cold, rainy night. It was a voice that promised things, that you could find yourself listening to with absolute intensity. It filled the room as if she'd been using a PA system, even though she wasn't.

"Children, children, children," she murmured, shaking her head in disapproval. "The world has gone to the children." Her gaze reached Ferrovax and paused. One of her cheeks ticked. She looked from the dragon to Vadderung, and when she saw him her teeth showed white and perfect. "One-Eye. Are you *that* involved in the Game, still? Are you still that arrogant? Look how far you've fallen. Consorting with insects, as if you're barely more than mortal yourself."

No one moved.

No one spoke.

And then footsteps sounded on the stone floor.

Gentleman John Marcone stepped out from behind the unmoving Gard, impeccable in his suit. He didn't look frightened, though he had to be. He simply stepped forward, clear of his guards, and said, "Good evening, madam. I am Baron John Marcone. This is my home. Might I have the pleasure of knowing how you wish to be addressed?"

The goddess narrowed her eyes, watching Marcone with the kind of revulsion that one normally sees reserved for a swarm of maggots. She shook her head, dismissing Marcone from her attention as she fixed her gaze on Vadderung again.

"*This* is your host?" she demanded. "You permit a mortal among you? Where is your dignity? Where is your pride?" She shook her head. "This world has gone astray. We have failed it. And I will no longer huddle fearfully in the seas and watch the mortals turn it into their filthy hive."

The goddess walked forward, staring down at Marcone. She circled him, shaking her head in judgment—and *still* no one moved. She pointed a finger at Ferrovax without looking at him and said, "Introduce me to this ephemeral."

For a few seconds there was silence. Then Ferrovax spoke in a ragged voice that sounded like it was being dragged out through his teeth. "This is Ethniu. Daughter of Balor. The Last Titan."

Ethniu lowered her pointing finger. Ferrovax gasped and staggered, putting a hand on the back of his chair to balance himself as he breathed heavily.

"This world has manifestly failed," she continued, now addressing the room. "You thought yourselves wise to band together. To live quietly. To embrace"—her lip lifted in a sneer—"civility. With the *mortals* that used to tremble at the sound of our footsteps."

I was trembling pretty damned hard right about then. And I still couldn't make a voluntary motion.

"I have stood by doing nothing for too much of my life," Ethniu said, pacing slowly. "I have watched holy place after holy place fall to the mortals. Forest after forest. Sea after sea. They dare to walk where they were never meant to walk. And as they do, the divine retreats, withers, dies." She paused for a moment, and that emerald eye landed on me like a truckload of lead, regarded me, and dismissed me all within half of a heartbeat. "They grow more numerous, more petty, more vicious, while they foul the world we helped to create with their filth, their noise, their buildings, and their machines."

She came to a stop beside King Corb and laid a hand on his shoulder almost fondly. "This ends. Tonight."

She turned and strode to Vadderung. She dropped to one knee in order to speak to him eye to eye. "I remember what you were. Because I respect you, I assume you have seen some redeeming value among these . . ." She waved a hand at the room. "Children. And because of that respect, I offer you something I was never given: a choice."

She looked around the room. "I offer it to all of the divine here. At the witching hour tonight, we who you thought fallen, defeated, banished, and humbled march upon the mortal world—starting with this fetid hive around us." She smiled, very slowly. "Finally."

Vadderung spoke, as if someone had superglued his tongue to the back of his teeth. "Ethniu. Do not do this."

She stared down at him for a moment with something almost like pity. "I remember that once you were great," she said quietly. "For the sake of the being I remember, I offer you this one chance: Do not interfere. My quarrel is with the mortals. Stand aside and there need be no conflict." She gestured at the hole in the wall behind the high seat.

"That creature cannot protect you. Cannot enforce her justice. Each of the divine here must choose: abandon the mortal world—or burn with it."

Her closed eye quivered, and suddenly there was a light behind the scarred eyelid, red and pulsing through the thin skin. She leaned back her head, took a breath, and opened that eye, the Eye, screaming.

The scream itself threatened to deafen me by sheer volume, but it was far, far more painful than that. I could feel it press against the vaults of my mind, emotion so violent and intense that it would tear my sanity to pieces if I let even a portion of it into my head.

Light erupted from Ethniu, lashing out furiously at the ceiling. Where it touched the hanging swaths of fabric, they rotted and flaked away, scorching at the edges and bursting into flame. When it touched the ceiling, there was an enormous concussion, and the dark grey stone of the castle suddenly erupted with cold blue glowing light emanating from previously unseen runes and sigils written on every surface. I could feel a surge of pressure, which might have put out my ears had it been physical, as the castle's magical defenses pitted themselves against the power of a goddess.

They failed.

Stone shattered to dust, and energy exploded upward through the ceiling, through the upper floor, and through the roof into the summer night. Pure magical energy surged out with it, through the room, into the night, in a wave of such breadth and power that five minutes before, I would have considered it impossible.

Looking back, that was the moment everything started to change.

Magic ran rampant into the air. It howled through the streets and alleys of Chicago. It thundered through tunnels and roadways, a tsunami of raw power.

And wherever it went, the mortal world fell into darkness.

Power stations exploded. Electronic devices screamed and showered sparks. Screens played diabolical images and screeched in demonic voices before dying. Cars died; systems failed; trains went powerless and slowed. I heard later that there were nearly fifteen hundred automobile collisions in that single moment, resulting in scores of deaths.

Chicago fell into total darkness.

I found myself on my knees, sometime after, breathing hard, making pained sounds. Others were making similar noises. The lighting in the great hall hadn't changed—not when it had been firelight in the first place.

King Corb and the Last Titan were gone.

I found myself staring at Vadderung as he fell heavily back into his chair, his expression stunned.

30

Asolid quarter minute of stunned silence followed before Gentleman John Marcone hauled himself to his feet, looked around at the destruction and confusion in the hall, and mused, "It would seem we have the Fomor's answer with regards to the peace process."

Ebenezar was the next one up. He looked around the room and said, "Is anyone hurt?"

"The dead, it would appear," Marcone said. He started for the high seat and offered a hand to Molly. She glowered at him but took his hand and rose with a polite nod. He spoke in a low, intent voice that wouldn't be overheard by most of the room. "Assess Mab, please, Winter Lady."

Molly stared at him for a second. Then she went over to the hole in the stone wall behind the high seat. She stared for a moment and said, "What's on the other side of the wall?"

"Storage," Marcone said.

"On the other side of *that*," Molly said, and vanished into the hole.

Etri and his sister stood up together. Voices rose in a babble of confusion and anxiety. Everyone had begun to recover and no one looked like they were happy about what was going on.

My grandfather looked around, eyes searching. He leaned over to Ramirez and muttered something. The Warden nodded and spoke quietly to the rest of the security team.

Carter LaChaise and his ghouls got up and were heading toward the exit.

"LaChaise," Marcone said in a voice that very much was meant to carry to the rest of the room.

The ghoul looked over his shoulder at Marcone.

"Where are you going, sir?" Marcone asked.

LaChaise pointed a finger at the hole in the rear wall. His voice was a low, rich Louisiana gumbo with some whiskey added in. "You heard that monster. You saw what she did."

"Yes," Marcone said, his tone bored. "I also saw your signature at the bottom of the Unseelie Accords, I believe."

"And?"

Marcone's voice was mild. "And mutual defense in the case of an aggressor nation is stipulated therein."

"Mab was the Accords," LaChaise spat. "You saw what the Titan did to her."

"And so I did," Marcone replied.

"If she can do that to Mab, what chance do any of us have?" LaChaise asked. He looked around at the rest of the room. "All of us signed because all of us fear Mab. Do any of you think you can stand up to Corb and Ethniu when even *Mab* gets swatted down like a fly? Let this mortal throw away his short life if that is his desire. The rest of us were doing business long before these recent Accords, and we can do it again quite comfortably."

LaChaise turned to leave, trailing half a dozen ghouls in the wake of his massive presence.

"Are you a coward, sir?" Marcone asked, his voice deadly quiet.

The ghoul whirled, light and fast for all his bulk, and a low growl bubbled across the room.

"A question, sir," Marcone said. "Not a statement."

"Tread carefully, mortal," LaChaise said. "I would be pleased to use your own entrails to make sausage links."

"I ask the question," Marcone said, "because your next actions will show everyone here what you are, LaChaise."

LaChaise quivered, his face contorting in rage. Actually, it started contorting from human form into something more bestial, uncomfortable crackling sounds coming from the ghoul's bulky form as his shoulders rounded and hunched and his back kinked.

Marcone's voice cracked out. "You are a *guest*, sir. In my *house*."

LaChaise's eyes had already gone hideous and vaguely serpentine. His weight had shifted to take a step toward Marcone, but the words locked him into place as rigidly as bonds of steel. He looked around the room to see the entirety of the leadership of the Accorded nations staring hard at him.

"Baron Marcone is correct," Etri said. "You are signatories of the Accords, as are we all. You are obligated to come to Mab's defense. As are we all."

LaChaise's jaw had extended slightly, and it made his voice a snarling, gobbling thing. "Your people are bleeding from a tussle with a mere White Court assassin," the ghoul hissed. "Do you think you can challenge a *Titan*, Etri?"

"Not alone," Etri said calmly. He turned to Marcone and nodded firmly. "Svartalfheim does not make commitments lightly. We will stand in defense of this city."

Marcone returned the nod.

"Fools," LaChaise said. "This is *hopeless*. The enemy has been given free reign to prepare. We have mere hours to assemble our own forces, assuming the attack has not already begun. Do you think Corb means to fight fairly?"

"Obviously not," Marcone said. "Which tends to make me think that he is not invincible—otherwise, he should simply have attacked, without any of this . . . drama. It is an attempt to destroy the Accords without firing a shot—to divide us, make us easily taken one at a time."

"And the Titan?" LaChaise demanded. "Did you see what she was wearing?"

"Titanic bronze," Etri noted. "An alloy beyond the skill of even my people. Only the Hundred-Handed Ones knew its secret." He looked at Marcone and clarified, "Mere physical force will never stop her. Only the most puissant of powers stands any chance of doing more than annoying her."

"A problem to be overcome," Marcone said, and looked at Cristos. "Perhaps our clever friends of the White Council have a solution."

Cristos looked at Ebenezar. The two of them traded looks with Martha Liberty and Listens-to-Wind, and the Senior Council put their heads together for a brief conference. Listens-to-Wind looked up from it and nodded at Marcone. "Perhaps. And in any case, we will stand with you and summon a complement of Wardens to the city's defense."

"Perhaps they can do something," LaChaise scoffed. He looked around at the rest of the room. "What does this city, this mortal, mean to any of you? I say it's better to let the Fomor expend their strength on the mortals."

"Idiot," snapped Ferrovax, a plume of thick volcanic-smelling smoke rushing from his nostrils. "You know the mortals as well as I do. Once you awaken them, frighten them, you anger them. They will lash out at any supernatural threat they can find—and may I remind you, LaChaise, that you do not enjoy the safety of dwelling beneath an ocean they have barely explored."

"The *wurm* is right," Vadderung said. He exchanged a nod with Ferrovax. "We must stop Ethniu here and now. If she is allowed to sack a mortal city of this size, there will be no way to contain their rage. Blind and foolish as they are, they are *many*, and full of the courage of ignorance. None of us will be able to carry on business in the face of that—and Corb and Ethniu will simply sit in their palace under the sea and laugh while the rest of us try to survive."

"I don't see how all of us dying in a foolish battle is an improvement," LaChaise said in an acid tone. "If Ethniu can do that to *Mab*, what can any of us do against her? What weapon do we have against her?"

Marcone stared at LaChaise as if the ghoul were a simpleton. "Courage, sir," the robber baron of Chicago said. "Skill. And will." He turned to Vadderung and said, "I wish to hire the entirety of the available Einherjaren for a night."

"I can have five hundred here in the next few hours," Vadderung said.

Marcone nodded. "Etri?"

The King of the Svartalves folded his fingers into a steeple. "My people are artisans, not warriors. We will fight—but our assistance in establishing defenses and providing appropriate equipment will prove a greater boon. Our armories are open to you, Baron."

Marcone nodded and regarded Ferrovax. "Sir?"

"My contribution to the defenses must be subtle," Ferrovax said. "To do otherwise would be to risk destroying more of the city than I save." He nodded thoughtfully. "With Etri's counsel and consent, I will close the underworld to them, prevent them from moving through or beneath the earth. One-Eye?"

Vadderung nodded slowly, evidently tracking Ferrovax's line of thought. "I will close all the Ways to them within the city itself. Given who they are, that will leave them only one viable avenue of approach."

"The water?" Marcone asked.

"Aye," Vadderung said. "Their power is greater beneath the water. They'll be able to bore through the defenses beneath the lake."

"Then we'll be able to deploy our forces against an attack from the lake," Marcone said. "I will bring the full strength of my own organization here."

There was a polite cough. Or it would have been a polite cough if a human had been making it. Considering it came out of River Shoulders's chest, it sounded more like a small cannon going off. The Sasquatch straightened his bow tie, stepped forward, and pushed his wire-rim spectacles up higher on his broad nose. "My people," he rumbled, "are not signatories of the Accords. Not yet. But if I understand things correctly, what is happening here has the potential to bring them harm. I will stand with you."

"Hah," said Listens-to-Wind. His worn teeth showed in a broad smile. "Be good to work with you again, River."

River Shoulders looked toward Listens-to-Wind and winked. I was impressed. River wasn't the kind to rush into things—and offhand, I couldn't remember going up against anything more dangerous than one of the Forest People who meant business.

"What of the White Court?" Ebenezar asked. "Where is Ms. Raith?"

At that, there was a murmur of confusion and then all eyes fell onto the White Court's sitting area, where only Riley was there to speak. "Ms. Raith had matters of state to attend to," he said, his voice steady.

"I'll need her authorization before engaging, but I've already sent a runner with orders to bring her local forces to combat readiness—a hundred guns, plus whichever members of the house are in residence at the château."

"Communications, transportation," Marcone said. "If that hex Ethniu threw was anything like what I've seen from others, and is as effective at destroying technology, we're going to have difficulty reaching everyone and bringing them together in the proper place."

There was a cough from the far end of the hall, where the Summer Lady had been sitting quietly with her security team, including the Summer Knight, gathered around her. Sarissa's hair had become a cloud of silken white tresses over a dress that had been leaf green before I had drunk the blending potion. She . . . looked a scary amount like Molly, honestly. Or maybe Molly looked more like her.

Sarissa rose, looking intensely uncomfortable, and said, "I can help with communications. The Little Folk are well suited for such tasks. I would recommend the roof of this castle, I think, for a command center, for easy access."

There was a rustle and then Molly slid out of the hole behind the high seat. "I've been handling transport for Winter troops for some time now. I can bring more of them in, as long as I know where they will be needed."

"Excellent," Marcone said. "Communications are, I think, the place to begin."

"As well as a centralized collection of our military assets," came a ragged voice.

Mab came out of the hole in the wall. She was . . . broken. Literally. Half her body had been crushed and mangled as if in some kind of industrial accident. She came through the hole in the wall with jerky, too-quick motions, once more the queen in purple and white, though coated with stone dust, her skin dimpled in dozens of places, as if it had been made of some kind of mostly rigid material that showed some hail damage. As I watched, there was a hideous crackling sound, and her broken shoulder snapped unnaturally in its socket and then resolved into its normal pale perfection.

She looked around the room, slowly. LaChaise avoided her gaze and looked as if he wanted to sink into the floor.

"Queen Mab," Marcone said. "It would be good to know what forces the Winter Court intends to commit to the city's defense."

Mab stared at Marcone for a moment in silence, before she said, "I am informed by my second that as of one hour past, all of the forces of Winter are urgently required elsewhere. The Gates are under intense attack."

I felt my stomach lurch at that. The Outer Gates were . . . the ultimate boundaries of reality, way out in the far reaches of the Nevernever. Beyond them was elemental chaos, the Outside of creation, filled with the beings known as Outsiders, who eternally hungered to break in and devour all of reality, mortal and otherwise. If the Outer Gates were suddenly being attacked, it meant that there was no way the timing of Ethniu's actions could be a coincidence.

It meant that the Last Titan was in league with the Outsiders.

It meant that more than a few powerful entities had evidently decided that the Accorded nations had to go, and they were making their intentions known in no uncertain terms.

Not everyone in the room got what was happening, but I could see who had the information to translate what Mab had said, very clearly. One-Eye and Ferrovax, the Senior Council, River Shoulders, Etri, and a few others suddenly went as pale as I felt. They understood just as well as I did what would happen if that battle was lost.

Mab looked across the hall at Fix, the Summer Knight, a wiry little guy with a shock of white hair, the knobby hands of a mechanic, and hard eyes that were green whenever I wasn't viewing the world in monochrome. "Sir Knight. I believe Queen Titania should be informed of the situation immediately."

"Then why don't you do it?" Fix asked in a very polite, mild tone. "Your Majesty."

"She is unwilling to . . . take my calls," Mab said. "She will do as she will—but she should be informed. It is her right."

Fix frowned, but Sarissa lifted a finger and said, "She's right. Go now."

The Summer Knight nodded, bowed to her, and immediately withdrew. I was impressed with that. He'd been unwilling to expose the previous Summer Lady to danger, to a paranoid degree. Sarissa had evidently established a different dynamic to their relationship.

"Queen Mab," came Ebenezar's voice. The old man sounded calm but respectful. Mab didn't react well to aggression, and even worse to weakness. "If I may ask . . . where is the Winter Knight?"

"He was last seen consorting with Ms. Raith," Mab said in an offhand voice. She glanced in my direction, and her eyes suddenly became bright green and very cold. "Rest assured he will participate in the defense of the city as soon as he has concluded his business."

Ebenezar's jaw hardened. "Ma'am, with respect. I will need to coordinate with him. The sooner the better."

"I will send him to you," Mab said, turning a cool gaze to the old man.

Ebenezar met her eyes for a moment and then nodded a stiff-necked acceptance.

Great. Now I had this to explain.

"Very well, then," Marcone said. "Ladies and gentlemen, if you could each send someone with executive decision-making capability with me, we will establish a command center for the city's defense. . . ."

The room stirred, generally speaking, voices rising as people started moving, and I took Mab's hint. I also had business to conclude. The evening had gone completely sideways, sure—but whatever the result of the battle, if Etri was still around afterward, he'd be after my brother. Right now, the only thing keeping him from hunting down and killing Thomas was Ethniu's major distraction, and the fact that no one had yet realized that Thomas had escaped. It had just become even more urgent that I get him clear.

There was only one place that I could do that, and there was little time to do it in. Mab's instructions had been crystalline, even to me— get it done and get back.

I headed for the door through a sea of worried monochrome faces, and hit the night running.

31

Being the Winter Knight mostly sucks, but it comes with a few perks that can be damned handy.

First, I'm strong. Not like Spider-Man strong, but I'm about as strong as someone built like me can be, and I'm not exactly a tiny guy. I'd gotten myself mostly dead as part of the deal, and by the time I'd gotten back to the world of the living, my body had wasted down to nothing. Part of recovery had been physical training—a whole hell of a lot of it. And since the constant primal pressure of the mantle could be safely eased through intense exercise, I'd kept it up.

It didn't turn me into an instant superhero or anything, but you don't want me punching you in the nose, either.

Second, I can have issues noticing pain and discomfort. Mostly, that means things like cutting myself a lot while shaving. Sometimes when I stand up after reading for a long time, I don't notice that my leg has gone to sleep and I fall down. I have to really pay attention to notice pain, most of the time. It's probably been good for me to work on a little more self-awareness, but it isn't much fun.

On the other hand, when you're doing something to which pain is a serious obstacle, like running, it can be really convenient.

The average fit young person can manage about sixteen or eighteen miles an hour over a short distance. Top human sprint speed is about twenty-eight miles an hour. I can't run that fast. But I can run considerably faster than average, maybe twenty-two or twenty-four miles an hour, and I can do it without slowing down for more or less as long as is necessary.

So when I hit the streets, I was really moving. I knew it wouldn't take me long to reach the waterfront. In fact, my biggest worry was that I would break an ankle and not notice it until I'd kept running and pounded my foot to pulp.

But Chicago's streets had changed.

Cars had simply come to a halt, dead in their rows. There were no streetlights, no lights in buildings, no signs, no traffic lights. No nothing. People had gotten out of their cars and were standing together in small groups, nervously talking. Everyone was holding a phone in their hands. None of the devices were working. The only human-made illumination came from, here and there, emergency road flares that people had deployed as light sources. If there hadn't been a waxing moon, it would have been too dark to move as fast as I was.

It was eerily silent. Chicago was a busy place. At any time of the day or night, you could hear any number of the sounds of the modern world: radios blaring, deep bass notes from someone's tricked-out car stereo, traffic, horns, sirens, construction equipment, public announcements, tests of the emergency broadcast system, what have you.

All of that was gone.

The only sounds were worried voices and my running footsteps.

There weren't any screams. There wasn't any smoke.

Not yet.

But it was coming. My God, it was coming. If Ethniu and the Fomor hit the city during the blackout, the resulting chaos could kill tens of thousands independently of whether anyone swung a blade or fired a shot. The sudden blackout had to have killed people in hospitals, in automobile collisions, maybe even in airplanes. I mean, how would I know? I couldn't see the highways. A plane could have gone down a few blocks away and if I hadn't seen it happen, and if there weren't any fires to mark it, I'd never be able to tell from here.

The Accorded nations were preparing for all-out war. Freaking *Ferrovax* was involved.

I ran for the docks, and as I did, I realized something truly terrifying:

I had no idea what was coming next.

This was out of my experience, beyond what I knew of the world. The supernatural nations might have their issues, and when we fought sometimes there was collateral damage—but for the most part, we kept it among us. Old ruins, jungles, deserts, underground caverns, that was where we did most of our fighting.

Not in cities.

Not in the streets of freaking Chicago.

I mean, my God, she had kicked Mab through walls. *Mab. Walls*, plural. Ethniu had gone through her as if she didn't *exist*.

A creature with power like that might not be impressed by a mere seven or eight billion mortals. She might very well be determined to play this one old-school, and a protogod's idea of *old-school* probably checked in around the same weight class as Sodom and Gomorrah.

Before the night was out, the city would fight for its life. My grandfather and my friends and allies on the Council would be in the middle of it. My God, I had to get Thomas clear of it before it got started. I had to warn people. I mean, the supernatural-community grapevine would be spreading *this* one like wildfire, and everyone would be paying attention because I'd spread the word for everyone to keep their eyes open— but that left the rest of Chicago. Ninety-nine percent and then some of the city's populace would have no idea what was going on when the attack began.

Like, *zero* idea.

And being initiated to the supernatural world was difficult even when it happened gently—much less when it rolled up and ripped someone's face off.

About eight *million* people would react with panic. With *terror*. With violence.

And my daughter would be in the middle of it.

The very thought gave my feet wings.

Only two things kept me from going to her. First, where she was staying. She was a guest in the house of Michael Carpenter, and under his protection. And that meant that while she was there, she had a mostly retired hero and a squad of literal guardian angels looking out for her. I don't care how badass you might be, even on the kind of scales I use—you don't want to tussle with an angel. Those beings are absolute forces of the universe, and they are freaking Old Testament.

Tangling with one would be less like getting into a street fight than like getting into a fight *with the street*—it's difficult to picture, you're almost certain to look incredibly foolish, and however you approach that fight, things are probably not going to go your way. Maggie could hardly be in a safer place in the city than under their protection.

And the second reason was my brother. I had been trying to keep cool while we executed the rescue plan, but I was terrified for him. He was in bad shape. I could . . . not save him, exactly, but I could keep him alive, on the island. That was the whole point. Out there, I had a lot more say about what happened. Out there, I could keep him shielded from tracking magic, from deadly spells, from hostile sendings, could forbid the presence of the svartalves and enforce it. Out there, he'd have a chance.

With luck, I could save my brother and make it back to town before Ethniu and Corb did. I hated the thought, but the imminent attack ought to provide us with a damned fine distraction. We just had to get him to the island before anyone caught us.

But he wasn't there yet.

I rounded the last corner at my best pace, feet pounding hard against the concrete, dashed across the street, and made it to the entrance of the docks at Burnham Harbor, where the *Water Beetle* was moored. I flew through the gates, guided through the dark by the white paint on the stairs and floorboards of the walkway. There was no one else here, no one else trying to get away from the city.

Not yet.

My footsteps on the dock hammered out over the open water, loud and clear, and I didn't bother trying to be quiet. Speed was everything.

I flew down the last length of dock to the boat and saw green glowing light coming from belowdecks and from the cabin. The *Water Beetle* was a worn-out little old blue-water fishing trawler, pretty much a twin to the *Orca* in *Jaws*. As I slowed, panting, my footsteps got even louder, and Freydis's slim form appeared on the deck, holding a green chemical emergency light in her hand. Murphy came limping out of the cabin a second later, her P90 riding on its harness across her chest, holding a second glow light.

"Jesus, Mary, and Joseph, Harry," she breathed. "That blast of light. Was it an EMP?"

"Or a hex," I said. "Or both. Where's Lara?"

"She took Thomas below," Murphy said, her voice tense. "He's in rough shape."

I nodded and put a foot on the gangplank. "Okay, then let's—"

And from behind me came a deep, warbling, throbbing hum, like nothing I'd heard before.

My dad, the illusionist. I slipped the dark opal ring I'd gotten from Molly off my hand and palmed it.

Then I turned.

Hovering maybe twenty feet up, with his feet planted firmly on a stone the size of a Buick, was the Blackstaff, Ebenezar McCoy. One hand was spread out to one side for balance, fingers crooked in a mystic sign, sort of a kinetic shorthand for whatever spell was keeping that boulder in the air.

The other gripped his staff, carved with runes like mine, and they glowed with sullen red-orange energy. His face had twisted into a rictus of cold, hard fury. Flickers of static electricity played along the surface of the stone.

"You fool," he said. "You damned fool."

I put my feet back on the dock. Then I knelt down and tied my shoe.

"Boy," he said. "They're using you."

I set the palmed ring down behind my heel, out of sight. Breathed a word in barely a whisper.

There was a moment of dizziness and then I stood up and faced my grandfather. I gathered in my will. The shield bracelet on my left wrist began drizzling a rain of green and gold sparks of light. The runes of my staff began to glow with the same energy.

"Sir," I said. "What are your intentions?"

"To salvage something out of this mess, boy," he snapped. "The jaws of the trap are already closing in. I'm going to open your eyes." His gaze flicked past me to the ship, and a flicker of electricity along the stone made a thrumming crack like a miniature thunderbolt. "The vampire's in there, isn't he?"

"You haven't seen him there," I said. "You have no idea."

"Don't play games with me, boy," the old man spat. "I'm not one of your new Fae friends. And I'm not a lawyer."

"He's working for me," came a clear, calm voice.

I glanced over my shoulder to see Lara Raith, still dressed in her party gown, standing on the *Water Beetle*'s deck, arms akimbo. I didn't see any weapons on her. I didn't see where the dress would have allowed her to *hide* any weapons. But she stood there like she was ready to draw and fire, and all things considered I would judge it the better part of valor to assume the implied threat was valid.

"I worked with Mab on some visa issues some of her people were having," Lara said. "She owed me a favor. He's it."

The old man's gaze remained on mine for a moment, growing harder and hotter and more hostile. I saw the rage gathering behind his eyes, before he moved them, slowly, to Lara.

"Vampire," he said, "the Accords are the only reason I haven't relieved you of your arms and legs and kicked you into the lake. Your brother stands accused of murder. He's going to answer for that."

The voice that came out of my grandfather when he said that . . . I'd heard it before.

I'd *been* that voice before.

I thought of ghouls buried to their necks in the earth. I thought of the savage satisfaction that had filled me while I did it. Because they had done wrong, and I had seen them do it. To children. And to deliver just retribution for that crime had been to be the right arm of the Almighty Himself, to be filled with pure, righteous, unarguably *just* hatred.

My God, I knew how he felt. I knew how bright and pure that fire burned. But when it was happening, I hadn't been able to feel it burning *me*.

I just had to live with the scars afterward.

The vampires of the White Court had hurt my grandfather to the heart. And he was determined that it would not happen again. And that they would pay for what they had done.

If Mab had been standing there advising me, she would have said something like, *It is his weakness. Use it against him.*

And she wouldn't have been wrong.

Ebenezar glared his hatred at Lara, and I realized with a sinking heart that there was only one way this was going to play out. His eyes were full of hate. It made him blind. There wasn't room in them for anything else.

"Cast off," I said in a calm, firm voice, my eyes never leaving my grandfather. "Go ahead with the plan. I'll catch up."

"Dresden?" Lara asked. "Are you sure?"

"Dammit, Lara!" I said, exasperated.

I checked over my shoulder in time to see Murphy step up beside Lara, catch her eye, and nod firmly.

"Freydis," Lara said.

The Valkyrie moved for the ropes.

"Do that," Ebenezar called, "and I'll sink this boat right now."

"No," I said, calmly, firmly. I swallowed and faced the old man. "You won't."

The old man's brows furrowed, and the air suddenly became as brittle and jagged as broken glass.

"If I let you do this," the old man said to me, his voice desperate, "you're out of the Council. You're an outlaw. The svartalves won't care about who hired who. They'll know you prevented them from having justice. And they'll kill you for it. It's the only outcome their worldview will accept. Don't you see, boy? You'll be vulnerable, compromised. Mab, and this creature, they're *isolating* you. That's what abusers *do*."

My heart broke.

"I think," I said quietly, "that I'm just about done making my choices based on your mistakes."

He stared at me.

"You don't know me," I said quietly. "Not really. You haven't been there for most of it. And you don't know Thomas."

Behind me were two quiet thumps, as lines were dropped on the deck of the ship.

"I know enough to know a frog with a scorpion when I see one," he replied. "You've been around them for a decade and change, and you think you know them. But I've dealt with their ilk for *centuries*. They'll turn on you, frog. Even if it destroys them. They don't get a choice about it. It's what they *are*."

Lara stared at the old man with furious . . .

. . . haunted . . .

. . . eyes.

Murphy strode into the wheelhouse and started the *Water Beetle*'s ancient engine. It was an old diesel, didn't even have spark plugs. Hexes, EMP, none of it mattered. If a one-eyed, palsied squirrel was all you had to do maintenance, that engine would run until its molecules decayed into their component atoms.

Ebenezar's eye flickered to the ship and hardened.

I sucked in a breath, ready to unleash Power.

My God.

Was this really about to happen? Was the old man really about to throw down with me?

He wouldn't *listen*. Stars and stones, I couldn't get him to accept that a White Court vampire might be partially *human*. If I told him that Thomas was his *grandson*, he would . . . not receive the news well.

The old man had a volcanic temper.

That wasn't a metaphor.

If that happened . . . I really wasn't sure what came next.

The *Water Beetle*'s engine didn't roar so much as sputter and cough loudly to life. Compared with the almost-silent murmur of the water against the docks and the ships, the sound was deafening in the unnatural silence over the city.

Ebenezar McCoy snapped his staff across his body, held vertically—a duelist's salute.

My heart lurched into overdrive.

I returned my grandfather's salute with my own staff.

And then me and the old man went to war.

32

Some free advice for you: Never fight an old man.

They've been there, done that, written the book, made and starred in the movie, designed the T-shirt, and they've got no ego at all about how the fight gets won.

And never fight family.

They know you too well.

Ebenezar slashed his hand down at the boulder beneath him with a word, and in the same spell a blade of unseen force slashed a three-hundred-pound section of rock free of the boulder he stood on and sent it zipping toward my boat at several hundred feet per second.

I wasn't even going to try to stop it. It was just too much energy, too much momentum. It would be like lifting a medieval shield to block a descending war maul. Sure, you can *do* it, but if you do, you're gonna wish you hadn't.

No. The smart thing to do is to give that war maul a single sharp lateral tap just as it begins its forward momentum. A few pounds of pressure in the right place, at the right time, are often more effective than expending heroic levels of energy.

And besides. If I tried to match the old man swing for swing, he'd bury me. Not so much because he was stronger, although he was, but because he was *better* than me, more energy efficient, milking twice the efficacy out of every single spell while expending half the energy to do it. Wizard fights between the old and the young were a reverse image of mundane confrontations between the same. *I* was the one who was weaker, slower, limited in what moves I could attempt, and had to play it smart if I wanted to win.

So as the old man sent the section of boulder at the *Water Beetle*, I lifted my staff, modifying the formula of my simple force-blow spell to send it in from the side instead of straight ahead, and smacked the projectile firmly in the flank as it got moving.

It streaked forward at an angle, wobbling and tumbling as a result, and smashed into one of the boats farther down the dock, plunging through the hull and part of the deck, straight on through the hold and out the other side, with such force that water splashed a hundred feet.

The old man brought his boulder around in a swooping arc, studying me through narrowed eyes, his voice bitter. "*Now* you learn that you don't have to swing for the fences every time."

"Yeah," I said, studying him right back. The cleave mark where the boulder had been cut was a slightly darker grey than the surface—living rock, with water still inside, then. "Don't tell anybody. You'll ruin my maverick rep."

He looked from me to the *Water Beetle*, chugging out into the open lake. "But you still ain't using your brain."

And he flicked a wrist and started sailing over me, out over the lake toward the boat.

The second his eyes were off me, I unlimbered my blasting rod from the sewn pocket inside my suit coat, aimed for the damp stone of the boulder, and shouted, "*Fuego!*"

Green-gold fire lanced from the blasting rod and smashed into the boulder—and I poured it on in a steady stream.

The boulder beneath my grandfather's feet began to let out a kind of hissing, whistling scream, and the old man flung himself off into open air half a second before the water in the stone began to boil and shattered it into dozens of pieces. Some plummeted into the lake, and some onto and through the decks of more of the boats parked in the marina.

That should have been it. The old man should have fallen into the lake, become immersed in deep water, and had the lion's share of his power washed away for a time. But instead, he barked a pair of words, hurling a blast of force at the surface of the lake that pushed back just as hard against him. He was flung to one side, falling toward the dock. He hurled a second, weaker blast at the dock, slowing his fall without shattering it, and landed with one foot stomping down so hard that I heard the board crack, dropping to one knee for balance, his staff still held in his hands, his pate gleaming, his eyes bright.

Hell's *bells*, was he better than me.

That was Ebenezar McCoy, the Blackstaff, the most feared wizard on planet Earth.

Without pause the old man's staff struck the boards of the dock, and they bowed up in a straight line coming toward me, as if an enormous shark was swimming toward me beneath the dock, its dorsal fin bumping up the wood.

I slammed *my* staff down and vaulted over the oncoming wave of energy as it passed, and as I came down, I beckoned the winds, focused my will, shouted, *"Ventas arctis!"*

At my command the air stirred, and gale winds suddenly lashed the surface of the lake with vicious, frozen spite. A miniature cyclone of spraying ice and water engulfed the end of the dock around the old man, clouding him from sight as fog billowed out from the sudden temperature change in the sullen night air, and while it blinded him, I did the last thing wizards generally do in a duel.

I sprinted right at him.

I crashed through the sleet and frozen air and ice as if they weren't there at all, spotted the old man when I was five feet away, and let him have it with a swift, speeding thrust of my quarterstaff, aiming for his gut.

But the old man had learned his quarterstaff in Britain, long enough ago that it had still been a common weapon in widespread use, and his teachers had been masters. His own staff caught mine in a parry, and he followed up with an advance and a circling sweeping motion that would have taken my weapon out of my hands if I hadn't disengaged properly.

He came at me in a blur of attacks. If we'd been on solid ground, he'd have knocked my punk ass out cold. But now we were standing on intermittent patches of sleet and ice, and while his feet slipped and faltered, mine just seemed always to find the ideal footing. The conditions provided just enough hesitation in his forward motion that I was able to retreat a little faster, until I could use my reach to good advantage, stop his advance, and, with a quick, snapping combo Murphy had taught me, put him on his back foot.

He shifted his grip on the staff, both hands at shoulder width, and raised it defensively as he came in on me like a bull. He didn't have any choice. He could probably defend against me forever, but as long as I had the footwork advantage, I'd be able to swing at him while he couldn't reach me in reply. If he diverted his attention to summon the energy for a spell, I'd be able to feel it coming, and I'd brain him. So his only option was to come at me hard.

I had a brief shot at his head when his foot slipped a little, but I was too slow to take it.

Or maybe I just didn't want to.

He caught it on his upraised staff, and then there was a whirlwind of blows coming at me from both sides and all angles.

I defended. Barely. If my foot had slipped once, the old man would have made me pay for it. He almost nailed me twice, anyway, and only the treacherous footing he had to endure gave me time enough to manage a defense.

You know. Or maybe he just didn't want to, either.

But he drove me *back* up the dock, forcing me out of the miniature freeze I'd laid on him. Once he had his feet under him again, I wasn't going to do very well. I checked the progress of the *Water Beetle* as it chugged out of the harbor. It had a hundred yards' lead now.

So, yeah. This was the right time.

Ebenezar's foot slid off the last patch of ice, and he promptly threw a stomp kick at the bridge of my left foot as he came in. I avoided that, but it put me off-balance, and the old man's staff hit my shoulder with enough force to shatter concrete.

Molly did good work. There was a flash of light from the spider-silk suit, the scent of something putrid burning, and instead it merely felt like getting smacked by a particularly proficient Little Leaguer.

I cried out in pain and staggered back.

"Don't make this anything it doesn't have to be, Hoss," my grandfather said, his voice hard. His next blow hit my right foot, and evidently Molly hadn't specifically enchanted the shoes. Which the old man had probably been able to sense. The strike wasn't as strong as it could have been, but it broke toes, flashes of vicious, stabbing heat that quickly vanished into the rippling chill of the Winter mantle, and I staggered to a knee.

The old man stomp-kicked me in the center of the chest, driving the wind out of my lungs with a sickly gasp and slamming my shoulder blades and the back of my skull against the dock.

Ebenezar shoved the end of his staff against my Adam's apple with a snarl and said, "Yield!"

"No," I croaked.

The old man's eyes widened. "Dammit, boy, you are about to make me angry."

"Go ahead," I said, baring my teeth. "Do it. Kill me. Because that's what it's going to take."

His jaw clenched, and he slowly bared his teeth. "You . . . arrogant . . . foolish, egomaniacal drama queen!"

"I'm not the one who *flew* in on a baby mountain!" I complained.

He shoved the staff a quarter inch forward.

"Glurk," I said.

His face was red. Too red. The veins stood out sharply in his head, his neck.

And the ground was shaking. I could feel it through the dock.

When he spoke, his voice came out in a register so calm and measured that it completely terrified me. If he was doing that, it was because he was employing mental discipline techniques to contain his, gulp, rage.

"I will ask you a question," he said. "You will answer me, clearly and honestly. Nod if you understand."

I nodded. Glurk.

"How did they get to you, boy?" he asked, his voice still unnaturally calm. "What do they have on you? It can't be so bad that I can't help you get out of it." His eyes softened for just a second. "Talk to me."

I glanced down at the end of his staff.

"Ah," he said, and took the pressure off.

I swallowed a couple of times. Then I croaked, "They don't have anything on me."

His eyes went furious again, and . . .

And tears formed in them.

Oh God.

"Then why?" he demanded. The calm in his voice was fraying. "Why are you *doing* this? Why are you destroying yourself for that *thing*?"

I knew exactly what I was about to do.

But he deserved the truth. Had to have it, really.

"Because I've only got one brother," I said. "And I'm not going to lose him."

The old man went very still.

"Mom," I said in a dull, flat voice. "She gave each of us one of her amulets, with a memory recorded on them, so we'd know each other."

Ebenezar's mouth opened and closed a few times.

"Half brother, technically," I said. "But blood all the same. He's got my back. I've got his. That's all there is to it."

The old man closed his eyes.

"You're . . . saying . . . that *pig*, Raith . . . with *my* daughter."

The ground shook harder. The surface of the lake began to dance, droplets flying up.

"Sir," I said, trying to keep my voice calm, "you have a second grandson."

If I'd punched him, I don't think I could have staggered him more. He fell back a step. He started shaking his head.

I sat up. "Look, whatever happened, it's over now. Thomas didn't have anything to do with that. But he *has* saved my life on multiple occasions. He is *not* your enemy, sir." I blinked my eyes a couple of times. "He's family."

And the night went still.

"Family," came the old man's voice, a primordial growl lurking in it. "One. Of those *things*."

He whirled toward the retreating boat, barely visible from the shore by now, and his staff burst into incandescent blue flame as he lifted it in his right hand, the hand that projects energy, drawing it back.

"No!" I shouted, and lurched toward him.

He spun, eyes surrounded by white, his face scarlet, his teeth bared in a snarl, snapping his staff out . . .

And what looked like a comet about the size of a quarter, blazing like a star, leapt from the staff, like some kind of bizarre random static spark, and plunged into my ribs and out my spine.

I tumbled down to the dock on my back, the stars suddenly unusually bright above me.

I tried to breathe.

Nothing much happened.

"Ach, God," the old man whispered, his breath creaking.

His staff clattered to the dock. It sounded like it came from very far away.

"Harry?" he said. "Harry?"

His face appeared at the end of a little black tunnel.

"Oh, lad," he said, tears in his eyes. "Oh, lad. Didn't think you were going to come at me again. Didn't think it would trigger."

I could feel his hands on my face, distantly.

"That's why you were so big on teaching me control," I slurred dully. "You're barely holding it together yourself."

"I'm a hotheaded fool," he said. "I'm trying to *help* you."

"You knew you were losing it," I said weakly. "And you kept going anyway. You could have backed me up." Blood came out of the hole in my chest in rhythmic little spurts. "And instead it ends like this."

Shame touched his eyes.

And he looked away from mine.

The pain we feel in life always grows. When we're little, little pains hurt us. When we get bigger, we learn to handle more and more pain and carry on regardless.

Old people are the hands-down champions of enduring pain.

And my grandfather was *centuries* old.

This pain, though.

This hurt him.

This broke him.

He bowed his head. His tears fell to the dock.

Then he paused.

Then his expression changed.

He looked up at me. His eyes widened, and then his face twisted into rage and disbelief. "Why, you *sneaky*—"

"Good talk," I said, "Wizard McCoy."

And I let go of the Winter glamour Lady Molly had crafted for me.

I felt my consciousness retreating back down that black tunnel, down to where I had laid Molly's opal pinky ring on the dock, while I felt the ultimate construct of glamour, my doppelgänger, collapsing and deflating into ectoplasm behind me. My awareness rushed into the stone in the ring, found the thread of my consciousness I'd bound to it, and then went rushing swiftly back toward my body.

My eyes flew open and I was on the deck of the *Water Beetle*, on the far side of the cabin from where Ebenezar had been, where I'd taken cover after dropping the ring and beginning the illusion. Once I'd activated the ring, the veil around me had let me slip aboard the *Water Beetle*, take cover, and then project my consciousness back into the construct.

I'd blown up my relationship with my grandfather by remote control.

But at least I hadn't taken a comet to the lung.

As I came all the way back into my body, I was gripped by a weariness so intense that it was its own entirely new form of pain. I could feel myself thrashing in spasms. Murphy had one of those face masks with a rubber pump over my mouth and was forcing air in. Freydis was trying to hold me down.

I fought for control of my body and eventually reasserted it, sagging down to the deck in utter weariness. Freydis lay half across me, panting. Murphy, all business, peeled back one of my eyelids and shone a light on my eye. "Harry? Can you hear me?"

"Yeah," I said, and brushed the mask off my face. "Ugh."

"Od's bodkin, *seidermadr*," Freydis breathed. She rose off me wearily. "You cut that one close."

"What the hell is she talking about?" Murphy asked.

"A construct," I said. "For the illusion. Um. Molly made a really, really good ectoplasmic body for me, stored the pattern for it in the ring, and linked it to me. Everything you need to drop a fake double of yourself in place as a decoy and simultaneously make yourself unseen. Then I . . . kind of possessed the construct. Projected my awareness into it. Sent all that energy into it, all the way from here, which is exhausting as hell. Had a *wonderful* chat with McCoy."

Murphy helped me sit up, staring at my face intently. "What happened?" she asked.

I looked at her and said in a lifeless voice, "I won."

"Oh my God," she said. "Is he . . ."

"Pissed," I said, with drawn-out, heavy emphasis.

She frowned and touched my temple with one hand for a moment. "He hurt you."

I closed my eyes. "You should see the other guy."

"You two are just precious," the Valkyrie quipped.

"Freydis," Murphy said, not unkindly, "fuck off."

Freydis looked back and forth between us, frowned, and said, "Fucking off, ma'am." And she left us as much privacy as she could on the little ship as the *Water Beetle* chugged forward.

"Harry," Murph said gently.

I kept my eyes closed. They were overflowing anyway.

"He's . . . he's not . . ."

"Not quite the hero you thought he was?"

I pressed my lips together.

"Yeah," she said. She leaned down and lifted my head into her lap. "He's human. What a shock."

"I told him," I said. "About Thomas."

"Seems like he reacted a little," she said.

"He killed me," I said quietly. "The fake me, I mean. If the fake me had been me me, I would now be dead me. He didn't mean to do it. But it happened. And he's not who I thought he was. He was out of control."

My voice kind of choked on the last sentence. My chest felt like it should have had knives sticking out of it. I leaned my shoulders back against the bulkhead of the wheelhouse and clamped my left hand over my eyes while I sat on the deck. "He was out of control."

"Oh God, Harry," Murphy said, her voice full of pain.

"It *hurts,*" I said quietly. "Oh God. It *hurts.*"

She put her hand on my forehead, stroking. I lowered my hand and leaned down toward her. And I cried.

That went on until it was quiet.

Then she said, "I heard the beginning of the conversation. And you're both wrong about each other, you know. You don't really know who he is. Not yet. And he doesn't know you. And you both hurt each other terribly, because you're family. Because what you say and do matters so much more than anyone else." She leaned down and put her cheek against my forehead. "Listen to me. I know it hurts right now. But the reason it hurts so much is because you care about each other so much. And that pain will eventually fade. But you'll both still care."

She was right. I did hurt. The kind of pain a magical mantle can't do jack about. The real pain, of the heart, the kind that can kill you in about a million ways.

Damn the stubborn old fool.

"I know this is hard, Harry. I remember when I first realized my dad was just human," she said. "When he shot himself."

She let that hang in the air for a while.

Then she straightened, framed my face with her hands, and stared out over the darkened lake, her eyes filled with tears. "You can still talk to him, Harry. Something I never got to do. I want you to promise me, for my sake, that you'll talk to him when tempers have cooled."

"Karrin," I said.

She gave one of my cheeks a little slap, annoyed. "Did that sound like a request? Do it. If my advice means a goddamned thing, do it right now. That's how important this is."

"What if . . ." I swallowed. "What if that's me, one day? What if that's what I'm like?"

"There's a difference between you and him," Murph said.

"Yeah?"

She moved a bit, leaned down, and kissed my forehead. "Yeah. You've got me."

And . . . something little and warm kindled in my heart. It didn't stop the pain. Oh God, did it not stop the pain.

But it told me the pain wouldn't be there forever.

"Fine," I said. "I'll talk to him."

I made a weary X over my heart.

She patted my cheek approvingly and said, "Good man."

And I reached for her hand, closed my eyes, and spent a few minutes with tears less bitter.

33

I pulled myself together after a bit. There was a cabinet in the wheel-house where I kept a bunch of long-term-storage snacks. Nuts and beef jerky, mostly, plus bottled water. Nothing fancy, but projecting your consciousness was an exhausting activity, and my body needed the calories so badly that the stale nuts and dried jerky tasted freaking delicious. I chomped and guzzled.

It took most of an hour to get to the island on a normal trip, but I opened the throttle all the way, so we would get there in slightly less than most of an hour.

Murphy limped into the boathouse and kept me company in steady silence, watching my face. After about ten minutes of that, she said, "You're scared."

I shot her a glance. Shrugged a shoulder.

"That bad?"

I thought about it for a moment, while trying not to think about how sick I felt, how worried. Then I said, "I can do things. You know? I can burn down buildings if I want to. I can blow up cars. Call up things from the Nevernever."

She nodded.

"Right now, right under my feet, my brother is dying. And maybe the people who want to kill him are already on the way and we won't even get him to the island. And what's about to start happening back in town . . ." I didn't quite manage to suppress a shudder. "I feel very small."

Murphy looked at me evenly for a moment. And then her face twisted and she choked down chortling laughter.

"You . . . you . . ." She shook her head and slammed her shoulder gently against me, still laughing.

"What?" I asked.

"Welcome to the club," she said. "Tiny."

"I mean it," I said. "This is bad stuff."

"Right now," she said, "every precinct in Chicago is scrambling to round up every officer it can get. They'll be doing everything they can to get ahead of the chaos that's going to come from the blackout. Fire-fighters, too, for all the good it will do them." She shook her head. "They don't feel too big, either. And they don't even have a magic island."

I thought about footprints on a beach.

"Maybe they're about to feel a whole lot smaller," I said. "Maybe we all are."

Karrin frowned at that. She folded her coat closed around her a little more tightly and leaned against me. I put my arm around her.

"Just how bad are we talking, here?" she asked me.

"The Fomor think they can wipe out the city, whether we know they're coming or not," I said. "They seem sincere."

"Wipe out," Murphy said.

"Old-school. Think Attila. Genghis Khan."

"Jesus Christ," she breathed, and leaned against me. "The radio's out. So is the Internet, in town. How do we warn them?"

"If only we'd put out the word to be on guard already," I said wryly. "The Paranetters are used to surviving the big kids slugging it out. They'll get together at their safe houses, Mac's, places like that."

"And everyone else?" Murphy asked.

"Hey, everybody," I said, "mythological monsters are coming to kill you. Please evacuate."

She pressed her lips together in frustration but acknowledged the point. "So what do we do?"

I shook my head. "I don't know."

"What's going to happen?

I stared out at the darkness ahead of us, tracking the location of the island as surely as I would the progress of an ant across my arm, and pushed emotion away from things, thought through the matter as I would any mathematical problem.

"What makes this different," I said, "is Ethniu. And this weapon she has. The Eye of Balor."

"Yeah," Murphy said. "What's up with that thing?"

I blew out a breath. "Hell of a lot of variants in Celtic traditional folklore. It's hard to say. Balor was kind of an equivalent to a Greek Titan, up in Celt territory. He had this eye that could be used to wither the world, to destroy everything it saw, to set it on fire. He kept it covered behind a bunch of eye patches and veils, and he could remove a few of them at a time to get different kinds of destructive effects, from making things rot to setting them on fire to blasting them to dust."

"Kind of like gradually reducing the shielding around a radioactive core," Murphy noted.

"I . . ." I blinked. "Ugh. That's unpleasant to consider. But yes. I don't know how accurate the folklore is, and I haven't talked to anyone with direct knowledge yet. But it's safe to assume that the Eye is a weapon of mass destruction," I said. "There's a city-killer coming to our town."

"How will they do it?" she asked.

"Come in from the lake," I said. "After that, it's old-school."

"Kill everyone they see," she said.

"And use the Eye to blow away any points of hard resistance," I said, nodding. "They'll kill or take anyone they can, while the mortal authorities flounder in the blackout. Do their worst with the Eye, and I have no idea how bad that could be. Then they'll be gone before the National Guard can get there."

"The people," Murphy said quietly. "Tonight. There's no one to protect them."

"The hell there isn't," I said, and coaxed a little more speed out of the old engine. "I'll be back before they get here."

"You, huh," Murphy said, and I could hear the smile in her voice. "Against a protogod with a pocket nuke and an army of monsters."

"Not *just* me," I said. "But if it had to be just me, yeah. I'd be good with that. It's home. You gotta die somehow. Standing up to a monster at the door isn't a bad way to do it."

She was quiet for a moment before she said, "I feel you."

I squeezed her against me a little harder. "Here I am, getting all dramatic. How are you holding up?"

She shrugged one shoulder. Her voice was heavy and tired. "Everything hurts. But I can move some."

"Maybe you should take shelter," I said. "The Paranetters are going to head for Mac's place. They'll need someone to keep a cool head and a sharp watch."

She snorted. "You think I can't handle myself?"

"Don't," I said quietly. "I was ready to take you with me into literal Hell and you know it. Every warrior gets hurt. Has limits. There's no shame in acknowledging that."

She was quiet for a moment. Then she asked, "If you were hurt, would you sit this one out?"

I said nothing.

"It's my home, too, Harry."

I clenched my teeth.

"And," she said, leaning her cheek against my biceps, "if you try to strand me on that damned island to keep me safe, I swear to God I will shoot you in the leg."

I stiffened and gave her a quick guilty glance.

She smiled wanly in the green chemical light, widened her eyes, and said in a dramatic impersonation of my voice, "I'll be back in time." She snorted. "Get over yourself. You are who you are. And mostly I like it. But let's treat each other like grown-ups. Promise me."

I felt sick.

Karrin was smart, tough, and capable. She was also hurt. She was also right. And what was coming would give her no special consideration whatsoever.

But she was who she was. Karrin Murphy could no more have sat quietly by while Chicago burned than she could grow wings and fly. She would fight for her home. She would die for it.

Some part of me made whimpering animal sounds, way down deep inside.

At the end of the day, people have to be who they are. If you try to take that from them, you diminish them. You reduce them to children, unable to make decisions for themselves. There's no way to poison your relationship with someone else faster.

I didn't want to lose her.

If she fought, she might well be taken from me.

If I tried to keep her from fighting, I would lose her for sure.

So while my heart and some enormous portion of my soul quailed in terror, my mouth said, "I promise."

I felt her arm go around my lower back and she squeezed gently for a moment. "Thank you."

"Promise me you'll fight smart," I said.

She bumped her head against my arm and said, "How would you know if I did?"

I huffed out part of a laugh. And we stood together.

34

The little cheap plastic compass swung and bobbed as the boat did, but I didn't need it. Now that I had acquainted myself with the island's arcane functions, I had my own personal compass, a subtle, tiny sensation in my head that always told me where I could find the place.

That was part and parcel of being the Warden of Demonreach.

I felt it when the *Water Beetle* hit the outer ring of defenses, about a mile out from the island. With a few words and an effort of will, I could have had the island causing treacherous currents, frigid vortexes that would pull intruders down to sharp rocks below. The lake would have boiled like a sea under a storm.

I could tell that Karrin felt the island's influence as well, a subtle presence that caused unease in all who entered. It prevented casual visitors: No one who came into these waters would feel at ease until they'd changed course to go around the island. Hell, planes didn't fly directly overhead; that's how powerful the island's influence was.

That wasn't a planned defense, exactly. It was simply the natural presence of the things held prisoner there—a menagerie of supernatural terrors that started with some of the foulest beings I'd ever faced and progressed down into the depths of nightmare from there. Demonreach was the Alcatraz of the supernatural world—and I was the guy holding all the keys.

I could have found that place blindfolded and in the dark. Hell, I *was* finding it in the dark, piloting the ship without much need to turn the wheel until the looming mass of the island rose above us.

We'd prepared for arriving at night—the floating dock my brother and I had built, the Whatsup Dock, had been lined with luminescent marine tape. I cut the throttle and came in slow and careful. Even without the possibility of aquatic bad guys, operating a boat was a damned dangerous occupation for fools, so I had to be extra cautious.

I saw Freydis move up to the prow of the ship as we approached the dock, skin glowing in the green chemical light. She rubbed her arms a few times as the shadow of the island fell over her, as if the place chilled her. Beside me, Karrin shifted restlessly.

"It's that bad?" I asked her.

"You don't feel it at all, do you?" she asked. "Ugh. It's . . . You know that feeling, when you're dreaming, and you realize that you're in a nightmare?" She nodded toward the island. "It's that. In IMAX."

"Yeah," I said. "Well, it's not supposed to be a place where visitors are welcome."

"I worry about you, when you're out here," she said. "What it's doing to you."

"It's not doing anything to me," I said. "I'm the Warden."

"Maybe," she said. "Or maybe it's something you can't feel happening to you. Something else."

A disturbing thought.

But not one I hadn't had before.

"You're just going to have to trust me."

"Yeah. That's why I'm standing here."

I brought the ship in carefully to the dock and Freydis leapt like a doe down from the ship and started making her fast.

"Is the cabin still livable?" Karrin asked. "It has supplies?"

"Everything we need," I said. I cut the motor and headed out of the wheelhouse. "I'll check on Thomas."

I cracked a fresh light and took it down belowdecks with me, to the boat's little living compartment, and into a tableau from some kind of Renaissance painting.

The boat had a couple of bunks, nothing fancy, generally covered in

white sheets and heavy red plaid blankets. Thomas and Lara were reclining on one of them. She sat up at the head of the bunk, and he was
sprawled back, his shoulders across her upper body. Both were naked,
and there was nothing sexual in the moment at all. One of her hands
held his broken ones upon his chest. The other simply cupped his cheek.
Her head was bowed, as if in exhaustion, and her shoulders sagged. Her
hair spilled across her face, hiding all but a bit of her profile, and brushed
across his forehead.

My brother's eyes were open, unfocused. They had acquired faint
hints of grey among the silver in his gaze.

He looked like some poor broken knight, being gathered into the
gentle arms of an angel of death.

"What the hell?" I asked.

Lara lifted her gaze to me, her eyes flickering with bits of mirror-
bright silver that shifted even as I took note of them, sending the eerie
light of the chemical stick dancing about them in fluttering, kaleido-
scope changes of all shades of otherworldly green. . . .

I tore my eyes away before something bad happened.

"Lara. What are you doing?"

It took her a moment to speak. Her voice came out furry and delicious. "I'm giving him the energy I took earlier. It's . . . slowing down
the damage his Hunger is inflicting. But it's very bad. And I'm almost . . ."

She licked her lips. The sight of it made me want to rip off my shirt
and start boasting of my many manly deeds.

". . . empty." She made the word sound like a sin. "I'll need to feed if
I'm to give him more."

"Not really an option," I said. I had to clear my throat in the middle.
"We're here."

She looked up at me, her silver eyes sharp and clear. "And you're sure
you can protect him here? Even from his own Hunger?"

"Everything we need," I said. "Give him to me."

She nodded and said, "Take him."

She transferred Thomas to me, wrapped in a blanket. The air around
her was cold. Like, gorgeously cold. Like, I wanted to take my shirt off
and stretch out in it and cool off. And the Winter mantle let out a low

growl in my mind that suggested that a number of terrible ideas were in fact the most interesting concepts I had ever considered.

"Dammit, Lara," I snapped in irritation. "We're working."

She blinked at me for a moment at that, as I wrapped a blanket around him and gathered Thomas up like a child. Then she said, "Involuntary. Honestly. We can always choose to use the Hunger. We can't always choose not to."

"Well, it's annoying," I said grumpily.

She lifted her hand and quickly covered a smile. "Oh. You know, I've . . . never been told that before. Not once."

I rolled my eyes and said, "I believe you." It would be a trick to carry my brother up the narrow stairwell to the deck, but whatever. I growled in irritation and toted him out. He was still barely conscious, and he felt entirely too light.

Stupid svartalves.

Stupid vampires.

Stupid Titans.

Stupid Thomas. Why in the hell had my brother gotten himself into this mess?

I got him up on the deck and Freydis was there to steady me. The redheaded Valkyrie eyed me in the light and nodded toward the island. "Not much here."

"Everything we need," I said. "Don't step off the dock. I'm not sure what would happen to you."

Freydis looked at me and shuddered. "I won't."

I brushed past her and carried my brother down the dock toward the island itself. No one stopped me. Everyone was too worried about what was happening back in Chicago. Which was just as well.

I had told everyone Thomas would be safe on the island. I hadn't yet told them where he'd be staying.

See, the thing about keeping people safe is that, in the end, if you really want to keep someone truly protected, your only option is to lock them up. Fortresses are prisons.

And vice versa.

I started up the dock and stepped onto the rough ground of the island, walking with perfectly sure footing, my *intellectus* of the place making it impossible to slip or fall. I knew Demonreach, every tree and stone, as thoroughly as I knew my own body.

I had taken fewer than a dozen steps onto the stones of the island before there was a massive movement in the trees. I came to a halt, waiting, as the figure came gliding out of the darkness. It was enormous, as tall as the Titan, and far broader, a menacing shape in a billowing, shadowy cloak and hood that hid its form from the human eye. A pair of green flames burned somewhere back in the hood, supernaturally bright eyes that were currently narrowed in something like concern.

The vast figure drifted out to a halt in front of me and bowed slowly, formally, from the waist.

"WARDEN," it said. Its voice was a grating rumble of stone and tearing earth, heard as much inside my head and chest as with my ears. "YOU HAVE RETURNED."

"Alfred," I said. "We've got trouble right here in River City."

The genius loci of the island regarded me in stillness for a moment before it said, "THE ISLAND IS IN A LAKE."

The supernatural crowd is not generally up on any cultural reference that has occurred since the Renaissance. "Human reference, Alfred. Pay it no mind."

"AS YOU COMMAND, WARDEN." The enormous hood tilted to one side, verdant gaze fixing on my brother's unmoving form. "YOUR BLOOD KIN IS DYING."

"I know," I said. "We're going to help him."

"I AM NOT MADE TO HELP," Alfred said. There wasn't any passion to the statement. There was no mercy, either. Alfred was . . . the spirit of the prison itself, a place constructed to contain magical threats too dangerous to be permitted to roam the world. Over the millennia, more than six thousand beings of terrible power had been consigned to the oubliette tunnels beneath the island: They were a legion of nightmares, the least of which made me shudder in a very real fear I could never quite shake.

Alfred was the being created to maintain their isolation. He wasn't what you call easygoing.

"Right," I said. "We're going to place him in stasis."

Alfred's eyes blazed several shades brighter with eagerness. "IT HAS BEEN OVERLONG SINCE THE LAST FOULNESS WAS CONSIGNED TO MY EVERLASTING CARE," it said. "THIS PARASITE-RIDDLED VERMIN SCARCELY QUALIFIES FOR MINIMUM SECURITY."

"I want him held," I said. "I want his Hunger held helpless as well, until such time as I return to release him."

"WHICH PENITENCE PROTOCOL SHALL HE SUFFER, WARDEN?"

There were several that could be inflicted on the inmates of the prison. Some were bound in darkness. Some in torment. Some in simple confinement. The various Wardens of Demonreach had tinkered with the cells for a very, very long time. Some of the protocols had been developed before civilization had been more than a few collections of huts and fires in the darkness, and they were not kind.

There was one prisoner held below in a kind of unique stasis, something that could most closely be considered sleep, though he could also awaken and perform limited communications for short periods of time. It was, as best as I could understand, the only protocol with sanity-saving sleep built into it.

The prison had never been meant for something as frail and nearly mortal as my brother.

Thomas made a soft, ugly little sound, as if only his utter exhaustion was holding him back from screaming in pain.

"Contemplation," I responded quietly. "He is to be shielded from any communication with other prisoners not enduring the same protocol. Give me the crystal."

The great spirit bowed again. When it straightened, a shard of crystal about the length of a socket wrench, like quartz but pulsing with a quiet green light, lay shimmering upon the earth.

I lowered my brother to the ground. He groaned as I settled him down. The grey in his eyes had faded again, as his Hunger apparently renewed its assault on his life force. He had slowly begun to show signs of helpless agony as whatever palliative energy Lara had given him began to fade.

"Hey, man," I said. "Can you hear me?"

He might have focused his eyes on me for a second. Only sounds of pain came out of his mouth.

"Look," I said quietly. I drew a pocketknife I'd stuffed in my suit pants before leaving and used the needle point to pink the pad of flesh between thumb and forefinger. After a second, droplets of blood welled up, and I smeared the blade of the pocketknife over them, staining its length with a shade of scarlet just a little too pale to be human. "I can keep your demon from hurting you. Keep you alive. But going in will be rough."

One of his ruined hands landed on my arm. He squeezed weakly. It was barely there, but it was there. He'd heard me.

"Part of the process of being taken into the cells is . . ." I took a deep breath. "You suffer the pain you've inflicted on others," I said. "It was meant to get through to the most alien of beings, why they were being imprisoned. It's not fair. It's not meant for people. It could hurt you. But if I don't do it, you're going to die."

My brother forced his eyes open and tried to find me. "J . . . J . . ."

"Justine," I said. "I know. I'm on it."

He sobbed. That was all he had left in him.

I stood away from him, leaving him within the light of the crystal.

Alfred loomed over Thomas. "YOU HAVE THE CAGE. YOU HAVE THE BLOOD. DRAW THE CIRCLE AND SPEAK THE WORDS, WARDEN."

My instincts twitched. I looked back over my shoulder.

Freydis stood at the very edge of the dock, staring up the slope at me. Even as I watched, she turned and rushed back to the ship, leaping up onto the deck and vanishing into the hold.

There wasn't much time. My brother was fading, being devoured by his own demon.

I rose and drew in my will, while I used my staff to gouge a circle into the earth around my brother. Once that was done, I bent over, touched the little trench with my fingers, and raised the circle by unleashing a tiny amount of energy into it. It snapped up in an invisible screen around my fallen brother and began to gather and focus magical energy.

Then I raised the pocketknife overhead in one hand.

"Bound be Thomas Raith," I hissed. I felt resistance against my will begin to rise, the reluctance of this world to open a passage to another. "Bound be my wounded brother," I growled, forcing my will into my voice, making it ring from the stones and trees and water. "Fallen warrior, father-to-be, I name him *bound*, consigned to thee."

I heard a brief cry from behind me.

I released my will with the third repetition of the binding.

And Demonreach went to work.

I didn't have the kind of power it would have taken to do what the genius loci did. The energy I'd had to pour into the incantation had simply been to release a portion of the spirit's power—like turning the key in an enormous, stiff, stubborn lock. Demonreach was not meant to be used by the weak-minded or the uncertain, and the effort it had taken to set it into motion was not one I would care to repeat on a regular basis for exercise.

The crystal flared with light. It bathed Thomas so brightly that I could see his bones through his skin.

And then my poor, battered brother began to scream. It was a thin, shrieking sound, a sound that embraced more emotion, more agony, than his broken body could possibly bear. It ripped at me, that sound, causing me pain that the Winter mantle could do absolutely nothing about. I had just condemned my brother to a punishment that I would have been terrified to face myself.

Thomas screamed and screamed, and the vast form of the genius loci towered over him, bending down.

And then the screams ended.

The light vanished.

I stood alone on the cold stones.

Where my wounded brother had been, there was nothing but a very faintly glowing cloud of green mist, dispersing rapidly, sinking into the stone and earth of Demonreach.

I sagged, dropping down to one knee and bracing my arms on the ground.

Stars and stones.

What I had just done . . . there had been no choice, especially not now. But my brother.

I heard a single low cry, raw and ugly with pain.

I turned to see Lara land on the dock and rush toward me, a pale blur of supernatural speed, something that gleamed and caught the moonlight in her hand.

35

Lara Raith didn't like to fight—it was what made her such a deadly opponent when she had to do it. Once the knives were out, she didn't let pride come into it at all. If she decided to kill you, it was going to happen as quickly and efficiently as she could arrange, and that would be that.

I had personally seen her walk through a battlefield full of ancient foes armed with nothing but a pair of long knives. She hadn't just beaten them—she'd made it look easy. She was older than my brother, and she'd taught him to fight. Thomas had walked into a svartalf fortress and damn near assassinated its chief executive, through all the security, all by himself. Lara was faster than my brother, stronger than him, and more experienced.

And now she was coming for me.

I got it. I mean, this was the only place on the planet I was sure Thomas would be safe, but if she'd known the details she'd have fought me on it, and there just hadn't been *time*. For all she knew, I'd just disintegrated her brother. If I'd been in Lara's shoes, I'd have been freaking out, too.

She probably didn't realize she'd chosen her ground even more poorly than my brother had.

Demonreach had been constructed by Merlin. *The* Merlin, the original, Camelot and Excalibur, *that* Merlin. He'd broken at least one of the Laws of Magic to build the place, romping about through time in order to lay a foundation strong enough to bear the supernatural weight of the prison. As a result, the island absolutely seethed with power—and if one knew the layout of the defenses, and the painstaking geomancy that had gone into laying all that energy into usable patterns, it was possible to use that energy at almost no cost to one's own store of personal power.

Behind Lara, Freydis and her shotgun vaulted off the ship and onto the shore, the Valkyrie following her boss into battle.

Except it wasn't a battle.

It wasn't even close.

I made a gesture, hissed part of a word, and the soft ground beneath Lara's feet abruptly gave way and then snapped back, sending her into a sprawl in the air. She hit the ground, and the brush and grass of the island wrapped her swiftly and completely.

I made a swatting gesture with my right hand, sent out a mental command to utilize some of the waiting energy of the island, and a hickory tree that towered above the landing site abruptly swept down like an angry giant and slammed an enormous branch into the ground a few feet in front of Freydis. The impact knocked the Valkyrie from her feet—and at a second gesture the tree hit her hard enough to send her flying back into the water of the lake.

I turned back to find Lara tearing her way wildly out of the grass and brush, and I had to lift both hands and expend a mild effort of will to have the ground simply swallow her to the neck.

Lara struggled briefly, savagely, and silently, her silver eyes bright. It took her about half as long as it would have taken me to realize the hopelessness of her position. The struggle ceased then, and she went cold and so still that her head might have been something severed from a statue rather than part of an actual near-human being. Only her eyes moved, tracking me. There was nothing playful in her expression now. It was like looking at the eyes of a big cat. An angry one.

"That wasn't necessary," I said, turning to track Freydis's progress in the water. My *intellectus* was a little fuzzier out there, like peering through smudged glass, which was probably the penalty for my merely human brain struggling to be aware of the constant shifting of every individual molecule of water in the area.

I found Freydis just as she kicked off the bottom of the lake, churning the water into swirling helixes with the power of her limbs as she stroked for the surface, and flew out of it with enough momentum to clear the railing of the *Water Beetle*—and collide with Murphy on the deck.

"No!" I shouted, and with an effort of will and another flick of my wrists, a pair of trees bent and reached for the ship, wood straining, limbs creaking with threat.

Freydis was fast as hell—and Murphy didn't even try to fight her. The Valkyrie got behind Murphy, close, one hand on her waist and another on her throat. I knew how strong she was—she could just rake a pound of meat out of Murphy's neck with a flick of her wrist. Freydis's eyes were bright and cold. "Back off!" she screamed.

The power of Demonreach was vast and terrible—and not much good for surgery. The only chance I'd have would be something that killed Freydis so fast that she didn't have time to react, and the Valkyrie was damned quick. I'd be aiming trees (for God's sake, I should have *practiced* smashing things with trees) at targets on a floating, bobbing platform, and an inch's difference in any direction could mean Murphy's life or death.

So I backed off, the trees groaning threateningly as they retreated.

"Trade time, *seidrmadr*," Freydis called to me. "Yours for mine."

"Why should I?" I called back.

Freydis tightened her hand, and I saw Murphy tense up with pain.

"This is not the fight that is destined to be her last," the Valkyrie called. "Unless you make me kill her."

Murphy simply lifted her arms. There were a couple of clinking sounds, and a pair of metal bits flew up from her hands and arched out to either side of the *Water Beetle*, landing in the water with little splashes.

They were little metal handles. Soldiers called them spoons.

Murphy was holding a live grenade to either side of their heads.

Freydis's eyes went very wide.

"Frags," Murphy said calmly. "Your move, bitch."

There was an instant of frozen silence.

"Gods, that's hot," Freydis said, and blurred as she dove over the railing, hitting the water like a thrown spear.

Murphy turned and pitched the grenades over the far side of the

Water Beetle. She had to lob one of them underhand, with her wounded arm. They hit the drink maybe seven or eight yards out, and a couple of seconds later they went off with a roar of displaced liquid that sent a geyser of water twenty feet in the air.

I ignored that. The frags were no danger to anything when they were surrounded by that much water, and instead I tracked the evasive Valkyrie, until I found her.

I raised my voice and called out to where Freydis had tried to swim silently back to shore in the shadows and shelter of some huge old shaggy willows. She came out of the water and picked up a rock and was about to start through the trees and rocks on a least-time course for the back of my skull.

"Hey, Red!" I called. "Your client is fine, there's no reason to fight me, and if you make me spend what's left of my money on weregild for your boss, I'm going to be really annoyed."

Freydis paused in the darkness in confusion. I didn't blame her. There was no way I could have seen her from where I was standing, no way I could have heard her stealthy movements. But while I stood on Demonreach, I was as aware of the island as of my own body. I could have chucked a rock, bounced it off a couple of trees, and landed it right on the Valkyrie's head.

Sometimes actions speak louder than words. I lifted a hand and willed the earth of the island to cooperate. Freydis found herself sunk to her waist in the ground in the space of a heartbeat. I heard her let out a short choked sound.

"See?" I called to her. "This is . . . just a terrible idea. Just awful. For you, I mean. Maybe we can talk instead."

Freydis's voice came out a little breathless. "Lara?"

I looked at Lara and made an impatient gesture with one hand. "Come on."

"I'm alive," Lara called back to her. Then she looked at me and said evenly. "You traitor."

"Hey," I said, lifting an annoyed finger. "*I'm* not the one who came running at *you* with a knife."

"What did you do to him?" Lara asked, her voice cold and measured.

I'd heard the tone before. Back when I'd had to put the fear of, well, me, into a vampire named Bianca. We'd sort of been amicable opponents up until that point. Things changed when I'd made her feel helpless. Things had gotten a little complicated.

And I'd just repeated history.

Only Lara was smarter and stronger and a great deal more dangerous than Bianca had ever thought about being.

This was one of those situations where it would maybe be wise to use my words.

I walked over to Lara and settled down on my haunches next to her. "I did exactly what I said I would do," I said. "He's safe. Locator spells won't be able to lock onto him here. His demon can't hurt him. The svartalves can't get to him. We did it."

"I want to see him," Lara hissed. "I want to talk to him."

I rubbed at my eyes. "You can't," I said. I frowned and reached for my *intellectus* of the island.

I felt what my brother felt. Which was not much. There was distant pain, but mostly he had simply sunk into an exhausted stupor. His mind had been overwhelmed by physical stimuli. Now he sought blessed shelter in oblivion. "He's . . . unconscious."

She stared at the middle distance, refusing to look up at me. "Unconscious?"

"He's locked in one of the cells," I said. "He's safe. But he's stuck, too. And right now he's exhausted. Resting."

"You never said anything about locking him in a cell."

"I said he'd have to stay here."

Lara let out a small bitter laugh. "You did. And you kept your word. To think I believed you'd come into Mab's service as a result of misfortune rather than aptitude."

I winced at that one.

Ow.

"You've made your point, I believe, Dresden," Lara said somewhat stiffly. "The current balance of power does not favor me. Is it really necessary to keep me in this . . . position?"

"Are you done with the knife play?" I asked.

"I am ready to negotiate rationally," she said.

I gave her a professionally suspicious look.

Her poker face was much better than mine.

"Fine," I said. I stepped back and gestured.

The ground just sort of slid away from her, bringing her back to her feet without any effort needed on her part. As her right hand came free, she lifted a small practical knife that she'd been hiding . . . somewhere. She put it back into the sheath she held in the other hand and then tossed the knife down onto the ground between us.

"Thank you," she said stiffly. "I'd appreciate it if we could deal frankly with one another at this point."

"Sure," I said.

"What do you want?" she asked.

"For what?"

"Don't be coy, Dresden," Lara said. "You hold my brother's life in your hand now. What is your price?"

I lifted my eyebrows. "Wait—you think that . . . Wow."

She tilted her head.

"Lara, look," I said. "I'm slowly growing more aware of things, but . . . you're giving me too much of what you probably think is credit. I don't play the game like that."

"A cursory review of your defeated foes begs to differ, wizard."

"I'll play hardball," I acknowledged. "But I play it clean. Or at least, I don't sell my own damned brother up the river for gain."

"You're not that much of an idealist, Dresden," Lara said with a faint hard smile on her mouth. "At the end of the day, you'll commit genocide if you think it's the proper thing to do."

"You're goddamned right I will," I said, because the empirical evidence was pretty tough to dispute. "But if I was as hard-core as you think I am, you wouldn't be walking off this island with your own mind. And maybe not at all."

Lara narrowed her eyes. "What do you mean by that?"

I threw up my hands. "Hell's bells, Lara. Look, if I wanted to do something bad to you, I could right now. You're standing in the wrong place, I have the advantage, and if I wanted to wreak some manner of skullduggery upon you, you aren't in a position to stop me from do-ing it."

Words could not be more rigid than the ones she spoke. "I am aware."

"No!" I said. "That's not . . . Augh! Look, I'm not saying that because I'm trying to leverage you. I'm pointing out that I *can* do it, but I'm not going to because it's just . . . dickish. And I try to avoid acting like that whenever I can."

Lara frowned. "What?"

"Look, I know you play the game real hard," I said. "That's in your nature. But you also understand family."

She tilted her head, frowning. "What do you mean by that?"

"That Thomas is my family, too," I said. "I won't do anything to know-ingly harm him. Um, again. And if he needs me, I'll be there for him."

"And," Lara murmured thoughtfully, "I suppose if anything happens to you, terrible things happen to my brother."

"Not terrible," I said. "Just . . . nothing." Unless the next Warden decided to free him. I hadn't yet finished reviewing the inmates of the island. The filing system of the island, such as it was, was a psychic one. Reviewing the inmates meant *reviewing* the inmates. The first half dozen or so had left me with nightmares for a couple of weeks, and there's only so much masochism I can keep all to myself.

"He's trapped there forever," Lara said.

"No. He's *safe* there until we can find a way to cure him," I said.

She regarded me with flat eyes. "And as a happy side effect, if I wish to protect his life, now I must invest resources in protecting yours."

That hadn't been what I'd been planning at all.

And yet . . . by Lara's standards, that's exactly what I'd done.

There is plenty of daylight between intentions and results. Inten-tions are fine things, but they don't stanch bleeding or remove scars.

Or heal broken brothers.

Man. I hadn't planned it like that.

Had I?

Maybe I'd been hanging around Mab too much.

"Lara," I said tiredly, "I'll grant you, yes, that's how things stand. We can talk all night about how they got there. But I swear to you, I didn't do it to try to get a handle on you. Of every person you have had to deal with, which of them has tried harder to avoid even *touching* your . . . handles?"

She stared at me with that unreadable expression for a good minute. Then she said, "Empty Night, wizard. Either you're sincere, in which case"—she shook her head, baffled—"I feel I do not understand you very well at all. Or you're a person capable of using even your brother's misfortune and possible death to secure gain for yourself while simultaneously cladding your actions in such moral armor as to make them practically unassailable. In which case, I suppose . . . I admire your skill in arranging matters."

"I figure you can look at this two ways," I said.

She arched an eyebrow.

"You can write this down in your little black book and remember it," I said, "because I took a cheap shot at you when you needed help, when you earned it, and when you came to ask for it, you deserved getting it. And instead, I leveraged you."

"That is one way to look at it," Lara concurred.

"Or," I said, "you can take it as a bit of circumstance that happened because circumstances are *bugnuts*, absolutely *insane*, and you and I do *not* have reasonable jobs for sane and rational people. Both of us are making it up as we go along, as best we know how. Both of us look for the knives coming at our backs, and both of us take action to prevent them. That includes being suspicious-minded enough to take out a little insurance even when you aren't consciously thinking about doing so."

Something like grudging understanding tinged her gaze for a second. She let out a soft snort through her nose.

"So," she said. "You agree with the old man. And decided to be a very clever frog with this scorpion."

"I respect what you can do, Lara," I said quietly. "You're one of my favorite frenemies. But if we both want to survive, a certain amount of moving past these rough spots is going to be necessary."

She let out a hard little laugh. "I suppose, then, I shall expect a similar amount of tolerance from you when, one day, I have the upper hand."

I winced at her tone. It was hard, unforgiving.

I'm pretty sure I could have thought of a number of terrible things I could do to Lara Raith that wouldn't have made her blink. But making her feel helpless was not on that list.

I definitely did not want to think about Lara gaining the upper hand between us. I didn't want to think about that for more than a couple of reasons.

"Yeah, that's fair," I breathed. "When it's my turn, I'll have to take it with grace. But look: You got what you wanted. Our brother is safe. He's hidden from any tracking spells and he'll at least not be in any worse shape while he's a guest here. Yes, you're going to have to watch my back until we can get him out of there, but since Mab's got me covering yours anyway, that shouldn't be too much of a stretch for you—and we've got bigger fish to fry right now. Let's survive the night, and we'll sort out Thomas tomorrow. Agreed?"

She kept at it with those flat eyes for another minute before she shook her head and pushed her dark hair back out of her eyes. "Fine," she said. "Yes, all right. Your reasoning is sound. We have larger issues to face. They must take priority. I accept your terms. You have my word."

"Thank you," I said.

Lara recovered her knife and turned away from me. "And after that," she said, starting back for the boat, "my first prerogative shall be balancing any scales between us that seem less than level. Beginning with my bodyguard. You will release her, please."

I gestured, muttered to the island, and felt Freydis's tension ease as she escaped the sinkhole I'd put her in. The redheaded Valkyrie melted out of the shadows. She paced over to Lara's side, checking her client for injury, before giving me the kind of steady, cautious look people normally reserve for dangerous animals.

"Shall we return to the city, then?" Lara asked. Her voice was its normal velvet loveliness again, but I could feel the sharp edges underneath.

Fabulous. This was just what I needed. To provide people like Lara with motivation.

"Go ahead and board," I said. "I need to grab a couple things. We'll leave in five minutes."

Lara nodded stiffly and turned to walk back to the ship. She was limping slightly and had been thoroughly muddied. I watched her go.

"SHALL I PREPARE ANOTHER CELL FOR THAT ONE?"

I turned to find the island's spirit looming over my shoulder—and I hadn't sensed Alfred's approach.

Which . . . bothered me. I mean, my *intellectus* of the island was essentially without limit. With a minor effort of concentration, I could have known how many ants were on the island, how many birds, how many fish in the waters off its shores. But I couldn't find out more about the inhabitants of the cells without dragging my brain through their psychic rap sheets, experiencing to some degree everything they were and had done. And I couldn't sense Alfred or his movements. I mean, the spirit had come every time I'd called.

And I'd been assuming this whole time that it *had* to.

But Alfred was apparently able to hide things from me. The spirit could hide its presence from my *intellectus* of the island, for example. And it could hide the innate terror of the island's inmates, preventing it from taking a toll on my psyche.

So I kind of had to wonder—what else could Demonreach be hiding from me?

"That won't be necessary," I muttered back to the spirit. "Alfred, how big a being can the cells contain?"

"PHYSICAL SIZE IS NOT A FACTOR," the spirit replied. "META-PHYSICAL MASS IS A DIFFERENT CONSIDERATION." The creature's green eyes suddenly flashed fiercely. "THE LAST TITAN IS ON THE MOVE."

"Yes," I said simply. "Can you hold her?"

"IF YOU CAN PERFORM THE BINDING, I CAN HOLD HER," Alfred said.

"From how far out?" I asked.

"I AM A JAILER, NOT A BOUNTY HUNTER," Alfred replied. "PERHAPS TO THE SHORES OF THE LAKE—IF YOU USED THE ATHAME FROM THE ARMORY."

An athame is a magical tool—think magic wand, but in the form of a knife. They're powerful tools for ritual magic.

I had one locked up in the island's armory. I'd stolen it from the God of the Underworld, from the same shelf as the Shroud and the Crown of Thorns. If it truly was what I was pretty sure it was, then using it was going to put me in a long-term pickle.

But if the storm coming for Chicago was as bad as I thought it was going to be, *not* using it would be unthinkable.

"To the shore, eh?" I said. "All right. Get me the knife. And a binding crystal. And the placard."

"YOU WISH *TWO* OF THE WEAPONS?"

Alfred sounded . . . slightly intimidated.

That's the kind of power level we were talking about.

"Sure," I said in the most cavalier fashion I could. "After all, that's only half the arsenal. And as soon as I leave, I want the full defensive measures of the island activated. Nothing gets in or out. Understood?"

"UNDERSTOOD, WARDEN," the entity said with a bow.

"Great," I sighed. "Now, run and get me my toys, Alfred. I've got a long night coming up."

36

When I got back to the boat, Karrin was up on top of the boathouse, seated on the stool there. Her P90, a personal defense weapon that was the bastard child of an assault rifle and a box of Belgian chocolates, was resting on the safety railing, its barrel aimed in the same general direction as where I had been standing and negotiating moments before.

I checked. She had a good line of sight to where I'd been standing with Lara, as well as to where Freydis had come out of the water.

"Had them both lined up, huh?" I asked.

She shrugged. "I know who my friends are."

"But you didn't shoot."

She folded her arms as if cold. "I know who my enemies are, too." She glanced down, toward where Lara and Freydis were belowdecks, washing off mud and changing into some spare clothing. Some of it was Thomas's and would sort of fit. "Lara's tired and scared and running on instinct," Karrin continued. "She'd have never come at you the way she did, here, otherwise."

I regarded Karrin for a second. Then I said, surprised, "You like her."

"I find her terrifying," she replied calmly. "But I will acknowledge a certain amount of respect. When we worked together in the BFS, she always held up her end and always kept her word. That's not nothing."

"No, it isn't," I said. I opened up the boat so that the roar of the engine would prevent Lara from overhearing our conversation. Vampires and their hearing. "So, I made an enemy of her."

Karrin snorted. "Maybe. But I saw the whole thing. You beat her, but you didn't show her any disrespect. She's not as petty as most of the rest of the supernatural types I've met. Maybe she'll decide to overlook it." She shrugged. "And if she wants a fight, we fight her."

"Tonight was high-stress and special. I'm pretty sure any fight Lara starts in the future is going to be set up so that we don't get a turn," I said.

Karrin turned bright blue eyes up to me. "So? You want to kill her right here, drop her in the lake?"

"Course not," I said, annoyed.

"Then stop borrowing trouble," she said. "Either throw down right now, or accept the fact that by not doing so, you're giving her the upper hand. Either way, complaining isn't going to help you."

"If the Council gives me the boot," I said, "there's nothing stopping her from coming at me however she wants."

Karrin snorted. "Merely Mab."

I pursed my lips. True, that. Honestly, my long-term prognosis was for death by Mab, one way or another, but until I fell trying to do something for her, I had a certain advantage in my role as the official Thug of Winter. I was high-profile. Anyone who wanted to come at me outside of the various shadow games would have to run a table of serious risks to make the attempt—and even then, if they didn't pull it off perfectly, so that they could vanish the body and avoid my death curse, it would be bound to catch up to them sooner or later in the person of the Winter Queen.

Nobody particularly cared to cross anyone from Winter—much less the Sidhe who ruled over the other predatory fae by dint of sheer wickedness and power. Mab's reputation and force of personality had created the Unseelie Accords from whole cloth.

Mab was not a kind or gentle boss, but she'd never betrayed me, either.

When she made a promise, she meant it, and everyone knew it.

Everyone but Ethniu, apparently.

I found myself turning the binding crystal over and over in my hand. It was about six inches long and between an inch and two inches thick, and glowed with a very, very faint luminescence that one could see only indirectly.

"That like the one you used on Thomas?" Murph asked.

"Yeah."

"You think you can get a Titan inside one of those?"

"Sure," I lied.

She spat casually over the side of the boat and gave me a look.

I grimaced. "Bindings are difficult work. You pit your will against whatever you're trying to bind. If your will is stronger, it gets bound. If not . . ."

"Whatever you tried to bind comes to kill you?"

"She was doing that anyway," I pointed out.

Karrin bobbed her head to one side in a little gesture of acceptance. "So your head is harder than Thomas's?"

"He wasn't in much shape to fight," I said. I chewed on my lip thoughtfully. "He'd had a long, long day."

Karrin nodded. "You hurt him putting him in there. Didn't you."

"Maybe more than he's ever *been* hurt," I said. "Didn't have many options."

"Mother of God." She looked up at me and then out at the dark. "I'm sorry that you had to do that to him."

"Didn't hurt me."

"Sure. What happens to Thomas if you don't make it through the fight?"

"He stays there," I said. "Probably for good."

"Harry, I need your honesty here. Can he be healed? Or are you just buying him time?"

I shrugged a shoulder and shook my head. "I don't know."

"You don't?"

"Hey, I'm making this up as I go along." I thought of my brother, trapped in a crystal prison for the next foreseeable eternity. And Justine and his kid, alone. "But I have to try."

She exhaled through her teeth and nodded. "You do."

The boat chugged steadily through the water back toward town. We both stood, staring toward it, silent tension rising.

I felt her hand slip into mine.

There were lights shining in the city now, though we couldn't see them until we got within sight of shore—candles in windows. Larger fires, maybe in trash cans.

The city was silent and dim in the darkness, unnaturally still.

Waiting.

And somewhere inside it, my daughter would be asleep right now, with Mouse somewhere under her feet.

I thought of the hideous scarlet light of the Eye, tearing through Marcone's little fortress.

"This . . ." I breathed. "This is too big."

"What do you mean?" she asked.

"It's too big," I said. "This isn't a war-torn nation where it can be explained away. Or an odd-duck private investigator with a quirky shtick. It's *Chicago*. Ethniu and King Corb aren't even trying to keep this quiet. The kind of blood that's going to be spilled . . . It will cry out."

"People will be terrified," Murphy said.

"And they'll set out to destroy what frightens them," I said. "It'll make the Spanish Inquisition look like a bouncy castle."

Murphy shuddered. "If Ethniu and Corb pull this off, they'll set the mortal world and the supernatural world at war."

I stared ahead at the dim skyline of my city, ghostly in the darkness.

"Yeah," I growled. "If."

And I gave the old boat all it had.